DARK SKY ISLAND

ALSO AVAILABLE BY LARA DEARMAN

The Devil's Claw

DARK SKY ISLAND

A JENNIFER DOREY MYSTERY

Lara Dearman

CROOKED
LANE

NEW YORK

Copyright © 2018 by Lara Dearman

All rights reserved.

Published in the United States by Crooked Lane Books, an imprint of The Quick Brown Fox & Company LLC.

Crooked Lane Books and its logo are trademarks of The Quick Brown Fox & Company LLC.

Library of Congress Catalog-in-Publication data available upon request.
ISBN (hardcover): 978-1-68331-752-4
ISBN (ePub): 978-1-68331-753-1
ISBN (ePDF): 978-1-68331-754-8

Cover design by Blacksheep/Orion Books
Book design by Jennifer Canzone

Printed in the United States.

www.crookedlanebooks.com

Crooked Lane Books
34 West 27th St., 10th Floor
New York, NY 10001

First Edition: September 2018

10 9 8 7 6 5 4 3 2 1

To Andrew, Lily, Charlie and Lena—I love you more.

Prologue

The door to the cottage was ajar. The darkness from within seemed to spill out into the sunshine. But that was silly, because the dark didn't do that—it didn't travel, not like the light did. It was a shadow from the magnolia tree, that was all. Here and there, bright pink petals had fallen onto the path and were wilting in the sun, edges curled and brown. He picked one up.

He tiptoed up the steps, placed his hand on the door. The glossy red surface was warm. He ran his finger along a crack, felt the threat of a splinter, picked off a flake of paint. He held his breath. Listened. Something was wrong. The air sat heavy in his ears, like water. It seemed to have swallowed all sound. He felt a pain in his tummy, the one he always had when he was worried. It was the silence. The rage and the shouting and the smashing of plates he didn't mind so much, he could hide from it, hands over his head, curled under his bed or crouched behind a tree in the garden. It was the silence afterwards he feared. It settled over the house like fog, seeped into corners, lingered over him as he tried to sleep.

He rubbed the petal between his fingers nervously, rolling it back and forth into a tube until it disintegrated, leaving his fingers damp and perfumed. He held them to his nose. Sweet. Comforting. From somewhere in the distance, a lawnmower started up, cutting through the quiet and breaking its spell over him. The birds sang. The grass rustled. A dog barked. He pushed open the door.

The cool inside air settled on his sweaty face and bare arms, and he shivered. He blinked as his pupils dilated, adjusting to the dimness of the interior. He scanned the room, eye level first. Mugs on the breakfast bar; a newspaper, spread open; a glint, sunlight on metal—a teaspoon; dust swirling; the armchair, not where it should be, shifted, facing the wrong way.

And there, on the floor.

He'd seen it as soon as he'd walked in, but some instinct had forced him not to look, and now that he did, his brain was trying to process what he saw into something acceptable. A pile of clothes. But it had arms and legs and hair. A mannequin, then, like in a shop, with limbs so stiff and pale. Around its head was a dark shape. It was moving, very slowly. It was creeping towards him. He reached out and touched it.

Sticky. Warm.

He held his hand up to the light from the open door.

Red.

A shifting. A rustling of fabric. He was not alone. In that moment, he longed for the silence again. Because he knew that what had happened in this room was terrible. And someone was here, and they would see him, and now he was part of it. He glanced down at his hand. Worse. They would think it was his fault. He took a step back. Towards the door and the warmth and the barking dog, which he strained to hear above the racket his own heart was making as it pounded at such a rate he felt sure it would explode.

A moan. Somebody was crying. Muffled sobs. Behind the kitchen counter. He faltered. His teacher at school always said you should help people in need. He swallowed. Tried to push the fear back down to the bottom of his stomach. Tried to be brave. Walked towards the sound. One step. Softly. Slowly. Two steps. Remembered the time he found the cat with the bleeding leg. It had lashed out at him when he'd reached towards it, not knowing that he just wanted to help. He should let the person know he was here, so as not to startle them.

'Hello.' It came out as a whisper.
The sobbing continued. He tried again. Cleared his throat.
'Hello.'
A sharp intake of breath.
And he knew, from that single sound, that his help was not wanted.
That it was not welcome.
That he should run.

1

Michael

To the uninformed passer-by, the small, barrel-roofed building next to the visitor centre might look more like a public toilet than a prison. It was about the right size, and its door was painted the same shade of park-bench green as the conveniences opposite the church. A closer look, however, would reveal a heavy, iron padlock swinging from the door, and bars at the windows, which were small and set too high to see out of.

Inside, there were two cells, both around six feet square and containing a slatted bed frame topped with a thin, plastic mattress. The walls were whitewashed, the floors concrete. A narrow corridor ran the width of the building, and from here the prison guard, one of the many roles performed by Sark's volunteer police constable, could check in on detainees through the grille in each cell door. Locals called it the 'drunk tank' because it was mostly used to accommodate tourists who'd had a few too many and missed the last boat home. Only once, in all his years on the police force, had Michael had to come over and officially arrest someone held here—a man whose drunken night out had ended with him smashing a bottle over somebody's head.

All in all, then, Sark Prison was more frequently deployed as the butt of an islander's jokes than as a place of incarceration. Only, now, as

Michael lay shivering on the floor, bound and gagged, the wrong side of the locked cell door, it didn't seem very funny.

It felt as if the blood flowing through his brain were on fire. If he moved his head even an inch, the pain became overwhelming, flashes of light punctured his vision, and a deafening ringing he knew only he could hear filled his ears.

Then there was his side. He was still losing blood. Several times in the last hour, or two, or three, however long he'd been in here, he had passed into a horrifying semi-conscious state in which he had lost his grip on reality, imagined himself on a boat, the floor swaying beneath him, or caught up in an explosion, about to be ricocheted clean off the earth and thrown into the sea. He had forced his eyes to open and his brain to focus. The shifting floor was a product of his dizziness, the noise his exhausted brain's exaggeration of the thunder outside. But that in itself was enough to cause more panic.

Because the storm had arrived, and Jenny was on a boat, fleeing, from him, from his betrayal, from this godforsaken island. He hoped and prayed that she'd got home hours ago. Before the weather turned. Before the clouds that had been gathering for days, suffocating them all with this stale, unrelenting heat, finally split, unleashing their torrent of rain and thunder and lightning, whipping the waves into an unnavigable nightmare and drowning his stifled screams in their fury.

2

Jenny

Three days earlier . . .

Jenny picked her crumpled jeans and T-shirt off the floor and pulled them on.

'What time is it?' Elliot, his voice muffled, his face half covered by the duvet.

'Six fifteen. I've got to go home and get changed before work.' She put on her watch and picked up her phone.

'See you at the office?' He lifted his head, one eye closed against the early sunlight streaming through the thin curtains.

She nodded. He kept looking at her and she felt like he expected something more, that she should bring him a coffee and give him a lingering kiss goodbye, or whatever proper couples did when one of them left the bed in which they had both spent the night. She smiled instead.

'See you there.'

Elliot's flat was what an estate agent might call 'bijou'. A kitchen-cum-living room, a bedroom and a bathroom. But it was neat and cosy, and from the kitchen she could see out over the rooftops of St Peter Port to the sea, glittering in the distance. She turned on the tap. The pipes creaked and shuddered behind the walls, and after a few seconds, tepid water sputtered out. She waited until it flowed smoothly before she rinsed a cup from the sink and filled it. Last night's wine glasses were drying on the side, a half-drunk bottle of wine next to them; another, she knew, lay empty in the recycling bin under the sink.

They'd fallen into a pattern. A couple of drinks after work, a couple more back at his place. Bed. The first morning-after had been awkward, both acting like nothing had changed, laughing it off, neither of them expressing regret, neither of them suggesting it was anything more than a bit of fun. They had, she thought, crossed a line now. It had become routine. They hadn't discussed it. She wasn't seeing anyone else, but he hadn't asked her not to. He still flirted regularly with other women. She hadn't asked him not to.

She leaned against the breakfast bar. She should get her own place. Her mum, Margaret, had offered to lend her some money for a deposit. Even then she'd struggle to pay a mortgage on a flat like this on her reporter's salary. She needed a pay rise. Or a new job.

Elliot's alarm clock beeped from behind the bedroom door and she heard the bed shift and creak as he rose. She rinsed her cup, stood it on the draining board and left.

The flat was on the top floor of a terraced house halfway down Mount Durand, a steep, hill of a street. Next door, a broken front window and empty beer bottles still told of Saturday's party, which Elliot said had been broken up by the police in the early hours of yesterday morning. At the bottom of the road, the paved surface gave way to cobbles. Tiny alleyways led to flights of uneven steps and hidden rows of houses, washing lines strung between them, wheelie bins blocking the paths.

A few wisps of cirrus cloud streaked an otherwise clear sky. June had been warm and dry, and there was no sign of a change in store for July. The first week had seen record temperatures, thirty-two degrees yesterday; Channel News had ended on a clip of its weatherman attempting to fry an egg on the pavement outside the studio. The tourists on their summer holidays were loving it. So were the ice-cream vans and the shops selling beach supplies. But for the rest of the population, Jenny thought, a break in the heat would be welcome.

7

Her car was parked outside the Cove, a notoriously rowdy bar. A group of teenagers had stared at her, swigging from bottles of Breda, as she'd left it there the night before, one of them saying, 'Nice car,' and another muttering, 'Nice tits more like,' before they'd all sniggered like the schoolboys they probably were. She wouldn't have put it past them to have keyed her car for a laugh. She checked for damage before she got in. Other than the reek of piss and stale beer, all seemed well.

The inside of the car smelled of her damp swimming gear, left in a rucksack on the back seat. She'd been to the bathing pools last night, right before Elliot had called. She glanced at her watch. Only six thirty. Time for a quick swim before she went home to change.

Her phone pinged. Early for a message. It was from Stephen.

Bones found on Derrible. Poss. human remains. We are going over now. Will keep you updated.

The twist of excitement Jenny felt in her stomach every time she got wind of a new story was tempered with a sense of dread. Human remains. It had been only months since Amanda Guille's body had been found on the beach at Bordeaux Bay. But that case was closed. The killer was dead. The bullet wound in Jenny's shoulder had healed.

She read the message again. Derrible Bay was on Sark, a tiny island three miles long by a mile wide. It lay nine miles east of Guernsey, about an hour's journey on the boat. It had no airport and no cars either. The only way of getting around was on foot or bicycle or an overpriced horse-and-carriage ride. Jenny had spent weeks there every summer as a child, her parents' love of the peace and quiet combined with their dislike of travelling further than a few miles from home (and nowhere on an aeroplane if they could avoid it) making it the perfect family holiday destination.

The 'we' Stephen referred to undoubtedly included his colleague in the Guernsey Police Force DCI Michael Gilbert, the detective Jenny had worked closely with when investigating Amanda Guille's death. Since then, Michael had become a friend, and a frequent visitor at the house Jenny shared with her mother, first checking in on Jenny's recovery and afterwards, when she was well, dropping in for a cup of tea or, more often than not these days, for dinner. His visits were still under the auspices of making sure Jenny was all right, but both she and Michael knew he was far more interested in talking to her mother. Michael would help Margaret in the kitchen, the two of them chatting and laughing, the sound of the radio and the whoosh of the kettle coming to the boil muffling their words. Jenny wondered if they talked about their relationship. If once you were in your fifties, you could cut through the bullshit and have an honest conversation about where you were headed.

She glanced back at her swimming gear. It would have to wait. She was not going to miss an opportunity to cover this story, no matter how uncomfortable it made her feel. This time, she reassured herself, she would not make the news. She would just write it.

And besides, Jenny had another reason to want to go to Sark.

Ever since she'd found out that the investigation into her father's death may have been compromised, she'd wanted to retrace his steps, to talk to the people who saw him last. According to the police report, Charlie Dorey had died after falling overboard on his way back from Sark. That Charlie had been in Sark that day was indisputable. That his boat had been found floating in Sark waters hours after his disappearance was also fact. It was the falling-overboard bit that Jenny took issue with. Charlie would never have done that.

She let herself into the house. Margaret was sitting at the kitchen table, book in one hand, piece of toast and Marmite in the other.

'Morning, love.'

'Morning, Mum.' She kissed her mother on the cheek and helped herself to a cup of tea from the pot.

'How's Elliot?' Margaret's tone was light, but Jenny knew the question was loaded.

'He's fine, thank you. I'm going to grab a quick shower.'

'Would he not let you leave a few things at his place? Save you some time in the mornings.' Margaret turned a page nonchalantly.

'You trying to get rid of me?' Jenny meant it as a joke, but Margaret looked up, hurt.

'Of course not! I love having you here. So long as you're not staying on my account.'

'I know, Mum. You're back on your feet. So am I. I'm going to start looking for somewhere. Soon. I don't want to play gooseberry to you and Michael anymore anyway.'

'It's not like that, Jenny.' Margaret's cheeks coloured. She closed her book and bustled over to the sink, looking for dishes to wash. Finding none, she began to spray the surfaces with bleach, rubbing at stains invisible to Jenny's eyes.

'Mum, relax. I'm just teasing. Wouldn't be the worst thing in the world, though, would it?' She paused. 'It's been more than two years.'

Margaret was still for a moment, then turned, her eyes shining, too brightly. 'I just meant you're not a gooseberry.' She attempted a smile. 'Now, don't you have a job to go to?'

Before she left for work, Jenny went into Charlie's office. He'd spent hours in this room, writing letters to the *Guernsey News*, or doing his accounts on a bulky calculator that printed out receipts like a till in a shop. She had loved the whirring noise it made as it spat out reams of thin, shiny paper, the sort the chip shops used to wrap the fish and chips, only this was a long, narrow ribbon, wound tightly round a plastic tube. Sometimes he'd let her play with it—he'd 'buy' one of her teddies and she'd type in whatever price she'd decided was right, carefully tearing his receipt off against the jagged cutting edge. Margaret had packed it away. Stored it in the loft, one of the many of Charlie's things they were going to 'sort out later'.

Elliot had called the office her 'incident room' due to the fact that she had covered the walls with pictures and notes during the investigation into Amanda Guille's death. Margaret had taken them all down while Jenny had been in hospital recovering from her shoulder wound. She had placed everything neatly in a folder, put it in the desk drawer and moved Jenny's box full of articles and research from her time working as an investigative reporter in London from the bedroom into a corner of the office.

London. It was perverse, she knew, to miss it, after everything that had happened there. She needed to accept that she was an island girl after all, chewed up and spat out by the big city, still trying to wash herself clean, to shed the grit and the grime and the bad memories in the cold, clear water of the English Channel. She wondered if she'd have felt differently if she had managed to finish her last job there, instead of running back to Guernsey, frightened for her life.

She should put the box into storage. But something stopped her. A sense of disquiet that never truly settled, even when all else was well. The constant nagging of unfinished business. But there were issues closer to home that required her attention now. Bones on Derrible Bay. And finding out what had happened to her father.

She looked at the items she had pinned to the study wall. A photograph of Charlie—a close-up Jenny had taken, his face weathered, the lines on it deeper than his years warranted. He'd spent most of his life out on his boat, hauling in the catch, a permanent layer of salt seeming to toughen his skin and his hair, which lay in all directions, thick and wiry, poking out from beneath his hat. The obituary, pinned next to the photograph, had taken up half a page in the *Guernsey News* on account of Charlie being a local 'character'. *Could be found on his beloved* Jenny Wren *come rain or shine . . . always a friendly word . . . a great teller of island tales . . . leaves behind a wife and daughter.*

Next to this, pages from his sailing log, charting his fishing trips in the months before he died. These, she had colour-coded, looking for a pattern in his movements. The only thing she had noted of interest was the frequency with which he had visited Sark.

On the desk lay an open folder containing notes she'd made—interviews with his friends (or 'chats', as she'd called them, not wanting to alarm the people who loved him, or her mother, by hinting that she had her suspicions about his death). Next to the folder, a pile of his diaries.

Charlie had kept a diary ever since Jenny could remember, buying the same type each year, either red or black hardcover with the year printed in gold in the top right corner. Margaret had not wanted to read them, but told Jenny that she should, that Charlie would want her to.

The pages were lined, one per day, but the entries were irregular in length. Some days contained only appointments—*Dentist, 2 p.m.*—or observations about the weather, all in his strange, overly elaborate hand. Occasionally he wrote longer, more personal pieces. They were often sombre in tone: reflections on a bad mood he'd been in, or questioning a decision he had made, or the way he had spoken to Margaret over some trivial disagreement or other. Jenny had read them with tears in her eyes—the vulnerabilities of a man who had always seemed so sure and steadfast revealed.

The pages she focused on, though, the ones she had copied and highlighted and pored over, were the ones that, so far, revealed nothing. Numbers underlined—possibly times? Letters circled—initials? Brief notes—*Same as last time. Check again Friday.* All of these entries were made in the months before he died, and all of them coincided with his visits to Sark. Nothing about Charlie's death looked suspicious, Michael had assured her. But Roger Wilson's words still echoed in her ears: '*Fancied himself as a bit of a detective . . . We all thought it was rather funny . . . until somebody stopped laughing . . .*' The words of a psychopath and a killer, Michael had said. They were nonsense, the ramblings of a madman, uttered when Roger was cornered and desperate to confuse and disarm. Except, Jenny thought, something about them had rung true.

She remembered the first time she'd played detective with Charlie. They'd been walking round the reservoir at St Saviour's, following the shady wooded path that followed the perimeter of the water, long before the States, the island's government, tidied it all up and made it part of the 'Millennium Walk', with handy trail maps and 'What to Look Out For' guides, which brought hundreds of people to the area in the summer. Back then, it had just been Jenny and Charlie, maybe the odd twitcher—binoculars in hand, studying the banks of reeds, which sheltered nesting ducks and occasionally a heron or an egret. The path had been narrow and damp, gnarled tree roots twisting just under the surface. On the north shore, large steel gates had blocked the pathway, and walkers were redirected to the right, down a wide, grassy track that looped back to the reservoir a few hundred yards later. A foreboding 'Keep Out' was chained to one of the gate's crossbars. Jenny would stand, fingers pressed against the cold metal, staring through the trees, which seemed thicker beyond the gate than anywhere else in the woods. She'd been convinced there was something untoward hidden behind them: a covert science lab perhaps, conducting strange experiments on the Guernsey water supply, or a secret government facility.

When she'd relayed her suspicions to Charlie, he'd insisted they sneak round the gates to discover the truth. They owed it to the island, he'd said, to ensure there was nothing nefarious going on. She hadn't known what that meant, but it didn't sound good. They'd soon found themselves knee-deep in a bog, and Charlie had admitted the 'Keep Out' sign was probably there for benign reasons after all. 'Not a word to Mum,' he had said as he hauled her out of the swamp, holding on to a fallen tree to ensure he didn't fall back in. When they'd got home, they blamed their wet things on a misguided duck-rescue attempt. Margaret had been unconvinced and given Charlie her look, the one that begged him not to be reckless—the same one she gave Jenny even now every time she left the house.

The *Guernsey News*, the island's only daily newspaper, was housed in a bright, purpose-built space located on an industrial estate on the north coast, a short drive from both Jenny's house and the main town of St Peter Port. Its many glass walls afforded views over Belle Grève Bay, and beyond, on a clear day, to the islands of Herm and Sark.

The news editor, Graham Le Noury, was talking to Elliot about Rock-Cane, a hedonistic music festival held at Rocquaine Bay every August bank holiday. There was some pressure to cancel from parent and community groups, worried at the increase in drug-related activity on the island. The mother of a teenager who had spent several days in hospital after reacting badly to taking a Black Pearl, a particularly strong strain of ecstasy that had flooded the local club scene, was spearheading the movement.

Jenny attempted to interrupt Graham, as politely as possible, with the news of her lead. He waved her aside, gave her a look that told her to get in line, and she stood, fidgeting, waiting for an opportunity to get a word in without antagonising him.

Graham had worked for the *Guernsey News* for as long as anyone could remember. This was, in Jenny's opinion, the only reason he'd been given the news editor position when Mark Martel, a mild-mannered but diligent reporter with a keen sense of what made a good story, had been promoted to editor-in-chief following Brian Ozanne's unceremonious firing several months previously. Brian had narrowly avoided prison, charged with perverting the course of justice for not revealing what he'd known about key suspects in the biggest murder investigation the island had ever seen.

So the news team was stuck with Graham, a fine but dull reporter, the oldest member of the news team by at least twenty-five years. In fact, looking around the room, Jenny wouldn't have been surprised if Elliot was the next oldest, closely followed by her. The rest of the team were in their mid-twenties. The job didn't pay enough, and the hours were unsociable, and eventually most people went on to more lucrative positions doing marketing or PR at one of the banks. Graham finally finished his conversation and Jenny took the opportunity to grab his attention.

'Graham, just before you start, can I run something by you? It's time sensitive.'

Graham rolled his eyes: his resentment at her breaking the serial-killer story had nowhere near abated. He was not the only one, she thought. There was a shifting from the reporters, ten in all, who had gathered round Graham's desk, and an audible sigh from someone. Elliot had told her there had been some bitching behind her back, other reporters saying that she was Mark's favourite, and she could have sworn there was a palpable change in atmosphere whenever she stepped forward to speak. She carried on regardless.

'I've had a message from my police source.'

'You mean Cousin Steve, I presume?' Graham asked.

She laughed along with the others. There was not a hope in hell of keeping a source secret on Guernsey, not when everyone knew you were related to them.

'Yep, Cousin Steve has come through again. Well, maybe. Suspected human remains have been found on Derrible in Sark.'

'Not a body?' A tremor in the voice of the young female reporter who asked the question. Jenny knew why. None of them wanted to deal with the likes of last year again.

'I don't think so. At least, not a fresh one. Bones apparently.'

'How do they know they're human?'

'No idea, Graham. I've just got a text. If I go now, I can find out.'

'There was a big hoo-ha about bones found on Sark a couple of years ago, remember? Turned out to belong to a bloody great dog. It's probably something like that. Sarkees trying to add a bit of drama to a slow summer. Tourist numbers are shocking this season, I hear.'

'Could be, Graham. We won't know, though, will we, unless I get over there?'

Graham frowned at her, as though trying to work out if she was being impertinent. She smiled, as sweetly as she could, and he looked down at his notes, weighing up whether or not he could spare her.

'You've got the piece on the beach clean-up to finish,' he mused. 'Maybe we should send someone with more capacity.'

Several of the reporters in the room stood up straighter, shuffled forwards. She couldn't blame them. She'd had more than her fair share of good stories recently. But she'd worked for them.

'I can finish that on the way over. I'll have it filed by ten.'

He sighed heavily. 'OK. Let me know what's going on as soon as you get there. Right, on to the rest of the news.'

Jenny gathered her things. Elliot got up quietly and stopped her with a hand on her arm on the way out. She wondered how many of her colleagues had guessed that they were sleeping together.

'Are you OK?'

She nodded. 'Yes. Why?'

'You left in a hurry this morning. And you seem a bit agitated.'

'Everything's fine.'

'You want me to come with you?'

'Graham will throw a fit if I distract you from the Rock-Cane story. He seems to have his knickers in a right twist about it all. Although, I swear, if anyone else had brought him this tip, he'd have had a whole team on the way to Sark.'

'You sure you're OK on your own?'

She knew what he was thinking. Could see the concern on his face.

'Graham's probably right. I'll be back later with breaking news about a sheep that fell off a cliff twenty years ago.'

'And if Graham's wrong?'

'Then I'll be back later with a different story. A big one.'

3

Reg

He knew someone was there. Felt the familiar tingling at the back of his neck. He turned. But he was too slow to catch a glimpse.

He could not remember when he first saw that flicker of movement in his peripheral vision, when he first heard the crackling of dry grass stalks or the crush of stones behind him on an empty pathway. Weeks ago. Perhaps months. Or had it always been this way? He was never alone, not really. There was always someone nearby. A neighbour just beyond the hedge. A friend passing by on his way to work. A tourist wobbling on her bicycle. A ghost. So many ghosts. Whispering their accusations. Taunting him. Brushing the back of his neck with their icy fingers.

He shrugged. It was probably kids. The children of the children who used to follow him, daring each other to get as close as they could and then running away as soon as he caught a look at them. That's how old he was. The kids had kids already. He was too slow now to catch them, and he wouldn't even if he could. One of them had fainted once. Passed out cold as he'd grabbed the little bugger by the scruff of the neck. He'd only been going to give him a telling-off. He wondered what stories they told each other, what sort of bogeyman he was. He smiled. Nothing changed. Each generation had their monsters. Their horror stories. He and his friends had taunted an older lady way back when.

17

Convinced she was a witch, they'd muttered charms whenever she'd passed, or crossed themselves and spat over their shoulders, lest she cursed them with her evil eye. Poor woman. Just a spinster. Old and alone. Like him.

He looked at his shoes. Fine yellow dust coated the dull, scuffed leather. It had not rained for days and the main road through the village was dry; small clouds of the pressed, sandy surface surrounded his feet as he walked.

He had gone out with a purpose this morning and managed to follow it through to completion. No mean feat these days. He pulled a trolley behind him. It was red-and-black tartan and heavy with bread, eggs, milk and butter. No national papers. There was fog over in Guernsey and the mail plane from the mainland could not land there in time to make the eight-o'clock sailing to Sark. No matter. He never read the papers anyway. And he had a copy of the *Guernsey News*, which would do nicely.

His smile slipped as he tried to remember why he needed a newspaper that he wouldn't read. To start a fire, perhaps. No, that couldn't be right. It was summer. Hot. So hot that even now, early morning, sweat trickled down his brow and stung the corners of his eyes. He closed them. Shook his head. A sudden, sharp vision. A boy crying. He could hear him. Smell him. That's how it was now. Memories from years ago were clear as though they happened yesterday, and yet it was a struggle to hold on to a new thought for more than a few moments.

He wondered how long it would be before he stopped questioning his own behaviour. Before he was so lost there was no finding the way back, not even for a little bit. Perhaps one of his strolls would finish him off. He found himself in the strangest places at the strangest times. He would set out to watch the sunrise over the common and end up on La Coupée, the narrow, wind-battered isthmus that connected Sark to Little Sark, leaning on railings built by German prisoners of war, looking out over the sea to the sun rising from behind Jersey, the empty feeling in his stomach reminding him that he'd not yet had breakfast. It was a long way to walk without breakfast.

Or, in the dark, at the edge of the cliffs at Gouliot, acutely aware of the caves that riddled the earth beneath his feet, the island of Brecqhou rising out of the water before him. It had been deserted when he was a boy. Just seagulls and seagull shit, the odd puffin, sometimes a seal basking on the rocks. Now there was a mansion made of marble and gold, so they said, each step leading up to it costing hundreds of thousands of pounds. So they said.

Sometimes he would come round as if from sleep at Port du Moulin, sitting on the pebbles, the tide lapping at his feet, staring at the arch of rock that straddled land and sea, and reminded him of pictures he had seen in National Geographic magazine, of great stone arches in the American desert, Utah, or Nevada, he couldn't remember which. Somewhere he'd never been. Somewhere he would never go. His was a life measured in footsteps, not air miles.

He lived less than three miles from anywhere on the island. Less than one from the village. It would only have taken a few minutes on his bicycle, but he had left it somewhere. He had forgotten where. He'd posted a note up, a few days ago, at the Village Stores. The scrawny girl working there had laughed at him as she wrote it. She was one of those seasonal workers who came over for a few weeks every summer. She'd said all the islanders had funny names and he'd had to spell his out for her. She'd had a tattoo of a butterfly on the inside of her veiny wrist, and her T-shirt had lain flat and loose over her chest. He preferred a little meat on the bones. Large breasts and fleshy buttocks. Like Rachel.

It was still on the board. The note. There had been no sign of the bike. Truth be told, he'd been struggling to ride it anyway, with his knees. Better to walk. Maybe if his knees got really bad, he could get one of those motorised scooters the aged seigneur had used after his hip replacement. Sir William de Bordeaux, the island's feudal leader, was approaching ninety. There'd been a big to-do when he'd asked for permission to use a motorised vehicle. But after much consideration, the Chief Pleas, Sark's government, had agreed that it was impractical for the seigneur to be taken everywhere on a horse and cart, and that a mobility scooter was less intrusive than a tractor. They were right about that. Used to be hard to get a tractor licence on Sark. Now it seemed like anyone could get one.

There was one now. Not just one—two, three in a bloody row. That was unusual, truth be told. And they seemed to be going very fast. He turned to watch them, spewing thick fumes into the heavy air as they chugged up the Avenue.

Outside the new coffee shop, two women were talking animatedly. They pointed after the tractors. One was holding a mobile telephone to her ear, talking into it, then pausing every now and then to check something with her companion. Time was he would have tried to find out what all the fuss was about. But he didn't know the women. At least, he didn't think he did. It was difficult for him to sort out the familiar faces from the unfamiliar. People stopped and talked to him as if they knew him, but he could not place them. Each face seemed to blend into the next, their features blurred by the haze that settled on his eyes overnight and often didn't clear until lunchtime. He should get his eyes tested, at the very least, but that would mean a trip to Guernsey and he'd rather go blind than go there.

He passed the bank and some guesthouses. They were all covered in wisteria and advertised lobster rolls and afternoon tea and Prosecco in the garden on chalkboards outside. Fifteen pounds for a sandwich and a glass of wine. He shook his head, felt the sweat under his collar. It was like the desert sometimes. All the yellow roads and the sand and the dust and the shimmer of the heat up ahead. He would have liked to have seen a desert. The Sahara, perhaps. It froze there, sometimes, at night. Not many people knew that.

He set down his trolley and rested against the hedge, avoiding a patch of cow parsley, which on a day like today, with the sun blazing, would blister the skin if brushed against. The grass was cool. He closed his eyes for a moment, listened to the grasshoppers and the birds and felt like he could just drift off, right there.

The rumble of another tractor. It came into view and he stood and squinted at it. Ah, this one he knew. It was Malcolm Perré's boy. He had forgotten his name. Malcolm's boy raised a hand in greeting and he nodded his head in reply. He had never liked Malcolm, but the boy had been friends with Luke and was always polite, and he'd stayed here, to run a farm, which said something, he supposed, about the boy's character. He coughed as the dust churned up by the tractor hit the back of his throat.

The tractor stopped.

'Everything OK, Mr Carré?'

'Yes, yes. Just enjoying the sunshine.' He took hold of the trolley, made to continue on his way.

'Have you heard about the body?'

'What's that?' It seemed as if Malcolm's boy was looking at him very intently and he felt a frisson of fear.

'Well, not a body. Bones. Down on Derrible. The police are there now.'

The heat on his face was no longer from the sun but from the blood that rushed from his body and his limbs and surged into his head. His legs felt hollow and he did not trust them to hold his weight. He leaned back against the hedge again.

'Nothing to worry about, I'm sure. Probably washed up from somewhere else. Do you need a lift home?'

He shook his head. Waved a hand. 'I'm fine.' Benjamin. That was Malcolm's boy's name. 'Thank you, Benjamin.'

'OK, Mr Carré. Take care now.' The tractor rumbled away.

He stood up. Pulled his trolley, head down, one foot in front of the other. He needed to get home. To sit down in the cool darkness of the cottage.

Head still pounding. Legs still weak. The trolley felt heavy all of a sudden, a weight trailing behind him he could no longer bear.

Just get home.

But his vision blurred and the path began to resemble not earth but water, and he stumbled as the surface undulated, his feet continuing to travel through what his eyes believed was solid ground. He stopped. Searched his pockets for a handkerchief.

A rustle. The crushing of dry grass.

It was close now. He could feel it. Closer than it had ever been. The air thickened; the heat pressed down on him, hampered his breathing. He recalled the feeling of being buried on the beach, a game played as a child, sand shovelled on top of him, heavy as rocks piled on his chest.

And then he saw it. A dark flicker. In the field beside him.

He steadied himself. Swallowed down a gulp of the warm, heavy air. Turned. Let go of the trolley, which fell to the ground with a clatter.

It stood motionless, save for its tongue, which lolled out of its open, spittle-flecked jaws, rippling as it panted in the heat. Its coat was so black, so sleek, it shone almost blue in the sunlight, muscles quivering beneath it. Its eyes were fixed on him, flaming from within.

He felt sure if he moved, it would come for him. Even the flicker of an eyelash. The twitch of a hand. So he stood, tensing every aching muscle, holding every brittle bone in place. Still. So still. Until the breeze whispered through the undergrowth, sent leaves scuttling across the path and lifted his hair. It was enough. The beast stiffened. Crouched. Growled, long and low, and he could smell its breath, laden with dank and decay, like the soil in a graveyard. He had seen the Tchico. His time had come. It turned. Padded silently across the field and into the woods beyond.

He allowed himself to breathe. Felt the tension leave his body, only the old and familiar aches remaining in his bones. Not now, then. Not right now. But soon. He'd known all along that it would come to this. It wasn't children following him. It was fate. He'd always imagined when it caught up with him that he would scream and run, that he would fight against inevitability.

As it was, he picked up his trolley, put his head down. Kept on walking.

4

Michael

The boat flew over each wave, bouncing back onto the surface and showering them all with sea spray before taking off again. There were four of them in the RIB, a high-speed rigid inflatable boat, plus the captain. The pair from forensics—Cathy, a pretty woman in her mid-thirties, and Rob, a dependable, if slow-moving chap who had worked for them for years—were sat on one side of the boat taking in the scenery. They laughed as they wiped the water from their eyes. Opposite them, Detective Constable Stephen Marquis, who had been fiddling with his phone, hastily dried it on his trouser leg before prodding furiously at the screen, a panicked look on his face. Always texting someone, that boy was. It was bloody irritating.

Next to Marquis, DCI Michael Gilbert gripped the edge of his seat and wished that he'd eaten something before he'd left home. He was not prone to seasickness, but an empty stomach and a choppy patch taken at speed were not a good combination and he felt faintly nauseous. This was adding to his already bad mood, the result of the phone ringing late last night, just as he'd drifted off in front of *Hang 'Em High* (the last of the Clint Eastwood special DVD collection his ex-wife had sent him for Christmas). The constable in Sark had received an anonymous tip that bones had been found on Derrible Bay and would they send a team over to investigate?

There were no police on Sark—as part of the Bailiwick of Guernsey, it came under the jurisdiction of Guernsey Police, who hadn't had a full-time presence there for years. Time was, they'd send officers over on a two-week rotation during the summer, but it hadn't been cost-effective, because, quite frankly, nothing ever bloody happened there, and as Michael knew only too well, the officers tended to spend their two weeks propping up a bar and gossiping with the locals. So now they just had the constable, a voluntary position, who had responsibility for ensuring law and order among the island's population of approximately four hundred and fifty. An easy enough job. Until something like this happened.

Michael rubbed his forehead. Anonymous tips often came to nothing—bored kids making mischief, or disgruntled members of the public trying to get one over on the police. So best-case scenario, this whole thing was a wind-up. Which would be frustrating. But better than the worst-case scenario. And because his expectation of what a worst-case scenario might involve had been adjusted upwards several levels after last year, he had pulled out all the stops this morning. Police boat, forensics, the lot. All of this on top of the fact that he was already neck-deep in the investigation into this new drug flooding Guernsey. Black Pearls the kids were calling them, due to their colour and the little skull and crossbones printed on each one. Horrible things had already landed one kid in hospital, and they were no closer to finding out where the stuff was coming from. But Michael couldn't afford to miss a beat. Not on the drug investigation, and definitely not on whatever was going on in Sark.

Because the entire Guernsey Police Force was under review. Everything they did, everything they'd ever done was being scrutinised by a team of special investigators from Scotland Yard. That's how monumentally they'd fucked up last year—Scotland Yard were taking an interest in Guernsey, a sleepy little backwater.

So Michael was feeling jittery. Under pressure. Unable to relax on the short boat journey, because he was dreading dealing with whatever awaited him. Human bones or animal bones or no bones at all, he was still in for a difficult day.

The cool breeze that ruffled his hair as they sped over the water would be absent on Sark. It would be hotter than hell there today, he thought. He shook slightly. Felt a tingling in his back, like the beginnings of the flu. It was probably just the late night and the early morning and the three cups of coffee he'd drunk before 6 a.m. He needed a lie-in. And an end to the paperwork, and the weight of responsibility this job seemed to burden him with these days. The alternative was worse, though. Retirement. All that time to think. To dwell. He shrugged. He'd have to do it eventually. He'd adjust, he supposed. Many years ago, he'd never imagined life without his wife and daughter. And now look at him. Sheila had been married to her second husband for longer than she'd been married to Michael. And Ellen had been dead and buried for as many years as she'd walked the earth.

The roar of the engine faded to a growl as they reached the bay. Michael had never approached Derrible by sea before, only from the footpath, which wound steeply down the cliff from the headland, landing at a rocky plateau, the only place to sit at high tide. The path afforded a gentler introduction to this scenery, slowly enveloping the visitor in their surroundings, the scale of which Michael only really appreciated now. The cliffs appeared sinister and looming, black shadows in the early morning light, the cave openings gaping mouths. The beach was less than half exposed, a thin crescent of shingle and stones, the sand hidden by the retreating tide.

The captain, a taciturn chap called James Després, whose reticence had earned him the nickname 'Gobby Jim', took them as close to the shore as he could, turning towards a flat boulder and buffering the front of the boat against it. Michael stared distastefully at the two or so feet of water beneath them. It was an odd thing about Sark that no matter how warm the air, the water was always ice-cold. He took off his shoes and socks, and rolled up his trousers. He'd not had much time outdoors this summer and his legs were plucked-chicken pale. He let out a yelp as he slid off the side of the boat and plunged his feet into the water. He swayed from side to side, struggling to get a footing on the smooth pebbles of the seabed before finding his balance and striding to shore, the salt stinging his dry skin. When he reached the sand, he wiggled his toes, which looked to have entirely drained of blood, while he waited for Marquis, who was a good few inches shorter than Michael and had made a poor job of rolling up his trousers. They unfurled a little further with each step he took and were soaked through up to the knee before he reached dry land.

'Right.' Michael pulled his socks and shoes back onto still-wet feet. 'Where are these bloody things?' He raised his hand to shield his eyes against the sun, which had fully risen over Hogsback Cliffs in front of them.

'Would they not have been washed away by the tide since last night, sir?' Marquis scanned the small area of dry beach and seaweed not touched by the sea.

'According to our tipster, the bones are in a cave.' He pointed to a ledge protruding from the cliffs fifteen feet above the sand with a round opening about five feet across above it. 'That just about matches the description we were given.'

Michael went first, clambering up a series of wide, flat rocks before reaching the ledge. He hauled himself onto it and then sat for a moment to catch his breath. He stood at the mouth of the cave and shone the torch inside. It was larger than it looked from the outside, full head height, room for two people so long as they didn't want to move about too much. The floor was rock and shingle. No footprints. No bones. Wrong cave, maybe. Or crap information more like. He swept the light around one more time. Lingered on a pile of lighter-coloured stones in the corner. They looked out of place. One or two lay on the floor of the cave, as though they'd fallen from the stack.

'See anything, sir?'

'Hold this, will you? Shine it over here.' Michael poked at one of the stones. It was loose. He removed it, placed it behind him. Then took another. And another. Until an opening was revealed. A second, small cavern, a couple of feet high, perhaps three feet wide at most. Michael peered in. The shapes within were confusing, the light from behind bouncing off pale curves, absorbed into dark hollows.

'What's that, sir? Another cave?' Marquis squeezed himself next to Michael and shone the torch beam right into it. Edges sharpened.

Michael winced, stepped back.

'It's not a cave, Marquis. It's a tomb.'

5

Jenny

*T*he *Venture* was a small, cheerful-looking ferry with a bright blue hull, white cabin and red roof. There was plenty of indoor seating, and a coffee bar on the lower deck, but Jenny headed straight for the benches that lined the upper level. She found a seat right at the back, which offered the best views of Guernsey behind them. When she was little, she had sat in the same place on Charlie's boat, the *Jenny Wren*, waving goodbye to Guernsey as it first expanded into a panorama, stretched out before them, from the cliffs of St Martin's in the south to the chimneys of the power station in the north, and then shrank, slowly retreating into the distance, a green-grey dot on the horizon.

Two women came and sat next to Jenny. They were in their sixties, dressed for walking, both wearing sturdy boots, long socks and wide-brimmed sun hats with strings tied under their chins. One of them pulled out a map and started making suggestions as to a possible route round the island.

'Do you know Sark?' The lady next to Jenny turned to her.

Jenny nodded. 'Yes. A little.' Better than most, she thought.

'We've never been. We go away every year together.' She pointed to her friend, who smiled and nodded in agreement. 'Girls' break.'

'From our husbands,' her companion stage-whispered.

'Never quite long enough, is it, Irene?'

They both chuckled and began studying the map again.

Jenny listened to their chatter about the best places to visit and chipped in with a couple of ideas of her own, suggesting, to great controversy, that the ladies consider hiring bikes. She left them to their good-natured argument and stood, leaning against the railing. It was slick and sticky with salt and grease. Below, a crew member unwound the thick rope from the cleat that tethered them to the dock. A shout and a hand raised to the captain signalled that they were good to go. The noise from the boat's engines shifted from a hum to a rumble and they moved off, through the harbour and out onto the open sea. She breathed in the salty air and watched the beams of sunlight fragment into rainbows as they bounced off the sea spray.

After only fifteen minutes, they had reached the south coast of Herm, a tiny island a mile and a half long by half a mile wide, popular with locals and tourists alike for its beaches and winding coastal pathway. The sun's rays always seemed to seek out Herm, and as they passed it now, the island itself shone—the sand of Shell Beach an iridescent pearly pink, the cliffs golden, topped with lush green and bright purple echiums, known as 'Towers of Jewels' due to their tall, beautifully flowered stems.

As they left Herm behind them, Jenny looked for some of the familiar rock formations Charlie used to point out to her. She spotted two rocks, the larger one appearing to cradle the smaller, known as the Madonna and Child, and Le Chat, its ears poking out of the waves towards Sark, which they were now approaching.

Too beautiful to describe as 'looming', there was still something unsettling about the way the island rose out of the sea. It was ethereal, she thought, rather than sinister, three hundred feet of red-brown cliff towering above them. At the top, a lighthouse nestled among foliage, its parapet stark and white against a clear blue sky. You could almost be approaching an island in the Mediterranean, Mykonos or Santorini, rather than a wind-swept Channel isle.

The coast was riddled with caves. Charlie had taken her on the RIB, whizzed through the waves and then slowed to a crawl as he'd navigated the narrow openings into their gaping maws. He'd told her stories about pirates and smuggling years ago, and more recently, about a couple of tourists who had ventured off the cliff path down to the caves and been trapped by the tide and rescued, just in time, by *Flying Christine*, the marine ambulance. 'Cost a bloody fortune, those kinds of rescues,' Charlie had said. She'd had the impression he would have left them to drown.

The Venture's engines slowed as the captain manoeuvred round the jagged rocks that spilled off the cliffs and into the sea. Above the jarring screeches of the gulls wheeling around them, Jenny heard the panicked cries of an oystercatcher. It sounded like a child, calling out for its mother.

They moved slowly through a narrow passage between the cliffs, round into Maseline Harbour. Here, after the rugged north coast, it felt as if the island was opening its rocky arms to them, a welcoming display of wild flowers scattered over the grassy headland. Granite slabs clad the jetty, the only man-made part of the harbour, and rows of tyres lined the concrete posts they chugged towards, buffering the boat as the same crew member who had cast off in Guernsey hopped onto the dock, rope in hand, and tethered them to Sark.

A man in the Sark Shipping uniform—a navy polo shirt and shorts, which exposed weathered, muscular legs, one heavily tattooed, a dragon twisting round his calf—helped her off the boat with a 'Watch your step, love' as he held the crook of her arm and guided her onto the jetty.

She strung her bag across her shoulder and trod carefully up the damp steps. A lone tractor waited, engine running, to collect the luggage of the few visitors who were staying overnight and deliver it to hotels and guesthouses, while the passengers were left to walk through a tunnel that ran thirty feet under the towering rock face, and naturally separated the harbour from the rest of the island. A 'Welcome to Sark' sign hung cheerfully over the tunnel's mouth. Framed in the opening at the far end, a miniature view of verdant cliffs topped with yellow gorse drew pedestrians out onto Harbour Hill, the road leading to the village.

'The guidebook wasn't joking about it being steep, was it?' One of the women from the boat drew up alongside Jenny, quickly followed by the other.

'You could always take one of the toast-racks.' Jenny used the local nickname for the open-sided, tractor-drawn carts that would take visitors to the top of the hill for two pounds.

'Oh, I don't think so.' The lady called Irene looked at the carts distastefully.

Jenny smiled. Charlie had always derided the toast-racks as 'for tourists', and she was oddly pleased that the women had rejected them.

'Well, I'm in a bit of a hurry, so I'm going to hop on one, but the path is over there.' She showed them the steps to the woodland trail that ran parallel to the road. The ladies declared it quite lovely and waved Jenny off. She left them consulting their map and bickering about where they were stopping for lunch.

The bone-rattling toast-rack ride took Jenny as far as the crossroads at the brow of the hill, where a row of horses harnessed to old-fashioned cariages stood in front of a high-hedged field. The air was ripe with their scent, sweet hay and oat-laden manure, the drivers hastily stubbing out cigarettes or placing half-drunk cups of coffee in the carriage cabs, readying themselves to haggle over the cost of an island tour. The horses, heavy-hooved, pawed the ground and shook their heads in anticipation. Several people wandered over to them. Jenny checked her phone. Nothing from Stephen. They would have been down on Derrible for a couple of hours by now. If she didn't hurry, she might miss them. She didn't want to think about Graham's reaction if her journey turned out to be a complete waste of time.

The quickest way to Derrible—in fact the quickest way to anywhere on Sark—was on a bike, so she set off towards Alf's, the nearest of several cycle-hire shops, a brisk five-minute walk down the Avenue.

Wide enough for cyclists to pass in either direction, with room for a couple of pedestrians to meander down the centre, the Avenue was the closest thing to a main road on Sark. It was also flatter and smoother than the rest of the island's gravelly, potholed lanes and dirt tracks.

A row of single-storey buildings lined either side—the Village Stores, selling sunscreen and first-aid kits, local-interest books and souvenir tea towels, the tiny supermarket proudly advertising, 'Now stocking Waitrose!' Jenny passed a new café, its pastel-pink awning looking out of place on a street that otherwise displayed muted tones—dark green or blue doors, black-and-white signage. The sandwich board outside advertised expensive lattes and custom-made cupcakes. She wondered how long it would last. It had only been a year or so since she had last been here and several shops had closed since then. One building looked particularly dilapidated, its window obscured with white paint, the remains of a row of posters stuck all over it. It appeared that somebody had haphazardly torn at them, ripping off the middle sections but leaving the edges, curling towards the corners. Jenny flattened one of the larger remaining pieces—'Want' and the top of a picture of somebody's face. She smoothed out the bottom section—'Crimes Against Sark.'

'They were all over the place couple of weeks ago.'

An attractive woman in her forties, wearing a tight white T-shirt, arms tanned and muscular, leaned against the door of the next building, a souvenir shop. Her peroxide-blonde hair was pulled back in a ponytail, exposing dark roots. She lit a cigarette, took a deep drag and blew the smoke over her shoulder.

'Someone put 'em all over the island. Sent Monroe nuts. Thought he was going to pop a vein.' She had a London accent.

'He's the one on the poster?'

The woman nodded. 'You on holiday?'

'Just a day trip from Guernsey. I used to spend a lot of time here as a kid.'

'Heard about what's happened down on Derrible?'

'Someone said the police are there?' It wasn't a lie. Jenny always told people she was a reporter when she approached them, but when the conversation was being steered by someone else, it often paid not to reveal what she did, or how much she knew. This woman seemed like the naturally talkative type. Jenny just needed to listen.

'And the rest. Heard there was a body.'

'Any idea who it might be?'

'Well, I haven't done a full headcount since yesterday, but so far as I know nobody's missing.' She smiled. 'Wouldn't worry, love. Most of the gossip around here turns out to be three-parts speculation to two-parts bullshit. Still, you might want to steer clear of that end of the island.'

The woman turned her attention back to the posters. 'You know about Monroe?'

Jenny nodded. Corey Monroe, the shipping billionaire, had bought Brecqhou, a tiny island off the west coast of Sark, five years ago as the ultimate, private tax haven. He had built a huge estate, complete with manor house, pub, landscaped gardens, swimming pools and tennis courts, and then set about trying to buy property on Sark. The Sarkees had taken a disliking to Monroe, accusing him of trying to buy the island, to turn it into his own private playground, and they used Sark's ancient laws to block him every step of the way. Clearly a man not used to taking 'no' for an answer, Corey Monroe had faced off against the seigneur and the Chief Pleas, Sark's unelected, feudal government, and pushed for democratisation, challenging them in the European Court of Human Rights. He had won. Sark's first free and fair elections had been held the year before. The sale of several properties to Corey Monroe had followed soon after.

The woman shook her head. 'It's like that programme on the telly *Neighbours at War*. Only it's the whole bloody island. Bet it's changed since you was a kiddie?'

Jenny nodded.

The woman waved towards the empty storefronts. 'Monroe owns them. He hiked up the rents to punish the islanders for not voting for the candidates he wanted in the elections. Cancelled local supply contracts for his hotels as well. That's what people say, anyway.' She shook her head.

'Ironic, isn't it? He was the one got the whole system changed—all his challenges in the courts to the old ways, the articles in the newspapers about how the island's finally a democracy, and now he can't get anyone to rent his buildings or work for him. He's started with this charm offensive. Wanders around trying to be all pally with us, acting like he's one of the locals when we all know he practically shits diamonds.'

'You're not local?'

'Been here twenty-five years, but no, I'm not local.' She held out her hand. 'Tuesday Jones.' She rolled her eyes at Jenny's reaction. 'I know. My dad had a thing about Tuesday Weld. Arsehole that he was.' She laughed. 'Monroe tried to buy this place off me.' She gestured to the building behind her. 'He offered me a fortune, but I held out.' She shook her head. 'I worked hard for this. No one's taking it away from me, billionaire or otherwise. Here, hang on a minute.' She disappeared into the shop and came back with a flyer. 'Next time you're over, take a tour. See some of the island this bloody feud hasn't ruined.'

'Cave tours. You run these?'

'Certainly do. Did well last summer—introduced a couple of night-time sails. Now we're officially a "Dark Sky Island". Some of the darkest and clearest skies in the world here. Only a couple of street lights, see, no cars. Anyway, brings in a few extra tourists. I do a nice trip round the coast, show 'em the constellations. You should come on one. Place is different in the dark. Better, if you ask me. But then I'm a bit of a night owl.' She smiled and stubbed her cigarette out on the door frame. 'Right, I better get on. Enjoy your trip.' She stepped back into the shop once more.

Jenny folded the flyer and put it in her back pocket. She snapped a couple of pictures of the posters. Perhaps it was time the *News* ran an update on the dispute between the Sarkees and Corey Monroe.

Empty storefronts and posters aside, everything else on Sark was just as it had always been. Hanging baskets overflowing with geraniums, a notice board outside a shop announcing that the quilting club met in the church hall every third Wednesday, another offering a reward for information about a missing bike.

At Alf's Cycle Hire, she paid six pounds to take a rickety Mary Poppins-style shopper for the day, turning down a more practical mountain bike on account of its hard, narrow seat, which she knew,

34

from painful experience, would render an inexperienced rider unable to sit down for a week after a couple of hours on Sark roads.

She cycled back the way she'd walked, turning right at the crossroads, avoiding a pile of freshly dropped horse manure and a boy of no more than five or six years old on a battered bike, who cut the corner as he headed to the village, yelling a 'sorry' as Jenny wobbled towards the hedge. Balance regained, she freewheeled down the rough, gravel-strewn pathway towards the cliffs.

Hedgerows gave way to woodland and the path became shaded and cool. A wooden sign reading, 'The Coach House,' hung askew on an open gate. She glanced through it, down a short track to a low, white cottage with a thatched roof, pink roses growing up the walls and chickens scratching in the yard. She thought, as she had so often on visits to Sark, that its quaint beauty belonged to another age. It was too picture-perfect to be believed without seeing.

Before long, the landscape opened out again, lush green fields on either side, and she could feel the sea in the air. She knew the turn-off to the cliff path was nearby and slowed down. She passed a tractor that had pulled into an opening in the hedgerow. The cab was covered but open-sided. A man lounged back in it, cap pulled down over his eyes. A tinny radio played Tears for Fears. She slowed, concerned he had fallen ill, but the steady rise and fall of his chest suggested he was sleeping. Early for a nap, but the heat and the soothing birdsong were enough to make anyone drowsy. Round the corner, the path turned to grass and opened out to a clover-strewn field. Jenny, realising she'd gone too far, turned round, cycling uphill now, passing the tractor again. The driver, awake after all, sat up as she approached, pushed up his cap.

'You lost?' The words rumbled, heavy and wet, as if from deep within his chest. His skin was tanned, his eyes bloodshot.

'I'm looking for the path to Derrible.'

'You with the police?'

'No.'

'Well, they're down there. Body, apparently. Probably best you visit another day.'

'I'd still like to have a look. If you wouldn't mind pointing the way?'

He frowned at her. 'You look familiar. I've seen you. On the news.'

'I'm a reporter.'

'That's right. The one who got shot. Dorey.'

'That's me.'

'My gran was a Dorey.'

'Lots of us about.'

He seemed to think for a moment and then pursed his lips and pointed a grimy finger towards a field.

'You can cut through there,' he said. 'Go as far as the next hedge and follow it to the right until you come to a gate. Go straight across the next field. You'll pass a digger. Swing right down the cliffs just after that. The path is marked. If you come to Sark Henge, you've gone too far.'

'Thank you.'

'Be careful, though, eh?'

'Sorry?'

He smiled, revealing a row of teeth too small for his mouth.

'It's steep. Mind your step.'

She set off in the direction he had pointed, glancing back once, feeling like he was watching her. He had returned to his semi-prone position, hat pulled down, but this time, his eyes remained uncovered. She walked quickly, trying to shake off the unease he had provoked. She found the gate and fumbled with the blue twine that anchored it to a post in the hedge. It swung open with a screech. Only when she was through, the gate secured behind her, did she slow her pace.

She could see Sark Henge up ahead. Nine old gate stones of pink granite placed in a circle. They looked ancient and mysterious but had only been standing a year—to commemorate the four hundred and fifty years since Queen Elizabeth I had granted Sark to Hellier de Carteret, the seigneur of St Ouen. He, in turn, had split the island into forty parcels of land, known as the Quarantaine. Each of these tenements was given to a strong, healthy farmer and his family, who would not only work the barren, weather-battered soil and transform it into fertile farmland but protect it from marauding enemies: the French, or

Spanish, or Dutch, depending on the year. These landowners formed Sark's first parliament, the Chief Pleas, headed by the seigneur himself. Thus this tiny, feudal state, allegiant to the English Crown, had been born.

Jenny paused to get her bearings, then followed the edge of the cliff until the path dipped down, the grass thinning to earth and then gravel and rock, roughly hewn into steps. A length of yellow tape had been strung from the iron railing on one side to the gorse bush on the other: 'Police Line. Do Not Cross.'

Shit. She could just imagine Graham's face if she had to report that there was in fact a story but she couldn't get to it. And if she left now, she'd have no excuse to stick around and ask questions about Charlie. She stared at the police line. The end attached to the gorse bush had come untethered and was held in place only by the plant's spiky leaves. It flapped half-heartedly in the scant breeze. One strong gust would blow it right out of the way. If that happened, it would be unclear, really, where she shouldn't cross. She looked around. There was nobody in sight. She walked through the tape, pulling it free as she did so, leaving it hanging limply in her wake.

The descent was steep and she made good use of the railing. Derrible Bay itself was hidden from view until over halfway down the cliff, and Jenny used the time to think of a way of getting Michael on side when she reached the bottom. He would be displeased with her and unlikely to comment on the investigation unless she could persuade him it was in his interest. And apologise profusely and maybe offer him dinner. She grinned. Perhaps her colleagues were right to be exasperated by her. There were perks to being friends with one of the most senior detectives on Guernsey.

The steps curved sharply to the right and Derrible in all its glory was revealed. The tide level was perfect, low enough to reveal a butter-coloured curve of sand but high enough that the water was still easily accessible, a short walk to an arc of almost impossibly bright blue. Behind, the cliffs—jagged ochre rock splashed with acid-green lichen and patches of sticky black tar. Gulls perched nervously in crevices, skittering back and forth, one then another taking flight, screeching and cawing before coming back to rest, hard yellow eyes fixed nervously on the unwanted activity below.

There were several police officers combing the pebbles near the cliffs. She snapped a few pictures, then spotted Michael, on his phone. He looked stressed and his voice carried over to her. He was on the line to a superior, calling whoever it was 'sir', an almost pleading quality to his tone. He hung up and paused for a moment before marching towards a cave, from which, Jenny noticed, a forensics officer had just emerged. Michael stopped dead, however, when he caught sight of Jenny, a look of confusion quickly replaced with anger. Her stomach flipped. Her pathetic excuse about an unclear police line was not going to wash. She took the last few steps slowly, meeting him at the bottom.

'What the hell are you doing here, Jenny? This is a bloody crime scene! Marquis! Marquis!' he barked, looking around for the junior officer. 'I thought I told you to secure the steps?'

Jenny's cousin, Stephen Marquis, came running over. He was beet-red, whether from the exertion, stress or his near-permanent state of borderline embarrassment Jenny couldn't be sure.

'I did, sir!'

Jenny held up her hands. 'I'm sorry. I figured that was a preliminary line and all the real action was on the beach. I haven't disturbed anything important, have I?'

'That's not the point, as well you know. Leave this to me, Marquis.'

'Yes, sir.' He looked relieved to be getting out of the way but threw Jenny a frown as he left. She knew she'd landed him in it—it wouldn't take Michael long to work out who had tipped her off. She'd have to do some serious pint-buying to get back in his good books.

'I could have you arrested. There's only so far being a local hero will get you, you know. You've not got some carte bloody blanche to stick your nose into anything you feel like.'

He looked tired, she thought. More than that. Weary. The last time he'd come to the house, she'd sensed it too. The external investigation into the police force was taking its toll.

'You can't expect to keep something like this a secret.'

'Hmph,' he grunted, then sat on a damp rock with a deep sigh. She joined him. The pebbles beneath their feet were glossy.

'And you know if you give me the story, I'll at least write it up nicely. Proper grammar, full sentences.'

She saw the edges of his mouth twitch. He often complained about the quality of the writing in the *News*.

'You're bloody incorrigible, you are.'

She smiled. 'I was hoping for a quote about the investigation, but that's better than nothing.'

'I was going to call you. When we were finished.'

'But as I'm here . . .'

'You didn't get this from me. I've got enough on my bloody plate.'

'Absolutely not.'

He stood. 'Bones. In a cave. Looks like a full skeleton.'

She paused, considering what this meant. Spoke softly, knowing that the answers to her question would be anything but gentle.

'Any theory as to how it got there?'

The seagulls had momentarily stopped screeching. A drowsy bumblebee floated between them. Michael watched it land on a pink campion flower growing between the rocks. Then he turned to her, deep furrows in his brow.

'With help, presumably.'

She was hot and thirsty by the time she made it back to the top of the steps and could feel the first prickling of sunburn on the back of her neck. She was not looking forward to the uphill cycle ride back to the village. Michael had given her enough for tomorrow's front page, but his willingness to co-operate had fallen short of offering her a lift back to Guernsey. They'd be tied up on the beach for hours, he'd said. And then they'd have to think about setting up an incident room, questioning locals. He'd asked her not to share details about the discovery with the Sarkees, not until the police had made a formal statement.

But Jenny figured there was no harm in listening to the gossip, following up with a few questions while she waited for the next ferry back to Guernsey. As for her enquiries into Charlie's last visit to the island, they would have to wait. With a major story like this to work on, she'd soon be back.

On the path, the tractor she'd seen earlier was still parked up. The radio was still playing. But there was no sign of the driver. She looked around for him. The fields here were for grazing, but there were no cattle to tend. Perhaps he'd broken down and had been waiting for help, had got bored and walked back to the village. She approached the vehicle. Checked behind her before climbing up into the cab.

The smell of engine oil and stale body odour was overwhelming. A copy of the *Sunday Sport* had been trodden into the footwell, pages mud-stained and crumpled. On the dash was a spiral-bound notebook, the front page full of rows of tight writing in soft pencil. She turned it towards her. Scanned the numbers and words. They looked like names, perhaps times. The last note on the list read, *Dorey, 9.40.* She twisted the book back into position, clambered down, face flushed. Tried to think of a rational explanation. Maybe he liked to write down the names of everyone he met and the time he met them. There was no law against it. She climbed onto her bike, began to pedal, then stopped. She wasn't thinking straight. She should take a picture, see if she could figure out to whom the rest of the notes referred. She moved towards the tractor.

The screech of metal against metal.

The gate.

She cycled as quickly as she could, only stopping at the top of the hill, her cheeks burning, legs shaking from the exertion. She risked a look down, saw the sweeping panorama of the cliffs and the sea beyond. And the figure of the tractor driver, who was making his way back to the path. The same way she had come only minutes before.

He had followed her.

6

Michael

They'd searched every accessible cave they could find, but so far it was looking like there was only one body. *Only* one. His parameters of what constituted a disaster had shifted somewhat since last year. He counted seven police officers, plus the two from forensics, who having spent most of the morning crouched in the cave, had finally removed the remains and were back on the beach, hunched over their findings. He watched Cathy as she stood and stretched, rubbing the small of her back. She waved him over, her hand still blue-gloved.

'All done?' The bones were laid out on the pebbles, bagged and labelled.

She nodded. 'As much as we can from here. As we suspected, it's a complete skeleton. Impossible to say how old at this point. The damp environment no doubt hastened decomposition. No trace of clothing or shoes, but if the body's been here long enough, they could have decomposed.'

'How long for a pair of shoes to rot away, then?'

Cathy wrinkled her nose. 'Depends on the material and how much of it there was. Pair of leather sandals could be gone in twenty years. Boots would take longer. Maybe fifty. Of course, she could have been placed here naked.'

'It is a woman, then.' The words caught in his throat.

'I'm pretty certain it's female, judging by the size of the skull and the pelvis. We'll know for sure after we've got them back to the lab.'

He felt a knot forming in his stomach. It was cold and heavy. He'd dealt with enough dead girls to last ten lifetimes. 'Very impressive. But depressing.'

She seemed not to detect the melancholy in his words. 'That's not the impressive bit.' She picked up the bag containing the skull and carefully removed it. 'Look.' She held it up, pointed to a depression on the right side, above the ear cavity.

'Fractured?'

She nodded. 'Violently.'

'How can you tell this didn't happen afterwards? Rock falling on it or something?'

'The lines are too sharp for it to have happened any significant time after death. Post-mortem bones are dryer—any cracking would be jagged; the bone would crumble. And look at the shape of the break.' She traced it with her finger. 'Deeper and narrower at the top, wide and shallow at the bottom. That wasn't made by a rock.'

'Right.' He kneaded his brow. 'Not that it could have been anything other than murder, I suppose. Body stuffed in a bloody cave. Dammit!' He kicked at the pebbles, sending several flying towards Marquis, who was approaching in what looked like a panic.

'What is it, Marquis?' he snapped, and Marquis's face fell into the sort of expression Michael would expect to see on a faithful dog who had just been kicked, which only served to further exasperate him. 'Well, spit it out!'

'There's someone coming down to the beach.'

'Who the bloody hell is this now?' Michael squinted against the sun to see a tall, lean figure descending the steps down to the bay at a rate of knots.

'Hey!' Michael waved up at the figure. 'Hey, this is a crime scene!' He strode to the bottom of the steps, where the man stopped. He was sallow-faced and skeletally thin. His shirt stuck to his underarms, and his upper lip and brow shone with sweat. His voice trembled as he spoke.

'I'm Martin.' He coughed. 'Martin Langlais. The constable. There's a body.' He took deep, rattling breaths.

'I know that, Constable. We've been down here since first bloody light. Where have you been? You were supposed to meet us—'

'No, no,' Constable Langlais interrupted.

'You bloody were. Seven thirty we got here!'

'No, I mean not here.'

'The hell are you talking about?' Michael could feel a rare explosion of temper coming on. It was too much—the early start, another dead woman (so help him God) and now this blathering idiot.

'The body. Not here. It's Reg . . . old Reg Carré . . . Blood everywhere. I've never seen anything like it.'

And with that Martin Langlais slumped to his knees.

7

Jenny

The next ferry back to Guernsey left at two. Jenny ordered a coffee at the new café in the village and sat at a table outside. Snippets of conversation floated over to her as people walked past.

'. . . police have been down there for hours . . .'

'. . . you know what I think . . .'

Two men, voices low, conspiratorial—the tone and timbre of juicy gossip being shared. Jenny left her seat and approached them. They stopped mid-conversation.

'Can I help you?' The younger of the two, in his mid-forties, strong-featured, had an air of authority about him, but he spoke in a gentle, enquiring manner. He was dressed smartly, in chinos despite the heat, and a short-sleeved shirt.

'I couldn't help overhearing you. My name's Jenny Dorey. I'm here from the *Guernsey News*. I was wondering if you had a minute to talk?'

The older man, tall and red-faced with a mane of thick white hair, shook his head. 'You're not putting me in that rag. No offence, love. More of a broadsheet reader myself. I'll be in later, Joe, about the knee.' He gave a wave and hurried off, limping slightly.

'Don't mind him. He's a bit of a character.' The younger man extended a hand. 'Joe Lawton.' He paused. 'Seems more likely you

44

might know what's going on at Derrible. Presume you've been down there?' he asked.

'The area's sealed off. I believe the police will be making a statement later today,' she dodged. 'But I'm sure people are already talking.'

'They are. I'm not included in the gossip, though. Only been here since April. It's probably for the best—I'm the doctor. It can be a bit awkward knowing too much about people in such a small place. Everyone's shocked, though—I can tell you that much. Beyond that, there's a lot of speculation about who it might be, obviously.'

'Any names?'

He smiled. 'Like I said, nobody tells me.' He looked at his watch. 'I must be going. I'm late for my next appointment. Nice meeting you.'

Jenny returned to her coffee. She opened her laptop. Thought about a headline. Fought the urge to go with 'Terrible Derrible', which is what she'd called the beach as a kid. Knowing Graham's penchant for the melodramatic, he'd love it, but it seemed too glib for the seriousness of the situation. A sharp smell interrupted her thoughts—woody, overtly masculine. A shadow fell over her table.

'Ms Dorey?'

She looked up. A man stood across from her, scalp shining beneath closely shorn hair, large aviator-style sunglasses hiding his eyes.

'It is Ms Dorey, isn't it? I was wondering if I might join you?' He sat before she had a chance to say anything, folding his long, lean body into the wicker chair, stretching his legs out to the side. He motioned to the waitress.

'Cappuccino, please, Stacey.'

The waitress smiled. 'Coming right up, Mr Monroe.'

Jenny closed her laptop. 'I don't think we've met?'

'But you know who I am.' He took off his sunglasses and polished the lenses before placing them on the table. His eyes were large and bright green, framed with long, thick eyelashes, feminine almost, and completely at odds with his nose, which was bent out of shape. It had been broken, Jenny thought, more than once.

'Corey Monroe.'

'That's right.'

'How can I help you?'

He smiled, teeth bleached and gleaming. 'Shouldn't you be down on Derrible?'

'It's a crime scene. One of the officers is meeting me here,' she lied. Stupid. It was broad daylight; there were plenty of people about, but she'd already been followed this morning and there was something about this man. She didn't want him to think she was alone.

'All very dramatic.' He paused and turned his attention to the waitress as she placed his drink on the table. 'Thanks, love. You've changed your hair, haven't you? Suits you. Look a bit like that Scarlett Johansson now.' He winked at the girl, who giggled.

'I was wondering,' he said, still watching the girl as she walked back into the café, 'if you wouldn't mind giving me a call.' He turned his attention back to Jenny and slid a card across the table. He rolled his linen shirtsleeves up over his elbows. He had that easy, self-assured manner the wealthy often had. He was used to being listened to, to getting his own way.

Jenny picked up the card. 'What about?'

'Well, it occurred to me recently that with all of the bad blood between myself and a number of the islanders, it might be worth me telling my side of the story. I've tried talking to people one on one, arranged meetings, which nobody ever turns up to. Seems like once people have made up their minds, there's simply no changing them. I could go to one of the nationals, of course, if I wanted to. But I'd like to reach the locals. Everyone here reads the *Guernsey News*.' He took a sip of his drink, licked the foam from his top lip.

Jenny sat up a little straighter. Corey Monroe had never spoken to the *News*. He'd released statements—cursory comments about some of his properties being vandalised, soundbites about working together with the locals, quotes regarding his newly refurbished hotels being 'open for business'. But he'd never sat down with a journalist face to face.

'Why now? We've approached you many times asking for an interview. You've always refused.'

'As I'm sure you can see, Jenny, things have reached a bit of a stalemate. There are people here who, for some bizarre reason, think that I mean the island harm. It's virtually impossible to find people to work with me.' He shook his head. 'It makes no sense. Not to mention the personal attacks, which frankly have become libellous. I could sue, but I don't want to punish people.'

'I heard talk of rent hikes. Supply contracts cancelled?'

'Oh yes?' He smiled again. 'You see. This is why you're perfect for the job, Jenny. There'll be no accusations of sycophancy with you running the show. And that's all I want. A fair representation of what's happening over here.'

He finished his drink.

'Best coffee on the island. I own the place, so don't worry about paying.' He put his sunglasses back on and she saw herself reflected in them. She looked uncomfortable, unsure of herself. She tried to relax her shoulders, to smile professionally as he got up to leave.

'I'll be in touch. Probably best to wait until we have the full story about Derrible.'

'I don't know about that, Jenny. What better time to bring the island together than now, in the wake of a tragedy?' He took a five-pound note out of his wallet and placed it under his cup.

The waitress came out of the café and waved. 'See you tomorrow, Mr Monroe.' Her smile fell as soon as he'd left. She started to clear the table.

'Comes in regularly, does he?' Jenny asked.

'Every day.'

'You don't sound very happy about it.'

The girl stopped what she was doing and glared at Jenny. 'I know who you are. Don't you go writing anything I say about him—I need this job.'

Jenny held up her hands. 'I'm just making conversation! Is there anyone on this island who doesn't know who I am?'

The waitress shrugged. 'Probably not. People have been talking about the body on the beach. Someone said there was a reporter down by Derrible. Then I heard you talking with Monroe.' She pocketed the money he had left on the table.

'Well, he's a good tipper, if nothing else.' Jenny started to pack up her things.

'Everywhere else they spit in his coffee.'

'Not here, though?'

The girl glanced over her shoulder before replying. 'Not as far as he knows.'

Jenny stared at the empty cup, feeling slightly ill.

The girl noted her look of distaste. 'He deserves it. I've heard all sorts of rumours about what goes on over in his mansion. We all have.'

'Like what?'

The interesting turn in the conversation was stopped short by the sound of a shriek from the end of the street. Two older women, one with her hand pressed over her mouth. Another joined them. There was a rapid exchange of words.

'. . . just now . . .'

'. . . police have gone running up there . . .'

Jenny ran over to them. 'Is everything OK?'

These ladies at least did not seem concerned as to who she might be. They answered immediately with a volley of information.

'It's Reg Carré, up at his cottage.'

'Known him all my life!'

'Murdered!'

There was a moment of stunned silence, as though the whole street were listening.

'Murder? Are you sure? Where did you hear this?' Jenny asked. There must be some confusion, she reasoned, with the events on Derrible—small-town gossip gone into overdrive.

The smallest of the ladies answered. 'It's true! I saw Constable Langlais about twenty minutes ago. He'd stopped on his bike and he looked a terrible state and I asked him, "You all right, Martin?" and he said,

"Reg is dead."' She shook her head. 'Not "dead"—"killed", he said. Reg has been killed and we shouldn't go near his place, and that's when I saw the police were following him.'

'The Guernsey Police?'

The woman nodded. 'They were here already, weren't they? There's another body on Derrible. Good grief. I need to sit down. This isn't right. This is Sark! What's happening?'

She looked at Jenny, as if she might hold the answers.

'Where does Mr Carré live?'

'Off Rue du Fort. The path down to the common. Middle of nowhere. You're not to go there, though—Martin said!'

Jenny left the women to their disbelief and walked slowly back to the café. She checked her watch. Less than an hour until the ferry back to Guernsey. But there was a sailing at four, another at six. She picked up her things and walked with her bike to the crossroads. Straight down the hill to the harbour. Or left towards Rue du Fort. It was wide and straight, one of the main routes to the north and, as island roads went, busy—filled with the sounds of Sark. A horse and carriage plodded up ahead, the clip-clopping of hooves, rhythmical, comforting, like a nursery rhyme. The ringing of a bicycle bell. Glasses chinking, laughter from the beer garden opposite. In the distance, the chug of a tractor. And somewhere, beyond, the silence of a dead man.

8

Rachel

1978

Perhaps she could blame it on the island; the sunshine had turned her skin pink, then pale gold, bringing out the freckles on her cheeks and nose. The breeze lifted her hair and her skirts, and she felt, for the first time in years, carefree.

She and Meg spent the morning swimming at Venus Pool. It had taken them ages to find it: neither of them could follow the ramblers' map they'd picked up at the tourist information centre and they'd taken several wrong turns before they reached the shoreline. She wasn't even sure that this was the one—they'd passed other similar rock pools on the way. This was the deepest, though, deep enough to jump into, and the surface was polished like glass, bright seaweed and anemones scattered over the bottom.

They were hot and sweating, so they stripped down to their costumes and leaped in, screeching as they hit the water. She surfaced quickly, gasping with the cold, eyes stinging, skin tingling. Awake. She swam to the edge of the pool. Looked out to sea. Thought of the endless possibilities.

'Fuck. I'm not staying in here.' Meg's foul language was a new thing. It didn't suit her, with her private-school accent. She had one too, but it was cultivated. She had studied the silky-smooth vowels of her fellow students, speaking only when spoken to and very carefully, until she was sure she could fully replicate it. Only then did she join in, begin to make friends. Not that she had been ashamed of the way she spoke. She just understood the importance of fitting in. Of making other people feel comfortable. It had worked. She'd made good friends. Useful ones, with money, like Meg.

They hauled themselves out. The rocks were hot and they burned the soles of their feet, hopping from one to the other as they spread their towels across a huge, flat boulder and then lay on them, soaking up the warmth from beneath.

Meg took her top off, lay with her breasts shining like moons they were so white. She envied Meg's confidence but not her figure. Meg was one of those willowy blondes who looked good in magazines with the right make-up and lighting, but in real life she was all angles in slightly the wrong places.

She threw a towel at Meg. 'Cover up—you'll send someone blind if they see you!'

'No one's coming,' Meg said. 'This place is dead. Take yours off—go on, you big sissy.' Meg propped herself up on her elbow and searched through her pile of clothes, finding the cigarettes in the pocket of her shorts. She lit one and blew smoke towards her. 'Go on. Don't be shy,' she said, her voice lowered and breathy, batting her eyelashes like Marilyn Monroe.

She laughed. Unhooked the clasp at the back of her bikini. Her father would have died on the spot if he'd seen it, two little triangles of fabric tied at the neck in a bow. Hers was a figure that featured in the sort of magazines she'd seen discarded at the bus shelter at the back of the housing estate near school. She'd attracted whistles and catcalls since she was fourteen, no doubt the reason her father insisted she dress like a nun. He seemed to think it was her fault men shouted obscenities at her, despite the fact that the stiff white shirt, over-the-knee navy skirt and red tights of her school uniform were hardly provocative.

51

She lay back, enjoying the warmth on her nearly naked body, and she felt as though she had shed more than clothing, that she was lighter, freer than she'd ever been before. She reached for her T-shirt, used it to cover her eyes and drifted into sun-drenched sleep.

The sound of voices roused her. It took her a second to remember where she was, before she sat up, still drowsy, then scrambled around like a lunatic, pulling her T-shirt on just as an elderly couple appeared, heads bobbing up and down as they climbed over the rocks towards them, before unpacking a picnic and offering the girls a custard cream.

They were still laughing about it as they cycled back to the guest-house for a bath before tea. She was in front, out of breath after the walk over the bridge from Little Sark. (Even Meg, always the first one to break the rules, had peered over the sheer drop on either side and admitted the 'No cycling' warning should probably be adhered to.) It was downhill nearly all the way from here, though, and she let gravity do its thing. As she gathered speed, she played a game, counting in her head, challenging herself not to use the brakes until she reached twenty, then thirty, then fifty.

Eyes streaming, hair flying, she laughed, turned back to Meg. 'Come on, slowcoach!'

The road flattened and she slowed, but not enough to take the corner safely, and she pulled on the brakes, the back wheel skidding out to the centre of the path, the front one only feet away from an awkwardly parked tractor. She swerved, lost control, had no time to stop for the man pushing the wheelbarrow.

Her whole body jarred with the impact, the clanging of metal against metal rang through her ears, and she flew over the handlebars, landing against the relative softness of the hedge. Winded but embarrassed, she laughed, ignoring the pain she felt in her wrist as she brushed the hair out of her eyes, saw his hand, outstretched.

He was handsome, in a rugged, country sort of way, a way she was familiar with, having grown up in a village not much bigger than this place, but unlike the boys she knew from home, he was tanned and had something of the sea in him—his eyes sparkled as he helped her up, like light on water. His hair, thick and sun-bleached, fell in waves to his shoulders. Her father wouldn't have liked that. Anything below the ears was too long on a man according to him.

'You all right? Jesus, woman, you're lucky that wasn't a tractor—just because there's no cars, you can't ride around like a bloody maniac!'

He was shaken, she realised. And there was a dent in his wheelbarrow.

'I'm sorry. I was going too fast. I'll pay for the damage.' She had no idea how.

'Don't worry about that.' He seemed to calm down. To look at her properly. She stopped herself from tugging at the bottom of her shorts as his gaze flickered over her body and back up to her eyes. He reached out. Gently brushed a knuckle against her lip. He held it up, showed her a lick of crimson. 'You've damaged your face too.'

She tried to look confident, but shivered inside, shaken by the accident, and something else.

'Oh my God, are you OK?' Meg came squealing to a stop.

'I'm fine.' She winced as she picked up her bike. 'This man helped me. Thank you.'

'Reg,' he said. He smiled.

She smiled back.

'You got a name?'

'Rachel.'

Meg gave her a sideways glance, made a noise, like she was about to say something, but Rachel flashed her a look and she stopped.

'Well, Rachel. Suppose you could buy me a drink. For the damage. And nearly giving me a heart attack.' He grinned. 'I'll be at the Mermaid later. Along with half the island.'

She was flustered but didn't show it.

'Absolutely. We'll see you there.'

They could hardly say no. Not after he'd been so nice.

In the pub, the air was thick with smoke and heavy with beer and laughter. The accent here was funny. Long vowels, but not like hers, not 'grarse' and 'barth'; here, they were harsh and jarring—'graaas' and 'baaath'. There were words she didn't understand at all and she felt sure that some of the men (and it was mostly men) were talking about her and Meg. Maybe because they were overdressed, both in short skirts and blouses, everyone else in work gear, scruffy trousers and dirty T-shirts.

She drank three beers, which was two too many. She had no tolerance for alcohol. She was trying to impress him. He had changed his clothes since this morning, was wearing a button-up shirt and trousers, holes in the knees but clean at least. He was much older than her, thirty maybe, which was good. He'd know what he was doing.

He asked her questions. She lied. Just a little. Added a couple of years to her age, failed to mention that she had told her father she was on a trip organised by the Young Christian Association, that there was not a chance in hell she would have got away with this if he hadn't been still grieving her mother's death, only a year ago. He'd thrown himself into his work at the church, and the Christian Pregnancy Advice Centre, where he prayed with expectant single mothers, helping them follow the Lord's path. He had taken Rachel there a few times—she presumed in lieu of sex education. Most of the girls were her age, younger even, sad and desperate.

It got late and Meg wanted to go. But Reg asked if she'd like to take a walk. Meg hadn't had much luck: she'd been stuck next to a boy not much older than them who had barely said a word all evening. She told Meg to go back and she'd be home soon.

'Are you sure?' Meg whispered, eyebrow raised, looking at him as he drained his pint.

'Very.' She winked, hoping that the display of bravado was more convincing to others than herself. Her stomach churned. The bar seemed to have got even noisier, full of chat and people shouting across the room to each other and then groans as the landlord called 'time' and rang the bell.

He held his hand out and helped her down from the stool. She straightened her skirt, told him she had to pop to the loo.

'I'll wait right here,' he said, before lighting a cigarette. He looked handsome and confident, smoke curling around him, and if she hadn't been sure before, she was now.

She sat on the toilet and peed for what felt like an age, heart pounding. Her ears rang in the quiet, and she couldn't get a line from a song her granny used to croon out of her head: 'Sweet sixteen and never been kissed . . .'

She had been kissed. She'd done more than that, after the last dance she'd been to, surprising her date, who had been mercilessly teased by his friends that he wasn't getting anywhere with the vicar's daughter. Which was why she'd let him touch her, even though she hadn't particularly liked him. Just to prove his toffee-nosed friends wrong. It occurred to her that what she was about to do was no different, not really. The school motto was 'Seize the day.' Presumably losing your virginity to spite your father was not what Kent Country Girls had in mind when it had those words carved over the entrance two hundred-odd years ago. But where better, she thought, to seize the day than here?

She pulled up her things. She'd put on her nicest undies. Matching, white cotton, little daisies embroidered round the edges. She checked her reflection in the mirror. Ran her finger over the split in her bottom lip. Pushed her bra up, pulled her top down and popped a mint in her mouth.

Meg had gone by the time she got back, and the bar was nearly empty. He stubbed his cigarette out and took her hand. His was large and rough. She liked the feel of it. He wasn't a tall man, but she was short, only coming up to his shoulder. As they left the lights of the bar behind them, he put his arm around her, pulled her close to him. He smelled of smoke and beer and salt.

'Look at the stars.' He stopped. She looked up. She'd never seen so many.

'Beautiful.' She didn't know what else to say. She wanted it to happen, but she wanted it to be over with. Wanted him to kiss her, to put his tongue in her mouth, to put his hand up her skirt, to touch her breasts—she could tell that he wanted to, the way he'd been looking at them all night, but she wanted to be home too, back at the guesthouse with Meg, telling her all about it, the stress and tension and excitement done with already.

'You can see even better from here.' He led her off the main track, down a grass-covered path. They passed a small cottage, all in darkness, and came out into open fields.

'Sit down.' The grass was warm and dry and soft. In front of them, the land stopped, and from below, the sound of waves breaking against the cliffs, and next to her, the sound of him, breathing, then his hands on her, pulling at her clothes, and all at once she froze. She pressed her lips tightly together. She wanted this. She'd told him, with her eyes and her laughter and her hand on his leg.

He carried on, tugging and grabbing and breathing, and she couldn't help herself—she started to struggle against him, she tried to get up, but he took her hand, the injured one, and pinned it to the ground. She gave a gasp of pain.

That was when he kissed her. Pressed his mouth so tightly on hers that she could make no sound, and he kept it there, one hand heavy on her sore wrist, one fumbling with his trousers, and then he was on top of her and all the breath was squeezed out of her and she pushed the fear and the panic away and stared at the stars above her.

Afterwards, he walked her back to the guesthouse. He kissed her again. She let him.

'How about dinner tomorrow? I can come and meet you here after work?' He tucked a loose strand of hair behind her ear.

She nodded. Yes. Dinner. Of course.

As he walked away, she felt a wave of emotion washing over and over her, leaving remorse and shame in its wake.

9

Michael

'His throat's been slit.'

'I can see that.' You'd have to be blind not to, Michael thought, as he forced himself to look at the gaping wound that had loosened Reg Carré's head from his neck.

The body was lying in the kitchen, if it could even be called that. The cottage had just the one main room, an area to the left of the front door with a sofa and an armchair, to the right a small kitchenette and breakfast bar, a table with three chairs set to the side. The whole room was very dark, three small windows letting in three shafts of dust-filled light, the naked lightbulb hanging from the ceiling doing little to alleviate the dingy atmosphere.

'I'd guess he was facing the kitchen wall when it happened. Artery's been severed, hence the blood splatters—autopsy will confirm.' Cathy from forensics was kneeling next to the body and talking into a minuscule voice recorder. 'Making some tea maybe, attacked from behind?' She looked up at Michael and pointed at the kettle, which rested on the sideboard, immediately below the bloodstained wall. 'Then he staggered backwards, collapsed, fell forwards and bled out on the floor.'

'It's a theory,' Michael agreed. He was feeling a little queasy. He might be imagining it but the smell that had hit him when he'd walked into the tiny cottage, what seemed like hours ago, was even more intense now that the body had been turned over and the day's heat had finally started to permeate the stone walls. He forced himself to look at Reg's face. It was ghastly. Drained of blood, blue-lipped, that gash exposing God knows what bits of a man's throat to a daylight they should never see. Michael put his hand to his mouth briefly before rubbing his chin.

'If you and Rob have it covered, Cath, I'll go and take the constable's statement.'

He walked out into the sunshine. He had radioed down to Derrible for back-up as soon as he'd established that Constable Langlais was not raving mad, and three uniformed officers were waiting at the end of the overgrown garden path, still panting after the jog over.

'Came as soon as we could, sir. The rest of the lads are still wrapping up at the beach. Where do you want us?'

Michael held his hand up to shield his eyes as he surveyed the area. He pointed to the common, then the fields in front of the cottage, then the path to the main road.

'One of you in each direction for now. Gloves on, eyes peeled for anything unusual.'

'Like what, sir?' A young PC, not long out of training.

'It's Bachelet, isn't it?'

The PC nodded. 'Well, PC Bachelet, anyone covered in blood or wielding a weapon might want stopping for a start. Failing that, use your brains, eh? And watch where you walk—there's dog crap every-where. I've already trodden in one lot.'

Marquis jogged over to him from the edge of the cottage, where he'd been securing police tape to the hedge.

'Another boat is on its way over from Guernsey, sir. Ten officers on board.'

'Good. As soon as they get here, we'll want a thorough search of the area. When you're done securing the scene, Marquis, you can help out young Einstein over there.' He pointed to Bachelet, who was poking around in the hedgerow a few hundred yards away. Made Marquis look like Sherlock Holmes, that one did.

Michael found Martin Langlais sitting on an upturned flowerpot at the side of the house. Blotchy hives had broken out on his cheeks and over his forehead.

'You don't look very well, Martin.'

'I'm only a volunteer—you know that. I don't even get paid,' he snapped.

'I know, I know. There's no need to explain. I'm not feeling too good myself. I do need to take a statement, though.'

'Said to my wife yesterday, "I've had enough of this," I said. "I'm not doing this anymore, all for free an' all."'

'What happened yesterday?'

'Nothing in particular.' He rubbed his eyes. 'It's been building up for months. Used to be a nice job. People would come and make complaints about little things—littering, hedges not being cut back on time, tractors going too fast. You know how it is, stuff I could sort out. But recently there's been all this trouble with Monroe. Vandalism against his property, then him handing out those leaflets, then the posters.' He shook his head. 'Or maybe it was the posters, then the leaflets—I can't remember. Anyway, I thought that was bad. But this . . .' He rubbed at his brow. 'I need a drink.'

'You called in this vandalism, did you?'

'Of course I did! Report anything serious, don't I? I thought bricks through windows and burned crops might warrant a visit, but clearly you lot disagreed. I've been dealing with this all on my own.'

Michael had heard nothing about it. The report was probably sitting on a desk somewhere in Guernsey Police Station.

'Right. Well, we'll get onto it. But first we need to figure out what the hell has happened here. How did you come to find the body? Did someone call you? Not the kind of place you're just passing, is it?'

'Shit!' The constable's grey face went even greyer. 'Shit, I'm sorry.' He put his head in his hands. 'It was the Le Page kid. Arthur. He can't be more than six or seven. I caught him running out onto Rue du Fort, stopped him because he should have been at school. Soon as I saw his face, I could see something was wrong.' He paused. 'He wouldn't say anything, though, just ran here and I followed. I saw the front door was open—Reg isn't the type to leave his door open, so I went to check on him. After I saw . . . with all the stress . . . I panicked. I forgot about the kid. Where did he go?' He looked around wildly as if the child might magically appear in front of them. 'Round the back, I think. He's probably long gone. Shit.' He stood, wobbled, sat back down again. 'I think I'm going to throw up.'

'Take some deep breaths. I'll go and have a look.'

The back garden was as unkempt as the front. A small concrete area with a couple of dirty folding chairs and a round plastic table with a hole in the middle for a sunshade, covered in empty bottles and an ashtray overflowing with cigar butts. On a patch of scrubby grass, in front of the overgrown hedge that marked the edge of the property was an enclosure made of wood and wire, and a small hut with a ramp that led down to an open run. A chicken coop, Michael thought. He peered in, wrinkled his nose at the sharp, sweet smell of urine and something else, something damp and decaying–rotting wood, perhaps. Guinea pigs, not chickens, munched at the few strands of green grass that peppered the dry earth. They were dull-eyed and mangy-looking. A food bowl in the corner had been tipped over and some sort of grain was spread over the surrounding area. A plastic water container that looked like a baby's bottle but with a metal spout in place of a rubber teat was attached to the outside of the enclosure. It was empty.

A rustling noise. The hedge behind the hut shook. A knot of sparrows fluttered into the air. Michael took a few steps backwards. Listened. The blood in the house had been freshly spilled. Whoever had killed Reg Carré was undoubtedly still on the island. He picked up an empty beer bottle from the table, held it at his side.

'Hello?' he called out softly.

More rustling.

'Arthur? Come on out now.' He tried to sound firm but friendly. Likely it was a frightened little boy back there. His hand shook. There was no reason why the killer would have stuck around, not here, at the scene of the crime. That would make no sense. But there was a madness about all of this. Michael sensed it. This tiny island. The body on Derrible. An old man brutally murdered. He felt a darkness approaching like a rolling fog. He gripped the bottle. Walked slowly round the hut, setting the guinea pigs to a nervous shrieking. Peered into the narrow, dank space between the enclosure and the hedge.

He dropped the makeshift weapon to the floor. 'Hello there.'

The boy was curled up, knees hugged to his chest, mop of hair flopped over his face.

'It's Arthur, isn't it?'

Movement. Perhaps a nodding of the head.

'Have you been here all this time? There's nothing to be frightened of, not now. Where do you live?' he tried. 'Is it far from here? Let's find your mum, shall we?'

A whimper.

Michael crouched down. Squinted to try and get a better look at him. 'My name's Michael. I'm a policeman. I think you've had a bit of a shock, haven't you? What do you say we go and find your mum and then get you some ice cream? What about that, eh? And then when you're feeling a bit better, we can have a little chat. Does that sound OK?'

The young boy murmured something.

'What was that, fella?' Michael shuffled towards him, unsteady, his knees aching.

'Beast Man.' Louder this time. 'Beast Man.' Then he was shouting. 'Beast Man, Beast Man, Beast Man!' He jumped up and ran past Michael, who fell backwards into the hedge.

'Shit!' By the time he'd scrambled to his feet and got to the front of the house, the boy was tearing across the fields, towards the village.

'What's going on?' Langlais asked. He was still sitting on the flowerpot and had, Michael noted, made no effort to stop the boy. 'Who's a beast?'

'Kid's terrified. How long must he have been hiding back there? It's been hours, poor little sod.' *And it's your bloody fault*, he wanted to add, but he bit his lip. 'Do you know where he lives?'

'The island has a population of four hundred and fifty. I know where everyone lives.'

'Well, bloody good job! God knows what that kid saw—he might know who did this. I need to speak to him. Now. Make yourself useful, will you, and find my DC, Marquis? Give him the kid's address and tell him to go straight there. I'll have the other lads search the fields. And I need you to pull yourself together now, get on your bike and talk to the residents here. Tell everyone, very calmly, to stay where they are or, if they're out and about, to get back to their houses. They'll take it better coming from you. Tell them there's been an incident and the police will be with them with more information as soon as possible.'

'What are you going to do?' He sounded petulant, and Michael couldn't help raising his voice.

'I'm going to wait here until back-up arrives, and then I'm going to come and talk to the boy. Is that all right with you?'

'All right, all right!' Langlais got up. Started towards the road.

Michael took a breath. Reminded himself that Martin Langlais was a volunteer and doing all of this for the good of his community.

'Martin,' he called after him.

'Yes?'

'Four hundred and fifty people on the island, you say?'

'Give or take. There's a handful of tourists, some seasonal workers.'

'You probably socialise with a lot of them?'

He nodded. 'Of course. It's a small island.'

'Well, be careful. Could be one of your friends is a killer.'

10

Jenny

The fields were dry. Grasshoppers jumped out of the way of each footstep she took, their tiny, brittle bodies whizzing through the air and instantly disappearing into the surroundings. A cool breeze only served to draw attention to the rapidly burning skin on her arms and she cursed that she hadn't picked up some sunscreen in the village. It was always like this on Sark. Like the sun's strength was magnified somehow. Day trippers often returned to Guernsey lobster-red, shoulders emblazoned with white strap marks, noses peeling.

Hoping to avoid another police line, she'd left her bike propped up against a hedge and walked through the fields towards the common. She'd had a garbled conversation with Graham, in which she'd tried to relay the morning's dramatic developments, but was unsure how much of it he'd understood, the signal dropping out three times during the short conversation. From his excited tone before he'd cut out the final time, she assumed he'd understood there'd been a murder. Fresh blood made for better headlines than old bones. It was unlikely anyone else from the *News* would make it over today, so it was down to Jenny to get a start on the story.

After walking for five minutes, she stopped. Tried to get her bearings. It had been years since she'd been to the common, and she'd never crossed the fields to get there. She might even be trespassing, although the stile she had just climbed over indicated ramblers were tolerated. She could see the sea, in the distance to her right, and figured that was east, adjusted her course so that she was heading north. She pulled her hair out of its ponytail so at least the back of her neck was protected from the sun and climbed over the next stile.

Right into the path of a small, sobbing child.

'Whoa!' Jenny held her arms out to steady herself as he catapulted into her legs. She failed and tumbled forwards, taking the child down with her. He yelped, whether in surprise or pain she didn't know, but started to struggle to his feet, scrambling to get away.

'Hey, wait there!' She grabbed his ankle. 'Stop. What's the matter with you?'

He turned and looked at her through wide, red-rimmed eyes, his grubby cheeks tear-stained. He trembled. His shorts were damp. He was terrified.

'Are you OK? What are you doing out here by yourself?' He looked to be about seven. Surely too young to be out on his own, even on Sark. She looked in the direction he had come from. The common. Reg Carré's house.

'Are you running from something? Did somebody hurt you?' She crouched down, shielding him.

He shook his head. She relaxed. Just a little.

'I want to go home.' It was a whisper.

'Here. Let me help you.' She smiled. Reached out, gently brushed his hair out of his eyes, offered him her hand.

He looked at her for a moment, unsure, but must have decided that she looked trustworthy because he nodded. Took her hand in his. A cold ripple flowed through Jenny, right from the point where his hand touched hers.

It was soaked in blood.

The boy stopped outside a large granite house on Rue de la Seigneurie. Beau Séjour Guesthouse. Jenny had called Michael, but the conversation

64

had yielded no information beyond the boy's name, Arthur, and a barked order—'Take him home and *do not* leave until I get there,' his tone a mixture of exasperation and relief that she had found the child, who she presumed was somehow involved in what had happened to Reg Carré.

'This is where you live?'

He nodded. The front door was unlocked. He opened it and Jenny followed him into a wide hallway, a staircase to the right leading to an open landing, a sitting room on her left. A low table displayed leaflets advertising carriage rides and restaurants and Tuesday Jones's boat tours.

'Hello! Hello?' She listened. The sound of water rushing through pipes. A shower running, perhaps. She was under police instruction to stay put, but she'd scare whoever it was stupid if she disturbed them in the bathroom.

Arthur headed down the corridor, towards the back of the house. Jenny followed him to a door with powder-blue letters affixed in higgledy-piggledy fashion: 'Arthur's Room.' She glimpsed a bed and a small desk covered in paper and crayons before the door slammed shut. She knocked gently.

'Arthur? Are you OK?'

No response. The sound of papers shuffling. She opened the door, just a crack, saw him hunched over the desk, scribbling. From above, she heard the shudder of pipes. The water had stopped. Creaking floorboards. Jenny walked quickly back to the front door, picked up a leaflet from the cabinet, flicked through it.

A door opening. Soft footsteps on carpet.

'Oh! I'm so sorry. I thought you were on the last ferry in?' A small, dark-haired woman in a low-cut blue dress, hair dripping wet, stood at the top of the stairs. She was classically beautiful: creamy skin, full lips, large eyes, like her son's.

She saw Jenny's confused look. 'It is Mrs Jacobs? Staying for three nights?'

65

'No. I'm Jennifer Dorey. I'm sorry for the intrusion. I found your little boy in the fields over by the common. He seemed quite distressed, so I walked him home.'

The woman wrinkled her brow. 'What was he doing over there? He should have been at school. Why didn't they call me?' Confident, well spoken. A woman used to getting her own way.

'I really don't know. I just bumped into him.' She hesitated. 'There's been an incident.'

'What sort of incident?' A flash of mother's panic.

'I don't know all the details. But it was a house near the common. Involving a man called Reg Carré.'

'What's happened to Reg?'

'I think Arthur may have seen something. The police are on their way over to talk to you.'

'Oh my God. Where is he? Where's Arthur?'

'He went that way.' Jenny pointed down the hall. 'He's fine, honestly. A little shaken, I think.'

The woman started down the corridor, then stopped, turned back to Jenny.

'I'm so sorry. How rude of me. Thank you for your help. I don't want to keep you. But thank you.'

'Actually, the police asked me to wait until they got here.'

The woman paled. 'Why? What on earth can have happened?' She didn't wait for an answer but hurried towards Arthur's room.

Jenny listened. Heard the woman's raised voice. She walked soft-footed towards the door, straining to hear the words.

'. . . But what? What did you see?'

The boy was sobbing. The woman sounded exasperated.

'. . . straight to school! How many times have I told you? And what have you done?'

Murmuring. A tap running.

A sharp knocking on the front door. Jenny hurried back into the hallway and opened it.

'Where's the boy?' Michael was out of breath.

She pointed towards Arthur's room.

'His mother here?'

She nodded.

'Right. I need to speak to you before you go. I'll meet you in the Mermaid. About an hour. Don't you file a word of any of this until we've spoken. Or you can kiss this police source goodbye.'

She looked at her watch. It was nearly four. The last ferry back to Guernsey was at six and she wasn't even sure there were any tickets left.

'I don't know how I'm going to get back.'

'Should have thought of that before you got yourself mixed up in another murder investigation, shouldn't you?'

'It's a murder investigation? Is that official?'

He sighed. 'I'll speak to you later. And we'll have a launch heading back this evening. I'm sure we can make room for one more. Thank you for helping with the boy. Now bugger off.'

The Mermaid Tavern was tucked away on Rue Hotton, a minute's bike ride from the village. An arch in a high wall led to a small courtyard, with picnic benches and a barbeque grill. Vines and clematis covered the entrance porch of the building and crept up its bright yellow walls. While she was waiting for Michael, it seemed as good a place as any to ask about Reg Carré.

It was busy. Busier than it usually would be on a weekday, Jenny guessed, but eerily quiet. Conversations were hushed; heads were shaking; faces were pale. She sat at the tiny bar and ordered a cider. Next to her, a man sat alone, gulping down a pint. She introduced herself. Asked him if he knew Reg.

'You're from the papers.' It was a statement, not a question. 'Don't waste any time, do you? Man's only been dead a couple of hours, from what I heard.' He slurred. This wasn't his first pint.

'I was here already to report on the bones down on Derrible.'

'Right. That as well. Bit of a day we're having, that's for sure. You spoken to the police, then? They're sure it was murder?'

67

'I don't know all the details.' Michael was not going to pin the spreading of gossip on her—there were plenty of others who could take the blame for that. 'You knew Mr Carré?' she asked.

'Course I knew him. Everyone knew him. Three square miles we live on. You know people. Whether you want to or not.'

'This must be such a shock.'

He shrugged his shoulders. 'I said I knew him. He was no great friend of mine.' He put his pint down. Looked at her. His eyes were small and black, like a bird's.

'What sort of man was he? Was he popular? Had he fallen out with anyone recently?'

The man laughed. 'Oh, that's a good one!' He slapped the bar and turned on his stool so he was speaking to the room. 'You all hear that? She wants to know if Reg has fallen out with anyone. Can someone please tell this young lady how it works around here?'

The shifting of a chair in the corner. 'All right, Mal. Everyone's upset. Let's keep it together, eh?' The voice belonged to a man in a Metallica T-shirt, sleeves rolled up over his shoulders. His fists rested on the table; the muscles in his arms were taut.

'You might be upset. I'm not fucking upset. Doing a fucking inter-view, aren't I, love?' He threw Jenny a sly glance. 'Nobody gonna tell her? No? Down to me, then, as always.'

She could smell the alcohol fumes on his breath. A hum of con-versation had restarted behind them, but Jenny could feel the room watching, listening. 'Round here, see, if falling out with someone led to murder, we'd all be fucking dead.'

He took a swig from his pint. 'You want to talk to Len Mauger.' The menace in his voice had completely disappeared. 'Len keeps himself to himself, 'specially the last couple of years, but him and Reg used to be great friends.'

'Not anymore?'

'I imagine it'd be a bit difficult to be friends with Reg right about now, love.' He laughed. 'They had a bit of a falling-out over one of their little card games. He knew your old man as well.'

'What?'

'Len. Knew your dad. You're Charlie Dorey's girl, aren't you?'

She nodded. There was something jarring about her father's name being spoken in this place by this man.

'Heard you were over. You've got his eyes. And a way about you. All the questions. I knew him too. Saw him around, like. Nice chap. Played euchre against him a few times in Guernsey, had a beer with him every now and then when he was over here. But him and Len was quite tight. At least, towards, well, you know, before the accident and that.' He shook his head and went quiet, as if thinking about Charlie, or perhaps his death, in detail. 'Now *that* was a shame.'

'Did you speak to my father around the time of the accident?' She tried to keep her tone light.

'Can't say I did.' He looked away. 'Like I said, you want to talk to Len.' The man looked at his watch, moved his wrist back and forth as if struggling to focus. 'He'll be home now, I shouldn't wonder.'

'Where's home?'

'Little Sark. The road down to the silver mines. Granite house, red door.'

'Do you have a number for him?'

He shook his head. 'You'll not be getting Len on the telephone,' he said cryptically.

'Oh?'

He drained his pint. 'Mind how you go, eh? Some folk around here don't like being asked too many questions. Not me. Happy to talk. In fact, I'll even leave you with a quote.' He got down from his stool, put a hand on the bar, steadying himself. He widened his eyes dramatically, looked over Jenny's shoulder, into the distance. 'We're all devastated and praying the police find whoever did this to poor Reg soon.' He relaxed his pose and laughed sharply again. 'That do you?'

'I'll need a name?' She smiled, despite his bizarre behaviour, not wanting to provoke him.

'Malcolm Perré. *Acquaintance* of the deceased.'

'Thank you, Mr Perré.'

'Not at all, *Ms* Dorey. And like I said. Mind how you go.'

Jenny didn't relax until he'd shuffled across the room and out of the bar. He was drunk, no doubt, but his reaction to the murder of a neighbour had been strange. Enough to make anyone feel uncomfortable. And the fact that he'd known Charlie, the way that he'd spoken about him had been stranger still.

But it wasn't just that causing her disquiet. *Mind how you go.*

It was the second time today someone had warned her to be careful.

11

Michael

Detective Sergeant Richard Fallaize, Michael's least favourite colleague and all round cocky shit, sat on a white wicker sofa in Tanya Le Page's rather elegant sitting room. He was leaning forward, as alert and interested as Michael had ever seen him. It was just Michael's luck that of all the officers on board the police boat, it was Fallaize who had accompanied the family liaison officer to the Le Page house. The rest of the officers had gone straight to Reg Carré's to conduct a thorough crime-scene investigation. The FLO, Sergeant Emily Gerard, a middle-aged lady with a pinched face, her hair pulled back into a neat ponytail, had a stern outward demeanour, only barely concealing a warmth that spilled out as soon as she smiled. She did so now, as Michael entered the room carefully balancing two mugs of tea in each hand.

The object of Fallaize's attention was the beautiful woman sitting opposite him. Tanya Le Page's long, dark hair was damp. Freshly washed. Michael could smell the shampoo, a clean, herbal scent, so pleasant, in fact, it was difficult not to obviously breathe it in. Her deep brown eyes were wide and frightened, just as her son's had been that morning. Her powder-blue sundress, cut low, complimented her pale skin. There were two damp patches just below where her hair rested, which, Michael noted, with some discomfort, was just above her breasts. She had her feet tucked behind her on the sofa. They were small and bare,

71

and seemed to add an air of almost painful vulnerability to the woman. He placed the mugs on the low coffee table in front of the sofa and sat next to her.

'Right. Nice cuppa makes everything better.' Not true, but there was something about the ritual of making tea that was soothing, and something about the drinking of it that undoubtedly settled the nerves.

Tanya Le Page took a sip.

'I can't believe this is happening. Not here. I moved back so Arthur could have the sort of childhood I had. Not this.'

'Local, are you?' Michael was surprised. She had no hint of an accent.

'This was my parents' business. I grew up here, in this house. I went to boarding school when I was eleven. By the time I'd finished, Mum and Dad had moved to Guernsey. They kept the business—had someone else running it, but when that didn't work out, I came and took over. It's ideal for a kid. No cars, outdoors all the time. We've no TV, no iPad, none of that. Arthur loves it.' She looked as if she was about to cry. 'I can't believe this. It's horrific.'

'We're going to have to talk to Arthur, Ms Le Page. The sooner the better.'

She nodded. 'The doctor's coming over as fast as he can.'

'I completely understand you want him checked over. We recommend it, in fact, don't we, Sergeant Gerard?'

'Absolutely.' Emily nodded and flashed another one of her reassuring smiles. 'Essential to have a doctor see him.'

'But you see, Ms Le Page, this is time sensitive. There's a chance Arthur might have seen who killed Mr Carré.'

Tanya shuddered. 'I understand, Detective. But I'm not risking my child's health. He's hardly said a word to me since he came home. He's obviously traumatised. What makes you think he'll talk to a complete stranger?'

'Emily here, our FLO, she's trained in this sort of thing.'

Tanya sighed, eyes heavy with tears. 'This is a nightmare.'

'We'll be out of your hair soon as we can speak to the boy.'

'If we don't speak to him now, love,' Emily ventured, 'we'll have to speak to him later. Best to get it out of the way, while it's all fresh in his mind. It might even help him, to talk about it. Chances are, he's scared. He might feel responsible in some way for what's happened.' Emily noted Tanya's incredulous look. 'Kids can convince themselves of the funniest things. If we get him to talk, we can reassure him—tell him he's safe, he's not in trouble, everything will be OK.' She smiled encouragingly.

Tanya ran her hands through her hair. 'Five minutes?'

'We'll be as quick as we can,' Michael said.

She nodded. 'OK. I'll get him. But first sign he's distressed, you stop.'

'Of course.'

As soon as she'd left the room, Fallaize piped up. 'Maybe we should wait for the doctor. She looks the type that might sue.'

'What on earth makes you say that?' Michael tipped his head back, tried to work a crick out of his neck.

'Look at this place. Nice stuff. And she sounds, well, you know. Bit stuck-up.'

'If you mean she speaks nicely, you're right, Fallaize. Not an indication she's going to be litigious as far as I'm aware.' He had a point, though, Michael thought. She certainly didn't seem the type to suffer fools. And too many people in the room would intimidate the boy.

'I need you in the village, Fallaize. See how Marquis is getting on taking statements.'

Fallaize frowned. 'Might be better if I'm here. Verify what happens in case, you know, she gets difficult.'

'I think Sergeant Gerard and I can handle it. Thanks anyway. Now get a move on!' He shook his head as Fallaize left, obviously put out.

'He's very enthusiastic, isn't he?' Emily said. 'Volunteered to come up with me. Talks a lot.'

'All about himself, I suppose.' Michael was sure Fallaize was angling for a promotion. He'd been ever so slightly less antagonistic towards Michael than usual. Seemed to have finally grasped who was boss. Michael moved to sit next to Emily just as the door opened. Tanya entered, her son trailing behind her.

Michael sat forward. 'Hello there, Chief. How are you feeling?'

Arthur gave no sign he'd heard Michael but sat next to his mother, mimicking her position, arms crossed, legs tucked behind him.

She put an arm around him. 'It's OK, sweetheart. The policeman needs to ask you a few questions. You just tell the truth.'

'Nothing you say here is going to get you in any trouble,' Emily said gently. 'Nothing at all.'

'First things first, then. How did you end up at Mr Carré's house this morning? I'm guessing you were supposed to be at school, eh?'

Arthur looked at his mother.

'I hated going to school on days like this. Who wants to sit in a stuffy classroom when the sun's shining, eh?' Michael smiled. 'And you walk to school by yourself, do you?'

'All the kids do here.' Tanya sounded defensive. 'I'd just told him this morning that this was his last chance, that if he didn't go straight there, I was going to start walking with him again. He's been late a couple of times. But this is the first time he's played truant. It is, isn't it, Arthur?'

'I get it,' Michael reassured her. 'Nobody is judging you. Or Arthur. That's not why we're here.'

Arthur stared at the floor, hair covering his face.

'You ended up at Mr Carré's house, Arthur.' Michael paused. 'Did you see him? When you got there. Did he let you in?'

Silence.

'Did you see anyone else, Arthur? Someone you recognised?' Michael pressed. 'You shouted something when I found you. Do you remember? You shouted, "Beast Man."' He held his breath. Come on.

Silence. The boy's shoulders shook and he emitted a snot-laden sniff.

'Tell them, sweetheart.' Tanya nudged him gently, but it was as though she'd poked him with a cattle prod. He threw his head back, leaped from the sofa, screaming.

'I didn't see him! I didn't see him!'

'It's OK!' Tanya pulled her son towards her, wrapped her arms around him, rocked him, whispering, 'It's OK. It's OK, baby.'

She looked at Michael. 'Enough.'

He held his hands up. 'Absolutely.' Shit. Shit, shit, shit.

Tanya carried the boy out of the room.

'Fuck. I thought we had a chance there. Now what, eh?'

'You can't question him anymore. Not now.'

'I know. Poor kid. But what a pain in the arse.'

Tanya returned. Michael was relieved to see she looked upset but not furious. She paced around the back of the sofa, chewing her thumbnail.

'He just climbed into bed. Pulled the covers over his head.'

'I'm sorry, love.'

She shook her head. 'I know you had to ask him.'

'If it's any consolation, children recover from this sort of trauma far more quickly than adults do,' Emily reassured her. 'We've an excellent counsellor—we'll arrange for her to come and speak with you as soon as possible.'

Tanya didn't seem to hear her. 'I kept asking him what he'd done—he's always getting into scrapes—but he wouldn't say anything. I thought he'd hurt himself. But when I washed the blood off, there was nothing. Was it Reg's? The blood?'

'I presume so.'

'You probably wanted to test it. Sorry.'

'You've nothing to be sorry about.' He paused. 'Do you have any idea why Arthur might have been at Reg's cottage, Ms Le Page?'

'No. No. We didn't know him. Well, we knew him, of course. But not really. Except . . .' She hesitated.

'Please, go on.'

'It's going to sound awful. When I was a kid, we used to follow Reg. It was a game. To see who could get closest to him without him noticing. He was such a grumpy man, complaining to our parents even when we weren't doing anything wrong. He drank a lot too, and would yell at us when he'd had too much. We were a bit scared of him. But that was what made it so much fun. You had to see how close you could get without him catching you. It's probably my fault Arthur was there this morning. Reg shouted at him a few weeks ago—Arthur was going too fast on his bike, something like that, and he came back scared. So I told him what we used to do. I was trying to make Reg seem less scary, make a joke of the whole thing. I think he told his friends at school and they started playing the game again. I've seen them whispering in little groups when Reg walks past.'

'He wasn't a well-liked man, then?'

'He was difficult. Bad-tempered. Between you and me, I think his mental health was suffering recently. Dementia, perhaps. He'd been behaving even more oddly than usual. I've seen him walking around muttering to himself.' She looked embarrassed. 'Probably should have checked in on him, shouldn't I? He'd been on his own for years. His wife left him. Left the son, Luke, here with Reg. It must have been hard for him.'

'You knew him, the son?'

Tanya nodded. 'He's a few years older than me. He lives in Guernsey too. Left Sark before I went away to school. He must have been about sixteen. He was never happy here. Not after all the stuff with his mum.'

'What stuff with his mum?'

'Her disappearing.'

'Disappearing?'

'Well, leaving them both. Not very often you hear of a mum walking out on her family, is it? I can't even imagine it. I saw him a couple of days ago.'

'The son? Here? In Sark?'

'Yes. I didn't speak to him. He was on his own, reading a book. I didn't want to disturb him.'

'He come over often?'

'Yes, to visit his dad.' She stopped, frozen to the spot, a sudden realisation apparently dawning on her.

'If Arthur saw something, are we in danger? What if whoever did this saw him and wants to keep him quiet?'

Emily moved over to Tanya and put her hand on her shoulder. 'It's very likely that Arthur arrived on the scene after the murder was committed. The blood on his hand certainly points towards that. And nobody else knows he was there. Just us.'

'There was a woman. The one who brought him home?'

'I'll be speaking with her shortly,' Michael said. 'She's an acquaintance of mine. I trust her not to say anything. But regardless, we're going to keep you safe. We'll post someone here. For your peace of mind.'

She nodded, seemed to relax, just a little.

'Tanya, what Arthur shouted this morning, before he ran off, "Beast Man." Does that mean anything to you? Perhaps it was something the children called Reg?'

She shook her head. 'Oh God. No, no, that's nothing to do with Reg. It's . . . You're going to think we're all crazy.'

'Of course not,' he reassured her. Although, at this rate, he thought, she was probably right.

'You have to understand it's different here. Kids have to make their own entertainment. They tell stories, make up games. One of them is the Beast of Sark.'

Michael furrowed his brow. 'Like the Beast of Jersey?' It was the name the press had given the notorious sex attacker who had terrorised the neighbouring island of Jersey in the 1960s, creeping into people's houses at night in a rubber mask and nail-studded wristbands.

'That must be where it came from originally. The story's been doing the rounds since I was a kid. Someone probably heard the news stories from Jersey at the time and then it got passed down. Now it's a bit of an urban legend. Or an island one, I suppose. We didn't know anything about the real Beast of Jersey stuff, not back then. Just that if you were naughty, or mean to your friends, the Beast would come and get you. Arthur and his friends are always chasing each other, and whoever gets caught is the Beast Man and has to chase everyone else. It's just a game.'

'And what does he look like, this beast?'

'Well, like I said, he's not real, Detective. Just a story kids scare each other with.'

'Of course. I understand. But Arthur seemed to think he saw this Beast Man this morning. What might he *think* he looks like? From the stories?'

She sighed. 'He dresses all in black. And according to the legend, his features are twisted and stretched beyond all recognition. That's why he's so scary. The Beast of Sark has no face.'

Michael was used to a room going quiet when he entered—years spent as the subject of gossip after Ellen's death, his subsequent fall from grace and, later, his public calling-out of unscrupulous colleagues had made sure of that. It felt different here, though. The stares of the Sarkees as he made his way to Jenny at the bar, the whispered 'Copper' from somewhere at the back of the room as he sat next to her.

'Everything all right here?' He spoke quietly.

'Brilliant.' Jenny's tone was dry. 'Best hour and a half in a tiny bar full of potentially hostile people I've ever spent.'

Michael motioned to the barman and ordered a lemonade.

'Spoken to anyone interesting?'

'Maybe. How about you?'

'You know the drill, Jenny. Ongoing investigation, waiting for forensics, post-mortem, et cetera, et cetera.'

'I heard there was a lot of blood.'

He raised his eyebrows. 'From who?'

'Someone in the corner. Over there.'

He followed her gaze. 'Bloke in the metal T-shirt?'

She nodded. 'But everyone's been talking. It was a frenzied stabbing according to one account. Another woman said she'd heard it had all the marks of a professional hit job.'

'Why the bloody hell would anyone think that? Bloody gossip. I bet that constable's been running his mouth.'

'So was it?'

'Was it what?'

She shrugged. 'A frenzied stabbing? A hit job? Listen, Michael, this place is ten times worse than Guernsey. Unless you tell people what's going on, there's going to be panic. There already is. You need to set the record straight, and soon.'

He tugged at his chin. 'You're probably right. But I can't say anything until I've cleared it with the super.'

'Course not. Anything I run with at this point would be from an anonymous source.'

He nodded. Lowered his voice even further. 'Knife wound to the throat. Police are following several leads. That's all I can give you now. I'll organise a press conference as soon as practical. Need to set up a space here first. Write that every available resource will be directed to this inquiry and we won't rest until we found who did this.'

'What about the bones on the beach?'

'Reg Carré's murder is a priority, but every effort will be made to identify the remains found on Derrible. Once we've established who it is, we'll try to figure out what happened to them. That do you?'

Jenny nodded.

'Right. What have you got for me, then?' If he knew Jennifer Dorey, and he thought he did, she'd have more than just pub gossip to show for sitting here.

'There's a friend of Reg's over on Little Sark.'

'Name?'

Jenny looked down at her notes. 'Len Mauger. Thought I might go and talk to him. Just for a bit of background.'

'Who gave you his name, then?'

'A Mr Malcolm Perré. You might want to speak with him. He was a bit strange.'

'In what way?'

'Well, there didn't seem to be any love lost between him and Reg Carré.'

Michael wrote down the names she had given him. 'You're not going to see this Len now? Not by yourself?' As much as Michael

79

trusted Jenny's instinct on a story, he was less sure about her instinct for self-preservation.

'He was a friend of Reg's.'

'Jenny, how many people do you think get killed by strangers?' The look on her face said she knew the statistics. Reg Carré was likely to have been murdered by someone he knew. 'The police boat leaves at eight. Stay out of trouble for the next couple of hours, will you?'

He left her sitting at the bar. If he'd had any spare resources, he'd have been tempted to have someone watch her, make sure she didn't do anything daft. But that would be overstepping. It wasn't his place. Even if it had been, he'd not proved himself particularly adept when it came to protecting young women. He tried to shake off the thought but it jabbed at the corner of his brain. Seeing Reg Carré's body had been disturbing, but Reg had been an old man. There was something so much easier to digest about a death in old age, even a brutal one. It was the scene down at Derrible that was playing on Michael's mind. Those bones laid out like that, brittle and dry, all that was left of a young woman. She'd been young, Michael felt sure of it. And now she was just bones. It had shaken him to the very core. Because it had been nearly twenty years since Ellen had died, and he knew, beneath the well-tended grave, that was all that was left of her.

12

Rachel

She refused to sit, even though he found her an empty seat. She stood in the open doorway, looking out at the lashing waves as they battered the back of the boat. Cases and packages had been thrown off the seats onto the floor, sticky and wet from the spray that washed in. Most of the other passengers had been shopping. It was the last ferry service from Guernsey before Christmas. She was shunted from side to side as the boat swayed, and her hand fluttered to her aching belly.

Three times she'd made this journey, and each time she'd left something behind. It was hard to recall the joy she'd felt on that first sailing to Sark. Summer. Only six months ago. How happy she'd been to say goodbye to her childhood. Ironic, then, that her second journey had been made at the behest of her father, the very man whose tether she had tried so desperately to escape. She'd thought he might kill her when he'd found out. But when he'd calmed down, he'd made her pray with him. Said she would go back and marry him, whoever he was, and if she needed persuading, she could come with him to the centre and talk to some of the girls there. And then he'd packed her bag and thrown her out. If she hadn't felt so sick, so alone, she would have laughed at his hypocrisy.

She'd had no choice but to go to Reg.

She'd stood in the same place on that journey, looking at Guernsey disappear into the distance, that small island, with its roads and cars, looking like a beacon of hope and opportunity compared to where she was headed.

Now this crossing. A whole week in the Princess Elizabeth Hospital. She'd lost the baby. She should feel relieved, but she felt hollow. She wanted it back with a ferocity she'd never before experienced.

He had Len pick them up in the tractor. She sat in the cab, he in the trailer. She was relieved at the break from the unbearable intensity of his stare. Len helped her out at the house. She wondered how much he knew, if men talked about things like women did—or like she assumed women did. She had not spoken to Meg since she'd left home, and had exchanged no more than a few words with the island women.

He held the door open for her and followed her into the bedroom. He had replaced the sheets—no amount of scrubbing would have got the stains out of the old ones. She sat on the edge of the bed, ran her hands over the fabric. The bright swirls of the pattern looked out of place in this small, sombre room.

'Can I get you anything?'

She shook her head.

'Tea?'

'There's no reason for me to be here now. I'll leave. Soon as I feel better.'

He looked confused. 'Said I'd marry you. Still will.'

'Why? Why would you do that? There's no baby.'

He was quiet for a moment. 'Stay. Please.'

She lay on the bed. Turned her back to him.

He was sleeping. Snoring in the armchair. A tumbler at his feet, bottle of whisky half drunk. She picked up the glass. Drained it of the last drop. It burned her throat. A log glowed in the fireplace, a slash of bright gold shining in the centre of the charred wood. She prodded at it with the poker, watched the shower of sparks float to the floor and shrivel to grey. He stirred. It was cold and she thought about covering him with a blanket. That would be a wifely thing to do. Instead, she took her coat from the peg next to the door and walked out into the night.

The road was empty. The gritty earth crunched beneath her feet. The only light came from a sliver of moon and the stars. There were so many stars in the sky; they swirled across the blackness, like spilt milk. She told herself she walked without purpose, without destination, but her feet said otherwise, taking her in a particular direction: left at the crossroads, right at the gate, towards La Moinerie, where he'd told her a monastery once stood.

The path here became uneven, rutted by tractors, broken by the twisted roots of the beech trees lining the way. They thickened as she walked. This was a wood, she supposed. Or the closest thing to one on this island of meadows and hedges, of bracken and gorse. It was rocky underfoot. It was rocky everywhere—the paths, the cliffs, the houses, the walls—all hard and grey and unforgiving.

It was darker under the branches. Hard to see the way down rough steps carved out of the earth and stone. She stumbled. Sat. Felt her way forwards with her hands, her frozen fingertips grazing against sharp edges, feeling damp hollows. She pulled herself down, blind save for the glint of moonlight through the branches, down into the valley, the earth tipping towards the sea, until she emerged from the shelter of the trees, onto open land, exposed to a biting wind, which struck her face with icy fingers. The path tapered, and at its point, more rock, a wall of it, blocked the way.

Except for the window.

It was one of the first places Reg had shown her. Someone had blasted through, many years ago—a mad seigneur's folly. He'd had people blow a hole with dynamite to frame a perfect view—an azure sea, passing ships, Guernsey in the distance. From here, in the dark, it looked like a way out. There was light at the end of the tunnel, a strange luminescence, the glow of moonlight on water.

She walked through. The gale battered her body. A few feet in front of her was a sheer drop. She stepped forward, held herself stiff against the gale. Looked down at the white horses turned silver, the blue water black.

This whole thing was madness. Island madness. That's what he'd called it, that first night. After the drinks. After the walk and the hot, uncomfortable mess that followed, and then dinner and more of the same, because after the first time, she'd thought, Why not? Why not see him again, spend a week pretending that her life was her own, to do as she pleased, that she was happy, having fun, in control? She shook herself. What a fool she had been. Everything about her life had been decided by other people. As a child, she'd had no choice. She had listened to Mother, and Mother had listened to Father, and hellfire and damnation would surely have followed if they hadn't. She'd wandered into adulthood in something like dream, she realised. Or more like an enchantment, one that made her powerless, bound to follow the orders of others. She felt like she'd woken up a week ago. Her screams had broken the spell.

She took a step forward. Disturbed the unstable ground at the edge of the cliff. Heard a pebble clatter, crack-cracking as it bounced off the rock face to the sea. She lifted a foot. Waved it in the nothingness. Was blown back, towards the window. She wondered if it might hold her and she spread her arms, eyes streaming, vision blurred, so at first she thought she imagined it.

Flashing lights. A little way out. She stepped back, pulled her coat tightly around herself, rubbed her eyes, squinted. Surely nobody in their right mind would be sailing or fishing in this weather.

On, off, on, off.

There was a pattern to it. Some kind of signal. As she focused on the light, sharp and bright, the scale of her surroundings seemed to magnify—the height of the cliffs, the depth of the ocean, the breadth of the sky above, the ferocity of the cold and the wind—and she wanted nothing more than to be back at the cottage, to wrap herself in a blanket, to lie in front of the warm embers of the dying fire.

She turned.

She was not alone.

A shape, on the other side, a black figure, edges defined only by the moonlight. It was him, she thought, come to bring her home, but as she took another step towards the tunnel, she faltered. The shape was all wrong. Too short, too stout. She pressed her back against the rock face. Heard shuffling. A cough. The smell of cigarette smoke.

'Someone's going to get killed, out in this.'

'Can you see it or what? I'm fucking freezing.'

Two of them. Their voices echoed in the tunnel. Her coat flapped about her legs. She tried not to move, not to breathe.

'I see it.'

'It's done?'

'Wait a minute. Gotta count them.'

Out to sea, the light flashed. On, off, on, off.

'It's done. Fuck me, in this weather. Not messing about, are they?'

Another cough. Voices faded.

She waited. Five minutes. Ten. She was so cold, so stiff, she dropped to her hands and knees for fear she would fall and bounce like a rock, crack-crack, into the sea below. She crawled through the tunnel, over the grass, into the woods, stumbled up the path and then ran to the cottage, stopping only when she reached it. She tried to quiet her breathing. Pushed gently so the door would not murmur. Shook uncontrollably, felt like the cold had frozen her bones. He was still in the chair. Still snoring. The fire had burned to ash. She unbuttoned her coat. Her ears were ringing; her hands were numb and bleeding, her trousers filthy and ripped. She couldn't stay here, in this tiny house on this tiny island. There was something dark about this place, something wrong and sinister.

She had to get away before it consumed her.

13

Jenny

She paused at the top of the steep approach to La Coupée. The cycle from the village had been short but arduous, the ascent over the last quarter of a mile relentless. She pushed forward, head down, finally getting off her bike and walking the last few feet before the main island ended abruptly in an outcrop of red and ochre rocks. Between them, the path narrowed and then dropped, sharply, a three-hundred-foot taper of land forming an isthmus between the main island and Little Sark. On either side, sheer cliffs tumbled into clear, cold blue.

She pushed her bike down onto the bridge, squeezing the brakes to hold it back as the loose, dry grit that dusted the concrete path slipped beneath her shoes. After several feet, the decline flattened. She stopped. It was impossible not to.

To the left, the water stretched to the coast of Jersey, hazy on the horizon. To the right, several boats were moored in the turquoise waters of La Grande Grève, a wide, shallow bay that met the sandy beach nestled into the bottom of the cliffs two hundred and fifty feet below. Steps hacked into the rock led down to it, a faded sign warning of soil erosion and telling visitors to attempt the descent at their own risk. There was somebody down there now. Jenny watched the tiny black speck picking its way across the white sand.

There were stories of hauntings here. The moans and screeches of the dead heard at dusk. There had been no railings until 1900. No road until German prisoners of war laid one after the Second World War. Before then, this bridge had been only five feet across, the path rough and crumbling. Children had crawled over on their hands and knees. One man, a farmer, attempting to bring his tithe of corn to the main island during a storm, had been blown clean off. Charlie had shown her, marked on a map in the bay below, La Caverne des Lamentes. That was where the eerie wailing sound came from, he said—one of the island's many *souffleurs*, made by the tide sucking in and out of a narrow passage below and driving pockets of air through stone channels. Or perhaps, he had said with a smile, it was that poor farmer, looking for his scattered corn. There was nothing ghostly about the place now, Jenny thought. With the sun shining, the cliffs lush and green with heather and gorse, the spectacular view; it was a picture straight out of a tourist brochure.

There was no time to linger. La Coupée finished with a steep incline up to Little Sark, matching the descent on the opposite side. She pushed the bike up, then freewheeled down the hill. After half a mile, the road forked. A sign pointed the way to the silver mines. She checked her watch. Less than an hour before she'd have to head back to the main island if she was going to take advantage of Michael's offer of a lift home. Plus she needed time to come up with a story about where she'd been—Michael wouldn't be impressed if he found out she'd visited Len Mauger against his advice. But she had a job to do and could hardly ignore a lead connected to both Reg Carré and her father. *Both dead*, Michael's voice whispered in her ear. She would find the house. Decide what to do when she got there. She followed the sign to the silver mines.

She soon found what she was looking for: a small, granite house with a bright red door. She set her bike against the hedge. Wind chimes hung from an apple tree in the front garden, ringing softly. On the doorstep were a pair of black wellington boots, wet nearly two-thirds of the way up, and a faded blue bucket, rim buckled. The same scene had greeted her countless times at her own house, Charlie having returned from a day on the boat with something for tea, or perhaps some ormers he'd promised a friend. From somewhere nearby, she heard a shrieking and then a laugh. Next door was a few hundred yards away, but close enough that she could see the children playing in the front garden. Close enough to run to, should the need arise.

She approached Len's house. Peered into the bucket. It was empty save for a puddle of water and a frond of seaweed. She knocked on the door. A sharp clang. Footsteps. Then, to Jenny's surprise, the turning of a key. Hardly anyone on Guernsey locked the doors, not even when they went out, never mind in Sark. The door opened, but only a crack. Only as far as the security chain on the inside would allow.

'What?' A voice from behind it. Dry, raspy.

'Mr Mauger? I was wondering if I could talk to you?'

'Fuck off. Keep telling you lot. I don't need any help. Leave me alone.' The door slammed shut. She knocked again.

'I'm not here to help you, Mr Mauger. I was hoping you could help me.'

He was still standing behind the door, she thought. His words came through muffled but loud enough that she could hear.

'What are you talking about? Why can't you all leave me in peace?'

'I don't know who you think I am, Mr Mauger. I was wondering if you'd mind answering a few questions.' She hesitated. This was not a man who would talk to a reporter. 'Mr Mauger, I'm Jenny Dorey. I just . . . I wanted to ask you about my dad. About Charlie Dorey.'

There was silence. A gentle thud. The door shifted in its frame. He was leaning against it. She waited. One minute. Two.

Next door, she heard somebody call the children inside. It was still bright as noon, but the sun had dipped in the sky; the heat abated, just a little. She would need to head back to the main island soon.

'Mr Mauger?' She knocked again. 'I really won't take up too much of your time.'

A creak. A rattling of the chain. The door opened.

'You'd better come in.'

*

The house smelled like a boat. Like the *Jenny Wren* the day after Charlie had brought in a big catch—not just fish but sand and salt, the faintest hint of tar and engine oil. In the low-ceilinged kitchen, a large pot of water was coming to the boil on an ancient-looking Aga. Next to the sink, a door led out to a back garden. It was open, but Jenny couldn't help noticing the bolt above the handle. Still shiny. A much later addition than the scuffed and rusted barrel lock beneath it.

'Sit down.' Len Mauger pointed to a stool tucked under a low, square table. He reached into the sink and pulled out a chancre crab, one hand on either side of its wide, flat shell. The crab waved its front pincers wildly in the air. Len dropped it into the pot and slammed on the lid.

'I'll enjoy eating that little bastard. Got my thumb earlier. Hasn't happened for years.' He shook his head. 'Must be losing my touch. You want something to drink? I've got beer. Some milk?' He was a short man, in his sixties, Jenny would guess, a little stout round the middle, but his shirt hung loosely from his shoulders. He seemed nervous, fidgeting with his pocket as he opened a narrow door to an old-fashioned pantry. A slab of butter wrapped in waxed paper on a shelf, a loaf of bread, a carton of milk next to it, bottles arranged in a rack, a box of vegetables on the floor and too many cans to count—peas and tomatoes, sweetcorn, mandarin slices, fruit cocktail. She looked around the kitchen. No fridge. No microwave. No kettle. No light fittings. She wondered if he was some sort of survivalist, with his over-the-top security, stockpiling food in case of disaster, living without electricity in preparation for a time when the grid failed and the world was plunged into darkness. She wondered what else someone like Len might have stashed around his isolated house. Nets and rope. Tools for working on his boat. Knives for gutting fish.

The room darkened. The small windows and low ceilings typical in these old farmhouses seemed designed to keep out as much daylight as possible. She rose from her seat, stood in the open doorway, looked out onto an overgrown field with a large greenhouse at the bottom. A patch of cloud slid over the sun just as a small, bright blue La Manche propeller plane came into view, engines roaring.

'Bloody pain, they are.' Len appeared beside her. 'Disturbing the peace how many times a day as they come in to land on Guernsey. Not as bad as that Monroe's helicopter, mind you. Whole house shakes when he flies over. Don't know who he thinks he is. Bloody helipad on Brecqhou.' He shook his head. 'Come on. Let's sit.' He motioned her back inside. She hesitated. There was a pallor to his olive skin, a frailness about him. He held on to the door frame as if he needed the support. He didn't look like a madman. Or a dangerous one.

She followed him back inside.

'Have you heard the news, Mr Mauger?'

'Not if it happened in the last three days. Last time I spoke to anyone.' He took a swig of his beer.

'You don't have a telephone?'

'No telephone, no TV. No internet.'

'Mr Mauger.' It was not her place to break this sort of news. She spoke gently. 'Reg Carré is dead. He was killed.'

The lid on the crab pot tremored as the water bubbled beneath it. Len sat, pale and silent, staring at her, unblinking.

'I'm sorry. I know you were friends.'

'Killed how?'

'I don't know, not exactly.'

'Not an accident?'

She shook her head. 'No. Not an accident. You don't seem surprised.'

He got up, angry. 'What are you telling me about this for? I thought you wanted to talk about your dad.'

'I did. I was asking about Reg and someone mentioned you knew him, and my dad too.'

'Asking about Reg why? And who told you I knew him?'

She checked her notebook. 'A Mr Malcolm Perré.'

'Course it was.' He looked at the notebook, then at her. 'Are you police? Charlie never said you were police.'

She shook her head. 'I'm a journalist. With the *Guernsey News*.'

'That's right. I remember now.'

'Was Reg a friend of yours, Mr Mauger?'

'He was.' He sniffed. Wiped his nose on his sleeve. There was no sign of tears, but his voice wavered. 'I worked for him. Years ago. Helped him out with his gardening.' He turned away from her, carefully folded a tea towel and wrapped it round his hands before lifting the pot off the boil. He drained it and brine-scented steam billowed out. He placed the pot into the sink and used the tea towel to wipe his eyes and brow before pulling the chancre out, its shell transformed from muddy brown to fiery red, the tips of its claws black and shining. He placed it on the side, remained with his back to her, his hands resting on the counter.

'Liked a crab did Reg. I used to take him one every now and then.'

'Had you seen him recently?'

He turned. 'Course I'd seen him. See everyone. Little as possible suits me, but I have to go into the village sometimes. We didn't really talk much. Two old men. Nothing to say to each other, not anymore. We drifted apart a bit after he and his wife had a baby. That was thirty-odd years ago. Then played a bit of cards together, up at the Seigneurie.' He stopped. 'What is all this? I don't want to be in the bloody paper. Don't know why I'm talking to you. You caught me off guard, saying you wanted to ask me about Charlie. You just say that to get in the door?' He spoke quickly now, as though agitated.

She put her pen down. 'No.'

'Well, good. I'm not doing an interview about Reg bloody Carré, I'll tell you that much.'

'I'm sorry. All the questions are a force of habit. I really did want to ask you about my dad.'

He picked up the tea towel, twisting it in his hands. 'He was a good man.'

'Thank you. How did you know him?'

'He fished. I fish. Saw him all the time, unloading in Guernsey. I used to sell to some of the restaurants, same as he did. We'd chat. He'd come over for a drink, play some cards. Sometimes when he was supposed to be out working.'

'He spent more time over here, I think, those last months before he died. Did you see more of him?' *And what was he doing*, she wanted to ask, *scribbling nonsense in his diary after his trips over?* but she forced herself to take it slowly. She did not want to risk rattling Len again.

He shifted. Winced. 'I suppose I did.'

'Anything you can tell me about that time? Not for a story, obviously. I . . . I have so many questions about what happened to him. How the accident happened. You'll know, if you ever saw him on his boat, he was better on sea than on land . . . or perhaps I'm wrong.' She attempted a smile. 'Perhaps I just saw what I wanted to see and you're going to tell me he was clumsy and getting old and you're not surprised he fell overboard.'

He stared at her for what felt like minutes.

'I'm dying. Cancer.'

'I'm sorry to hear that.'

'I thought you were from the hospital. They've sent a couple of people to try to persuade me to come over for treatment.'

'You're not having treatment?'

'It's in my bones. Terminal. The doctor here can prescribe me pain medication. I'm not taking too much just yet, but they say it will get worse quickly. They say if I go to Guernsey, they could *prolong* my life. But that's different to living, don't you think? I've a few good months left. I want to spend them here.'

He looked her in the eye for the first time, she realised, since she'd entered his house.

'Do you know your Bible?'

She shook her head.

'I do. Methodist. Lapsed. No surprise I've been thinking on it all a bit more recently, eh? Thinking about getting back to church, making my peace with God. Asking for forgiveness. Too late, though, eh? Too late.'

'Forgiveness?' Her voice caught in her throat. 'For what?'

'Too late.' He appeared not to have heard her. '"He is chastened also with pain upon his bed, and the multitude of his bones with strong pain." That's me, isn't it? Chastened, with pain in my bones. Better or worse than what Reg got? I wonder.'

'You're losing me, Mr Mauger.' He was rambling, she thought. Too much time spent alone and ill—he was losing his mind. Or he knew something.

'What did Reg get, exactly?'

'Wait here.' He got up, walked out of the room.

She heard the stairs creaking, then footsteps from above. She had made a mistake coming here, but she couldn't leave, not if there was a chance Len knew something, anything about Charlie's death. She checked her phone, wanting some connection to the outside world. No messages. No signal. She walked to the back door, held her phone in the air.

'Here.'

He'd come back so quietly he startled her and she turned sharply.

'This was delivered to me a couple of years ago. Slipped under my door.' He laid a piece of paper on the table.

She stepped towards it, blinking to refocus in the dim interior after the glare of the sunlight outside.

She stared at the words. Block capitals. Black pen on grubby paper.

YOU'RE NEXT.

'A couple of years ago?' Jenny's words caught in the back of her throat. 'When exactly?'

Len's expression was grim.

'The day after your father disappeared.'

14

Michael

The boat journey back to Guernsey was mercifully short and quiet. Even Jenny was unusually subdued and did not linger to talk to him beyond a brief goodbye and a thank you, exhausted, presumably, like he was. And his day wasn't over yet.

Luke Carré had been notified of his father's death by telephone. Michael had given him as little information as he could, mentioning only that there were 'extraordinary circumstances' surrounding Reg's death and that he needed to speak to Luke in person as soon as possible. Which meant going there now, straight from the ferry. Michael got into his car and peered into his rear-view mirror. He ran a hand through his hair, which felt stiff and wiry after his day in the sun and the salt air. Sand had settled on his scalp. He gave it a rub and the grains sprinkled his shoulders and lap. He closed his eyes, thought about sinking into the sofa, or, better still, standing under a cool shower, washing away the grime of the day. He could drift off here, he thought, warm and quiet, cocooned in his car. He could almost feel himself slipping into a dream and he shook himself awake, started the engine. One more job before home.

The Carré residence was situated halfway down the narrow and twisting Icart Road. Mackintosh roses adorned a glass panel set in the top half of the front door. Behind it, a hazy glow from the hallway light threw red and green glimmers onto the doorstep. He glanced up at the rest of the house—large Victorian shutters, well-stocked planters on the ground floor sills, shaped bay trees on either side of the front door. Luke Carré might only have moved a few miles away from his home, but he could hardly have been further away from that tiny cottage on Sark. Intrigued, Michael rang the doorbell.

'Nice place.' Michael surveyed the tastefully decorated living room. Even the paint looked expensive, the tones richer than anything he'd ever put on his walls, all navies and neutrals. A delicate chandelier hung in the middle of the room; the fireplace was tiled with the sort of tiles you saw in home décor magazines, intricately patterned, the glaze cracked—chic, rather than shabby.

'Thank you.'

Michael took a sip of his coffee, which had been produced from a gleaming piece of machinery that ground beans and steamed milk all with the press of a polished chrome button, and studied the man sitting opposite him. Tall and athletically built, with just enough stubble to look rakish, Michael thought the word was, not scruffy. Very tired eyes, though. And his demeanour, sort of defeated, round-shouldered, slumped back in the chair. Not a happy man. Which was understandable, what with him having just found out that his father had been brutally murdered.

'I understand that you were in Sark only a few days ago, Mr Carré. Visiting your dad, were you?'

Luke nodded.

'You went over to see him often, did you?'

'Fairly often. More so recently. When I realised he was struggling. Getting muddled. I was starting to think he had dementia.'

'I see. What were his symptoms?'

'Oh, going on about things that happened years ago. Not making any sense. Forgetting what he'd done last week. He lost his bike. Forgot where he put it but was convinced somebody had stolen it. That sort of thing.'

'Sounds like me on a good day.' Michael smiled.

Luke shrugged. 'Perhaps it was nothing. Old age. Still. I felt like I should check in on him. It was just the two of us, family-wise.'

'You were close, then?'

'Yes.'

'I understand your mother left when you were young.'

'That's right.'

'Are you in touch with her?'

He shook his head.

'Any idea why she left? Her relationship with your dad, how was it?'

'I was only nine, Inspector. I'm not sure I understood the first thing about their relationship. I never saw my dad hit her, if that's what you mean. He wasn't violent, not ever. I presume my mother was just unhappy.'

'Why's that, then?'

'She barely knew my father when they got married. They had a holiday romance. A wedding a few months later. Then I came along soon after. I was a very fussy child apparently. Hardly slept, cried all the time. Drove her half mad, Dad said. He worked; she stayed at home with me. She was lonely, depressed.'

'Must have been very difficult for you after she left.'

'I missed her, obviously. But I had Dad. He did his best.'

'Anything in particular prompt your visit last week? Had your dad seemed more confused than usual? Did he mention he was worried about anything? Or anyone?'

He hesitated, looked uncomfortable for the first time. 'Dad helped me out. Sent me money every month, has done since I left home. Last month, it didn't come, and usually I wouldn't have asked for it, but with Anna, my wife, leaving and I'm between jobs . . . I tried calling him about it, but he sounded confused. I've got a lot of time on my hands at the moment, so I thought I'd go over, check on Dad, do some fishing.'

'Ah, a fisherman.'

'Spear fishing.'

'Bass?'

'Mostly.'

'So you did a bit of diving and then went and checked on your dad?'

Luke nodded.

'How was he?'

'He seemed a little confused. No more so than usual. He was rambling on about all sorts. Wanted to show me the guinea pigs. I've never liked those bloody things. Anyway, I helped him clean up a bit. Asked him about the money. He thought he'd sent it already.'

'Did he mention anything that might have made you think he was in danger? Any arguments he'd had recently, anything out of the ordinary that had happened to him?'

'Not really. He said he thought he was being followed, but honestly, he's always been paranoid, and like I said, it seemed pretty obvious to me he was losing his marbles. He told me he'd heard the bloody Tchico howling in the night. Thought it was coming for him. Maybe he was right.' He shook his head.

'The Tchico, eh? Ghost dog, isn't it? There I was thinking it lived on Guernsey.'

'Oh, there's one on Sark too. Red eyes and fangs and jangling chains, apparently. If you get a glimpse of him, your time's up. I told Dad it was more likely to be a living, breathing dog he heard. There was nothing ghostly about the dog shit all over his front garden.'

'You weren't worried enough to get him to the doctor, or think about having someone check in on him?'

'What was going to happen to him on Sark?' Luke seemed to realise what he'd said. 'I mean, how could I have known anything like this would happen? I thought the worst case was he'd have a fall or wander into the wrong house or something, but everyone knows him over there. They all look out for each other.'

'Even though he wasn't a popular man, from what I've heard.'

'I don't think that's true. Who said that?'

'Oh, just overheard locals talking. Said he could be a bit difficult.'

'He was a touch temperamental. More so in his old age. But he had friends. It wasn't easy for him either. Marrying Mum, me coming along. He had big plans, he always told me. Wanted to see the world. Ended up stuck his whole life on three square miles in the English Channel.'

Michael nodded slowly. 'His friends. Anyone we should talk to?'

Luke was visibly upset. 'I shouldn't have left him there. Should have made him come home with me. Not like I don't have the room.' He sighed. 'Len Mauger. He and Dad were friends for years. And then there was Malcolm Perré. Me and his son, Ben, were friends. Mum and Dad used to spend time with Malcolm and his wife, Sharon. Whether or not they were still friendly I don't know.'

A phone ringing from the hallway.

'Excuse me a minute.'

Michael wandered over to the fireplace, looking at the photographs standing on the mantelpiece. Wedding picture. Arty, black and white. Her, bare foot on the sand, him with his dickie bow untied laughing. One of Luke at the finish line of the London Marathon. Michael heard Luke, voice raised, then silence, the lounge door opening.

Luke joined him at the mantelpiece, pointed to the wedding picture. 'My wife's moved back to her parents' in Shropshire.'

'Sorry to hear that. Been married long?'

'Six years.'

'Any chance of you patching things up?'

He shrugged. 'She hated it here.'

'Really?' Michael looked around the room. 'In this lovely house?'

'Not the house. Guernsey. When I lost my job, she said there was nothing keeping us here, wanted to move. History repeating itself. Thank fuck we don't have any kids.' He gave another of those world-weary sighs.

Michael gave him a genuinely sympathetic smile. 'Do you have any pictures of your mum? There were none at your dad's place.'

Luke shook his head. 'Dad burned them all after she left.'

'There's none of you, either.'

Luke shrugged. 'He wasn't the sentimental type.'

'Where were you this morning, Mr Carré?' As intended, Michael caught Luke off guard and he flinched. But that didn't mean anything, not necessarily.

'I . . . This morning, I was running. I'm training for a triathlon.'

'All morning?'

'Went out early. Was back here by nine, I suppose.'

'You train alone?'

'No. With my friend. Seb. Sebastian Clarke.'

'Very good. If you could just write down his contact details, the times you were with him and where, and we'll get that all verified.'

He passed Luke the notebook and pen, and Luke scribbled down the details.

'After your run, you do anything? See anyone?'

Luke shook his head. 'I've been . . . I've not been getting out so much recently, with everything that's been going on.'

'I understand. Divorce is a tough gig, I don't mind telling you. Just a couple more things, Mr Carré, and then I'll leave you in peace. Your dad sent you money every month, you said?'

'That's right.'

'How much?'

'A thousand pounds.'

Michael raised his eyebrows. 'Where was a retired gardener finding that sort of money?'

'Dad never really talked about it.'

'And you weren't curious?'

Luke shrugged. 'His father owned a lot of land. Dad was from a wealthy family. He could trace them all the way back to the original tenement holders. I think he just lived the way he did to spite himself.'

'Hm. Well, we'll soon find out, I suppose. And as his only known relative, I'm guessing you'll inherit anything he did have. Doesn't make anything right, but it'll come in handy, what with you losing your job and the divorce. They're bloody expensive, by the way—I forgot to mention that.'

'Like I said, Inspector, we never discussed money. Besides, considering the way he was acting this week, Dad may well have left everything to his guinea pigs.' A muscle in Luke's cheek flexed.

Michael studied the young man in front of him. There was something behind his eyes, pain or anger, something he was struggling to keep in check.

'You know, they say there's a very fine line between love and hate, and it's true. I've seen people do terrible things to those that they love. Terrible things. Worse than they'd do to a stranger. Family, eh?' He shook his head. 'I'll be in touch, Mr Carré.'

15

Jenny

She waded through the warm shallows. Overnight cloud cover had prevented yesterday's heat from fully escaping. As she went deeper, she could feel the colder water below wrapping round her ankles, then her thighs. She dived in, disrupting the layers, needing the cold this morning, something to shock her system, to shake the lack of sleep from her bones.

She'd not spoken to Michael on the boat journey back from Sark the previous evening. She'd sensed his exhaustion, and that of the officers around him, but more importantly, she had wanted to avoid talking about her conversation with Len Mauger. She needed time to figure out what everything meant. She needed to speak with him again.

Out in the bay, the air was sticky and opaque. She could barely see the loophole tower on the headland at L'Ancresse, the point she always swam towards, keeping her parallel to the beach. Several times she stopped, trod water, trying to get her bearings, waiting for the flash of red and gold, the Guernsey flag, flickering at the top of the tower. She swam until her arms began to ache, then stopped. Floated. Faced outwards, to the Channel. There was a space between the water and the cloud. It was colourless; neither the dark of the water nor the light of the sky. It was nothingness, she thought. She stretched out her limbs and floated in it.

She took her time getting dried. She felt wearier than when she'd woken, after only a couple of hours' sleep, disturbed by fragments of vivid dreams and the sensation that the room was shifting, rolling from side to side, the carpet transformed to water, the bed to a boat, as she slept.

She dressed, pulling an old Guernsey over her T-shirt. It was a rough-textured sweater, knitted from yarns soaked in oils to water-proof them, then twisted to make them stronger, able to withstand years of exposure to damp air. When she was younger, she'd refused to wear one; it was itchy she'd said, when Charlie had presented her with her first. Now, she had several—she'd grown to love the feel of the coarse fibres against her skin, the smell of the sea that seemed to settle into the wool over time.

She watched the sun rising, diminished to a hazy patch of light by the heavy, sombre sky. Today was different, she thought. Today was the first day she'd woken up knowing that something she'd suspected for so long was true. She wasn't crazy. She wasn't imagining things. Charlie had been murdered. She didn't know why. But she was going to find out. And she was going to bring his killer to justice.

Mark had taken over the running of the morning meeting and had called it for 7 a.m. Everyone was bleary-eyed but on time. Jenny gave a rundown of her day in Sark. Focusing on Reg's murder and the reaction of the locals.

'We need a detailed look at his background,' Mark interrupted her. 'Family, friends, job, involvement in the community. Sounds like you've got a fair bit of info already, but we need to flesh it out. There's a son, you said?'

'Yes. Lives on Guernsey.'

'Right. We'll need to try for a comment. He might have some pho-tos? Tell him it will help jog some memories, assist with the investiga-tion if he needs some encouragement. Which it might, obviously. Elliot, I want you in Sark with Jenny. Graham, you sort someone out to track down the son. And the bones on Derrible—we need someone working on that, find out when we should expect a steer on who it was and how they got there.' He paused. 'Do we think there's a connection?'

'Police haven't given any indication they think so. But difficult to rule it out one way or another until we know who the body is. There's another thing, Mark.'

'What the hell else can have happened on Sark in the last twenty-four hours?'

'It's probably for another time, but Corey Monroe approached me yesterday. He wants to give an interview. Seems the tension between him and the locals has reached a bit of a head. He wants to set the record straight.'

'Jesus. It's raining news.' Mark looked delighted. 'Right, we'll set that up. Have to put a senior reporter on it, Graham.'

'I got the impression he wanted me to do it.'

'Are you fucking serious?' It was a whisper.

Jenny looked around, unsure if she'd been meant to hear it.

'I can suggest someone else to him. Maybe Graham should do it.'

'No, no,' Mark said. 'We don't want to fuck Corey Monroe off. Let's do it as soon as we can. Get his take on the island, the murder. Outsider on the inside, something along those lines.' He was excited now. 'That's going to be massive. Might get some interest from the nationals. Right. Quick rundown of the rest of the news, Graham.'

Graham went through the regular daily items, assigning stories to reporters depending on which parish they covered. Jade, the new reporter, who was wearing a low-cut top and knee-high boots—ironically, Jenny suspected—had been allocated Torteval. She rolled her eyes as she was assigned a story about a dog that had escaped and attacked a neighbour's chickens.

'Seriously? There's been a murder on Sark, two probably, there's an exclusive interview to be conducted, and I get landed with some dead chickens? I had to wade through a field of cow shit last week so some old bloke could show me a nest of feral ferrets.'

'Don't knock it, Jade. "Living on the Hedge" was one of my favourite stories last week.' Elliot grinned over at her and she responded with an exaggerated pout and, Jenny couldn't help noticing, a blush of the cheeks.

'All right,' Graham admonished. 'You've been here five minutes, Jade. There'll be plenty more cow shit to wade through before you're on to the big stuff.'

Mark concluded the meeting. 'Right, let's get on with it. Jenny, I want front page ready to review by mid-afternoon. You'd better get a move on if you're going to make the eight-o'clock sailing.'

She glanced up at the clock. 'Shit.' She shut her laptop and shoved it into her rucksack.

'I'll drive.' Elliot followed her out.

'You all right?' Elliot asked. He put the keys in the ignition but didn't start the engine, turned to look at her.

'Fine. Why?'

'You look exhausted.'

'I couldn't sleep.'

'OK.' He shrugged and started the car.

'Sounds like it's not OK.'

'You don't want to talk to me. Nothing I can do to make you. I've learned that much.'

They said nothing for the rest of the five-minute drive to North Beach. He dropped her outside the ticket office.

'I'll meet you at the jetty.'

He over-revved and managed a wheel spin before pulling a U-turn and driving back towards the car park. He was pissed off. She was fucking things up, she knew it. Didn't mean she knew what to do about it.

She bought the tickets. The woman at the desk slid them over the counter.

'You'd better hurry up—it's due to leave any minute.'

She ran the short distance to the boat, waiting for Elliot before they both ran down the jetty, the boards shaking beneath their feet.

A crew member took their tickets. 'Feeling brave, are you?'

'Is it rough?' The sea looked calm.

He shook his head.

'Bit of a swell, nothing major. I meant the murder. Or should I say murders? Scared everyone off, I think. There's only you and a couple of others on board.'

'We'll have the best seat for a change, then.' She smiled.

'That's the spirit.' He took her rucksack and held her arm as she jumped over the gap between the pontoon and the deck.

She was the only person outside. Elliot had gone in after only a few minutes, wanting to talk to the captain and crew about the effect of the murder on business. He insisted everything was fine between them, but she could tell there was something on his mind. She suspected it was her.

Guernsey had disappeared from view, obscured by a thick haze. Everything was quiet. No chatter from other passengers. Even the boat's engines seemed muffled, as if the heavy air were dampening not just surfaces but sound. The benches were wet with condensation, the railings slippery beneath her grip.

A cough. She turned. Another passenger, come up from the cabin.

'Morning.' He leaned against the railing. He had the beginnings of a beard—patchy, flecked with grey. The collar of his denim jacket was turned up. His hands shook as he lit a cigarette. He offered her one.

'Pretty sure it's not allowed.' She pointed to the large 'No smoking' sign he stood next to.

He looked concerned. 'Reckon they'll take me straight to Sark Prison?'

She mirrored his expression. 'Reckon you'll get five years, minimum.'

He laughed. 'I don't even smoke. Not really. This is a ritual of mine. Hangover from when I was a rebellious teenager. All the sea air takes the smell off you. I try to have a sneaky cigarette out here every time I come over. I've usually been scolded by an old lady by now.'

'Well, I don't want to spoil your moment. I can scold you, if it would add to the atmosphere?'

'Wouldn't be the same. You're not an old lady.' He half finished the cigarette, then ground it out on the railing and threw it in the bin. 'You staying out here? Not much to see.'

'I always sit outside.'

'Hm. I've been on too many boats. Novelty wears off. Enjoy.' He held on to the top of the door frame, ducked his head to get back into the cabin.

For some reason she wanted to go after him. To tell him she'd been on lots of boats too and there was always something to see. The cry of a seagull cut through the rumble of the engine and she glimpsed its silhouette as it threaded its way through the opaque air. No fish for you here. There would be clouds of gulls behind the *Jenny Wren* when Charlie hauled in a catch. 'Clever birds, seagulls,' he'd said. 'Ruthless opportunists, too. They learned to follow the boats,' he'd told her. 'Surely they were following the fish?' she'd asked. He'd shaken his head. 'Just you watch them,' he'd said. 'They follow the boats first.'

'I've changed my mind.' He was back.

'About what?'

'Novelty never wears off. I don't know why I said that. And there's a guy in there talking really loudly on his phone. Besides, the sun's coming out.'

He stood next to her. He was right. The fog was thinning. The water turning from black to green.

'You just going for the day?' she asked him.

'I'm not sure. I think so. You?'

'Same.'

'You're a reporter.'

'I am. How did you know?'

'One of the crew knows you. Said you were over yesterday.' He paused. Looked at her intently. 'I'm Luke Carré. Reg was my dad.'

'I'm so sorry.' She kicked herself for nearly missing him.

'Are you writing about him?'

'Yes.'

'Are you writing about me?'

'Well, I was going to mention that Reg had a son. Nothing else so far. I'm not going to print anything you say here, for example. Unless you want to talk on the record.'

He smiled. 'You really say shit like that?' He shook his head.

The boat shifted, the swell intensifying as they entered the treacherous current of the Big Russel, the channel that ran between Herm and Sark.

'Let's sit,' he said. 'It's always choppy here.'

She sat beside him, feet planted firmly on the deck to steady herself.

'So would you be happy to speak on the record? One of our reporters was going to contact you today. You can just talk to me now, get it over with.' Jenny tried not to think about how much shit she was going to get from her colleagues for delivering a reaction from the dead man's son as well as the front-page story and an interview with Corey Monroe.

He nodded. 'I'm not sure what I can say that's worth reporting. Other than my father's dead and I'm devastated and I'd like to be left to grieve in peace without the *News* hanging around like vultures.' He glanced at her. 'I'm half joking.'

'OK if I slightly rephrase, then?' She smiled gently. 'Nobody from the *News* will hassle you. We're not like the tabloids on the mainland. As the case progresses, we'll ask for your take on the investigation, how you think things are going.'

'That's why I'm going over. I've spoken to the detective in charge. He has no idea what happened. Or if he does, he didn't share it with me. I haven't lived in Sark for twenty years, but it's still home. I know it. Only a Sarkee really can. Thought I might speak to some people. See if I could make a bit more sense of things. It's a fuck of a funny feeling.'

'What is?'

'Losing a parent.'

107

'I know.'

'You do?'

'My dad died just over two years ago.'

He nodded, seemed to be deep in thought. The boat pitched from side to side as they approached the jetty.

'I mean, you know they're going to go at some point,' he said. 'That you're going to have to deal with it. I just didn't expect to feel like this.'

'How do you feel?'

'Exposed.' He paused. 'It's like a barrier's been removed. Or a safety net. Depressing, eh?'

'It is,' she agreed.

'Sorry.' His voice cracked. 'I should have known Dad needed help, last time I was here. I was avoiding the fact that he seemed frail, that he wasn't with it.'

'He was murdered. You couldn't have prevented that.'

'I could. If I'd been there.'

'You couldn't possibly have known what was going to happen.'

He didn't respond.

'Did you have any idea he was in trouble? That someone might have meant him harm?'

'On the record, are we?'

'Jenny?' Elliot, holding two coffees. He handed one to her. Nodded at Luke. 'Sorry—I'd have bought a third if I'd known.' He looked at her quizzically.

'Elliot, this is Luke Carré, Reg Carré's son. Luke, this is my colleague Elliot.' She thought Elliot's flinched a little when she said 'colleague' but put it down to paranoia on her part. They had never introduced each other as anything other than friends or workmates.

'I'm so sorry for your loss.' Elliot shook Luke's hand.

'Appreciate it.' There was a moment of awkward silence. 'Well, it was nice talking to you, Jenny. I'll leave you both to your coffees.'

Elliot waited until Luke had disappeared down the stairs into the cabin. 'That all looked very cosy.'

'About as cosy as an interview with a bereaved person ever gets, I suppose,' she shot back, too sharply.

He stared at her. 'I was joking, Jenny. Jesus.'

She flushed. 'I know you were. So was I.' But she hadn't been. She'd felt defensive. As if Elliot were accusing her of something. As if she were guilty of it.

16

Rachel

1980

Icicles clung to the window. When she woke, the first thing she saw was her breath. It was rare, Reg had told her, even in mid-January, to have a cold snap like this. They slept in vests and socks and pyjamas, a duvet and a blanket on the bed. The nights were long, and heavy with the silence of winter.

But she was happy. Even as it froze outside, something inside her thawed. She reached down and scooped Luke up from the basket and brought him into the bed. He wasn't even crying yet, had just made a few mewling noises. He was soft and hot, and she held him close to her cold chest, pulling the bedclothes up around them. Next to her, Reg was awake, she knew, but he gave no sign, lying still and quiet, his breathing low and regular.

It was a miracle she thought, that something so small could effect so much change. She was exhausted and yet more awake than she'd ever been. She rose the instant Luke cried, warmed bottles, hummed and sang, made soothing noises.

Last night, for the first time, Reg had got up when she did. He'd held Luke, the baby wriggling and screaming and purple-faced. She'd warmed the milk, and Reg had handed Luke to her in the armchair, then stood behind her. The blanket she had wrapped around herself slipped as she shifted to get comfortable, exposing her shoulder, and he had placed his hand on her bare skin. She had not flinched. It was the first time he'd touched her since she'd returned.

As soon as Reg left for work, she showered. She put Luke on a towel on the floor, next to the tub, so she could see him. He kicked his legs and screwed up his face, made angry, grunting noises. He was never still, never settled—even when he slept, he fussed and whimpered. Sometimes he would wake suddenly, as if from a terrible nightmare, screaming and gasping. He was too little for dreams, she knew, too little even to focus. It would be another week or so until he would be able to see her properly. Imagine that, she thought. All the love and energy a mother gives her newborn and it doesn't even know what she looks like.

The shower was always either too hot or too cold, and she chose, according to the temperature outside, whether she wanted to be frozen or scalded. He said she exaggerated, that hardly anyone over here had a shower at all, as if she should be grateful, which she supposed she should—better here on this tiny rock in the ocean with a shower than without one.

He thought things were different. She'd come back. He thought that meant she loved him. Perhaps he was right. She had not been able to sort out the conflicting feelings he stirred up in her. Somewhere in there, she thought, there might be love, or some version of it. A flicker. Enough to build on. Enough to come back. The look on his face when he'd opened the door to them. She'd almost wanted to laugh. He'd stared at her standing on the step, shivering, her bag at her feet, the baby secured to her with a length of stretchy fabric. She had no pram. No pushchair. Luke had started to cry.

'Are you going to let us in?'

He'd stepped aside without a word.

Afterwards, he'd watched her while she'd unpacked her things, clearing space for Luke's tiny babygrows in one of her drawers. When

Luke grizzled, he'd bent over the basket and picked him up, held him awkwardly.

'Did you know, when you left?'

'After . . . what happened . . . my cycle hadn't gone back to normal.' Her cheeks had burned at sharing so intimate a detail. Stupid, after everything that had happened. 'I had no idea. And when I realised . . . I was scared. I didn't know how to tell you.'

'I've a telephone, you know.' He'd sounded bemused but not angry.

'I'm sorry.' She looked up from her folding. 'He looks like you.'

He'd stared down at Luke. 'The eyes, maybe. All babies look the same.' But he'd had the whisper of a smile about him. 'You're here to stay, then?'

'Of course. I wasn't well when I left. I wasn't thinking straight. I am now.'

He hadn't looked convinced. But he'd lain Luke gently in the Moses basket, adjusted the blanket around him and helped her to unpack.

17

Michael

The foghorn had been going since the early hours. He lay in bed waiting for each muffled blast. Lucky he wasn't flying anywhere today. The horn was the harbinger of doom for anyone who had a flight booked: heavy fog invariably meant cancellations and delays at the airport. Frustrating if you had a business meeting on the mainland; devastating if you had flight connections to Disney World, Florida, as he and Sheila had one year. Fortunately, they'd not told Ellen where they were going and the insurance paid out. They'd managed a week at Center Parcs instead.

He gave up on sleep at 5 a.m. Made himself a coffee and sipped at it while it was still scalding-hot, standing in the back doorway, watching as night lifted, the sky shifting, black to grey, before settling on a dense, sickly yellow. The fog was so thick he could hardly see the trunk of the apple tree, only feet away, just the branches, twigs laden with fruit, pointing at him accusatorily. *It's all on you*, it seemed to be saying. *The safety of an entire island is in your hands.* He rubbed his eyes. He needed to get back to Sark and get this nightmare sorted.

The kitchen table was covered in paperwork, mostly pertaining to the investigation into the Black Pearl case. He'd wanted to review it all last night, but after getting back from Luke Carré's house, he'd had energy only for a quick shower before he'd collapsed into bed. Not that there was much to review. They had no idea how the stuff was getting in. They were keeping an eye on all the usual suspects, watching the ferry terminal, tracking private planes, but this operation felt different to the usual smuggling they encountered. Slicker. The pills came in little paper envelopes, three in each packet, a simple design printed on the front. They'd found four different ones so far—a pirate, a ship, a treasure chest, a parrot. Together with the fact they were pushing them under a glamorous-sounding name, and putting God knew what in them to make them black, Michael felt sure it was all designed to appeal to youngsters. Teenagers, kids back from university. And it was working. It was very clever. And very wrong. And he didn't have time to deal with it today.

He finished his coffee. Picked up the other file on his kitchen table. An unexplained death at sea. It was slim—a missing person report, a couple of interviews, a copy of the post-mortem and one of the open verdict from the magistrates' court. An open verdict meant nobody knew what happened. It could have been an accident or a suicide; there was not enough evidence to point to one or the other conclusively. But there were 'inconsistencies' in the investigation, apparently. Reference made, in the initial report, to fingerprints found on the boat that did not match the victim's. Enough, according to the review team, to have flagged the death as suspicious. But the fingerprints were never run through the system. And now there was no trace of them in the evidence room. It was like they'd never existed.

Michael had known all this before it was brought to his attention by the UK taskforce. He'd noticed the discrepancy months ago. He'd already spent hours poring over the paperwork. He'd already lied to Jenny about it. Because his signature was there, next to the magistrate's, closing Charlie Dorey's case. He'd missed something, two years ago. And it had come back to haunt him.

Michael threw the file back on the table. Wished, once again, that he'd retired years ago.

He arrived in Sark on the police launch well before 8 a.m. and went straight to the tiny community centre next to St Peter's Church, where they had decided to set up the incident room. It was a jarringly pictur-esque location to base a murder inquiry. Michael had been to a wed-ding here once, one of Sheila's friends. He thought it had all been a bit pretentious really, making everyone go to Sark even though neither the bride nor the groom had anything to do with the place. Still, it had been a good do ('Magical,' Sheila had said) with a horse-drawn car-riage and a nice meal at Stocks afterwards. Hard to imagine now, him and Sheila, in their twenties, in love, before life fucked everything up. He'd been in good shape back then. Solid, but she'd liked that. Said he made her feel safe. She was still a fine-looking woman. He'd seen her in Guernsey last month, with her new husband.

Marquis coughed behind him, interrupting his thoughts, and Michael saw that there were a group of officers waiting outside. He counted them in. Ten. Eleven including him. The room was small and dusty, with unpolished floorboards, chairs arranged in a circle ready for the knitting group's weekly meeting. Michael had Marquis stack them in the corner, while two other officers requisitioned a spare desk from the tourist information centre in the village. The rest of the team set up laptops, a telephone. As Michael explained to them, they didn't need much: this was an exercise in public relations more than anything—the locals needed somewhere they could come for updates, or with any information they might have. They wouldn't like being told to call Guernsey, though that was the first thing the officer on duty here was instructed to do on receiving anything relevant to the inquiry.

'Marquis, I want Reg Carré's bank statements, pension information, whatever you can find. He appears to have had a significant amount of money. I want to know how much and where it came from. And find out if he made a will. As far as suspects are concerned, I want to know about anyone who Reg Carré ever had an argument with, anyone who he had a relationship with. So far, the only person who seems to have spoken with him recently is his son, Luke Carré. Says he was out run-ning with a friend yesterday morning—one of the lads in Guernsey is checking that out for us. Meanwhile, over here, we're going to continue with door-to-doors. There are four hundred and fifty-odd people on this island, less if you discount the kids. We should be able to get a statement and an alibi from every one over the next couple of days. Where are we with ferry passenger lists for the last couple of weeks?'

'I'm on it, sir. Already contacted them,' Marquis said.

'Good. And I want guest lists from all the hotels and guesthouses. Does the campsite have a register? It must do. I want to know every single person who has travelled to and from this island in the last couple of months. There's only one way to get on and off of here—that's got to work to our advantage. And everyone knows each other. Any strangers hanging around, any unusual behaviour, it will have been noticed.'

There was a snigger from the back of the room.

'Something funny about a bloody murder now, is there?' He looked for Fallaize, who could usually be relied upon to be an arse, but it was PC Bachelet who was beet-red.

'Sorry, sir. It's just, you know, people here are a bit unusual at the best of times.'

'Bloody hell's that supposed to mean?'

'Nothing, sir.'

'I should hope so. Folks in Jersey think everyone in Guernsey's weird, and we all know that's a load of bollocks. It's just different here, that's all. You will treat everyone on this island with respect. And as a potential killer. Now get to work.'

He'd hardly finished organising the place when there was a rap on the open door and Michael turned to see an overweight, pink-cheeked man wearing corduroy trousers and a polo shirt with 'Florence's' embroidered on the breast pocket. Florence's was the name of the tea-rooms at the Seigneurie, the ancestral home of the seigneur of Sark.

'I'm looking for Inspector Gilbert?' He had a high-pitched, nasal voice.

'I'm Detective Chief Inspector Gilbert. How can I help you?'

'My name is Jeremy Botham. I'm Sir William de Bordeaux's private secretary. Sir William was wondering when you might find the time to come and speak with him. He's rather anxious to find out what's going on.'

'I'm sure he is.'

The man looked affronted by Michael's tone. 'He's the seigneur. He needs to draft a statement. People here still look to him for leadership, despite all the recent political upheaval.' He wrinkled his nose, as though the recent democratisation of Sark was an unpleasant aroma.

'He's next on my list. I'll be there in twenty minutes. We've been a little busy, as I'm sure you understand.'

The man nodded. 'I shall tell him you're on your way.'

'You do that.' Michael watched the man walk up the road. He could have gone with him but didn't want Sir William to think the Guernsey Police Force were at his beck and call. Michael was already at the mercy of too many chiefs.

'This Sebastian Clarke, sir, Luke Carré's alibi—he confirmed that he was out running with Luke yesterday morning.'

'When exactly?'

'Early. He said Luke met him at six and he was back home by eight, in time to get ready for work. But that still wouldn't leave Luke enough time to get over to Sark.'

'Hm. I suppose not. In any event, let's keep an eye on Luke Carré. There's something about him. Can't put my finger on it. He was definitely holding back. Right. I'm going to talk to Sir William de bloody Beauvoir, or whatever his name is. Wish me luck.'

Hidden behind high walls, the Seigneurie Gardens were the biggest tourist attraction on Sark. The fertile soil and mild climate in this sheltered oasis meant that many plants that would have been killed by frost and rain on the mainland thrived here. Rose-covered archways, a bed of Singapore orchids, exotic clematises climbing up trellises, a greenhouse full of cacti; in the summertime, it drew hundreds of visitors, who included it on their European garden tours, right after Kew and Wisley.

Michael made his way to the house through a section of garden marked 'Private'. Here, it was less cultivated, borders full of lavender and sweet-smelling herbs spilling over onto the pathway. Mist still lingered, hovering over shrubs and threading its way between the flowers. Through the trees, Michael glimpsed the pond—a misnomer, really, for the ancient body of water that predated the rest of the property by hundreds, perhaps thousands of years. It was, as always, Michael noted, in shadow. He shivered. It had always given him the creeps.

The house itself was beautiful. The modern section at the front similar to that of an old Guernsey farmhouse but grander in scale. Behind, the turrets and towers of the original building rose above the rooftop. Up close, though, the dilapidation was more evident. There had been articles in the *Guernsey News* about the state of the house, the need for repair and renovation—Sir William had insisted it was up to the States of Guernsey to pay for the repairs, despite him being some sort of third cousin to the Queen and presumably loaded. Typical rich person, Michael had thought, never wanting to spend their own money. Paint was peeling round cracked window frames, a layer of lichen yellowing the blue stonework, the front door creaking on its hinges as it opened at his approach.

Inside, Michael's footsteps echoed on cold flagstones. Dark wood balustrades curved round a staircase leading to the top floor. Jeremy Botham showed Michael into a drawing room, where Sir William de Bordeaux sat tall and straight in a wing-backed chair. He was a man evidently blessed with good genes. Now in his eighties, he was well known for walking everywhere, with the help of only a highly polished walnut cane, eschewing the use of the motorised scooter he'd been granted special permission to use on Sark's traffic-free roads. He delighted tourists by turning up to island events in his full, now antique RAF uniform, medals sparkling at his breast.

'Ah! Here you are. I've been waiting for you. I need an update. People are going to expect me to make a statement. Forty-five years I've been seigneur of Sark. Never had anything like this. It's appalling. What's going on? And what are you all doing about it?'

Michael contemplated telling him that he was unable to discuss the details of the case. He'd be quite within his rights, too. The seigneur no longer had any official role on the island, was merely a figurehead. But it struck Michael that the man might be useful. He'd certainly have a different insight into island affairs than the rest of the population. So he gave him a very short précis of the previous day's events.

'This really is most distressing. You're to keep me informed. Any developments, as soon as an arrest is made, you must let me know.'

'We'll certainly do that, sir.'

'You'll be calling a meeting, presumably, updating the islanders in person? One can only imagine how worried everyone will be. You'll need to reassure them. This place is so small, Inspector—any one of us could be living within feet of a killer!'

'We're going to call a meeting, yes,' Michael agreed. 'As soon as we're up and running here.'

'I'll make a statement. Something the press can report, along the lines of "I'm shocked and distressed, and urge the public to help the police with their enquiries."'

'Thank you. That would be very helpful.'

'Although I'm not, you know. Not really.'

Michael furrowed his brow. 'You're not going to make a statement?'

'I'm not shocked.' He reached over to a side table and rang a small brass bell. Jeremy peered in from behind the door. 'Fetch us some tea, please, Jeremy.'

'Certainly, sir.'

Michael waited until the door was closed again. 'What do you mean by that?'

'You know how a pressure cooker works, Inspector?'

Michael tried to suppress a sigh of frustration and did not entirely succeed.

Sir William continued oblivious. 'You put all the ingredients into the pot and turn it on, and over time, they cook. Given the right amount of pressure, the right amount of time, at the end, you have a delicious meal. But under the wrong circumstances, forgotten, for example, or set incorrectly, what do you get? An explosion, Inspector. That's what. Broken glass and boiling-hot matter all over the kitchen.'

'I see.' Michael paused. 'Sir William, do you have any idea who killed Reg Carré? Or how his death might be related to the situation you've just described?'

'Goodness me, no. Hardly even knew the man.'

'But you're saying that circumstances are such that you're not shocked by his violent murder?'

'Inspector, Sark is not what it was. I have no power now, I realise that. It was always very limited. My grandmother Dame Florence was the last true ruler of Sark. Democratisation was inevitable. I don't resent it. But with it has come something else. The vandalism, the posters—there's so much ill will. More than that. Bad blood, Inspector. There's so much bad blood. It's flowing through us all now. Turning neighbour against neighbour, brother against sister. It was only a matter of time before somebody got hurt.'

18

Jenny

Jenny knocked on Len Mauger's door for the third time. She pushed open the letterbox, called his name. There was a good chance, she thought, that he was ignoring her. She'd frightened him the day before with her relentless questions, had left in a hurry with too many of them unanswered. She was on borrowed time once more, having asked Elliot to touch base with the police while she 'tied up a couple of loose ends'. He, rightly, suspected she was up to something. She'd have to tell him what eventually.

She walked the perimeter of Len's house, peering in through grimy windows. Back at the front, she stood on the path, realised something was missing. The boots and bucket she had seen at the door yesterday were gone. Len must have crab pots somewhere nearby. Somewhere accessible from land, judging by the wet wellies she'd seen yesterday. The quickest way to the coast from here was straight on, past the silver mines.

She walked downhill, through an arch of trees. The sunshine was scant, the air clammy, leaves throwing dappled shadows at her feet, and she was relieved to emerge out into the open countryside.

Long grass rippled in the fields on either side of her. Soon they would be shorn, bales of sweet-smelling hay rolled into the corners. A track led to a farmhouse and a barn, the last inhabited buildings on Little Sark before the land fell into the sea. She wondered if Len

Mauger's neighbours looked out for him, if they knew where he was, but stopped short of going to ask. Too many of Sark's residents seemed to know her business already, or at least were suspicious enough of her to warn her off, to discourage her questions. And it was obvious, from the note she had seen yesterday, that at least one person might not stop there. There was no sign that anyone was home anyway, just a fat ginger cat looking at her through half-closed eyes as she walked towards the ruined mines.

Ill fated. That was how the mining endeavour on Sark was most often described. It had started with a glister. A farmer picking up a rock, glinting in the sunlight. The caves were explored. A shining seam as wide as a man's arm found running through black rock. Riches were discussed in fevered conversations. Land bought and sold. Whole families shipped over from Cornwall, lured by the promise of a steady wage paid in silver. Four shafts were sunk at Port Gorey, with eight galleries mined under the seabed. Steam pumping engines were installed to clear out water and rubble. At some points, only a few feet of rock lay between the miners and the ocean. It was said they could hear the waves rolling back and forth above them. It made the locals nervous. It wasn't right to be beneath the sea. It wasn't natural.

There were whispers of bad luck. Accidents, not in the mines themselves but after the day was done. Shipwrecks in fine weather. Sickness. A stillborn child. Then one night, on his way home from a day at the mines, a Sarkee saw the Tchico. It stood on La Coupée, teeth bared, eyes glowing red, chains rattling at its neck. Hackles risen, it crouched on its haunches, growling, barring the man's way home. Terrified, he ran back to the camp. The curse was on all of them, he said, and while the mines were open, no one on Sark was safe. Half mad with terror, he took a boat, intending to sail back to the main island, avoiding the walk across La Coupée and the dog, which had surely been sent as a message from hell. He never made it home. Pieces of the boat washed ashore the next morning.

No one wanted to work the mines after that, so the story went. Eventually they were abandoned. All that was left of them were the chimneys, moss-covered stacks of granite protruding from the scrubby heather and gorse, some almost completely intact, others crumbling.

There was no clear path to the shore, just a lowering of the land as it reached into the Channel, its covering of springy grass thinning to rubble and rock as it met the water. Patches of wild flowers—delicate pink thrift, stark white sea campion—and mustard-coloured lichen peppered the yellows and browns of the cliff edge. Jenny took what appeared to be the easiest route down, treading carefully over loose shale, descending into a cleft between two rocky outcrops. The further she went, the less likely it seemed she would find Len Mauger. There was no nowhere to drop a crab pot from here, let alone pull one in.

She picked her way round a deep rock pool. Blood red, jelly-like anemones clung to the sides. The water disappeared into a black crevice on one side, flowing under the cliffs. Charlie had told her octopus could be found under rocks like these. The proper way to catch one, he'd said, was to stretch an arm into the space underneath the rock and wait. The octopus would attack, wrapping tentacles round the offending limb; at which point, you had to whip it out and bash it on the nearest hard surface. 'Simple as that,' he'd grinned. She had no idea if he'd been joking or not, but her arms still tingled at the thought of it. That was the thing about Charlie. The lines between truth and fiction blurred. Not intentionally, but he told all his stories with the same enthusiasm. Jokes became legends, legends became facts, and she'd never had the opportunity to ask him which was which. She had, she corrected herself. She'd had the opportunity. She'd never taken it.

She stopped at the water's edge, balancing on a flat boulder, which pitched back and forth under her weight, the cliff face behind her casting a shadow out onto the water. On the horizon, hidden behind thick cloud, lay Paimpol and Saint-Brieuc. Behind her, to the north, Carteret and Cherbourg. It was an anomaly of history that these islands, with their Gallic habits, embraced by the arm of Normandy on one side, of Brittany on the other, should call England the 'mainland'. She'd never felt English, felt much more at home on the quaint, cobbled streets of Saint-Malo, so like those of St Peter Port, than she ever did on the streets of Brighton, with its garish gaming arcades and the fume-spewing traffic and the beach—pebbled and littered and too busy to sit on whenever the sun shone.

A wave broke at her feet and she realised the tide was rising, the stones around her, which had been grey and dry only moments before, were now slick and black, not yet immersed, the water tentative, gaining more ground as it flowed forward, retreating a little less with each ebb. She turned, saw to her dismay that the water had risen behind her—the tide had filled the rock pools to overflowing and they now spilled over the surface she had walked across only five minutes previously.

Shit. It was embarrassment, not panic, that made her scramble back the way she came; only now, she was ankle-deep in freezing seawater. A tourist's mistake: failing to appreciate the unpredictability of the tide. She reached the headland, feet squelching in her shoes.

'What on earth are you doing?' Len Mauger stood holding a bucket in one hand, a fishing rod in the other.

'I was looking for you.'

'Well, I wouldn't be down there, would I? Those rocks are cursed. Least they were, according to the miners. One of the children from the barracks drowned down there. Not long before they wound the whole operation up.'

'That's why you don't go down there?'

'I don't go down there because it's a bloody deathtrap. Tide rushes in out of nowhere.'

She felt her cheeks redden. 'So I gather.'

She walked alongside him. They went slowly, her wet shoes chafing against her heels. He stopped every minute or so.

'Can I carry the bucket?'

He nodded. Handed it to her. She baulked at the weight of it. A conger eel curled inside, grey-green skin glistening. She grimaced.

'Don't like conger?' Len asked.

'I've only had it once. I didn't like it much.'

'You've got to fillet it right. It's bony.'

124

'You caught this from the shore?' Congers preferred deeper water. He nodded.

'Off Venus Pool. Couple of good spots there. Bugger reeling it in, though. Must weigh fifteen pounds. I'm a bit knackered, to be honest with you.' His face was pale, beads of sweat on his forehead despite the cool weather. She wondered how long he would be able to keep going. Out here, alone, sick, shunning help. He seemed to read her thoughts.

'I'll not be able to do this much longer.'

'You should go to Guernsey. Have the treatment they've offered you. Do you have any family there?'

'I've only one relative anywhere. A sister. Lives in Perth. Haven't seen her in nearly ten years.'

'Does she know you're sick?'

'I doubt she knows I'm alive. We were never close,' he offered as an explanation. 'I've always had my friends. Just the last couple of years I've kept myself to myself. Ever since . . .' he stopped walking, wiped his brow, 'your dad. Before he died, he saw something.'

'Yes?' She gripped the handle of the bucket.

'The waters around Brecqhou. No one's allowed to sail within a certain distance of the island. It's a privacy thing Monroe managed to sort out when he bought the place. Must have paid a fortune to someone. Not sure how you go about making the sea private property.' He shrugged. 'Anyway, he wanted to stop the press taking pictures of his castle, or whatever he's got going on there.' He paused again. 'Your dad saw a boat one evening. Right off the coast, on the castle side. He thought maybe it was one of the tabloids trying to get pictures, decided to follow it.'

'It was probably Monroe's. He must use a boat to get to and from Sark.'

'It wasn't Monroe's. His is practically gold-plated, not hard to mistake. This was a regular fishing boat. Anyway, over by Port du Moulin, this boat starts flashing a light. Your dad reckoned it was some sort of signal. He got a bit obsessed about it, truth be told. I'm sure you know what he was like. Anyway, he started asking around about it. Thought he was on to something.'

'What did he think was going on?'

He shook his head. 'I really don't know.'

'You think Corey Monroe has something to do with this?'

'I don't think anything, and I have no idea what *this* is,' he said sharply. 'I'm telling you what Charlie told me over a couple of pints at the Mermaid. It's probably a load of rubbish.' He took the bucket from her, wincing at its weight. 'I've nothing else to tell you.'

They had reached his house, and he walked through the gate, took a few steps up the path.

'What the . . . ?' He dropped the bucket. It fell onto its side. The eel's head slid out onto the paving; its dead black eyes sheened with blue. A trickle of water followed it, drawing a dark line across the dry stones, stopping only when it reached the doorstep.

Jenny followed Len's gaze to the front door and walls of his house. All smeared brown. A blowfly buzzed in front of her face. Jenny took a few steps closer. The smell burned the back of her throat.

'It's manure. From the farm. Must be. It's happened before. Kids throw it around. Messing about.' Len's voice was unsteady.

Jenny shook her head. 'It's not manure. It's dog shit.'

'Jesus. It's her.'

'Who?' Jenny put an arm out to steady him as he swayed on his feet.

'None of this would have happened before. Not your dad, not Reg. She came over and changed it all. It's not the Sark way.' His voice faded and he took deep, rasping gasps of breath.

'Who did? For God's sake, please tell me what you know!'

'Just leave, will you? Leave here and don't come back.' His face was ashen, his skin clammy. He slumped into her arms and Jenny buckled under his weight.

'We need to get you inside. You need to lie down.'

She half dragged, half pulled him to the house, ignoring the dog shit on the door handle as she tried to open it.

'It's locked. Where's the key? Where's the key, Len?'

His eyes were closed, his breathing shallow. She lowered him as gently as she could to the ground. Flies immediately buzzed around his face and she swiped at them. 'Fuck off!'

She was panicking. Not thinking straight. She took out her phone. No signal.

Fuck.

19

Michael

'This is a monumental screw-up if ever I saw one.' Michael took off his jacket and threw it at the chair. He missed and it fell to the floor, edges instantly made white with dust. 'Martin Langlais mentioned he reported vandalism months ago. Now the seigneur's telling me the same story. If it turns out Reg's murder is connected to some sort of neighbours' feud that we did nothing about, we are well and truly fucked.' Michael was not one for swearing; his language worsened with his mood. From the look on Marquis's face, he knew the last statement meant trouble was brewing.

'Did the seigneur have any other useful information?'

'I've no idea, Marquis. It was all exploding pressure cookers and bad blood. Well, it's all over Reg Carré's kitchen walls now, isn't it, eh?'

'I don't quite understand, sir.' Marquis was fiddling with his belt loops. He did that when he was nervous.

'Well, could be the seigneur's lost the plot, Marquis. That's entirely possible, I grant you. Let's face it, he's knocking on a bit. Didn't strike me as a rambling pensioner, though. Quite the opposite. And he seemed to think this whole island has gone to hell. Based on the day and a half we've spent here, I'm inclined to agree.' He pulled at his chin. 'We're no closer to finding Reg's killer. We're calling for calm, obviously, but whoever did that is dangerous. Every hour that goes by . . .' He shook his head. 'Doesn't bear thinking about. And we've not had a single tip off about the bones. It'll be days, weeks maybe before we get anything back from the lab on them.'

There was a shuffling in the doorway. Michael swung round. 'Yes?'

A man stood on the step, looking awkward.

'Can we help you?' Michael had no time for dawdlers this morning.

'Yes. I didn't want to interrupt.' The man stepped into the incident room. He was well over six feet tall, broad-shouldered and clean-shaven, a tan line visible below the open collar of his checked shirt. He scratched the back of his neck.

'I saw Mr Carré. Yesterday morning, first thing. He was on his way back from the shop, I think.'

Michael picked up the pile of statements taken from residents who had come forward the day before.

'Did you speak to someone about this yesterday?' he asked.

'Yes, I gave a statement. Benjamin Perré.'

'Got it.' Michael pulled it out and glanced over it. Nodded as he read it. 'It's all here.'

Benjamin shifted. 'I'm not sure it is.'

'Take a seat, Mr Perré. Marquis, sort out some coffee, will you? Get a couple from the village and keep the receipt.

'Says here you passed Mr Carré in your tractor. He was resting against a hedge; you were concerned he was unwell; you exchanged pleasantries and made sure he was OK. This was shortly after nine yesterday morning.' Michael looked up. 'What have we missed?'

Benjamin sighed. 'This is stupid. I told my wife it was going to sound stupid.'

'Well, you're here now, and I've heard stupid too many times for you to need to feel embarrassed about it. If something's bothering you, let's hear it.'

'I've known Mr Carré all my life. Luke and I—that's Reg's son—we're friends. Spoke to him Sunday night actually.'

'You spoke to Luke? What about?'

'Oh, just told him about the bones down on Derrible.'

'You knew about the bones Sunday night?'

'Course. Martin, you know—the constable, he was in the Mermaid having a pint.'

'You call Luke often?'

'Every now and then. Keep him up to date on all the island gossip.' He stopped. A worried expression crossed his face. 'Was I not supposed to say anything? About the bones? Only Martin didn't say it was confidential or anything. We were all talking about it in the pub.'

'No, no. It's fine. You were telling me about Reg.'

'Yes. That's right. Yesterday, when I passed Reg, I stopped, like I said. He was fine, just taking a rest. It was warm. Only, when I mentioned the bones on Derrible, well, he looked very . . . distressed.'

'In what way?'

'Well, it's hard to say. It just seemed to affect him.'

'More than the average person on hearing a dead body's been discovered in a cave?'

Benjamin nodded. 'I'd say so. He didn't seem surprised. More panicked.' He looked up at Michael. 'This *is* stupid. I probably imagined it. Poor man. Can't get away from the old gossip even when he's dead.'

'What old gossip? You didn't mention that yesterday.'

'Well, it's not on, is it? And they were just nasty rumours. My dad started them, so I should know.'

'What rumours?'

'When Reg's wife disappeared.'

'Disappeared? I thought she left him?'

'Right. Yes, see, this is the problem. She did leave him. But it was very sudden. And she never came back, to visit Luke or anything. So people talked.'

'And what did they say?'

'That Reg had bumped her off, you know. I mean, nobody *really* thought that. It was a bit of a joke. But it came back to me yesterday, when I told him about the bones. Saw his face. Remembered my dad, twenty-five years ago, just after Mrs Carré left. He was talking to my mum about it. "Wouldn't surprise me if he'd done her in," he said, "and buried her in the back garden," and Mum said something like, "Don't be daft. There are better places to hide a body round here."'

He caught Michael's incredulous expression. 'They were joking, Inspector. They laughed. But I was only about ten, and I remember not finding it very funny.'

'Right. I see.' Michael could feel the beginnings of a headache. 'You did the right thing coming to us. We'll need to follow up. Talk to your parents—do they know you've told us about this?'

Benjamin shook his head. 'No. It shouldn't be a problem. They'd be happy to help. Well, Mum will.'

Marquis came in with the coffees just as Benjamin Perré left.

'Everything all right, sir?'

'Not really.'

'What was that all about?'

'More gossip and bad blood, Marquis. Reckon we've got a way to go before we get through it all.'

'Well, I've got something interesting. From the Sark Shipping ticket office. They sold a ticket back to Guernsey on the twelve-noon sailing yesterday.'

'Right. Carry on.'

'Well, the girl at the ticket office is not from Sark, so she couldn't be sure if the woman who purchased it was local or not, but she didn't recognise her.'

'OK. It would be unusual for a visitor not to have a return ticket—that's what you're getting at?'

'Exactly. And the timing—few hours after Reg Carré was killed. Thought it might be worth pursuing.'

'True bloody right, Marquis. Did we get a name, a description?'

'They don't take names on the Sark ferry, boss—it's still paper tickets. The crew tear one half off when you board. We could look at credit-card sales, but this woman paid cash, and the girl at the ticket office wasn't the best witness, boss. Said it was a woman wearing a sun hat, sunglasses. She couldn't see her face or her hair. Average height and weight.'

'I see. Well, let's put out an appeal. See if whoever it was comes forward. And let's talk to anyone we do know was on that sailing—in fact, any sailing from Sark yesterday—check the credit-card sales, like you said, ask anyone who paid cash to come forward, cross-check against numbers, see if we're missing anyone. Might be someone was acting strangely; people might have noticed.' He nodded, almost to himself. 'Good work, Marquis.'

The phone on the desk rang. It was a weighty, old-fashioned brick of a thing and you could almost hear the bell shaking inside the casing. Michael picked it up. Listened. Sighed. Grunted. Put his hand to his forehead.

'OK. OK. Yes, got it. We'll be there in ten minutes.'

'What's up, sir?'

Michael stared out of the door, brow furrowed. 'More vandalism. House over on Little Sark. Chap's collapsed.'

'Shouldn't we be focusing on all this?' Marquis pointed to the pile of interview notes, beneath which they both knew were pictures of Reg Carré's body, and the crime scene photographs of Derrible Bay.

'We should. But we'll not be hearing anything from the lab until Friday at the earliest. And this man, Len Mauger, he's on my list of people to speak to. Was a friend of Reg's. Jenny Dorey's with him. That was her on the phone.'

Michael left the room, stepping out onto the street.

'Come on, then!' he called over his shoulder. 'Let's find out what trouble that cousin of yours has been causing this time.'

20

Rachel

1984

If only you could get shoes on Sark. It was easy to guess the sizes for his clothes—if a T-shirt was a little big, it could be tucked in, the ends of trousers rolled up—but the shoes were a different story. She had to buy a couple of sizes each time and return the ones that didn't fit. But this time the smaller size was much too tight, and the bigger ones were the right length but too narrow and they pinched his feet.

'Just take him over. Get him properly fitted. There's only a week before he starts. First pair of school shoes are a bit of a big deal, anyway. I remember getting mine.' He ruffled Luke's hair. 'What do you say, Luke? Fancy a trip to Guernsey?'

Luke nodded. 'Can we go in a car when we get there?' He'd never been in one. He'd never left the island.

She felt sick at the thought of it, out among all those people. The High Street, the shops, the crowds. It would be too hard to keep him safe.

Reg sensed how nervous she was. 'I'll come. We'll make a day of it. It'll do the boy good. We'll show him all the sights,' he joked.

She didn't laugh. Didn't even crack a smile.

'He's a strong, healthy lad, Rachel. You've got to stop all this fussing. He's not going to break.'

Reg was right. Luke was strong and healthy. He was smart, too, and curious, full of questions about the world around him, about nature and the weather and the sky at night. A trip to Guernsey wouldn't break him. She was another matter.

They went on a Thursday. Luke's grip on her hand was too slight and she had to keep pulling him back, towards her. She had thought that having Reg there would be useful, an extra pair of eyes on the child. Instead, he hindered her efforts.

'Let him go.'

'He's four years old.'

'He just wants to look at everything. We're right beside him.'

'He's not used to the cobbles. He might fall.'

'Well, then we'll pick him up.' He was getting exasperated, but she held on to Luke's hand anyway. Tighter.

To make matters worse, it was the town carnival. Colourful bunting fluttered between the buildings. As they walked from the seafront onto Le Pollet, the cobbled road that led to the High Street, they passed a man dressed as a clown. He held a bunch of bright helium balloons in one hand. He bent down, smiled at Luke.

'Are you coming to see the show?'

Luke looked at her. He was a good boy, knew not to talk to strangers.

'I don't think so, thank you.'

She started to walk, pulling Luke with her.

'When is it?' Reg asked.

'Eleven o'clock in front of the Town Church. There's a Punch and Judy.'

Luke's eyes widened. 'Can we go?' he whispered.

It was so hard to say no to him.

'We'll see,' she said.

Beghin's was the only place for school shoes, Reg said. It was right next to the Town Church, the red-and-white-striped Punch and Judy tent already erected and catching Luke's eye.

'We've got plenty of time, Luke,' Reg reassured him. 'Let's get you sorted in here first. Then we'll find a good spot to watch the show, eh?'

It was decided, then. She could hardly say no now. She glared at Reg. He pretended not to notice. They went into the shop.

A stern-looking assistant dressed in a sombre suit with a dark green tie and a pair of wire-framed glasses perched on the end of his nose placed Luke's feet in an unwieldy metal measuring contraption. He told him to stand up straight, slide his heels back, then disappeared without a word. He returned a few minutes later with boxes stacked to his chin. Luke dutifully tried each pair, walking the length of the shop and back, wiggling his toes so the assistant could feel them through the stiff leather. The fourth pair he tried were declared a perfect fit, and Luke agreed that they were not too big, too small, too tight or too slippy and that he would probably be able to run quite fast in them. The assistant packed them back into the box, carefully folding the tissue paper over the top.

'I'll ring them up for you.' He smiled.

'Can we take the next size up?' she asked.

He wrinkled his brow. 'But these fit perfectly.'

'As well as those. Two pairs.' She'd have asked for the size after that too but was worried that Reg would baulk at the cost. As it was, he just gave her a look, then rolled his eyes. Much as her eccentricities seemed to perplex him, he liked to see her happy.

Luke roared with laughter at the Punch and Judy, right until Mr Punch put the baby in the sausage machine. Then he looked at her confused as the string of fabric sausages flowed over the side of the tent.

'Is the baby dead?' He had tears in his eyes.

'It's just pretend, sweetheart. And look.' She pointed to the show. The sausages disappeared back into the grinder; the baby was removed, paraded back and forth, unharmed but still unsafe, wobbling precariously in Mr Punch's arms.

'He shouldn't have done that,' Luke said quietly.

'It's just pretend,' she said. 'And anyway, wait until you see what happens at the end.'

With the baby safely returned to Judy, Luke started to laugh again, and by the time the devil had walloped him off the stage, he was clapping and cheering.

Rachel looked around for Reg, who had been standing at the back, a shopping bag in each hand.

'Come on,' she said. 'Time to go home.'

He was tired on the way back to the ferry and she carried him, his head nestled into her neck.

'It would have been better if the policeman had got him,' he said. There was a note of anxiety in his voice.

'What do you mean?'

'It would have been better if Mr Punch had gone to jail. Because after the devil hit him, he was OK and he might be mean to the baby again and to Mrs Punch.'

'Her name's Judy. I don't think he was mean to them anymore. Not after seeing the devil. I think that would be enough to teach anyone a lesson, don't you?'

'Have you ever seen the devil, mummy? Does he really look like that?' He held her tighter.

'Don't be a silly billy.'

She felt him relax a little. His eyelashes fluttered against her cheek. 'He probably only comes for bad people, doesn't he?'

'That's right Luke. So we have nothing to worry about.

It hurt to swallow past the lump in her throat.

21

Jenny

She paced the path in front of the small front garden, nose wrinkled against the smell, mouth closed firmly against the flies. Michael arrived, looking too large for his bicycle, and wobbled to a stop. He embraced her awkwardly, half hug, half pat on the back, his usual greeting. The usual smile was missing, though.

'Not like you to get in the middle of everything,' he said shortly. 'How's the poor chap doing? And what exactly is going on?'

She pointed to the house. He took a few steps towards it.

'Is that . . . ?'

'Smeared all over the house. The back too. Mr Mauger collapsed not long after he saw it. Chest pains.'

'Any sign of a break-in? Any damage inside the house?'

'Not that I could see. I don't know for sure. I ran next door and used the phone, then sat with Len until the doctor arrived. He's sick. Cancer. He should be in hospital, but he refuses to go.'

'And what does all of this have to do with you?'

'I was speaking to him about Mr Carré. They were friends. Was just looking for a bit of background.'

'Hm. Find out anything interesting?'

She hesitated. This wasn't the time to bring up Charlie's death. Michael had too much going on. She tightened her grip on her backpack.

The note Len received two years earlier was tucked inside. She needed more than that before she asked Michael for help. She shook her head.

'They'd grown apart. I'm not sure why.'

'And this.' Michael nodded towards the house. 'What the hell is all this about?'

Jenny shrugged. 'Your guess is as good as mine. There's been a lot of trouble over here recently. Maybe this is just more of the same.'

Michael furrowed his brow. 'This is disgusting, though. Who does something like this? Someone's taken the time to collect a load of crap and then rub it all over this poor sod's house. That's something else. He didn't have any idea what it was about?'

Jenny shook her head. 'No. As soon as he realised what it was, he went into shock, started shaking and panting. I thought it was stress, but then he collapsed. He needs an ECG but is refusing to go to Guernsey. I think he's scared he might never come back.'

'Because it's so bloody brilliant over here, eh? I don't know about you, Jenny, but I'm getting the impression that no bugger on this island is being entirely honest with me.' He stared at her for a moment too long and she felt her cheeks flush. She was glad to hear the creak of the front door. Joe Lawton held his nose as he walked over to them.

'How's he doing, Doctor?' Jenny asked.

'I'm fairly sure he's had a mild heart attack. I've arranged a bed for him at the Princess Elizabeth Hospital. *Flying Christine* is on her way over now.' The St John Ambulance boat was the only way to transfer patients to Guernsey.

'He's agreed to go?' Jenny was surprised.

'I told him he might not last the night if he stayed here alone without any treatment. That together with the sedative I gave him seems to have had the right effect.'

'Is he well enough to give a statement?' Michael asked. 'I don't mean to be callous, but if Mr Mauger knows anything about who might have done this, I need to speak with him.'

'He's not in a state to talk now. He's very drowsy. And we need to get him in the ambulance as soon as it arrives. I wouldn't have thought you'd be bothered about this sort of thing anyway, Chief Inspector. Haven't you got enough on your plate?'

'I've got plenty on my plate. I'm just not quite sure what it all is. Have you seen anything else like this recently?'

'I've only been here a few months, and in that time I'm delighted to say I've not had the misfortune to venture into a house covered in dog excrement before. Surely just kids, though—nothing to do with what you're investigating?'

'This the sort of thing kids get up to on Sark, is it?'

Joe Lawton shrugged. 'Kids here don't seem to be particularly different to anywhere else. A little more independent, maybe. They have more freedom than almost anywhere else I can think of. And they get bored. Leads to a certain wildness sometimes. I imagine this is just a prank that got out of hand.'

The rumble of a tractor signalled the arrival of the ambulance. The driver got down from the cab at the same moment that a paramedic jumped out of the trailer and they both began wrangling a stretcher.

'I need to get Len moved now. If you have any further questions, I'll be at the surgery the rest of the afternoon.'

'Where would that be, then?'

'The big house just before the turn-off to La Moinerie.'

'That massive place with the pillars? You live there?' Michael queried.

'It's ridiculous, isn't it? I'm a bit lost in it, but it came with the job.' Joe Lawton walked over to the ambulance and began to give directions.

'Very sure of himself, isn't he?' Michael muttered.

Jenny smiled.

'What?'

'For a policeman, you have a surprising problem with authority figures.'

'What's that supposed to mean?' He glared at her. 'Eh? Bloody doctor has no authority over me.'

'If you say so.' She looked at her watch. 'Shit. I was supposed to meet Elliot nearly an hour ago.'

'Ah. Brought your partner in crime this time. Glad to hear it. You stay out of trouble, all right? And you never finished telling me what you and Len were talking about.'

'I've got to run. Mum says hello, by the way. You should give her a call, organise that dinner?'

He cleared his throat. 'Yes. Yes. Should do. Will do. Anyway. Best get on with this, eh?'

It was a cheap trick, but it worked. Michael, distracted, turned back to the house, forgetting his question about Len Mauger. At least for now.

Elliot was pissed off. Again. The fact that she'd turned up to the café over an hour late hadn't helped.

'What do you mean you're staying over? We've got everything we need, haven't we? It's going to take hours to write all of this up.' He waved at the waitress, the same one who had served Jenny the day before, and asked for the bill.

'I can do it from here. And there's someone else I need to speak to.'

'About Reg Carré? Or your dad? Jenny, this is getting out of hand. I know that's what you've been up to—I'm not stupid. He was in Sark right before he died, and you're acting the way you always do when you're obsessing about something.' He stopped at her look. Lowered his tone. 'Look, there's a murder investigation underway here. We need to be focused on that.'

'I am. This isn't about my dad. Not entirely. Len Mauger was a friend of Reg's too, remember.'

Elliot's face softened. 'I'm worried about you, Jen.' He reached out and tucked a strand of hair behind her ear. 'This stuff with your dad . . . Wait.' He held out a hand as she started to interrupt. 'I'm not saying it's nothing, or that you're looking for answers that don't exist. I'm not saying that. I'm just asking you to slow down. You don't have to do this now. We've got enough to do. The police are holding a conference tomorrow in which they'll give an update on the investigation and appeal for information. We'll need to be here to cover that.'

'Fine. What else have you got?'

Elliot flipped through his notebook. 'Spoken to a few residents. All said pretty much the same thing. Shocked and appalled, et cetera, et cetera. Your cousin told me they were checking passenger lists on the ferry, so looks like one line of enquiry is that the killer has scarpered. We can follow up on that at the press conference tomorrow. Oh, and one lady mentioned gambling. She was very upset about it. Said there were people here who should know better than playing card games for money. It's the devil's work, apparently.'

'This is a Methodist island. A lot of the older folks are still very devout. Who did she say was gambling?'

'Well, I was asking about Reg. I presume she meant him. Can't see how it's relevant to anything.'

'Could be.'

'You think she slit his throat for breaking the Methodist code?'

'Very funny.'

'OK, some sort of row, then. A feud over a card game? Seems a bit intense.'

'Everything about this place is intense.' She rubbed her eyes. 'I'm sorry. I know I've been shutting you out. And I have been obsessing. I'll stop. Or I'll let you obsess with me.'

'That's more like it. I don't want you doing this alone. But for now, one of us is going to have to get these reports filed.' He leaned over and kissed her.

His lips were warm and dry, and he smelled fresh and clean, like he always did, and she felt so stupid that she hadn't just shared all of this with him from the start.

He sat back and his phone pinged. She caught a glimpse of the screen as he pulled it out of his pocket.

'I'm going to have to go.'

'OK. I'll call you later.'

'Sure.' He squeezed her shoulders as he left. 'Get some sleep, will you? You look exhausted. And for God's sake, be careful. This place gives me the creeps at the best of times.'

She watched him walk away, head bent as he looked at his phone. She didn't know if she was sad or angry, just that she was alone and Jade was texting Elliot about a drink at the Cock and Bull, and Jenny was sure that was why he had to be back in Guernsey in such a hurry, and there was nothing she could do or say about it because it was her fault. She had pushed him away, spending all her time wrapped up in the past, so caught up in other people's stories that she had no energy left to tell her own.

The waitress came over with the bill. 'You don't need to pay it.'

'Hm?'

'Mr Monroe said it's on the house. And will you please go and meet him at the steps to Havre Gosselin when you're done.'

'He was here?'

'About ten minutes ago. He was watching you and your boyfriend. Looked a bit put out, actually. Lucky you.'

'What do you mean?'

'Well, the bloke's a complete wanker, but he's also a billionaire. He leaves me five quid every time he has a drink here. Imagine what you'd get for making him breakfast in the morning.'

Jenny was rendered temporarily speechless.

'You'd better get a move on. He doesn't like to be kept waiting. Not even for coffee,' she added slyly.

Corey Monroe stretched, catlike, when he saw Jenny approaching. He was muscular, she noted, well-honed biceps barely concealed beneath a Fred Perry tennis shirt. There must be a gym somewhere in his mansion on Brecqhou. He rose from the bench overlooking Havre Gosselin, the tiny, rock-bound harbour between Sark and Brecqhou, and stretched out a hand. His mirrored sunglasses were perched on top of his head, reflecting the grey of the sky above. He looked tired, she thought, the skin under his eyes pale and puffy, but the smile was undiminished, confident. Aggressively so.

'So, so pleased we could make this happen.' He took her hand. Dry, firm grip.

'Thank you for suggesting we speak, Mr Monroe. My editor was delighted when I told him you were prepared to do an interview. But I'm really under pressure to finish a report for this afternoon. I was wondering if we could possibly do this another day? There's a lot going on right now, as I'm sure you can imagine.'

'Quite.' His smile loosened at the edges. 'These are terrible circumstances to be meeting under. But there's nothing wrong with making the best of a bad situation. I thought you might like to come across to Brecqhou. Have a look at the place. It won't take long. I'll have you back here in an hour or so.'

'You'd allow me into the house?' Jenny's reasons for asking to delay the interview were genuine—she had no time to work on a profile, no matter how interesting the subject—but a glimpse into the mansion on Brecqhou was not an opportunity to be missed.

'I've never really understood people's fascination with my home. But my longing for privacy has backfired on me. It's difficult to make friends when I'm considered aloof, at best. At worst, well, God knows what they say about me. Or maybe you do.'

She sensed he was showing her his best side. That this willingness to co-operate was fleeting and could quickly be replaced with hostility if she failed to meet his expectations. Which seemed to be that she would do as he wanted.

'Why are you doing this, Mr Monroe? Why talk to the *News* after years of taking such great efforts to stay out of the papers?'

'It's like I said yesterday, Jenny. The situation on Sark has become untenable. It's bad for business. My previous attempts to reach out to the population have proved unsuccessful. I've decided to try something else. And as someone with a considerable stake in the island, I believe what I have to say is relevant to yesterday's tragic events.'

'I can ask whatever I like?'

'You can ask. I don't have to answer.' She had the impression he was amused. 'Shall we get going?' He gestured towards the path. 'There's something I want to show you before we get in the boat.'

She followed him, away from Havre Gosselin, down a grass track to a field. He stopped at a gate. It was made of a bright amber timber. It looked brand new, and too pristine for its position, in the middle of an unruly hedge covered in long grass and brambles. She looked over it, into the field. Most of it was full of neat rows of olive trees, leaves silvery green. But closest to them, the trees were withered and black. She thought at first it must be the result of some disease, but the breeze provided another explanation.

'Petrol?'

'Two weeks ago and you can still smell it. You can imagine how much they must have used.'

'Who did this?'

'I've a fair idea but no proof, so I wouldn't like to say. The Sark Olive Oil Company has the potential to employ up to twenty people. But the Sarkees would rather cut off their own noses than work for me. It's such a shame. The island's dying, Jenny. It was long before I got here. It's cheaper to get to Spain or Greece or the Canary Islands than it is to get here in the summer. It's a thousand times more beautiful here—don't get me wrong—but people want guaranteed sunshine and karaoke and sex on the beach'—he glanced at her—'not rock pools and cliff walks and fog.'

The path down to Havre Goselin was steep. Thick, wiry grass grew either side of it and they were forced to walk one behind the other, Jenny following his steady steps downwards. He was at home here, she thought. Sure-footed, not just physically. He felt that he belonged, even if the locals would do anything to get rid of him. He turned, without warning, back towards her. She stopped just short of him, so close she could see the pores in his skin. He pointed up, to a kestrel, hovering, wings twitching as it battled to stay in position over whatever prey it had spied in the long grass beneath.

'I could watch them for hours,' he said.

They stood, side by side, waiting for the bird to dive, but instead, it shifted slowly sideways, further and further away from them, before swooping out to sea.

'I saw one catch a baby rabbit once,' he said. 'It was amazing watching the kestrel struggle with it. They have a strength way beyond their size. The rabbit must have weighed nearly as much as the bird, but it wouldn't give up. Tore it to pieces.'

He continued down the path. Jenny waited until there was twenty feet between them. She felt uncomfortable standing too close to him. It was his aftershave, she decided. It had a metallic edge to it. Like blood.

Corey guided the RIB onto a jetty built of light stone. No uneven earth or untended grass here, but a wide path of polished granite, tone picked to match the pale jetty behind them. It wound upwards and round, boulders on one side, windswept grassland on the other, until it flattened. Low gateposts marked the beginning of a wall on either side, which increased in height the closer they got to the house now before them.

It was referred to as 'the Mansion' by everyone in Guernsey and Sark, but she could see now that it more closely resembled a French chateau. Built of the same stone as the path, the main building was three storeys high, and as wide as three or four regular houses. A taller, circular tower finished either end. The roof was pink slate, giving the whole place a fairy-tale quality. Jenny wanted to find it crass but had to admit that the effect, with the pale sky above and the sound of the waves crashing around them, was enchanting.

'What's that?' She pointed at a smaller building behind the main house.

'Guest quarters.'

'How many bedrooms does the main house have?'

'Twelve.'

He overtook her. Pointed out another building. 'That's the pub.'

145

'So there is a pub. I thought that was a rumour.'

'I only open it when guests are staying.'

'Where's the helipad?'

'Other side of the island.'

'Who flies the helicopter?'

'I do usually. I've offered it to the islanders for emergency use. Never been taken up on it. It's equipped for search and rescue too. Come on, let's go in.'

They entered the house through huge double doors, stepping into a bright, fresh entrance hall and then through to the 'reading room'. Monroe said it almost reverentially as he opened the door. He led her over to a bay window seat, billowing white curtains tied back to reveal a spectacular view of the Gouliot Passage and over to Sark.

A woman appeared from a side door, tall and slim with the air of an art gallery curator. 'Can I get you anything, Corey?'

'Tea, please, Margot. And whatever Jenny would like.'

She asked for coffee and waited until the woman had left. 'How many staff do you have?'

'A handful. Margot is my Girl Friday. Couldn't do without her.' He gestured for Jenny to sit, and she did so, taking out her notebook and pen.

'Mr Monroe, as time is of the essence, can I ask you now about the current state of affairs between you and the people of Sark? It's safe to say, I think, that relations have reached a crisis point. Can you tell our readers why you think this is the case?'

'Of course. As you'll probably remember, tensions were running high around election time. A lot of the locals took their first ever opportunity to run for government on an anti-Corey Monroe ticket. Which is a little ironic. Considering the only reason Sark has free and fair elections is me.' He paused. 'It was the young people who surprised me. Who'd have thought people your age would be so vehemently opposed to living in a democracy?'

'Can I ask, and I don't mean to sound rude, but why do you care whether Sark has "free and fair elections"? You knew what the island

146

was when you bought Brecqhou. Why get involved in island affairs at all? What's in it for you?'

'Nothing.' He saw her raised eyebrows. 'I find it hard to understand how anyone can defend a system of government that only offers representation to landowners. Where the leader of that government is born, not elected. Where a man can beat his wife so long as the stick is not too wide.'

'OK. That's all well and good, but those idiosyncrasies were part of what made the island special. Gave it that "land that time forgot" atmosphere.'

'It's still a land that time forgot, Jenny,' he said dryly. 'You have to walk everywhere. My helicopter—Jesus, you'd think I was using a fire-breathing dragon to get to and from the island, all the controversy it's caused. And that's fine. I can't change that. Nor do I want to. But I'm proud of the fact that wife-beating is now a crime.'

'But what's in it for you? There are empty storefronts up and down the Avenue. There's been talk of rent hikes.' She left the statement hanging.

He shook his head. 'No. I've poured millions into the Sark economy. Millions. Renovated hotels, used as much local workforce as I could. Tried to stock the kitchens with local produce. Tried to employ local people. It's all smoke and mirrors. They're trying to force me out.'

'Why would anyone do that?'

'It's a good question. One I'm trying to get to the bottom of. I know there was some crazy talk about me trying to turn this place into some sort of theme park.'

'You suggested building a railway round the island.'

He waved his hand dismissively. 'A misstep. And I was never serious, not really, was just floating around ideas, looking at ways to reinvigorate the tourist industry. Believe it or not, I'm not the bad guy here.'

'Who is?'

'It's never that simple, is it? But if I had to pin the problems on a particular person, I'd say the seigneur has done more damage to this island than anyone.'

She was shocked by his candour. 'But he's been broadly supportive of democratisation. At least in the interviews I've read.'

'He's said all the right things in public. In private, and among the islanders, it's been a different story.'

'You think he's behind the vandalism?'

'Not directly, obviously. But I think he encourages it.'

'You have proof?'

He shook his head.

'I can't print unsubstantiated allegations.'

'I'm not asking you to.' He looked out. 'It's murky today. A peasouper—that's what my dad would have called it. I grew up in the East End of London. Did you know that?'

'I did. I read somewhere that your dad knew the Krays. Is that true?'

He laughed. 'A gross exaggeration. The tabloids love to try to tar me with that brush. He was from the same part of town and lived there at the same time, but my dad was a grafter, not a gangster. Helped me buy my first boat. All this is as much to do with his hard work as it is mine.'

'It's a great story.'

'I sometimes think it's part of the problem people have with me.'

'How so?'

'As a rule, much as folks like to grumble about it, they're more comfortable with inherited wealth. It's so much easier to resent. Self-made billionaires make them feel inadequate. I'd rather you didn't quote me on that.' He was still staring out at the Channel.

'You have a great view of the passage over to Sark. Do you see a lot of boats?'

'Not on this side of the island.'

'People aren't allowed to sail past here, are they?'

'As I'm sure you know. Before I successfully argued that having people sail past my house with telescopic lenses was an invasion of privacy, it happened all the time. A boat from the *Jersey Star* ended up stranded just down there.' He pointed to a stack of jagged rocks between the jetty and the coast of Sark. 'Had to rescue them. I made them tea while they waited for the lifeboat.' He turned to her and smiled. 'Killing them with kindness.'

'What about at night?'

'What about it?'

'Have you ever seen anything unusual at night? Boats, flashing lights?'

He hesitated. Just enough for her to notice. 'You must mean the cave tours. That woman, Thursday something. She does a night-time sail a couple of times a week. They don't come here. They're not allowed. And anyway, the passage is too narrow. Too many rocks.'

'I've heard about the tours. You've never seen anything else?'

'Why do you ask?'

'I'm sure it's nothing. Some of the locals said they'd seen boats out after dark. Probably stargazers, like Tuesday Jones.'

She could feel his eyes still on her.

'Probably. Whoever they are, they should be careful. Can you imagine the amount of ships dashed on these rocks, smashed to pieces in the kind of storm that sends sea spray all the way up here?' He paused. 'I love it here. Did when I first visited twenty-five years ago. Still do. I'm hopeful, even after all of this, that Sark can once again be a happy, thriving community.' He stared at her now, and it was as though a shadow had passed over his face.

'Because we've all seen now, haven't we, Jenny, where animosity can lead? It starts with a brick through a window and ends with a dead body.'

The waves smashing against the rocks outside were the only sound in the room.

'You're implying Reg Carré's death is related to the political situation on the island?'

'I hear the man's head was practically severed from his body. Has to be the work of hate and anger. Or fear.'

There was a moment of silence, broken by the clinking of crockery as Margot arrived with the drinks.

'You know, I'm afraid I really don't have much time.' Jenny put her notebook back in her bag, desperate, suddenly, to get away from this strange place and this man whose demeanour had flipped from charming to unsettling in an instant. 'I have to get my report filed for tomorrow's *News*. Thank you. For speaking with me so candidly.'

'Of course. My pleasure. Let's get you back.'

The cloud was so thick she could only just see Havre Gosselin landing, a short jetty and steep steps carved out of a wall of solid rock. Monroe slowed the boat, before butting against the first of the steps. He cut the engine and jumped out, a move that looked to have been perfected over time. He tied up to a mooring ring and held out his hand. She had no choice but to take it: there was nothing else to hold on to. She stood next to him on the jetty.

'What did you mean when you talked about fear?'

'What?'

'You said the person who killed Reg could have done it out of fear. Only it sounded like you were speaking from personal experience.'

'Not particularly. It's human nature. Or is it animal instinct? Fight or flight. You know all about that, surely. I hear you offended a few people while you were working in London. Got some of them running scared. And fear makes people lash out. Look what happened to you.'

She froze.

'I hope we can talk again sometime, Jenny.' He untied the rope and jumped back down into the dinghy, started the engine and deftly manoeuvred out into the channel. He raised his hand in a goodbye salute and sped off into the fog.

Look what happened to you. He could only be referring to the assault. Anyone could find out about it within a couple of minutes on Google. How she'd been abducted, threatened, left in Epping Forest, blindfolded, hands bound behind her back. They wouldn't get the whole story, though. At the time, most of the press had reported it as a botched robbery. There had been some speculation her attackers meant to rape her but were disturbed by a passer-by. Only one or two sources mentioned that she was a journalist, that perhaps the assault was something to do with a story she'd been working on.

It was. But that story had never been published. There was nothing online about the real reason behind her attack. Only Jenny knew that. The police she'd reported it to. And the men who did it.

22

Michael

Malcolm and Sharon Perré owned Ariel's Grotto, the toyshop on Rue Hotton. The Mermaid was only a few hundred yards further down the road. Michael had spent many a night propping up the bar there while on one his two-week 'tours of duty' in Sark. Years ago now. The last one had been the summer after Ellen had died. He'd got so pissed he'd missed the boat coming in the next morning, which was the only real job that the officer on Sark had—checking that there were no troublemakers on board. It was Sod's Law that Peter Norman arrived that day. A well-known alcoholic (the irony) and petty thief, he'd been caught trying to nick a bike half an hour after landing. Michael's absence at the morning ferry was noted, and reported back by the rather zealous constable at the time. He wasn't asked to return the following year, and soon after, they stopped the trips altogether. There was never enough trouble to justify them being there. Until now.

'I used to come here as a kid,' Marquis said, before sneezing violently. He pulled a handkerchief out of his pocket and blew his nose.

'You all right?'

'Think it's just allergies. Hay fever.'

Michael rolled his eyes. He didn't know a single person his age who had an allergy. 'Let's get inside, then, shall we? Away from the hay.'

The ringing of the bell as they crossed the threshold reminded Michael that he had brought Ellen to this shop. She had jumped in and out, making the bell sound until the owner had asked her to stop. Not the same person, he was sure, who stood behind the counter now. A woman in her late fifties, unnaturally dark hair set in a style that even to Michael's untrained eye was at least twenty years out of date—short and choppy, the sides blown backwards to frame her face. A very nice face, he decided, the sort that smiled quickly and as often as possible, well-worn lines at the corners of her eyes, deep dimples in each cheek.

'Can I help you?' Her countenance wavered as she took in Michael and Marquis, side by side. 'Are you looking for anything in particular?'

'Mrs Perré?'

'Yes. You are?'

'DCI Gilbert, DC Marquis. Wanted to ask you a couple of questions about Reg Carré.'

'That poor bastard.' The voice was muffled and came from behind the counter. It was followed by a cough, and then shuffling and creaking. A hand grabbed the back of the countertop, belonging to a dusty-faced man, sharp black eyes shining.

'This is my husband, Malcolm. He was in the basement,' Sharon explained.

Michael peered over to see a trapdoor and the beginnings of a wooden staircase.

Malcolm placed a small box next to the till.

'That's the last one. You need to order some more, sharpish. And it's a shithole down there. Might want to take a duster to it, eh?' He wiped his hand across his face and then on the back of his trousers. 'Filthy it is.'

'Sorry. I'll get down there later.'

'You want to ask about old Reg, then, eh? Thought you might be over.' Malcolm looked at Michael expectantly.

'Yes. We spoke to your son, Benjamin, yesterday.'

Sharon's hand went up to her cheek, then to a stray strand of hair. She looked as though she was about to speak, but Malcolm got in first.

'Likes to talk, does Ben. Have anything interesting to say, did he?'

'Mentioned some rumours, actually. About Reg and his wife. Years ago.'

Malcolm walked out from behind the counter and leaned on the front of it, a hard smile pasted on his face. Behind him, Sharon paled. Michael watched her as Malcolm spoke.

'There were always rumours about Reg, weren't there, Shaz? Liked the old . . .' He mimed a glass being raised to his mouth. 'And the ladies. Liked the ladies, didn't he, Shaz?'

'I don't think that's true, Malcolm.' She played with her hair again, the other side this time. 'He was devoted to Rachel. Things were difficult for them. They lost a baby. Miscarriage. She was devastated. Left Sark for a while. She came back; they had Luke, but I'm not sure she ever fully recovered.'

'Women, eh?' Malcolm rolled his eyes. 'Go soft at the squeak of a baby. It's why this place is such a fucking mess—Ben and his missus just had one. Shaz here can't keep away, can you, love?'

'I've been a bit distracted. First grandchild.' She smiled, but there was no warmth in her expression now, rather a look of desperation. She was frightened. Of her husband or Michael's questions, or something else entirely, Michael couldn't be sure.

'Rachel's disappearance was very sudden, I understand.'

Neither Malcolm nor Sharon responded. Michael pushed.

'There was talk at the time, so I hear, that she might not have left after all.'

'Well, I think we'd all know if she was still here, wouldn't we, Detective? I mean, how ridiculous. You can't spend twenty-five years on Sark with no one knowing about it,' Sharon said.

'Unless she was holed up in a cave.' Malcolm seemed to relish saying the words.

'Malcolm, don't be stupid! It's absolutely irresponsible to talk like that now, with everything going on.' She looked at Michael pleadingly. 'At the time, there was some gossip. But it was only ever that. I helped Reg out from time to time after Rachel left.'

An intake of breath from Malcolm. The first genuine reaction from him, Michael thought. The man had something of the pantomime villain about him, a part he seemed to enjoy playing.

'Luke and Ben were friends, and Reg struggled, a single dad, twenty-odd years ago—it was hard for him,' Sharon continued. 'He was really a lovely man. Nobody knew what he dealt with, with Rachel. She had problems, you know?' She tapped the side of her head. 'Honestly, I think she did the best she could for that boy leaving when she did.'

'What my wife seems to be saying, Detective, is that even if he did get rid of her, she deserved it. That right, Shaz?' He turned to his wife, a sly look on his face.

'Don't do this, Malcolm. Not now.'

'Don't mind her.' Malcolm looked entirely relaxed. 'Been post-menopausal for the last ten years, haven't you, love? Plays havoc with her emotions.'

For the first time in many years, unprompted by any physical threat, Michael felt a twitch in his right hand. His fingers curled, as if they had a mind of their own, into a fist.

'So you think Mr Carré could have murdered his wife. Is that what you're saying, Mr Perré?' Marquis took a couple of steps forward, drawing level with Michael on his right side.

'Could have done. Course he could. Wouldn't blame him if he had. 'S'like my wife said. She was a fucking nightmare. Mooning around all the time. Always miserable. They had some blazing rows, you know. She had a vicious way about her, I always thought. Bet she was a right goer in the sack, but you always pay for that, I find, in other ways.' He laughed as though recalling fond memories but stopped abruptly as his wife slammed the trapdoor shut.

'Shut up, Malcolm.'

'All right, all right!' Malcolm held up his hands.

'I'm late for an appointment, Officer. Do you need anything else?' Her voice was strained.

'Not for now, Mrs Perré. Thank you.'

She picked up a large handbag and slung it over her shoulder before she left.

Malcolm whistled. 'Don't know what's got into her. She thought Rachel was a mad bitch as much as I did.'

'Care to elaborate, Mr Perré?'

'How so?'

'Well, was there any particular behaviour Mrs Carré displayed that would lead you to form that conclusion?'

'No. Nothing in particular. She was just that type of woman. I mean, look at her.' He pointed in the direction his wife had just gone. 'They're all the bloody same.'

Michael knocked over a basket of soft toys on the way out, so anxious was he to escape the presence of Malcolm Perré.

'Can we arrest someone for being an arsehole?' Marquis muttered as he righted the basket and replaced a pink-and-silver unicorn.

'Sadly not.'

'It's been a bit of a day.'

'Bloody hell, Stephen. You going for the Nobel Prize for Understatement? It's been a bastard of a day. And it's not over yet.'

They'd gone only a few steps before the sound of footsteps behind them stopped them in their tracks.

'Officers!' Sharon Perré was hurrying after them.

'You all right, love?'

She seemed taken aback by Michael's concerned manner. 'You mean because of Mal?' She waved a hand, dismissing him. 'Please. Takes more than him on one of his little rants to upset me these days.' She paused. 'He's really not that bad. His nose gets out of joint when, well, when anything upsets the status quo, I suppose.'

'Like Reg Carré getting killed?'

'Well, yes, of course that upset him. It's upset all of us. But what I meant was more . . . Well, it's difficult to explain.'

'Try your best.'

'It was when I helped Reg out after Rachel left. It was very sudden, you see. One day she was here, the next she'd packed her bag and left, leaving that poor boy. It broke my heart. I had to do something. So I started taking meals over a couple of times a week. I was cooking for us anyway, so it was no hassle. Only Malcolm didn't see it like that. Said I was spending too much time over there. He and Reg fought about it, actually.' She blushed deep red. 'It was awful. It was right here, in the street.'

'Can you tell us about it?'

'They'd both had too much to drink—Mal was right about that: Reg did drink too much, but because he was depressed, I think. People didn't get help for things–mental health stuff, you know—not like they do now. Anyway, Malcolm was accusing Reg of all sorts. I don't think he really believed any of it, and Reg denied it all, of course. But Malcolm wouldn't let it go. Said he wouldn't be surprised if Rachel's body washed up sometime soon, and even if Reg didn't want to . . . to fuck me, maybe he wanted to kill me.' She stopped. Her cheeks were scarlet. 'That was when Reg hit Malcolm. There was a crowd of people around them by this point. They fought. Reg broke Malcolm's nose. Eventually, someone pulled them apart. The rumours about Reg have flown around ever since.'

'And you stopped helping Reg out after this fight?'

A defiant look crossed her face. 'No. I did not. Why should I? I was still taking him meals up until last week.'

'And Malcolm knew about this?'

'I assume so. We never discussed it. We didn't discuss much after that fight. It took us a long time to get over it.'

'Mrs Perré, I have to ask, were you involved with Reg, romantically?'

'No.' She sounded emphatic but her eyes told another story.

'Do you think Reg Carré murdered his wife, Mrs Perré? Do you think it was her in that cave?'

She shook her head. 'He was a good man.'

'That doesn't answer my question.'

'No. I don't think he did. I wouldn't have helped him, I wouldn't have . . . spent time with him if I'd thought he was a killer.' She hesitated. 'I'm sorry. I'm wasting your time. I'd best go.'

'Your appointment.'

'I don't have an appointment. Not really. I'm going to help out Ben. The baby's a bit colicky, and Ben's wife's not coping so well.' She seemed angry all of a sudden. 'None of you men understand what it's like. It's so hard. You have a baby and you think you're gaining something, but you lose something too. A little piece of the you that you were before. It vanishes. Every mother I know has struggled. I did. And I'm sure Rachel did. I don't want you to think that what I said about her was unkind. She wasn't crazy. She was suffering. Thank God there's help for people nowadays.' She walked off in the direction of the village.

Marquis waited until she was out of earshot. 'Crikey. That was a bit intense.'

'She obviously puts up with a lot.'

'You think they were Rachel Carré's bones in that cave, sir?'

'Maybe.'

'And once they were found, perhaps it confirmed someone's suspicions after all these years that Reg murdered his wife. Someone like Malcolm Perré.'

'Let's not get ahead of ourselves, Marquis. Rachel Carré was never reported missing, was she? So nobody ever looked for her. Let's do that first—see if we can't eliminate her from our enquiries that way. Maybe she's happy as Larry somewhere, just never wanted to be found. Let's get a DNA sample from Luke Carré too. Cover both angles.'

'If the body in the cave is Rachel Carré, Luke would be the prime suspect, not Malcolm.'

'Talk me through the theory.' Always helped to have Marquis think out loud, especially when he was on the right track.

'Well, he must be aware of the rumours. The bones in the cave confirmed them to be true. He loved his mother, so he killed his father. Would all be a bit Shakespearean, wouldn't it?'

'You mean Freudian.'

Marquis looked confused.

'It was Freud who talked about sons wanting to kill their fathers and you know . . . with their mothers.'

'That's right. Othello.'

'Oedipus. It's a good theory. But Luke couldn't have got here quickly enough. Not if his alibi is telling the truth, at any rate. You all right?'

Marquis looked peaky as hell. 'I feel a bit faint, actually, boss.'

'Heat's getting to you, Marquis. Getting to me too as it happens. I think we'd better get a cold drink. Before we both pass out.'

23

Rachel

1986

He threw the money on the counter, sat in his chair, took off his boots. 'Where's Luke?'

'At Ben's house.' She picked up the money. 'You must be the world's best euchre player. Winning hands every month.'

He looked at her. 'You got something you want to say?' He was like this more and more these days. Ever since the letter. It was like all the warmth had drained out of him. Except when he was with Luke.

'I just want to know where you're getting it.'

'Why? What difference does it make?'

'Are you doing something illegal?'

He laughed softly. 'Rachel, please.'

'It's something to do with Len, isn't it? He's always flush. And Malcolm too, for that matter—he's always flashing his cash. I don't trust him, Reg. If it's anything to do with Malcolm, you should stop.'

He stood. Approached the counter. He had an odd look on his face. Angry. Frightening. She took a step back.

'Then what, Rachel? I stop doing what I'm doing, where are we going to find this kind of money?'

'I don't know. I'm sorry. I shouldn't have asked.'

'You're right. You shouldn't have. We're doing so well as we are. It would be a shame to spoil things.'

'What do you mean?'

'I mean it's better for everyone if we all just keep pretending.'

A knock at the door. He went to open it. She let out the breath that had caught in her chest.

'All right, buddy?' Just like that Reg was back to his old self. Luke came running in, followed by Sharon, holding his schoolbag and a piece of cardboard covered in lentils and macaroni.

'They've had a great time.' She smiled. Sharon was always smiling, despite being married to Malcolm.

'Thanks for having him, Sharon. What do you say, Luke?'

'Thank you, Mrs Perré.'

'You're welcome, darling. Bye, then.'

Rachel might have imagined it, but there was a look between Sharon and Reg, just before Sharon left. Of what she didn't know. Solidarity? Companionship? Complicity? *She knew.* He'd told her. But of course he wouldn't have done. How ridiculous. She wanted to laugh. And then all at once she wanted to cry.

Luke had snuggled up to Reg already; they were looking at his reading book, about Billy and his blue hat. Luke had been slow to start reading. Just like his dad, Reg had said. Nothing to worry about. He'd get there, in his own time. He was a smart boy.

'He needs a bath.' She walked over.

'I'll do it when we're finished with this.'

'It's getting late.'

He didn't look up from the book. 'You tired, Lukey?'

'No, Daddy.'

'Well, then. Like I said. Bath time when we're finished, eh?' His arm wound a little tighter around Luke's shoulder. His head bent a little lower, so his hair, coarse and dark, fell over Luke's, which was soft and shiny and honeyed brown.

Her heart shifted upwards, towards her throat.

He was using his love for the boy like a weapon.

He was showing her the power he had.

24

Jenny

The cobweb shone in the lamplight, the desiccated husk of a spider casting its spindly shadow on the wallpaper. The room wasn't dirty—the linen smelled fresh, and the toilet and sink in the tiny en suite sparkled—but clearly the elderly lady who ran the bed and breakfast Jenny had checked into an hour ago hadn't thought to dust the corners in a while. Or perhaps she'd thought it unnecessary, not anticipating that her guests would lie on the bed staring up at the ceiling, too tired to move, too anxious to approach anything close to sleep.

Jenny was familiar with anxiety. She tried to fight back the feeling that she was under threat. *Deep breaths. Think clearly. Be rational.* If it got worse, she would up the exercise. She'd missed her swim today: there'd been no time. She needed it to get the endorphins flowing, wash out the negative thoughts with serotonin. She'd seen a therapist, initially railing against the self-indulgence of it but realising after each session that she did indeed feel better, that talking was, if not a cure, a road to recovery. There had been pills. Each one washed down with an overwhelming feeling of failure, the argument that mental illness was no more under her control than a headache or a chest infection never quite convincing, her determination to 'beat it' without medication next time ever stronger.

It was this very determination that clouded her judgement. Because now her first reaction to the twist in her gut, the rise in her pulse was to ignore it. To crush it. To override the body's warning system.

Relax. Everything is fine. There is no danger.

Only sometimes there was. Sometimes the source of the anxiety was not imagined but all too real. A sick man and a threatening note. Dog shit smeared on walls. The whisper of violence beneath the rumble of an outboard motor, old bones and slit throats.

She rose from the bed, fully dressed, took the heavy front-door key from the bedside table and left the room, slamming the door behind her.

The dead spider, which was hanging by the finest of threads, shuddered.

'You going out, love?' Rosie, the owner of the guesthouse, shuffled out of the kitchen at the back of the house. She wore a baggy sweatshirt and deep red velvet tracksuit bottoms, her silver hair wrapped in a high beehive.

'Yes. I'm going to get some fresh air.'

'You should have a bite to eat while you're out. I can do you a sandwich later, an egg maybe, but I'm not cooking—not for one. Sorry, love.'

'No problem.'

'Was due to have a family of five in today, but they've cancelled.' She shook her head. 'It was bad enough before. July is my busiest month. I wonder if we'll ever recover.'

'I'm sure once the police have caught whoever did this, things will settle down.'

'You think?' Her eyes were sharp and an unsettling shade of violet. 'People round here have long memories. Especially the dead. They never let anything rest. Mark my words. It will be a long time before any of this is forgotten.'

Dusk was falling and the light on Jenny's rental bike was dim and flickering, doing little to illuminate the bumps and rocks on the narrow path. She had no plan, wanting only company, some other voice to interrupt the one in her head, to tell her that everything was going to be OK, to chase away the ghosts of which Rosie had spoken.

There was a gust of wind from the south, warm but fierce. It whipped at her hair and her bare arms. The hedgerows were black against an inky sky, long, dry tendrils of grass grazing her exposed legs as she swerved to avoid a pothole, coming to a stop at the gated entrance to a field. The sting of a nettle at her ankle made her swear out loud. There was no one to hear her. Only the cows, huddled by the steel bars of the gate, noses wet. They shied away from her, the whole group taking a step backwards, knees buckling, small eyes widening in fear. She saw the glimmer of the electric fence, the narrow red wire pulled taut between slim plastic posts, heard its gentle, menacing hum. She wondered how many shocks a cow would take, how many times it would brush against the wire before it recognised danger. Before it learned to stay away.

She pedalled harder, the thought of the encroaching darkness spurring her on towards the Avenue. She slowed when she saw the street lamp on the corner, the only one on Sark, and thought about where to go. There was nowhere on the Avenue, Jenny realised, as she pushed her bike past the shops and cafés, 'closed' signs hanging over darkened doors, blinds pulled down, shutters shut. Ahead, there was one illuminated window.

It was Tuesday Jones's shop. Posters on the wall advertised the times of her boat tours. Inside, Tuesday was sitting with her head bent over paperwork, her hair falling over her face. Jenny thought about going in, tried to think of an excuse, a question to ask her, when out of nowhere, Len Mauger's words rang in her ears: *She came over and changed it all. It's not the Sark way.* A woman. Not a Sarkee.

Tuesday looked up. Met Jenny's eyes. Smiled.

'They do a nice fish and chips at the bar. I wasn't planning to cook tonight anyway.' Tuesday blew cigarette smoke over her shoulder, away from Jenny, but the wind carried it back into her face and for the first time in years Jenny thought about smoking. She'd never really taken to it as a teenager but had had the odd one to calm her nerves before exams as a student. She still associated the smell with a forced state of relaxation, something she could do with right now.

Tuesday had seemed happy to see her, suggested a drink, professing how nice it would be to talk to someone different, perhaps picking up on Jenny's loneliness. Perhaps wanting to find out what she knew. Len's words still echoed. How many non-local women were there living on Sark? More than a handful. But with a boat? Tuesday knew the island waters—she'd said so herself. She knew the caves. And with her Dark Sky Island tours, she knew the night.

Heads turned as they walked into the tiny bar at the Mermaid, and the numbing tiredness Jenny had felt only an hour earlier was forgotten. She spotted Malcolm Carré, in the same stool he'd sat in only yesterday. This time a woman stood next to him, similar age to Malcolm, short dark hair, tired-looking, presumably his wife. Jenny had the impression that she'd either just arrived or was just leaving—she wore a jacket and had her handbag on her shoulder. She looked worried, for a second, as she looked at Jenny, then immediately relaxed, as though she'd been expecting someone else and was relieved not to see them. A young couple Jenny didn't recognise occupied a corner table. They openly stared. Probably standard, Jenny thought, when a stranger walked into a local bar hours after the last ferry had left for Guernsey. On the table closest to them, right opposite her was a familiar face.

Luke Carré put down his book and gestured to the empty seats at the table.

'You make friends quick, don't you?' Tuesday said. 'I'll get the drinks in.'

Jenny thanked her and took the chair next to Luke. not knowing what to make of the feeling she'd had when she'd first glimpsed him. She had wished, for more than a moment, that she had come to the pub alone.

'How are you feeling?'

'Lonely. Drowning in sympathy.'

'It's frustrating.' It had been the same after Charlie died. People insisted on telling her how sorry they were, offering help—like there was anything they could do. It wasn't their fault. Margaret seemed to appreciate it. Jenny just wanted to change the subject, to keep her grief to herself.

Her phone buzzed in her bag. Twelve messages, a whole day's worth.

'Only place on the island with decent phone reception *and* free Wi-Fi,' Luke said. 'Everyone buzzes as they walk through the door.'

She scrolled through the messages. Her mum. Work. Graham wanted some more interviews with locals. She knew the sort of thing he was after. Pictures of people, wide-eyed and frightened, declaring themselves in fear for their lives. She wondered why she stuck with the *Guernsey News*. She could blame it on the lack of options—her only other choice on the island would be a corporate publication, writing for the La Manche in-flight magazine or one of the upmarket estate agents' glossy monthlies, interviewing tax exiles in their three-million-pound post-modern glass-box houses on the cliffs. But it wasn't that. She could hardly argue that what she was doing was any better, not usually. Reporting on vandalised hedge veg boxes, interviewing States' deputies about planned changes to the education system. None of it was exciting. But every now and then, even on Guernsey, there was a story. And the *Guernsey News*, for all its small-town flaws, was the only place to tell one.

The last text was from Elliot: *Can't stop thinking about you. I should have stayed. Or not? Never know what you want! Let me know you're OK. E*

It was just past eight. According to the message she'd seen on his phone, the time he was seeing Jade for a drink. Perhaps he hadn't gone. Perhaps it was a work-related meeting. Perhaps he was about to take her back to his place. Just like he had taken Jenny. She threw her phone back into her bag. This was why she stopped herself caring too much. The self-doubt. The complications. The constant feeling that she was fucking things up. She needed a drink. Tuesday was still at the bar, deep in conversation with the barman.

'Bad news?' Luke looked concerned.

'Just work.'

'You must be busy. Any updates from the police? I hear you're friendly with DCI Gilbert.'

'It's a professional relationship,' she snapped.

He furrowed his brow. 'Obviously.' He smiled for the first time. 'Although you seem a bit touchy about it.'

'I'm sorry. Long day. Have you managed to get into your dad's place?'

'No. It's still a crime scene. I spent a couple of hours on the common. Used to play there as a kid. It was practically my back garden. One of my good memories. Lying in the sunshine, escaping my parents' rows for an hour or so.' He took a swig of his pint. 'It's funny. Sad, really. Back then, I never thought I'd miss them, you know? Thought if they'd both just disappear, my life would be brilliant. I'd be fine in the cottage by myself. And if anything went wrong, I could go and see Mrs Perré. She always looked out for me. Even before Mum really did disappear. God, I felt guilty after Mum left. Felt like I'd wished her away. I remember crying into my pillow a couple of weeks after she'd gone, convinced it was my fault.'

'Ah, you've always been a wimp, Luke Carré.' The sneering, slurred tones of Malcolm Perré, who had got down from his stool and was lounging against the bar, a short, heavy glass of what looked like whisky in his hand.

'Stop it, Malcolm.' The woman next to him looked mortified. 'I'm so sorry, Luke. We've had a stressful day; he's had too much to drink.'

'No problem, Mrs Perré.' Luke lifted his pint towards Malcolm. 'You're right, Mr Perré. And I was always grateful to your lovely wife for looking out for me.'

''S'actly right. Should be fucking grateful. Caused us enough fucking problems, didn't you?'

'Malcolm, stop!' Sharon's voice cut across the chatter in the bar, which had already fallen to a hum and was now completely silenced.

'Oooh, the missus is upset. I'm in for a right fucking ear-bashing when I get home.' He drained his glass and attempted to slam it back on the bar. He missed and it fell to the floor, shattering into pieces. He barely missed a beat. 'Sorry, Tom.' He waved to the barman. 'Sorry, mate. Missed the bar.' He looked genuinely aggrieved that he'd broken the glass, but when he turned to Luke, there was nothing close to regret on his face.

'And I'm sorry, Luke. Course none of this is your fault. Didn't ask to be born, now did you?'

Tears fell silently down Sharon Perré's cheeks.

'And really, if I was going to blame anyone, it should be your old man, eh? If he hadn't bumped off your mum, my Sharon wouldn't have had to look after you, would she? Wouldn't have had to look after your old man neither, would she? Fucking slag that she is.'

A fist came flying. A splatter of blood hit the table. Jenny cried out. Luke reached across and pulled her chair back, towards him and away from Malcolm Perré as the man crashed to the floor, moaning, hands held to a heavily bleeding nose.

Broken glass crunched beneath Tuesday Jones's feet as she stepped back to survey her handiwork.

'Sorry, darling'—Tuesday turned to Sharon, who stood shell-shocked—'but your husband is a first-class cunt.'

'Are you going to write about me in the paper, then?' Tuesday finished her third rum and Coke, and slammed the glass on the table.

'What would the headline be?' Jenny was halfway through her second pint of cider and could see Tom at the bar lining up another round. She'd tried to drink slowly, had intended to guide the conversation to Reg Carré's murder, to gauge Tuesday's reaction, perhaps even to mention Len Mauger, but it had been difficult, the talk dominated by Malcolm's outburst and Tuesday's reaction to it.

'How about "Mad Cow Hits Mad Bastard in Sark Pub"? Has a nice ring to it, don't you think? Joke! Don't hit me!' Luke had had too much to drink and half laughed, half sobbed as he slumped back in his chair.

'We've all listened to years of Malcolm's shit,' Tuesday said. 'He moans about everything and everyone. We just roll our eyes and ignore him, fine. But'—she pointed at Luke—'I'm not having talk like that about his wife. That's out of order. Sharon's a good woman. God knows how she puts up with him. And I'm betting that's not the worst of it either. It's time someone put that man in his place.'

'What do you mean?' Jenny asked.

'Man talks about his wife like that in front of other people? What do you think he's like behind closed doors?'

'Oh, I've seen him behind closed doors.' The trace of a smile still lingered on Luke's lips but faded as he cast his mind back. 'He came over once. Couple of years after Mum left. It wasn't pretty, believe me. Mouthing off. Think that's the worst of it, though. He's all talk.'

'All the nasty things he says to his wife—you think mouthing off is as far as it goes? I wouldn't be so sure.' Jenny sensed a malevolence in Malcolm Perré that went beyond words.

'Nor would I,' Tuesday added. 'You don't know the man, not anymore. How many years since you lived here?'

'Coming on twenty. But I do know Malcolm. I know this island. It never leaves you, doesn't matter how long you're away. If you're a local, of course. Born and raised. Different for an interloper like you.' He flashed another smile, but Tuesday was tense, eyes narrowed. For a moment, Jenny thought she was about to lash out again. The atmosphere was broken with the arrival of Tom, another tray of drinks balanced on one hand.

'Right, that's your lot. Drink up. Your help with the cleaning up was much appreciated, but the last thing I need is the police busting me for a lock-in.'

'Shit. Is that the time?' Past midnight. Jenny looked out onto the courtyard. Pitch-black. The thought of the dark, silent roads back to the guesthouse made her shudder.

'You all right?' Tuesday asked.

'Yes. I need to get back. I've still got work to do.'

'You're staying at Rosie's guesthouse?'

'Yes.'

'I'll come with you.'

'But that's silly. You live across the street.'

'Tell you what's silly—you riding around by yourself while there's a killer on the loose.'

'But then you'll have to get back to your place alone.'

'I think we all agree I can handle myself. Like Lukey here says—I'm a mad cow.' She downed her drink and picked up her bag. 'I'm going to have a quick cigarette. I'll see you outside.' She bade good night to Tom and strode out of the door.

'I offended her.' Luke shifted in his chair. 'Shit. I've had too much to drink. This place. I don't know why I came here. It's just making everything worse.' He put his head in his hands. 'Should have come more when he was alive. Waste of fucking time being here now. Calling myself a local. What a dick. Will you apologise for me?'

'To Tuesday?'

He nodded. '*I* should have punched him. Should have stood up for Sharon. Everything she did for me.'

She recognised his grief and the guilt he felt for leaving home, for never returning, for not being there for Reg, and she knew it was a weight he would carry for a long time, perhaps for ever. She reached across the table. Placed her hand over his.

'It gets easier.'

'Does it ever go away?'

She shook her head.

'Everybody out!' Tom switched off the main lights. The glow from the exit signs bathed them all in a dim, sickly green. Luke took her hand in his. Gave it a gentle squeeze.

'Time to go.' His expression was unreadable. He got up, pushed past her chair and left without another word.

They'd started walking, Jenny holding her torch, Tuesday smoking another cigarette, when Jenny remembered.

'Shit. I've left the bike.'

'No worries. Go back and get it. I'll wait here.' Tuesday settled back against the wall of Ariel's Grotto.

It was only fifty or so feet back to the Mermaid. She had left the bike in a rack at the rear of the pub. She entered the courtyard. Darker here. She shone her torch around quickly. Unnecessarily. She'd left only minutes ago.

Hers was the only bike there. The tyre was jammed into the stand and she had to rock it back and forth to work it loose. It popped out, suddenly, and she stumbled backwards, dropping her torch, which skittered over the paving stones and into a ditch, the border between the pub and the fields behind it.

She was in almost complete darkness. She resisted the urge to shout for help, to curl up in a ball, wrap her arms around her, to protect herself from the night. Instead, she took a deep breath, propped the bike against the wall, took tentative steps towards the faint glow of torchlight. The ditch was deep and wide, and the only way to reach the torch was to get in. She sank into leaves up to her knees. They were cool and damp round her ankles, brittle and dry on top. She waded over to retrieve the torch. It sank further into the leaves and the light dimmed until the blackness was almost unbearable. She could feel the scream growing in her chest, rising, her mouth open, ready to unleash it, when she felt the handle, grabbed the torch and shone it back and forth, side to side.

A noise from the field.

She stopped. Listened. Nothing. The gentle swishing of the grass in the meadow. The rustling of leaves at her feet. She'd imagined it. She turned to climb out of the ditch. Heard it again.

A low rumble. Not mechanical. Animal.

And then something else.

Closer, closer, until she could clearly hear the padding of feet over the thudding of her heart.

A deep, sustained growl.

It was a dog. But the sound was longer and lower than she'd ever heard before. It echoed around her, filling the air and her ears, making her skin tingle, the hairs on her arms stand straight. When it stopped, the silence was heavier than it had been before and loaded with menace.

Calm down. Her earlier panic at being alone in the dark had left her feeling vulnerable. Exposed. It was just a dog. Dogs acted on instinct. She had come too close to its territory; it wanted her to go, that was all. She was going. It had no reason to harm her.

No sudden movements. She turned, a slow pivot, trying to make as little noise as possible, and pulled herself out of the ditch, muscles tensed, elbows straining, legs trembling.

Slowly. Softly. A few steps back to the pub. She eased the bike away from the wall and waited until she was astride it before shining the torch back in the direction of the field.

It was empty. But that made no sense. She could still hear it breathing, each exhalation slow and heavy with moisture. It sounded so close she fancied she could feel it, warm and damp against her bare skin, the nape of her neck, the tops of her arms, round her ankles. It chilled her to the bone. That ever-present fist of disquiet that nestled within, already shaken by the day's events, opened, stretched its cold fingers upwards, grasped her round the throat, forcing out a strangled cry. With her feet on the ground, Jenny half ran, half rode the bike round the picnic tables and towards the front of the pub.

Behind her, the splashing of dry leaves. A thud, so heavy it felt like the ground vibrated beneath her. The scraping of claws on concrete.

She cycled as fast as she could, nearly coming off the bike as she came through the archway onto the loose earth of the path at too sharp an angle, righting herself just in time, screeching to a stop outside Ariel's Grotto. Tuesday was sitting astride a mountain bike that looked far too big for her, smoking another cigarette.

'Come on!'

'What's the matter?'

'Dog.'

'Where?' Tuesday peered into the darkness. 'I can't see nothing.'

'It was chasing me.' Jenny's hand shook as she held out the torch. The road was empty. 'I heard it.'

'What sort of dog?'

'Didn't see. Sounded big. Let's go.' She cycled ahead, imaging the feeling of those claws against her bare legs. Those teeth against her throat. She cycled faster, heard the creak of Tuesday's bike behind. Only when she reached the end of the Avenue did she slow down and check behind her. Nothing. Tuesday caught up. She had somehow managed to smoke and ride.

'Told you. There's nothing there.' She flicked her cigarette butt into the undergrowth.

There was nothing there. Not now.

They set off again, Jenny's heart still thumping, her stomach still cold, the familiar aftermath of an adrenaline rush. She felt exhausted. Like she'd been on the island for weeks. And she'd got nowhere. Achieved nothing. Her dad. The bones. Reg Carré. Len Mauger. The boats. Her brain was in overdrive, churning the facts and the fictions, imagining connections that didn't exist and creatures in the shadows. Get a grip, Jenny. Get a fucking grip.

They had left the village. The combined light from both bikes was just enough to keep them on the path. The cloud cover was still thick, the moon a milky blur. No stars. Tuesday wobbled alongside, barely able to steady herself, her feet several inches above the ground.

'Is that bike yours?'

Tuesday shook her head. 'Borrowed it.'

'Who from?'

'Whoever left it outside the pub.'

'You stole it?'

'Keep your hair on! I'll put it back. You're a right goody two-shoes, aren't you?'

'What? No. I'm not, actually. What makes you say that?'

'You remind me of a school prefect or something. Not that we had them at my school. You're what I imagine a school prefect would be like, though.'

'I was a prefect, actually.'

'Ha!' Tuesday cackled. 'Knew it.'

'But I've never stuck to the rules. Not when they needed breaking.'

'Is that right? Nosing around and selective rule-breaking—you should've been a copper.'

The track narrowed and steepened. Tuesday pulled ahead and Jenny followed, both of them silent as they put all of their effort into climbing the hill before freewheeling down the other side. Tuesday screeched to a stop outside Rosie's.

'Hope you've got a key? Old Rosie will have been in bed for hours.'

'Yes. I have, thank you. Thanks for coming back with me.' She paused. 'It's funny you saying I should have joined the police.'

'Is it?'

'I do like to investigate. Always have. I wanted to ask you about something, actually.'

'Oh yeah?' A hint of defensiveness.

'I've heard rumours about boats out at night. Lights flashing. Around Brecqhou.'

'I knew it. You listen to me—you can tell Corey Monroe I haven't taken my tours anywhere near his precious island, as well he knows.' Her face was in shadow, but her voice was clear as a bell.

She did not, Jenny thought, sound like a woman with something to hide. If anything, she'd shown a tendency to overshare. Both her feelings and her fists.

'I didn't hear it from Monroe.'

'Yeah, well, even so. Been chatting to him, haven't you?' She sounded calmer now. 'You need to watch that. People round here won't speak to you about anything if they think you've been cosying up to him.'

'I really haven't. Mr Monroe wanted to do an interview. I was with him for an hour, if that. He has a right to tell his side of the story.'

'If you say so.'

'So you don't know anything? Haven't seen any boats out while you've been doing your Dark Sky tours?'

'I never said that. Said I haven't taken my tours that way.' She started to wobble back down the hill.

'So what do you know about it?'

Tuesday came to a stop, brakes complaining with a high-pitched whine, tyres skidding on the loose surface. She twisted round on the seat, squinting in the glare from Jenny's torch. Jenny dropped it to her side and Tuesday's voice rang through the darkness.

'Is there nothing that will distract you from this, Jenny? I've just escorted you home. Protected you from the big, bad bogeyman. What more do you want? Blood?'

'No, I—' Jenny began.

'Because that's what it will cost us. It's too late, Jenny. We've tried. But they're all in too deep.'

'Who are?'

She didn't answer. 'I like you, Jenny. Do yourself a favour. Get the hell out of here. Have the *News* send over someone who's less likely to get us all killed.'

25

Rachel

1989

She read the letter again. It was the fourth one. But this one was different. She stared at the words, willing them to change. They were terrifying, black ink on white paper, etched on her brain. Indelible.

She heard his shuffling footsteps outside. Stuffed the letter down her top. Pressed her shaking hands to her hot cheeks. She would deal with it later. Somehow.

She could tell by the way he opened the door he was drunk. The fumbling of the latch, then pushing it too hard, so it shuddered and banged against the wall. He stood in the door frame, swaying.

'It's not even three o'clock.' She turned away from him, furiously washed clean dishes.

He shrugged. 'So?' He stumbled over. Tried to put his arms round her. He only ever did that when he was drunk.

'Luke will be home from school any minute.' She shook him off without looking at him. He smelled of whisky. Sometimes when he'd been drinking, he lost his temper and broke things. Plates, cups. Once, he'd put his fist through the door.

'Luke here, Luke not here. It's all the same to you.'

'He shouldn't see you like this. Why don't you go and lie down?'

176

'Look at me.'

She carried on scrubbing and scrubbing, catching her knuckles on the scouring pad.

'Shit.' The soapy water stung her raw skin.

'Rachel,' he said softly. He knew, of course, that it wasn't her name. She'd told him that very first week that she'd pulled it out of thin air, that she'd wanted to be someone else on Sark. He'd thought it was funny. 'You'll be Rachel, then, as long as you're here,' he'd laughed. And ten years later, she still was.

She stopped washing. Pressed her hands on her skirt to dry them. She turned to him.

'What's the matter with you?' he asked, not unkindly. It was infuriating, the way he knew her so well. She filled a glass of water from the tap. Drank. It soothed her throat, which was hot and scratchy with the effort of trying to subdue a scream. She took out the letter. Pushed it towards him.

He didn't pick it up. 'More money?'

She shook her head.

'Then what?' He picked up the letter.

'Please, Reg.'

As he read, the colour rose through his neck, then pooled, an angry circle of red on each cheek.

'We'll fix it,' she whispered, could barely hold back the tears, because she knew they couldn't. He knew it too.

He slammed his fist onto the counter.

'Reg, please. Luke will be home any minute.' She glanced at the clock. Past three already. Any minute now he'd come running through the door, chattering about his day, wanting a hug, a snack.

Reg shouted. No words, just rage and misery. It washed over her, freeing her tears, which spilled, unhindered, down her cheeks.

'Please. We can work this out.' But it was no good. She'd lost him. He swept his arm across the counter, sending dishes flying to the floor, glasses smashing, a saucepan clanging, the sound ringing in her ears. She ran from the kitchen. There was nowhere to hide in this tiny house.

'Enough!' he shouted, spittle flying. 'Enough.' Calmer. Just a little. He crouched on the floor. Put his hands over his head. 'Enough.' He shook.

'Reg?'

He remained crouched, shaking, silent.

'Reg?' She reached out. Touched his shoulder.

He looked up. His face was twisted with anger and grief and something else. Hate. She could see it now. He hated her. He stood, took a step towards her. She was frightened. There was nowhere to run. She closed her eyes. So many times she'd sat in church, repeated the meaningless words her father spoke from the pulpit, muttered the Lord's Prayer, the Collect, Communion, never thinking about what she was saying. But now she did. Now she searched her soul, gathered the lies, the deceit and the dishonesty, and sent it all to God. Prayed for His forgiveness.

26

Michael

One more blast of the horn and Michael was going to pull Fallaize out of the car by the scruff of his neck and give him what for.

'It's the crack of dawn. You're going to wake all the neighbours. You saw me wave at you from the front door,' Michael hissed when he reached the end of his driveway.

He clambered awkwardly into the passenger seat and tried to fit his feet and his overnight bag in the footwell. Fallaize drove a bright orange Lotus Elise, which was quite possibly the most ridiculous car a person could own on Guernsey. In fact, on the stupid-car scale, Michael would even put it ahead of those bloody great SUVs that some of the mums drove on the school run. They were far too big for the roads but at least had space and comfort going for them. The Elise had neither. Just a top speed of over a hundred and fifty miles an hour, as Fallaize had told everyone who would listen when he'd first bought it. Which was really impressive. And completely irrelevant on an island with a top speed *limit* of thirty-five miles per hour, and that was only on the coast road.

'Sorry, sir.' Fallaize didn't sound sorry at all but turned off the music. 'Didn't want us to be late.' He revved the engine like he was on the starting line at Silverstone, reaching a speed of ten miles an hour before coming to a halt at the yellow line at the end of Michael's road.

'How can we be late? It's not bloody going without us, is it?' Michael shifted in the seat, trying to position his legs in such a way that he didn't have to fold them into his lap.

'S'pose not. How long do you think we'll have to stay over, then?'

'End of the week at least. Maybe longer. Depends when we catch the bastard, doesn't it?'

'What's up with Marquis?'

'Sick.' Pain in the arse. Michael would have put up with Marquis's 'allergies' any day over having to deal with Fallaize's crap, but the hay fever had turned out to be some horrible strain of summer flu and so now, on top of everything else, Michael had this prat to deal with.

The Avenue was deserted. There was a thin cover of cloud, the sort that let the warmth of the sun seep through and then kept it there, pushing it down on everyone. A strong breeze had ensured the trip over was uncomfortable, but it was still a good five degrees warmer than it had been on Guernsey and he regretted wearing his long-sleeved shirt already. Sweat pricked at his brow.

The new coffee shop with the fancy cupcakes was still closed, despite a sign outside saying it opened at eight. Michael saw the twitch of a blind slat as they walked past. The chap who ran the grocery store stood in the window and openly stared. Alf from the cycle-hire shop was the only person who seemed to be up and about. Even he was quiet, handing over their bikes with little more than a nod.

They stopped in at the church hall, where they found a bleary-eyed Constable Bachelet at the desk.

'All quiet last night?' Michael asked.

'Too quiet, sir.'

'What do you mean by that?'

'Couldn't sleep, to be honest. Room was hot and stuffy. And I live in town. I'm used to hearing a bit of noise and bustle. There was nothing last night except crickets. And bats. Think they were bats. Squeaking.' He shuddered. Then yawned.

'Right. Well, we've got all that to look forward to. We're going to check into the B&B and then get set up over at the school. You man the desk here, all right?'

'Yep. No problem.' He yawned again.

He did not, Michael thought, have the demeanour of an officer involved in a major murder investigation.

'Oh, sir, just to warn you—press arrived late last night.'

'The *News*? Been here a couple of days already. Keep up, son.'

'No, couple of nationals.'

'How'd they get here?'

'Charter from Jersey. Suppose they wanted to be here for the meeting.'

Michael sighed. 'I suppose they did. Come on, Fallaize. Into the lion's den we go.'

Fallaize stopped on the way out, peering at his reflection in a dusty windowpane. Evidently wanting to be camera-ready, he swept his hair over to one side and straightened his blazer. He was looking a bit peaky, Michael thought. Lacking some of his usual wide-boy sparkle. Nothing dull about his cufflinks, though. They were tiny gold sports cars. Flash git.

Sark School assembly hall was the only place big enough to seat the amount of people Michael expected to attend the meeting. The press were already there, waiting outside. Not as many as he'd feared.

'Can you give us a comment, DCI Gilbert?'

'Are you close to finding the killer?'

'Any insight into possible motive?'

'Is Reg Carré's death connected to the gruesome discovery on Derrible Bay on Monday?'

Michael held up his hand.

'It is, as you know, very early days in this inquiry. This is a meeting for the residents of Sark. You can sit quietly at the back and I'll try to answer any questions you have as best I can at the end of it.'

'Jonathan Boswell, Channel News. Can you comment on the rumour that Reg Carré was murdered as a result of a twenty-year feud with a neighbour?' A microphone was shoved under his nose.

'I said I'll answer questions later!' Michael thundered. He pushed the mic away. 'And don't be so bloody irresponsible,' he hissed. 'People here are stressed enough without you stirring the pot.'

Bloody local press, he thought. Worse than the nationals by far, getting tied up with all the island gossip.

He stopped on the way into the hall. Scanned the small gathering of reporters. There was a notable absence.

'You expecting someone, sir?' Fallaize asked.

'No. Not particularly. Just Jennifer Dorey—I know she stayed over last night. Would have thought she'd be here.' He took out his phone. No bloody reception. 'Check in with the guesthouse, will you, Fallaize? Rosie's, I think it is. Make sure she's all right.'

'Absolutely, sir.' The edge, the ever-present touch of insolence was absent from Fallaize's tone. Which was, Michael thought, most disconcerting.

Several children cycled past chatting and laughing, parking their bikes in the stand to the left of the school entrance. They looked happy enough. Not a care, despite what was about to be discussed right next door to them. Michael remembered those blissful days, when bad news was something that only happened to grown-ups. In Guernsey, even the grown-ups were sheltered from the worst of world events. He'd visited London on a training course after a spate of IRA attacks in the early 1990s. It had been all over the news, but he had still been shocked to see his mainland colleagues checking under their cars before they got in and, later in the week, the moment of panic caused by an unaccompanied rucksack in the lunchroom.

Even now, Guernsey remained removed, the water that surrounded the island a buffer—a psychological cushion between it and the terrors of the wider world. Because on their small island, it was the small-scale horrors that were felt more keenly than elsewhere. The car crashes, the drug deaths, the suicides and, yes, the murders. Shock amplified, rippling through the community, each person touched in some way. It was bad enough on Guernsey. It would be even worse here. Everyone knew Reg Carré. Odds were a few of them knew why he was murdered. Perhaps they would be at the meeting this morning. Chances were the killer would be too.

Michael helped set up the chairs. Seating for two hundred or so and standing room at the back. The last time he'd done anything like this he'd had to admit to the crowd that a killer had gone about drowning young women undetected for decades. At least he would not have to face the sort of hostility that situation created. No, this time they were on top of things. They knew what they were dealing with. Murder. Two of them. Connected? They had to be. He didn't know how, but as he'd told countless junior officers over the years, there was no such thing as a coincidence. There was some thread, however thin, strung between the two bodies. Perhaps, he pondered, the bond between them was far greater than that. Not a thread at all but a band of gold.

Because the more he thought about it, the greater he considered the likelihood that the woman in the cave was Rachel Carré. Luke Carré had agreed to a DNA test already. The results would take a few days at least, the process of extracting DNA from bones time-consuming. A positive result would be, Michael considered, from a police perspective, the best possible outcome. Because, he reasoned, if those were Rachel's bones, he'd wage money on Reg Carré having put them there. Which made the whole case a family affair.

Michael checked his watch. Past ten and the hall was nearly full. Malcolm Perré was sporting an ugly black eye. Sharon sat in the same row but had left several empty chairs between them. Evidently there had been more trouble between those two. Constable Langlais looked worse than he had done two days ago, thinner, if that were even possible, his chin covered in patchy stubble. Luke Carré also looked a state—tired, bloodshot eyes. A hangover. Driven to alcohol by grief or guilt? Michael wondered. And just behind him, Jenny Dorey and her colleague-cum-boyfriend, Elliot. Michael had been relieved to see them arrive, although they both looked tired and stressed.

Tanya Le Page sat at the back. A lonely-looking figure, hair hanging limply, a drab-looking oversized cardigan wrapped around her slim shoulders. Several members of the Chief Pleas, Sark's now democratically elected government, were in attendance. They sat together, and talked among themselves, an air of officiousness about them. A woman he recognised from the village, dyed-blonde hair, very attractive, although her demeanour certainly discouraged any notion of conversation, stood at the back of the hall, arms folded in spite of the availability of several free seats.

He cleared his throat. The audience sat up straighter. Chair legs squeaked against the waxed wooden floor. Michael moved forward to speak.

'Wait a minute! Wait a minute.' Sir William de Bordeaux made his way through the hall, his cane tap-tapping beside him. He sat, slowly, in a front-row seat. 'Can't have an island meeting without the seigneur, now can we?'

Michael thought he might be attempting humour, but the reaction from the rest of the room was muted. Cool, even.

'Very pleased you could make it. I was just about to begin.'

'Well, don't let me stop you. Carry on.'

Michael bristled, then remembered Jenny's comment about his problem with authority figures and gave the old man a tight smile before launching into a summary of events, from the discovery of the bones on the beach to Reg Carré's body being found.

'The timings here are very important. Mr Carré was seen at just after nine a.m. making his way home from the village with his grocery shopping. Constable Langlais found his body shortly after eleven thirty a.m., by which point we believe he'd been dead for somewhere in the region of two hours. So whoever killed Mr Carré was most likely waiting for him at his house, or arrived very soon after. Mr Carré had been making tea right before he was killed, which leads us to believe the killer may have been known to him. Which means he's most likely known to you all too.'

There was a long, loaded silence while Michael let this sink in.

'Many of you have come forward and given statements regarding when you last saw Mr Carré, or spoken of his character, or contributed your theories about what might have happened, and we're very grateful for all of your co-operation. For now, we're interested in tracing a man who was seen on or near Mr Carré's property on Monday morning—'

'A man?' the seigneur interrupted. 'Is that the best you've got? What sort of man? Who saw him?' He looked behind him at the audience.

'I'm afraid that's not information I'm able to share with you all.' He saw Tanya Le Page shift in her seat, pull her cardigan a little tighter. 'And I appreciate the description is minimal,' Michael continued. 'But if anyone was in the vicinity of Reg's house on Monday morning, they should come forward, regardless of whether or not they saw anything suspicious.

'We're also looking for a woman in a large sun hat who bought a ticket for the twelve-noon sailing to Guernsey on Monday. Most likely a tourist on her way home, but due to the timing of the ticket purchase, we'd like to eliminate her from our enquiries.'

'What about the bones?' The woman at the back of the hall.

'We are trying to establish the identity of the body found on Derrible. If anyone has any information pertaining to that, we'd like to hear from you.'

'Who found them, then?' The same woman.

'It was an anonymous tip. We'd very much like to speak with whoever called it in.'

'What would someone be doing poking around in those caves, do you think?'

Michael was confused. 'I'm sorry, Ms . . . ?'

'Jones. Tuesday Jones.'

'Ms Jones, I really have no idea. It's not been a primary focus of the investigation so far.'

'Well, maybe it should be.'

'If you know something about this Ms Jones, you need to tell us.'

She shook her head, the hint of a smile on her lips.

Michael was suddenly aware that a tension had settled over the room. Nobody was talking, not even a whisper of conversation. Nobody was moving. They all sat straight and still. And nobody was looking. Not at him, not at the woman who was asking the questions.

A raised hand. 'Yes, Jennifer.'

'Are the police considering that the two cases might be connected?'

'I'm not able to comment on that until we've identified the body found in the cave.'

'Should people be locking their doors at night, Chief Inspector? Is there another serial killer on the loose?' It was that idiot from Channel News again.

'No, Mr Boswell, we do not suspect a serial killer is on the loose. And speculation of that nature is extremely unhelpful.' He paused. 'However, we always advise folk to lock their doors, and given the circumstances, I'd say people would be wise to follow that advice right now.'

'Rubbish.'

Michael flinched. 'You have something to add, Sir William?'

'Load of rubbish. This whole place has gone to hell and a locked door isn't going to make the blindest bit of difference.' He stood, turned to the crowd. 'I hope you're all satisfied. Made a deal with the devil, didn't you? And look where it's got us.' He spat, with surprising force, towards the group from the Chief Pleas.

'Hang on a minute!' Michael started towards him, but he raised his cane.

'I'm leaving. You should too. You're wasting your time. You'll get nothing out of this lot.'

The sound of gentle sobbing broke the silence. Tanya Le Page, shoulders shaking, head in hands.

'Let's everyone calm down now,' Michael said, although Tanya was the only one actually making any noise. 'Everything's going to be fine.'

'How can you say that?' She looked up. 'No one is safe.' She gestured around the room. 'No one.'

'We have no reason to believe that anyone else is in danger. Of course, if you know different, any of you, you should come forward immediately.'

'I need a cigarette.' Tuesday sounded bored. 'Thanks for your time, DCI Gilbert. I'm sure we all appreciate it.'

As she left, Michael could have sworn some of the tension in the room lifted. Enough, at least, for a murmur of conversation to start up, chairs to shift and squeak on the floor.

'That woman.' Michael spoke quietly. 'Tuesday Jones.'

'Stupid name.' Fallaize did not bother to keep his voice down.

'Get me some information. Background, how long she's been here. Then go and talk to her. Ask her about the cave comment. Whether she knows who tipped us off.'

'I'm on it.'

Everyone in this room, Michael thought, had been terrified. Even the seigneur's outburst seemed rooted in anxiety. Except Tuesday Jones. She hadn't seemed frightened at all.

Jenny and Elliot were waiting outside the school gates. She had that determined look on her face as she approached him.

'You all right?' he asked. 'Not letting all this get to you?'

'I'm fine.' She managed a tight smile. 'Heading to Tanya Le Page's. She just asked if she could speak to me.'

'What about? If she's any complaints about the investigation, she needs to come to us. You can't be printing anything that will under-mine public confidence, not now. You saw what it was like in there.' Michael could feel his blood pressure rising, his left eye twitching in synch with his elevated pulse.

'She looked worried. Not angry. I'll let you know what she says. Then I've pretty much covered everything I can on Reg's murder. Unless you've anything else for me?'

'Nothing at the moment. You going back to Guernsey, then, are you?'

She shook her head. 'Can we talk? Not now.' She glanced at Fallaize, who stood a few feet away and was obviously listening. 'Later this afternoon?'

'What about?' He looked at her quizzically.

'I've been making some enquiries. About my dad.' She winced as she said it, obviously anticipating his response.

He couldn't help delivering.

'For God's sake, Jenny.' Michael put a hand to his head, covered his eyes. 'I've got enough on my plate.'

'I know you don't have time for this now. But it might be relevant.'

Fallaize let out a sceptical-sounding huff.

'How so?' Michael asked.

'Later. At the Mermaid?'

'I'll not be able to take a break until five at the earliest.'

'Five, then.'

He sighed as she walked away.

'I know you're friends, sir, but I wouldn't take anything she says too seriously. She always looks halfway to a nervous breakdown.'

'Did I ask for your opinion, Fallaize? Go and speak to Tuesday Jones, will you?' Cheeky little bastard.

He waited until Fallaize had cycled off towards the incident room before sitting on the wall. These conferences always made him feel ill. He was all right while he was doing it, but afterwards, it was as if all of the tension he kept in check was unleashed. He felt it rising from his stomach and into his chest, like stress reflux.

He was going to have to tell Jenny what he knew about Charlie Dorey's death. He should have been honest months ago. As soon as the inconsistencies were brought to his attention. She would have understood. Everyone made mistakes. It was the not coming clean that caused problems. The cover-up. It was always worse than the crime.

27

Jenny

'Are you going to tell me what's wrong?'

They stopped at the crossroads before Tanya Le Page's house. It was the first time either of them had spoken since they'd left the school.

'I'm a bit distracted with everything that's going on, Elliot, that's all.'

'There's something else. I'm getting a bit tired of having to second-guess you all the time, Jenny. Why don't you just tell me what's on your mind so we can get on with things?'

'Were you out with Jade last night?'

He looked taken aback. 'Yes.'

'And I'm the one who's not being honest?'

'Jenny, I didn't want to upset you.'

'You're doing me a favour by not telling me you're sleeping with someone else? Fuck off, Elliot.'

He shook his head. 'I'm not sleeping with anyone else, Jenny. Jesus. It was team drinks. Jade organised it, that's all.'

It was too simple an explanation to be anything but the truth. She let it sink in for a moment, felt the sting of embarrassment behind her eyes.

'I'm sorry. I . . . misunderstood.'

He nodded. 'You did.'

'What team drinks?'

'It wasn't everyone.'

'Just the popular crowd?'

He sighed, exasperated. 'I didn't organise it. You were here, anyway.'

They stood next to each other in silence. The heat was oppressive.

'I need to speak to Tanya Le Page.'

'Let me guess. You need to do it alone?'

'Elliot, it's not because I don't want you there. But she won't talk to me if you are—she's very protective of her son.'

'It's fine, Jenny. I get it. You don't need me. No problem. I'll see you in Guernsey. Presuming, at some point, you decide to come back.'

There was something very final about the way he rode off, without so much as a goodbye or a glance over his shoulder.

Arthur Le Page was kneeling next to the coffee table, surrounded by colouring pencils, a vase of deep red roses pushed to one side. His head was bent over a sketchbook, long hair falling like a protective curtain about his face.

'He's hardly spoken all week,' Tanya whispered. She was still red-eyed after the meeting. 'Just the odd word. Nothing about what happened. The doctor says it's post-traumatic stress. Says we can't rush him. I know the police are desperate to get him to talk. But he didn't see anything. I'm sure about that.' Her voice cracked. 'Can we talk in the kitchen?'

'Of course.' Jenny followed her through the bright living room into a long, low-ceilinged room. Polished brass pots hung over a central island. Dishes spilled out of a ceramic sink. A gleaming range cooker hummed in the corner.

'Do you want some tea?' She got up but seemed to immediately forget why she had done so and sat back down again, put her head in her hands. 'This is a nightmare.'

'Here, let me do it.' Jenny filled the kettle and rinsed two mugs from the sink.

'Thank you.' She smiled weakly. 'I didn't know who you were when you brought Arthur home. Your dad was the man who drowned off Sark a couple of years ago.'

'That's right.'

'It must be hard for you, being here.'

Jenny shrugged. 'Not really. It's harder at home, where there are reminders of him. Besides, he loved Sark. I have happy memories of him here.'

'I'm sure there are lots of people who speak fondly of him.'

Jenny wasn't sure if it was a question or not. 'He had friends here. What was it you wanted to talk to me about, Ms Le Page?'

'Everyone knows it was Arthur who found Reg's body.'

'I haven't said a word,' Jenny protested. She had, under strict instruction from Michael, not told a soul about Arthur's involvement in the case, not even Elliot.

'I know it wasn't you. Constable Langlais is one of the most indiscreet men I've ever met. I'm sure he only volunteered for the job so he could satisfy his craving for gossip.' She paused. 'I want you to write about it but make a point of the fact that Arthur did not see who killed Reg Carré.' There was an edge to her voice now. 'The police keep saying we're safe, but how can they possibly know that? And now they've mentioned a witness who saw a man, it's only a matter of time before people work out it was Arthur.' Her big eyes glistened and she tore a piece of kitchen paper off a roll and dabbed at them. 'I'm sorry.'

'It's been two days,' Jenny said gently. 'Plenty of time for Arthur to have talked.'

'But he hasn't!' Tanya said sharply.

'I know that. And you know that. But the murderer doesn't. There would be no point in anyone trying to harm Arthur. And even if there was, they would have done it by now, wouldn't they?'

Tanya sighed. 'Maybe. Who knows. We're not dealing with a normal person, are we? Normal people don't do this sort of thing.' She shuddered. 'So will you do it? The article?'

'Of course.' Graham would love it, Jenny thought. Particularly with Tanya being so photogenic.

'Can I say a quick hello to Arthur before I go?'

'I don't think that's a very good idea. Sorry.' Tanya shook her head. 'He wet himself when the milkman rang the doorbell yesterday.'

'Poor thing. Of course, I don't want to upset him.'

A crash from the living room. A wail. Tanya paled and rushed out of the room. Jenny followed.

'What the . . . ? What are you playing at?'

The vase of flowers lay on its side, roses spilling out of it, water pooling on the table and dripping off the edge onto the cream carpet. Arthur stood, his sketchbook clutched to his chest. He looked, Jenny thought, defiant.

'Bloody hell, Arthur. As if I haven't got enough on my plate!' She started picking up the flowers. 'Shit! They would have to be roses, wouldn't they?' She sucked at the bead of blood that had appeared on the end of her thumb.

Jenny righted the vase.

The front door slammed.

'Oh God, no!' Tanya ran after her son. Jenny followed. The street was empty. 'He's got to stop running. Every time we fight, he runs.'

'Let me help you look for him,' Jenny offered.

'No. You've done enough. I'll find him. Usually I'd just leave him be, but not now. Not until they catch this madman. God knows how long that will take—the police don't seem to have a clue.'

'I wouldn't say that.' Jenny was instantly defensive of Michael. 'It's only been a couple of days. They haven't even had the forensic evidence back from the lab yet.'

'I forgot—you're friendly with DCI Gilbert, aren't you? I'm sorry. He seems like a nice man. But a couple of days feels like a long time when you're stuck on an island with a killer.'

*

It was Jenny who found Arthur, sitting in the entrance to a field just a few hundred yards from his house. He was still scribbling in his sketchbook.

'Hey.'

He looked up.

'What are you drawing?' She sat next to him. Glanced down at the page. 'That one's good. Is it Batman?' The boy put his hand over the picture. 'Do you like superheroes?'

''S'not Batman.' He did speak, after all.

'Oh. Well, it's very good.'

'It's bad.'

'Better than I could do. I'm rubbish at drawing.' She smiled.

'It's the bad man.'

Jenny felt a chill as the child's gaze met hers. 'You saw someone who looked like this?'

He nodded. 'Mummy said not to tell.'

Jenny gently moved the hand that covered the picture. The figure was dressed all in black, his face half covered in some sort of mask, the eyes wide and bug-like.

'He looks a bit like Batman.' Jenny wondered if the trauma had confused his memory. Perhaps it was easier for him to process an image of something he was familiar with than whatever the reality had been.

''S'not Batman. It's the Beast Man.'

'Arthur!' Tanya's voice.

He froze.

'Mummy said not to tell,' he whispered.

'About the Beast Man?' she whispered back.

'About anything.'

'Arthur!' Closer now.

Jenny couldn't tell if she sounded worried or angry. They were hidden from her view, but she would see them as soon as she drew level with the field entrance.

'You go to her. I'll stay here. She won't know you spoke to me.'

He seemed to think about this for a second, then nodded. 'OK.' He got up in a hurry and trotted out to meet his mother.

'There you are.' Tanya was mere feet away. A couple more steps and she would see Jenny. Their footsteps retreated, Tanya's voice a low murmur, Arthur silent once again.

Jenny waited until she could no longer hear them. Gave it another couple of minutes for them to make it back into the house. She got up. Dusted the dry grass off the back of her shorts. Picked up the sketchbook Arthur had left behind and slipped it into her bag.

She spent the afternoon in her room at the guesthouse finishing a report into the meeting Michael had held that morning ('Police Urge Vigilance but Islanders Should "Remain Calm"'), as well as starting on the interview with Tanya ('"This Is a Nightmare"—Sark Mother Speaks Out') and the piece about Corey Monroe ('Monroe: "I've Tried to Make Friends"'). Enough to keep Graham happy until tomorrow morning at the very least. She lay back on the bed. Thought about what she had to tell Michael. Malcolm's outburst. Tuesday's warning. Arthur's strange drawing. And Monroe. His reference to the assault she'd suffered in London. Or was it?

Fuck, she was tired. She scrolled through her messages. Nothing from Elliot.

She typed one. *I'm sorry. Can we talk when I get back?* She added an 'x'. Deleted it. Pressed 'send'. The Wi-Fi symbol flickered. One bar, then two, then none. An exclamation mark appeared. *Text not sent.* It would have to wait until she got to the pub.

Outside, the sound of trees swaying. She closed her eyes. Slept dreamlessly.

She woke with a start. There had been a sudden noise. A door slamming, maybe. It was oppressively warm, but the light in the room had a pale, silvery quality, and for one panicked moment Jenny thought she had slept through until nightfall. She checked her phone. Four thirty. She pulled open the curtains. Not darkness. But not quite light. The sky was overcast. The landscape drained of colour.

The noise again. She splashed her face with cold water. Changed into her last clean top and pulled on a pair of shorts. On the landing, she found the source of the disturbance. An open window, a door to one of the other bedrooms swinging back and forth in the draught. Jenny shut it and went down the stairs.

Shuffling. She wondered if Rosie sat in the kitchen all day just waiting for the sound of her guests' footsteps in the hallway.

'I shouldn't stay out too late tonight if I were you. Weather's coming in. I can feel the pressure.' She rubbed the top of her nose and then looked at Jenny's T-shirt with disapproval. 'Wait there.' Rosie disappeared into the kitchen and came back with a bright yellow cagoule. 'Take this with you.'

'Thank you.'

'You take care. It's treacherous out there in bad weather. Everyone's so happy about this Dark Sky Island status because they can see the stars. I'd rather have a couple more street lights. See what's right in front of me.'

Michael sat at a corner table sipping at what looked like a glass of lemonade. Fallaize was at the bar draining a pint. Jenny nodded a hello to him. He looked ill, she thought, sallow-skinned, his usually perfectly coifed hair unruly. He raised his chin in return and waved at the barman, tapping his finger on the top of his glass. Jenny joined Michael.

'He all right?' she asked, looking at Fallaize.

'God knows.' Michael rolled his eyes. 'He's off duty. Probably got the bloody flu. And not that I wish him ill but I'd be a damn sight happier if he buggered off home. Driving me nuts he is. Usually treats me with complete and utter contempt; now I can't shake the bugger off. Can't bloody do enough for me. Presume he's angling for promotion. As if a couple of days of not being an arrogant shit is going to make up for the last ten years. Anyway. Shall we take a walk? Too many people in here.'

She followed him towards the exit.

Fallaize slammed his pint on the bar.

'Where are you going?'

'None of your bloody business!' Michael barked. 'Listen,' he said, more gently, 'I know your shift's over, but I'm going to need you back on first thing. Why don't you get some rest, eh? Looks like you could do with it. And take it easy. You'll be no good to me with a hangover.'

'Yes, sir.' Fallaize saluted. He did not look like he had any intention of going home.

'Bloody hell, it's warm.' Michael held open the door for Jenny and then rolled up his shirtsleeves. 'Shall we go to the lighthouse? Shouldn't imagine we'll see many people out there now. And it will be cooler.'

Jenny agreed and they walked side by side, turning left at the end of the road and then right, past a number of deserted-looking farm buildings. The road narrowed, becoming a single-lane track, grassy in the middle, deep, gravelly trenches on either side. The hedgerows grew higher until they were under the cover of a row of tall yew trees, trunks gnarled, twisted branches shadowing the path. Pagans had planted yews near burial grounds—the seeds and needles that carpeted the earth were poisonous and discouraged animals from foraging in the freshly dug soil beneath. The tradition had continued. Yew trees were still silent mourners in most Christian churchyards. There was one a few feet from Charlie's grave.

'So, what have you got for me?' Michael broke the silence.

In low tones, Jenny caught him up with most of what she'd been doing—who she'd spoken to, what they'd told her, what they hadn't. Michael listened, hands dug into his pockets. He said nothing.

The path ended in a low white gate, padlocked, a 'closed' sign swinging off it in the breeze. Beyond, pale concrete steps led down to Point Robert and the lighthouse. Michael clambered over, jumping down and landing surprisingly daintily for a man of his size on the other side.

Jenny followed. 'Isn't this trespassing?'

'Hm. Maybe I'll arrest you when we're done talking.'

They started down the steps. It was fresher here, the air cooling on the water before it hit the land. The stark white of the octagonal light-house tower appeared before them. It had been automated for years, but before that had been a desirable posting. Considered a 'rock sta-tion' due to Sark's isolated position, keepers at Sark Lighthouse were paid well, compensated for the hardships such an apparently lonely post entailed. Jenny wondered how many other rock-station lighthouse keepers could walk to the pub within fifteen minutes. Not such a bad deal. And to wake up to this view every morning.

They were behind the tower, which rose straight out of the flat-roofed keeper's cottage and service shed below. Iron railings lined the edge of the concrete platform they now stood upon. The whole com-plex clung to the cliffs two hundred feet above the sea, which crashed around Blanchard Rocks beneath them, the very same rocks the Sark ferry navigated each time it sailed into Maseline Harbour.

Charlie had told her stories about pirates with precious cargo using Sark's network of caves to hide their loot. They would surely have arrived under cover of night, clambering over slippery rocks and sheer cliff faces in darkness, their spoils on their back. She'd always imag-ined they were hiding actual treasure, chests spilling over with silver and gold, goblets and jewels, like in fairy tales. But perhaps their cargo was precious in other ways. Barrels of rum or whisky. Ampoules of morphine.

'Why do you think the tip-off about the bones was anonymous?' She asked.

'What are you thinking, Jenny? I'm guessing you have a theory.' A gust of wind buffeted around them. The cry of an oystercatcher carried above it. Two of them, in flight, a flash of black and white, flying low over the surf.

'I'm thinking whoever found them was doing something they shouldn't have been.'

'You been talking to that woman, what was her name, Tuesday? Was it her? Does she know something?'

Jenny shook her head. 'This is all my own speculation. Maybe the person was trying to hide something of their own.'

'Go on.'

'It's all linked. The bones on the beach. Reg's death. My dad's.'

Michael said nothing.

'Well?'

'It would be a remarkable coincidence, the bones being discovered, Reg being murdered on the same day and the two events unconnected—I give you that. We're looking into it. Your dad, however . . . I'm not seeing it, Jenny.'

'Reg Carré and Len Mauger were friends. So were Len Mauger and my dad. Dad drowned in calm seas he'd fished in all his life. The next day, Len Mauger gets this.' She pulled the note out of her bag.

The colour drained from Michael's face. 'How long have you had this?'

'Since Monday.'

'Len Mauger received this the day after your dad died?'

'That's what he says.'

Michael stared at the note. 'We need to get it to forensics. Not that there's much chance of getting anything useful off it now.'

'So you accept there might be a connection?'

Michael did not respond. He looked like he was struggling with an idea, a thought he couldn't quite articulate. 'Jenny, I . . .' He shook his head. 'It's been two years since your dad died. How do you figure his death is connected to Reg's?'

'My dad saw something. Lights out to sea. Noticed a pattern.'

'What sort of pattern?'

'A signal of some description.'

'From where to where?'

'He followed a boat he saw near Brecqhou. He knew it shouldn't be there, suspected it was paparazzi. He probably wanted to come home with a great story about how he was going to be in the *Daily Mail*. But the boat stopped over by Port du Moulin and started flashing its lights.'

'Did he see anyone flash back?'

'I don't know. Len Mauger told me all of this. But it tallies up with what Dad wrote in his diary.'

'OK. For now, I'm going to presume all this is true—I'm not doubting your story, Jenny, but this is third-hand information—but let's just say your dad did see all this. What do we think was going on?'

'Something illegal.'

'Undoubtedly.'

'Something that involved boats.'

'You're stating the obvious now, but yes, something involving boats.'

'It's got to be drugs. They're stashing them in caves. That's how the bones were found.'

'You're right about the speculation Jenny.' Michael chewed his bottom lip. 'OK. Let's set the body in the cave aside, just for a minute. Say your dad, who I believe liked to share a good story, was telling Len about what he'd seen. Coming up with theories. Someone overheard them. Killed your dad. Reg is involved somehow, ends up brutally murdered. Type of person who would do that, why not just kill Len too? Why the note?'

Jenny shrugged. 'Maybe Len was a friend of whoever did it.'

Michael was quiet again. A touch of colour had come back to his cheeks.

'The bones are old, Jenny. Decades. If, and this is still a big if, Reg and Charlie's deaths are connected, how do you tie in a murder that took place twenty, thirty, forty years ago?'

'Maybe that's how long this has been going on.'

'A drug-smuggling ring run out of Sark for years on end?'

'Why not? How often do you check fishing boats for drugs?'

'All the time, Jenny. We've been aware of drugs coming in from France on boats for a very long time.'

'So you check boats coming from France?'

'Not just France—Jersey, the mainland . . .'

'Sark?'

'Boats from Sark get checked.'

'How often?'

'I'd have to check with Customs and Excise.'

'At a guess?'

'Rarely.'

'Would make sense, then, wouldn't it? Making a drop from France or the mainland in Sark first, then shipping to Jersey and Guernsey from there. Less chance of being seen dropping off in Sark, less chance of having your cargo checked in Guernsey.'

'Thing is, Jenny, this place is so small. How would you keep an operation like that secret? Hm?'

'You wouldn't.'

'What do you mean?'

'You get enough people involved that everyone is implicated in some way or other. Then nobody says anything.'

'That's crazy talk, Jenny.' He shook his head.

'Think about it. What have you really managed to find out these last two days? Nobody's talking. Not about anything that matters.'

'You're suggesting this whole island has managed to keep something like this hidden?'

She shrugged. 'Maybe not the whole island. Enough of them, though. I don't know. It's a theory. Would certainly explain some of the strange behaviour I've witnessed. The warnings. The passive-aggressive threats.' She shuddered at the thought of Corey Monroe, his silhouette disappearing into the fog as he'd sped off in the dinghy the previous afternoon.

'It can't last, though,' she said.

'What can't?'

'The collective silence. A secret like this? Somebody is going to tell.'

Michael seemed lost in thought. 'I wonder.'

'What?'

'The increased drug-dealing activity in Guernsey. Maybe someone has bitten off more than they can chew. Feeling the pressure, made a mistake.' He shook his head. 'I don't know. This is all speculation. We need something concrete.'

'Like a description of the killer?'

'Well, that would be bloody brilliant, wouldn't it, but that kid's gone mute, hasn't he?'

She held out the sketchbook.

'What's this?'

'Sketch of the Beast Man.'

Michael took it. Stared at the picture. 'The boy drew this?'

Jenny nodded. 'And he's not gone mute, either. Mummy told him not to talk.'

'What the . . . ?'

'I think she's terrified. Doesn't want him involved.'

'Shit. She had the bloody doctor tell us he was traumatised.'

'I'm sure he is. She's just trying to protect him.'

'Tell that to the next person who gets brutally murdered because no one could identify this psychopath the first time round! I need to get to the phones.'

She followed him, back up the steps and over the gate. His head was bent, shoulders stooped. He was brooding, she thought. Angry. At whom? Himself? Tanya? Her?

At the Mermaid, he stopped. 'I'll take it from here. Thank you. You've a way of getting people to open up. I'm not sure how, because you're a bloody pain in the neck.'

She shrugged. 'I just stole a sketchbook. But I'm glad it might be helpful.'

'This on its own, maybe not. But if we can get more details from the kid—what this mask was made of, what clothes he was wearing—well, that would be a start.'

'And the rest of it, Michael? My dad?'

'Jenny. Let's deal with this first. If you're right and it's all connected, we'll find this bastard and then go from there, OK? We'll talk. I promise. Later.'

The pub was rowdy. Jenny could hear laughter and yelling from outside. She needed to eat—she'd slept through lunch and her stomach grumbled noisily—but somewhere quiet, where she could think. She picked up her bike, cycled the short distance to Florence's tearooms in the Seigneurie Gardens. She sat under a wide green umbrella, a pile of paper napkins on the table, weighted down with a pebble. She ordered a crab sandwich, agreeing to the glass of Sauvignon Blanc the waiter suggested to accompany it, letting the sharp, cold wine soothe her parched throat and calm her nerves.

She had been scared sharing her suspicions about Charlie's death with Michael. Scared that he would laugh at her, tell her she was crazy. But he hadn't. He'd taken her seriously. That was all that she wanted. She took out her notebook. Started scribbling down a timeline. Charlie's visits to Sark, the flashing lights, the accident, the note to Len. The beginnings of an exposé into her father's death. The air was heavy with the scent of lavender, which trailed out of the borders and onto the terrace. Fat bumblebees hovered lazily around the flowers. A wasp whined around her empty glass and she batted it away, ordered another drink.

'We're closing in a few minutes, miss.' The waiter set her wine down with the bill.

She looked at her watch. Nearly seven. She drank the wine quickly. She'd had just enough to ensure she'd fall straight to sleep when she got back to Rosie's. One more night here, she determined. First thing tomorrow, she would get away from this twisted paradise, with its shadowy figures and their veiled threats. At least for a little while. Long enough for Michael to solve Reg Carré's murder. Long enough to reopen the investigation into Charlie's death.

She walked out through the gardens, past flowerbeds overflowing with roses and orchids and a maze, a signpost pointing the way to the pond. She felt a tug in her heart as a memory of Charlie, lost until now, resurfaced. He had brought her here once, had told her stories as they were 'hunting for ghosts'—his unique way of making a history lesson more interesting. The Priory of St Magloire had been on this site. The Magloirian monks had dammed a stream, creating a reservoir for water supply and fishing. She wanted to see it. To bring back Charlie's words, the sound of his voice, to fix the place in her brain so she wouldn't forget it again. Ahead of her, she could see one of the groundsmen rounding up the last few visitors. Charlie wouldn't have let that stop him. She put her head down, hurriedly took the path to the pond.

It was even warmer under the trees, the humidity trapped, almost visible as a haze, wrapping itself round branches, twisting through the leaves. The pond's surface was thick with algae and she could smell the dank water beneath. This was it. Here. Her hand in Charlie's.

'There's a ghost lives here.'

She'd been ten or eleven. Old enough not to be frightened of his stories, not anymore. Old enough to be sceptical too.

'Another ghost?'

He'd raised his eyebrows. 'True as I'm here. Not a scary one.'

'A friendly one. Like Casper?' She'd grinned.

'Not like Casper. A real one. A monk.'

'What does it want?' All ghosts wanted something, Charlie had explained. It was why they stuck around.

'This is holy land. The site of a monastery founded by St Magloire. He brought Christianity to the Channel Islands, but we'll let him off because he worked plenty of miracles while he was at it.' He'd smiled. 'There's a little shrine here somewhere. First one to find it gets an ice cream.'

She looked for it now, vaguely remembering a pebble-covered nook in the pond's bank, a tiny effigy of the Virgin Mary within. She was halfway round when a noise stopped her in her tracks.

Barking.

She froze.

Panting. A rustling of vegetation.

And then, right in front of her. A dog.

It was very big and very black and very real.

It stood still. Crouched low. Then bounded towards her, sniffing her legs and her feet, long tail wagging.

'Sybil! Sybil!'

A man appeared through the trees. He was overweight, rosy-cheeked and sweating profusely. 'She's friendly—don't worry.' He carried a small trowel in one hand and a bucket in the other, which he set down before wiping his brow. 'You shouldn't be here. The gardens closed twenty minutes ago.'

Jenny ruffled the dog's ears. 'I'm sorry. I was just about to get going. Is she a Lab?'

The man nodded.

'I think I've seen her. Over by the Mermaid.'

The man shrugged. 'I wouldn't have thought so. She's not mine, she's Sir William's. I'm his private secretary,' he added. 'You really need to leave now.' He gestured towards the path back to the exit.

She glanced down at the bucket as she passed him, wrinkled her nose in disgust.

'Sir William is very particular about keeping the gardens clean,' he said, noting the expression on her face.

The bucket was halfway full of dog shit.

She hurried through the gardens. She would stop in at the church hall, tell Michael what she'd just seen. Was the seigneur's private secretary somehow involved in what had happened at Len Mauger's house? Or perhaps the seigneur himself? Corey Monroe had said he suspected the man of encouraging acts of vandalism. Jenny regretted the second glass of wine now, wanted a clear head. The gates were closed but not locked. Her bicycle was where she'd left it, propped up against the wall. Next to it sat DS Fallaize.

'All right?' He clambered to his feet, attempted what was surely supposed to be a smile but came out somewhere between a leer and a grimace.

'Fine, thank you. Is everything OK? What are you doing here?'

'Went for a ride. Saw your bike. Thought we could have a chat.'

'What about?'

'Your hair's all messed up.'

She instinctively ran a hand through it, smoothed it down over her shoulders.

'No, looked nice. Like you just got out of bed.'

'You're drunk.'

'So what? You're always so uptight, aren't you? Relax when you're with Pretty Boy, do you? What's-his-face. Elliot?'

She flushed. First because she was uncomfortable, then annoyed. She shouldn't feel embarrassed because he was being an arsehole. She tried to keep her voice cool. 'I think you need to go and lie down. Sleep it off.'

The street was deserted, but she could hear the murmur of conversation behind the garden walls, the distant clattering of dishes—the staff at the tearooms clearing up for the day.

'Maybe I will. Why don't you come with me? Might do you good, eh?' He reached out. Tried to touch her hair. She took a step back.

'I'm too young? Is that it? Maybe it's the old boys that do it for you. That's all the talk, you know that? At the station. It's a joke, obviously. No way old Gilbert could keep up with you. You're fit, aren't you? Nice muscles.' He nodded towards her bare arms. 'I've seen you out running before. And swimming. Gilbert would have a heart attack before he'd even got started.'

'Fuck off, Fallaize.'

'But if I do that, I won't be able to tell you my secret. Well, it's not mine really. It's your boyfriend's. He's been keeping something from you.'

Jenny's stomach twisted. If Elliot really was sleeping around, the last person she wanted to hear it from was DS Fallaize.

'How would you know?' She couldn't help herself.

'Well, I work with him, don't I? See what he's up to, even if he tries to hide it.'

Jenny let out a breath. He was talking about Michael.

'Yep. He's been carrying that case file around with him. Ever since he met you. The whole time you've been harping on about it.'

'What case file?' Cold crept into the base of her spine, sending a shiver through her.

'Your daddy's,' he whispered. 'Every time you ask him about it, he tells you to stop fretting, doesn't he? Tells his little Jenny not to worry. Because he doesn't want you to know the truth.'

'Which is?'

'He's known for months your dad was murdered. And he's done fuck all about it.'

28

Michael

Michael paced the church hall. There was not a lot of room. They'd managed to cram four desks into the small space, plus a white-board covered with his barely legible scribblings and Post-it notes. It was noisy: two officers were on the phone; Bachelet was nose to his screen, furiously typing.

'Where are we with Tuesday Jones?'

Bachelet looked up. 'The background information and the inter-view notes are on your desk, sir. Me and DS Fallaize spoke to her this afternoon. She has alibis for Monday morning—several people went in and out of her shop booking tours. She said she took telephone book-ings as well during the morning. We're checking the records. All seems pretty watertight.'

'Still. There's something. What about the bones in the cave?' He picked up the notes and flicked through them.

'I don't believe we asked her about them, sir.'

'I specifically said I wanted to know why she'd asked that question at the meeting. And where are we with Reg Carré's bank statements?'

Bachelet looked blankly around the room.

'Where's DC Marquis when you bloody need him, eh? Apparently he's the only bugger around here who knows how to follow up a lead.'

'Oh, he called, sir.' Bachelet flicked through his notes and read them back to Michael. 'He said he had a Lemsip, managed to get into the station for a couple of hours—he's been looking into the whereabouts of Rachel Carré. Said he can't find any trace of her. There's no record of the marriage at the Greffe even, so he can't find a maiden name. Said it's like she never existed.'

'They weren't married. So she wasn't Carré? Who the bloody hell was she, then? Jesus wept. We're getting nowhere.'

He threw down the paperwork. Rubbed his forehead. It was no good. He had to talk to the kid. He wasn't supposed to. Not without the family liaison. But these were extraordinary circumstances. The boy was the only lead they had. The picture itself was no use. A child's drawing, no detail as to what the man looked like. But perhaps the kid had seen something else. Noticed the way the suspect walked, heard him speak, seen in which direction he'd gone. Perhaps he'd seen the weapon. A long, slim, curved blade, forensics had said. And as sharp as they come. No wonder he was terrified. And Michael understood that his mother wanted to protect him. But there was a killer on the loose. It was so irresponsible. He felt a wave of anger towards Tanya Le Page, and people like her, who deliberately held back information, for whatever reason. It was followed by a wave of shame. He was in no position to judge.

'I'm going out.'

'Do you want me to come, sir?' Bachelet, sounding like it was the last thing he wanted to do.

'No. I think it's best I do this one on my own.'

He rapped on Tanya Le Page's door. There was a light on upstairs. Shadows moving behind the closed curtains. Someone was definitely home. He knocked again. Still no answer. Just after seven. Tanya was probably putting the boy to bed. He tried the door. Locked. Of course. He didn't want to scare them. But this couldn't wait until the morning. He hammered on the door.

'Police! Open up!'

That did the trick.

'What's going on?'

'I need to speak with you and your son, Ms Le Page.'

'We've been through this. He won't say anything!'

'I have reason to doubt that.'

'What reason?' There was an edge to her voice now. He needed to tread carefully. To keep her on side.

'Ms Le Page. Please. Can I come in?'

She seemed to think about it for a moment, then nodded, opened the door fully. Stood opposite him in the hallway, arms folded.

'I understand you're trying to protect your son, Ms Le Page, I really do. But he won't need protecting once we've caught whoever he saw at Reg's house, now will he? And I have reason to believe Arthur can help us.' He took out the sketchbook. Showed her the drawing. She barely glanced at it, but her cheeks paled.

'Where did you get that?'

'A passer-by picked it up. Near your house. It is Arthur's, isn't it?'

'I don't think so.'

'Yes.' A small voice. Arthur stood at the top of the stairs, wrapped in a Spiderman dressing gown. 'I lost it.'

Michael smiled at him. 'Well, lucky for you it's been found. You can have it back. I just need to ask you a couple of questions about this picture. Would that be all right?'

Arthur looked at his mother.

She nodded at him. 'It's OK. Come on down, Arthur.'

She took her son's hand and pulled him close to her, led him through to the living room. Michael followed. All he needed was a description. Then he could leave the kid and his mum alone. There was no reason anyone on the force would even have to know he had come here.

'So you like drawing, do you, Arthur?'

He nodded.

'Well, I can see from this you're very good at it. Now, I know this is hard to talk about, but this is the man you saw, isn't it? The one you called the Beast Man?'

Arthur looked at his mother.

'You can tell him, sweetheart.' Her hands were clasped neatly in her lap. Her knuckles were white.

The boy nodded.

'And it looks to me that he's wearing a mask, doesn't it? Bit like a superhero, eh? Was he wearing it the whole time, Arthur?'

He nodded again.

'Great. You're good at this, eh? Doing very well you are. So, just a couple more questions. Was the man already there when you arrived at the house?'

'Yes.'

'And he was in the room? With Mr Carré?'

'Yes.'

'And what were they doing? Were they talking?'

A shake of the head this time.

'No? Were they fighting, maybe? Was this man hurting Mr Carré?'

Another shake. 'Mr Carré was on the floor.'

'When you got there? He was already on the floor?'

A nod.

'And this man, Arthur, where was he?'

Nothing. Eyes to the floor.

'Where in the room was he?'

A tear fell to the floor, leaving a tiny, dark splash on the carpet. 'He was bending over Mr Carré.'

'I see. Very good. And, Arthur, did he see you?'

A shake of the head. More tears. 'I don't think so. I was looking through the window.'

'Good stuff. So the man was bending over Mr Carré. Then what did he do?'

'He went.'

'Out the front or the back?'

He was quiet for a moment. 'The back. I think the back.'

'Brilliant! I'll be keeping an eye on you, I will—you'll be a detective before you know it. Now, what did you do after the man went out the back, Arthur?'

'I went into the house. To see if Mr Carré was all right and to—'

Tanya took a sharp breath. 'Do we have to make him relive this? For fuck's sake, this can't be bloody necessary!' She got up, went into the kitchen. Came back typing furiously into her phone.

'You pressured me into this. It was completely inappropriate, you coming here, bullying me into letting you in.'

'Now, Ms Le Page, I did no such thing.'

'I'm alone here—you know that. What am I supposed to do when a policeman hammers on my door? Refuse entry? How was I to know how you'd react?'

'I'm sorry if you felt that way, Mrs Le Page. I didn't mean to intimidate you in any way—I'm just desperate to catch this man. To make sure you and Arthur can sleep soundly again. And I'm done here. You've both been really helpful. Thank you.'

'Can I have my book back, please?' Arthur held out his hand.

'Of course you can. I'm going to borrow this page, though, OK?' Michael tore the page with the drawing of the Beast Man out and held the sketchbook out for Arthur. The poor little mite was shaking and the book fell open on the floor. 'Whoops. There you go, buddy.' Michael bent down and picked it up. 'Some other good drawings there, aren't there?' Michael looked at the pirate ship on the open page. He was filled with an odd feeling of familiarity. 'Very nice. Like pirates, do you?'

'Yes.'

Michael flicked through the book.

'Are you done?' Tanya demanded.

Michael's eyes met hers. Searched them for some recognition. Some acknowledgement of what he'd just seen. Her gaze was cool and steady. Her outstretched hand, however, trembled.

'I'm going to have to borrow this one too, Arthur. Hope that's all right.' He didn't wait for the boy's response but tore a second page out of the book. He handed it back to Tanya.

Outside the house, he took out his phone. Called the incident room. The signal was too weak: the call failed to collect. Shit. He wanted to watch the house. To make sure she stayed put. He searched for Wi-Fi. Found 'lepageguest'. No padlock. Sent a message to Fallaize, one to Bachelet. He walked a few feet away from the house and waited in the shadows.

29

Fallaize

Fallaize lay on a bed in the shitty B&B the force had put him in and tried to sleep. Every time he began to drift off, some fucked-up part of his brain jerked him back into consciousness. What the hell had he spoken to that Dorey bitch for? He'd had too much to drink, thought he'd try to throw Gilbert off his game, but it was just as likely to backfire. That woman was like a dog with a bone. She was never going to let it drop.

His phone pinged. He reached out for it, held it in front of his face, tried to focus on the words.

Shit. He sat up. She was panicking. If she was panicking, it was fucking bad. He tried to think of a vaguely reassuring response. He fumbled, pressing each letter firmly, deliberately.

I'll deal with it.

But he couldn't. He couldn't keep a lid on things. Not here.

He closed his eyes. The phone pinged again. He was tempted to ignore her. But that would be stupid. And dangerous. He squinted at the screen.

It wasn't her.

It was Gilbert.

Fuck.

30

Jenny

Michael had not been at the church hall, and nobody seemed to know where he'd gone. She'd cycled around for half an hour looking for him and eventually decided to sit in the Mermaid, where at least she had a decent phone signal. Not that it was doing her any good, because he wasn't picking up. She'd drunk two more glasses of wine and left him three voicemails, her tone shifting from questioning ('Fallaize just told me something. I'm sure it's nothing, but . . .') to challenging ('Did you, Michael? Did you know about this?') and, finally, accusatory ('You did, didn't you? You fucking knew. When I get my hands on those files, I'm going to blow this whole thing wide open, Michael! Answer the phone, goddamnit!'). After the last one, she'd slammed the phone on the bar in a fury.

'How do people live here, not able to bloody call each other or check their emails half the time?' She directed the question at Tom, but the answer came from behind.

'Most of the tourists love it. An escape from the stresses and strains of everyday life. Or some such bullshit.' Luke Carré slid onto the bar stool next to her.

'Well, I'm not on holiday. I'm trying to work.'

'Are you OK? You're shaking.'

Jenny placed her hands in her lap. 'Stressed. And strained. Sark's clearly not having the intended effect on me.'

'Well. You're not here under particularly relaxing circumstances, to be fair. Do you want a drink?'

She shook her head. 'I've had enough.' Her cheeks were warm and she already regretted that last voicemail to Michael. 'Rosie at the guest-house has warned me the weather's going to "come in" any minute, whatever that means. First thing tomorrow, I'm out of here. Need to get back to the office.' Back to some semblance of normalcy, she thought. It was a good thing Michael was not answering his phone. She needed to think. To run everything by Elliot. To get some perspective.

'I'm going tonight.'

Jenny looked at her watch. Squinted at it. 'The last ferry left ages ago.'

'Not taking the ferry. Got a boat. Give you a lift if you like.'

'Can you sail?'

'I can, as it happens. But I'm not sailing anything. It's a little motorboat.'

'Wait, I saw you on the ferry on the way over. Where did the boat come from?'

'Bloody hell, you are nosey, aren't you? Had some engine trouble when I was over visiting Dad last week. Left it here for repairs. Now I'm taking it back to Guernsey. Anyway, I'm leaving as soon as I've had something to eat. You're welcome to join me.'

'And you're all right . . . motorboating in the dark?' Her head was spinning slightly, and she wasn't sure she was getting her words quite right.

'I could get back to Guernsey with my eyes closed if I had to. I'll keep them open, though, don't worry.'

'And the weather?'

He shrugged. 'There's going to be a storm later. It's fine for now. Bit of a swell, nothing serious. If we leave in the next half-hour or so, we'll be back well ahead of it.'

There was nothing else she could do here. And the thought of another night staring at the ceiling in that dusty guesthouse bedroom, worrying about what Fallaize had said, what Michael had done, listening for noises in the night, might be just enough to send her mad. Emboldened by the alcohol, defiant in the face of Michael's apparent double-cross, she nodded.

'OK. Thank you. I'll go and get my stuff.' She jumped down from the stool. Swayed, just a little. Nothing that the ride back to the guesthouse wouldn't fix.

'Boat's at Dixcart. See you there?'

'See you there.'

The cool air outside the pub almost immediately cleared the spinning, but left in its place a dull, irritating ache. And the nagging feeling that everything was upside down, that she had made a stupid mistake. It was Michael, she decided. She should not have spoken to him that way. She called him, one last time. Still voicemail. She apologised for the previous message. Told him she was heading back to Guernsey with Luke.

They could talk, she said.

Tomorrow.

31

Michael

Michael's phone buzzed. His heart sank as he listened to each voice-mail, finally settling, a dead weight in his belly. He tucked the phone back in his pocket. There was no time to deal with Jenny now. Fallaize was another matter. Speak of the devil. The younger officer rounded the corner on his bike, coming to a messy stop in the entrance to the field a few hundred feet from Tanya Le Page's house.

'Are you drunk, man?' Michael hissed, as Fallaize seemed to struggle to keep himself upright. 'What is it with this bloody place? Nobody can stay sober for more than five minutes at a time!'

'I'm fine.'

'You stink of alcohol. How much have you had?'

'Just a couple of pints.'

'And the rest. What the hell have you been saying to Jennifer Dorey?'

Fallaize raised his hands. 'Boss, I'm sorry. She was asking me all these questions, and you two being so close, I thought she knew about the inconsistencies in her dad's case. Course, I realised, when I saw her face, that I'd made a big mistake. Makes sense. That you didn't tell her.'

Michael glared at him. 'Go back to the B&B. Sleep it off. I'll deal with you later.'

'I said I'm fine!' He lowered his voice in response to Michael's furious stare. 'I'm sorry. I had four or five pints. You know what it's like—the stress gets to you. But I stopped drinking over two hours ago. I've sobered up. You said this was urgent. I came as quickly as I could. There's nobody else here—you may as well make use of me. What's this about?'

'Tanya Le Page.'

'What about her?'

'She's involved in the Black Pearl racket.'

Silence. A clearing of the throat. 'Seems very unlikely.'

'It does, doesn't it? But unless that boy of hers is passing his little doodles to whoever is packaging up the pills that are landing on Guernsey by the boatload, Tanya Le Page has her hand in this operation.' He held out the drawing of the pirate ship. 'The latest packets we seized all had these motifs on them. Nearly identical ones, at least—pirate ships, same sails, same tiny flag. You've seen them; I know you have. They're the kid's drawings, I'm sure of it.'

'That's ridiculous. All kids' pictures look the same. What are you going to do, arrest her for letting her kid draw?' There was the old arrogance back in his voice now, and something else too. Aggression.

'I'm going to confront her about it. And you're going to back me up. Or else we'll be having words over at the station. In front of the chief.' They'd be doing that anyway, Michael thought, but it would be good to have Fallaize in the room with him when he confronted Tanya. That look she'd given him, just before he'd left. Cold and calculating. He couldn't risk her twisting his words or, God forbid, making official accusations about him, tainting any case they might build against her with false allegations. Everything needed to be above board.

'Wait. We should sit tight until the morning. Run everything by the chief first. That's standard, isn't it? High-profile case like this? And anyway, we'll want to search the place. We need a warrant.'

'She knows that I know, Fallaize. I saw it in her eyes. If we give her until the morning, I'll wager the place will be clean as a whistle. We've got to get in there now. If needs be, we'll arrest her and post someone here to watch the house. The search can wait until morning.' Every minute they stood out here was another minute Tanya Le Page had to hide evidence, to cover up whatever she was involved in.

'Come on,' Michael barked. He marched back towards the guesthouse.

Fallaize reluctantly followed.

'This is harassment. I've already called the station in Guernsey. Lodged a complaint. You shouldn't have spoken to Arthur without some sort of family officer here. Without his doctor signing off on it. I shouldn't have let you. I'm going to contact a lawyer too. You've caused us all sorts of distress.'

'With all due respect, Ms Le Page, any distress your son has suffered has been caused by whoever killed Reg Carré. I'm trying to find that person and bring them to justice. We're on the same side. At least, I thought we were.'

'What exactly is that supposed to mean?'

She did haughty very well, Michael thought, standing there, indignant and entitled, butter wouldn't melt.

Fallaize sat on the sofa opposite, obviously already in the midst of a hangover. He looked like death.

'OK if I have a quick look around, Ms Le Page?' Michael asked.

'No, it's not.' She stepped towards Michael.

Fallaize shifted in his seat.

'Something to hide, have you?' Michael asked softly.

He took Arthur's picture out of his pocket.

'How did your son's drawings make it onto the packaging of hundreds, maybe thousands of illegal pills being smuggled into Guernsey, Ms Le Page? And what do you know about Reg Carré's death? Why was your son there that morning?'

Because the more Michael had thought about it, the more suspicious he had become of Tanya Le Page's explanation for her son being at Reg's cottage that morning. Everything was connected. Tanya. The drugs. Reg. Arthur.

'You need to leave now.'

'We can leave. But you're coming with us.'

'Don't be ridiculous.'

'Ms Le Page, I'm going to need you to come and answer some questions at the incident room. We can call someone to watch Arthur for you.'

'I'm not going anywhere.'

'If you refuse to come of your own volition, I'm afraid I'm going to have to arrest you.' Michael nodded towards Fallaize, his cue to pull out the handcuffs.

Fallaize, however, remained seated, head bowed, and for a moment, Michael thought he had nodded off.

'DS Fallaize.' No response. 'Fallaize? Hell's wrong with you, man?'

'Oh, for fuck's sake, Rick, do something,' Tanya spat across the room.

It was as though Sergeant Fallaize had been slapped across the face. His head whipped round; his cheeks flamed red.

'Fuck do you want me to do, Tanya? You were always going to mess things up, way you are with that fucking kid.'

Michael tried to process this exchange. He looked at Tanya. She was furious, her face twisted with rage. And Fallaize, he wasn't hung-over, Michael realised. He was distraught.

Tanya darted forwards.

A cry from the doorway.

The boy.

Michael turned towards the sound.

A mistake.

A flash of silver. Then the agonising smash of glass against bone and he swore he could hear it, the crack of his skull reverberating in his ears. The last thing he saw before he struck the floor was a spray of his own blood hitting the sofa upholstery, a spatter of crimson spots among the delicate pink florals.

*

His head throbbed.

His wrists were bound.

Pins and needles in his arms and legs.

He opened his eyes. Blurred vision. Blurred thoughts. Pink roses. Red blood.

With a rush of adrenaline, the fractured pieces of his memory came together.

And he was scared.

Because hitting him with the vase was stupid and reckless but a result, surely, of panic. Tanya Le Page, involved—how deeply he didn't know—in a drug-smuggling operation, cornered and desperate, had acted on instinct, lashed out to protect herself. Leaving him here, however, wounded, bleeding, tied up, that was something else. The words he would use to build a case against her swam around his aching head.

Intent. Violence. Conspiracy.

Conspiracy. Fallaize.

Fallaize was in on it.

Even without a head injury, or his hands tied behind his back, there was no way Michael could beat Fallaize in a physical fight—the DS was younger, stronger and fitter than Michael. He was going to have to make a run for it.

He listened. Slowed his breathing. Cursed the pounding of the blood in his ears. He could hear them, their voices low and urgent. Tap running. They were in the kitchen. He tried to remember the layout of the house. Brain still sluggish. Eyes shut tight. The kitchen was at the back. The front door behind him, to the right. All he had to do was get to the door, open it somehow (it was an old house, he thought—a good kick might do it) and yell. Someone would hear. Might even be a passer-by he could send for back-up.

Michael tried to sit up, but a wave of nausea and dizziness forced him back to the floor.

A hammering. Someone at the door.

A clash from the kitchen.

Footsteps.

Strained voices. Door opened. Shut. Muttering. An exclamation.

'Tanya! What the fuck?'

Michael turned his head towards the voice, fighting back the dizziness. The figure spun before him. Tall and lean.

'Thank God. Help me, man.' Michael felt as though he were speaking underwater, his voice thick and slow, and he thought for a second that Martin Langlais had not understood him. The constable stood frozen in the doorway.

'Help me. My head . . . They've tied me up.'

Langlais moved towards him.

'No!' Tanya came into the room.

'Tanya. This is lunacy. What the fuck did you call me for? You've gone too far. You've got to give it up now. This . . . He's a policeman.'

'I need you to help us move him.'

Langlais blanched. 'Me? I'm not getting involved in this!'

'You're already involved.' Tanya spoke softly now. 'You've let all of this go on under your nose, never reported it, pocketed your share every month. You'll go away with us.'

'There's no proof.' Langlais didn't sound sure.

'None except DCI Gilbert here.' Tanya smiled. 'Pretty sure he's figured out you're involved.'

'Martin'—Michael struggled to a sitting position, propping himself up on the sofa behind—'you help me now and whatever your involvement in this, we can sort it. Come on, man. You've obviously got mixed up in this unwittingly—'

'Shut up.' Fallaize still looked like shit but seemed to have well and truly sobered up. He stood next to Michael. Looked at Tanya. 'Are you going to share this fucking plan? What the hell do we need Langlais for?'

'DCI Gilbert came here alone. He was in a rage. He'd found out from his journalist friend that I'd kept Arthur from talking to him. I was misguided, obviously, but acting in the best interests of my son. When I refused to let him talk to Arthur, he hit me. I was terrified.

222

Defended myself. Called Constable Langlais, who took DCI Gilbert to prison.'

'That's the best you can come up with!' Fallaize was incredulous. 'No fucking way anyone will believe he assaulted you. The man's got a clean record, thirty-odd years on the force. He's a fucking hero, for God's sake.'

'They don't have to believe me. They have to prove that I'm lying. And they won't be able to.'

Michael felt bile rising in his throat. He tried to move his wrists, to test the strength of the bindings.

Fallaize kicked the sofa. 'You should have let me handle this!'

'Because you've done such a good job handling things, haven't you, Rick? Want me to tell DCI Gilbert how you handled the last mess I asked you to clear up? Go on—tell him. Won't make any difference now.'

An intake of breath from Fallaize. 'Shut the fuck up.'

If Tanya felt threatened, she showed no sign of it. 'Messed it up something chronic he did, Chief Inspector. I only asked him to warn the man off.

'"Offer him a few hundred quid," I said, "and if that doesn't work, tell him we'll go after his family. His wife. His daughter."'

'Shut up, Tanya!' Fallaize lunged at her.

She dodged him and he tripped. She laughed. 'You'll have to try harder than that, Rick.'

Michael struggled to make sense of it all. Of Tanya. Of Fallaize, now on the floor, head on his knees.

'Whose wife and daughter?'

'I wouldn't have done it, you understand,' Tanya said. 'I just wanted him scared off. But Sergeant Fallaize fucked it all up. Went and killed the poor man. Not sure what caused him more distress—the fact that he'd done it or the effort it took to cover it up. Had to tamper with the paperwork, didn't you, Rick? Tell the chief inspector how you destroyed the evidence—made Charlie Dorey's death look like an accident.'

The silence that followed weighed down on Michael like a ten-ton blanket thrown over the room. It sucked the air out of his lungs and made his eyes water. It was broken, after what felt like hours but could only have been a matter of seconds, by a wretched sob.

'You bitch.' And with an ominous sense of déjà vu, for the second time that evening Michael saw a glint in the air. A piece of the broken vase, short and sharp and shining in Fallaize's outstretched hand. There were pieces of it, Michael noticed, all over the living-room floor.

'You fucking bitch.' Fallaize got to his feet.

Michael brushed the carpet behind him with his fingers. Back and forth. Side to side. Prayed they would find what he was looking for.

'Jesus Christ.' Langlais took a step back, towards the front door.

Tanya seemed unperturbed. 'I'd think carefully before you try to use that, Rick.'

'I've had enough of your bullshit, Tanya. Said I'd make sure your shipments weren't checked, would help out with a bit of paperwork. I never agreed to any of this.'

'You should have thought about that before you tipped Charlie Dorey off his boat, shouldn't you? There was no going back from there. You did that, Rick. I've never killed anyone.' Tanya looked at Langlais. 'How about you, Martin? You killed anyone recently?'

'Of course not!' He swung round to face Michael. 'I knew nothing about this—you have to believe me.'

Michael coughed. Shifted to the side. Kept his fingers moving. Felt cold, hard glass. 'Everyone needs to calm down.' He gripped the makeshift blade in his right hand. Winced as it sliced into his skin. He rubbed at the rope with it, struggling to hold on to it as his fingers became slick with blood.

He looked at Fallaize, who stood, outwardly defiant, shard of glass still held clenched in his trembling hand. Stupid, stupid bastard. He was in way over his head. Another man might have realised that, might have given up, been willing to face his fate, but Fallaize had always been an arrogant shit. He was never going to back down.

'Don't do it, Fallaize.' He tried to sound forceful, but his voice was weak and dry. 'Whatever else you've done. You can stop now. You can ask for forgiveness.' He could feel the tension on the rope lesson as he sawed through each strand.

Fallaize, eyes still fixed on Tanya's, slowly lowered the weapon.

Michael strained against the now-frayed bindings round his wrists. The rope snapped. Tanya saw him shift position. He had to move. He clambered to his feet, the shard of vase slipping from his bloodied hand as he did so. Tanya darted towards him. But before she could get to Michael, Fallaize, quick as a snake, had his arm wrapped round her neck, glass held to her cheek.

'It was an accident.' He directed it at Michael. Fallaize's voice shook as he gulped back a sob. 'You have to understand that. I went to talk to him. Maybe I came on a bit strong. He leaped at me. Wasn't expecting it. It was self-defence. Put my arm out, tried to restrain him. He fell, hit his head. I panicked. Of course, Tanya here didn't waste any time taking advantage of it. Sent threatening notes, warning other people they'd suffer the same if they didn't keep their mouth's shut. As though it was all planned. It wasn't. It was an accident. I swear it.'

Tanya's skin was white where the glass pressed against her cheek. Her eyes were fixed on Michael. Langlais whimpered.

'Put it down, Fallaize.' Michael struggled against the spinning in his head.

'Or what? I'll go to jail? I'm already going there, aren't I? This way, at least she gets what's coming to her.'

'Rick.' Tanya's voice was hoarse. 'Rick. We made plans, remember? Me and you, and Arthur. It's not too late. You're hurting me, Rick. Please.'

'I'm not buying that, Tanya. Not this time. Think I don't know you tart around with everyone? I've heard the lads who move the stuff talking. How you come down half dressed, acting like you've been caught off guard. It's what you do, isn't it? Flash a bit of tit here, bite your lip, all the while doing the "poor little me, all alone with my boy" act like some Virgin fucking Mary. Even had Gilbert here feeling sorry for you.'

He waved the glass in Michael's direction and in that moment, with a speed of movement that made Michael's head spin even faster, Tanya twisted away from Fallaize, kicking him hard in the groin as she did so. He doubled over but held on to the weapon, his hand bloodied.

'You fucked up, Rick.' Tanya stood with her back pressed against the wall.

Langlais now cowered in the corner. Michael and Fallaize faced each other, a few steps between them.

Tanya spoke as if to a small child. 'But it's OK. The only way out of this is if we all work together. Are you with me, baby?'

Michael kept his eyes fixed on Fallaize but appealed to Langlais, who was clearly the weak link in this unholy triumvirate.

'Martin, are you really going to go along with this? You think she's going to get her hands dirty, kill me herself? She'll have you do it, man. And you don't have the stomach for it. And you, Fallaize. Like she said, you fucked up. God knows there's no love lost between us, but you say it was an accident, I believe you. You can work out a deal. Bet you know a lot, eh? Bet you could get your sentence reduced. You'll be out after a few years. You're a young man. You go along with this'—he motioned his head towards Tanya—'it's over. You'll spend the rest of your life inside.'

'Don't listen to him.' Tanya's voice was steel.

'You're right,' Fallaize said. He looked dazed, as if he'd woken from a nightmare only to find himself still in the middle of it. 'I could proba- bly bargain my way to a fifteen-year sentence. Out in twelve. But you know what they do to coppers in prison. My life's over, whichever way you swing it.'

He took a step towards Michael, shard of glass pointing directly at his heart. Michael summoned every last bit of energy he had left. He balled his hand into a fist and swung at Fallaize.

Fallaize dodged.

Michael missed.

Fallaize lunged.

Sharp, hot pain in his side.

Michael staggered. Looked down at the shard of glass now sticking out of his waist.

'I'm sorry.' Fallaize held his hand to his mouth, smearing it with blood from his torn-up hands so he looked like some hellish clown. 'I'm so sorry.'

'Toughen the fuck up, Rick.' Tanya came forward. 'Let's get this shitshow over with.'

32

Jenny

Dixcart was easier to get to than the neighbouring Derrible, but no less beautiful. The tide was out, revealing a swathe of rocks, hewn from above. They tumbled towards the sea, diminishing as they did so, first broken and smoothed into pebbles, then mingled with the remains of long-dead sea creatures—mussel shells, winkles and limpets, cuttle-fish, coral—pounded to little more than dust, the fine, yellow sand of the shoreline.

A single boat, anchored a few hundred feet out to sea, swayed from side to side.

Luke Carré waited next to a grubby dinghy. He waved at her as she descended the final few steps onto the beach.

'Are we both going to fit in here?'

'It's a bit snug, but we're not going far.' Luke took off his shoes and threw them into the boat. She did the same. The two of them dragged the dinghy down to the shore. He held it steady, ankle-deep in the water, while she climbed in.

Luke manoeuvred the oars into place. He pulled them through the water with ease and they moved rapidly, arriving at the motorboat in a matter of minutes. At Luke's request, Jenny got out first, pulling herself up a loosely secured ladder before throwing back a line, which he tied on to the tender, leaving it floating behind the main boat. He took the ladder rungs two at a time and the boat swayed, not quite settling once he was on board. The swell was more noticeable here, though they were only a short distance from the shore. She felt the first drops of rain, fat and slow.

'I think Rosie might have been right.' He put a hand out onto the cabin roof, steadying himself. 'Weather is coming in.'

'Should we go back?'

He shook his head. 'Practically halfway there now,' he joked. 'We'll be fine. Might be a bit choppy, that's all.'

He stood in front of the wheel, turned the key in the ignition. The boat's engine growled feebly. He pushed the throttle forward. Jenny held on to the side, feet dropping away from her as the boat dipped and rose through the waves, a heavy mist of sea spray soaking her face and bare arms, the wind whipping her hair into a frenzy, stinging her eyes so she could hardly see where they were going. It was exhilarating and she laughed, sat down heavily, pulled her hair out of her eyes.

It was past nine and the sky was overcast, but it was still not fully dark. Here and there, cracks in the cloud cover revealed splashes of colour, the apricot glow of a setting sun. Just out of the shelter of Dixcart Bay, the land swept inwards, swallowed by the gaping Convanche Chasm on their right-hand side. Jenny could make out the railings of La Coupée hundreds of feet above them. Luke swung the boat out in a wide arc, following the lie of the land. She could see the chimneys of the silver mines on the headland now, and below, a series of rocky fingers reaching out into the ocean.

'Are you all right?' Luke shouted above the noise of the engine.

'I'm great. This is a much better way to travel than the Sark ferry.'

'Wait until we get out of the way of the rocks. I'll show you what she can really do.' He grinned. 'Actually, she doesn't go much faster than this. She's years old and had a bit of engine trouble. But you were impressed for a minute, eh?'

'Very. This is fast enough. How long will it take to get back?'

'Half an hour. Maybe less. Do you want to make some tea?' He pulled back on the throttle. 'There's a kettle down there.' He pointed down the steps towards the tiny cabin. 'Or I can do it, if you want to have a go?'

'God, no. Thanks. I never did learn to navigate properly. We'd end up in Jersey with me at the helm.'

'Shit. Not Jersey. That would be terrible,' he joked. 'You should definitely stick to making the tea.'

She had to duck her head to get into the dark cubbyhole of a cabin. She found a light switch. A single bulb flickered dimly in the ceiling. On one side, a counter held a small plastic kettle on a non-slip mat, next to a sink. On the other, a bench obviously used as a bed, with a pillow and a neatly folded blanket.

'You sleep here?' she called up.

'Sometimes. When I visited Dad. I don't like staying at the house. Didn't like staying there,' he corrected himself. 'Even before.'

She found two mugs stowed under the work surface, both faded and chipped, and teabags in a plastic pot.

'Do you have any milk?'

'Powdered. I don't have a fridge. I just got some more. It's in one of the bags at the end of the bed.'

She found two hessian shopping bags and a black holdall. She steadied herself, one hand on the wall. It was always unsettling below decks; down here, there was a disconnect—a domestic scene, a kitchen, a bed, thrown around unnaturally. It confused the senses. Made her feel sick.

She found the powdered milk and a packet of biscuits in one bag. The other was full of beer. The holdall was partially unzipped. She looked behind her. The bottom of Luke's legs were visible on the deck above. He was still at the helm. She opened the bag. Diving gear. Gloves. Flippers.

Black mask.

She lifted it out of the bag. It was larger than a snorkel mask, the rubber extending up onto the forehead and down over the nose. The lenses were wide and bug-like. Just like the one in Arthur's drawing of the Beast Man.

The kettle clicked.

Luke Carré had been in Guernsey when his father was murdered. She had checked with Michael after she had first met Luke—it was a professional responsibility—and a personal one too. He had an alibi, Michael had confirmed. Luke Carré was not a suspect in his father's death.

She dropped the mask back into the bag. Turned to make the tea. Noticed that the boat had slowed even further; the engine had quieted.

She carried the mugs up to the deck, glad that the motion of the boat disguised the shaking of her hands. Luke was sitting. It was cooler now, the rain heavier. He pointed ahead, to where the clouds were darkest. A flash of lightning.

'Shouldn't we hurry?'

'It's miles away yet.' A distant rumble of thunder. The wind gusted around them. He looked at her, eyes glinting.

'It's for spear fishing. The stuff you were looking at.'

Her cheeks burned. 'I shouldn't have been looking at your things. Sorry.'

He kept staring at her, as if searching her face for something.

'We need to get going, or go back.' Little Sark was behind them, Brecqhou scarcely more than a dark shadow on their right. 'We're never going to make it before dark. Or the storm.' A hint of the rising panic she felt broke through into her voice.

'It's not what you think,' he said softly.

She took a step backwards. With the rise and fall of the water beneath them, the boat climbed, then dipped, each time a little more forcefully. She swore as she spilled hot tea over her hand.

'It doesn't matter what I think. Only the facts matter.' He had to see her as an ally, not a threat. Until they got off this boat, he had to believe that she was his friend.

'And what are the facts, Jennifer?'

'You're not a suspect. You have an alibi. You have nothing to worry about. Not from me, not from the evidence.'

He laughed. 'I do have an alibi. You're right about that. The rest of it, I'm not so sure about.' He stood. She pressed herself against the side of the boat.

With the engine cut, they had drifted, the current sweeping them towards the Gouliot Passage, the narrow channel between Brecqhou and Sark. The sun had disappeared, leaving only an afterglow, light's shadow, playing on the horizon. The hull creaked. Sark loomed behind them. *Dark Sky Island*. No street lights. No streets, not over on this side. She couldn't even remember if there were any houses. Think. *Think*. There was a small hotel. Twenty minutes' walk from Havre Gosselin, the tiny harbour on the other side of the passage. Too far for anyone to hear her scream.

They were drifting closer to the passage, and to the rocks on either side of the opening.

'Luke. You need to get back to the helm. Start the engine. Get us out of here. Or it won't matter what anyone thinks.'

He didn't seem to hear her, and as the last remaining natural light died, the warmth on the horizon extinguished by the turning of the earth, he became a shadow—dark and expressionless—the dim glow of the cabin behind him failing to illuminate his face.

'Luke, what are you doing? You need to take us back.'

'What's the point?' Angry. Reckless.

'We'll be smashed on the rocks if you don't get us out of here! Or let me.' She made a move towards the helm.

'No.' He didn't even raise his voice. She could hear the waves breaking on the rocks now, but could see nothing, not even shapes or shadows, just black. It was difficult to keep a steady footing, the deck shifting beneath her feet, and slippery now, as the rain continued to fall. Her hip banged painfully against the side and she grasped on to it, stopping herself from going head first into the deep.

And then. To their left. A twinkle.

Brecqhou.

There were lights on Brecqhou.

The Mansion.

She was a strong swimmer. Went out in all seasons. She could deal with the cold; she could even deal with the swell, although it was stronger now than anything she had attempted to swim through before.

She was not sure she could deal with the dark.

The alternative was to get past Luke, to wrestle the throttle from him. But she was no match for him physically. He had not, so far, shown any signs he planned to harm her. But right now his were not the actions of a stable man. And the mask. His reaction to her seeing it. Like he'd been found out. She could only assume that he had killed his father. That his lack of violence towards her was a temporary state. She had to act accordingly. She had to get away.

There was only one way to do that.

A sickening scraping and tearing.

The jolt to the boat flung her forwards, straight into Luke, who seemed to wake out of a trance.

'Shit!' He grabbed at her, falling backwards as he did so. They both hit the deck. She scrambled to get up, but the boat jolted in the other direction. Water seeped through her shoes, weighing her down. She kicked them off. The light in the cabin flickered. Luke hauled himself up, grabbed the throttle, jerked at the keys. The engine sputtered to life. He was going to save them. Or at least try. Their only chance was Havre Gosselin. They might be able to make it that far. He turned back to her. He could see her, in the dim cabin light, but he was still in shadow, his expression unreadable. There was something in the way he stood, though. Something desperate.

Hopeless.

Dangerous.

At the next jolt, he stumbled. She slammed against the side of the boat. The side nearer to Brecqhou. To the lights.

The engine whined. She could hear him cursing. Water sloshed at her ankles. The next jolt, the next fall might break something. And if Luke got them out of this, where would he take her? What would he do?

She relaxed her grip. *Breathe.* And with the next roll of the boat towards the ocean, she let go.

Plunged into the deep.

Cold. Sharp, breath-stealing cold.

Silence.

No. Not silence. An absence of familiar sound. Ears and nose filled with saltwater. Echoes. The crash of the waves turned inside out. Muffled. Diminished. Comforting. She was cocooned, wrapped in the very thing that wreaked havoc just a few feet above, the swell reduced to a gentle swaying and rocking. The cold soothed her aching limbs. She had so often sought solace in the water. It wasn't the first time she'd thought how much easier it would be to stay down here.

A burning at the back of her throat.

A slow, steady trickle of saltwater.

She opened her eyes.

Twisted, panicked, focused on the glint of light.

The jump had winded her, the slap from the water's surface as she plummeted through as painful as any fall to the ground. Her lungs begged for air, for an intake of breath. Her brain screamed back, *Keep your mouth shut.*

Up. She had to swim up.

She kicked, hard, threw her arms down.

Broke the surface.

She'd been under only seconds, but she gulped down the air as though she hadn't breathed in days, coughing and gagging as more water washed over her. She had to swim, to work up some momentum, before the waves overpowered her. She trod water as best she could, battered one way, then pulled the other by sparring currents. Saw the light from the cabin, the boat, listing, bathed a sickly yellow, and Luke, a frenzied silhouette, first at the helm, then screaming over the side.

'Jenny! Jenny!' He sounded frantic. Broken.

Perhaps she'd got it all wrong—he was mixed up in all this some-how but not a killer. He thought she'd fallen, was desperate to save her.

Or maybe he knew she'd jumped. Maybe he wanted to make sure she was dead.

She dipped under. And again. Each time it was harder to get back up, each breath she took shallower than the one before, her limbs heavy, starved of oxygen.

She focused on the lights, still glinting on Brecqhou. On a calm day, she figured it was a fifteen-minute swim away. Today, perhaps thirty. If she made it at all. She struck out. Stayed clear of the feeble ring of light surrounding the boat. Luke's screams faded as she covered ten, twenty, thirty feet. The darkness intensified. Thickened.

But there was no room for fear.

Every cell in her body was focused on battling the waves and win-ning, making it to land, to warmth, to light.

Her only hope was Corey Monroe.

33

Michael

He was in a cell. They'd overpowered him. It wasn't hard, the state he was in. They'd retied his hands. Gagged him. Dragged him. He remembered the weight of a blanket over his head, the slamming of a door. They'd locked him in here. In the prison. It was part of the plan, to convince everyone that it was he, Michael, who was the criminal. They were going back to clean up. To destroy the evidence. Then they were going to deal with him. Tanya didn't know how. She hadn't said that, but Michael could tell, could hear the uncertainty in her voice even as she'd barked out orders to the two men who seemed entirely in her thrall.

He shook uncontrollably, which increased the pain in his side. He was exhausted, felt like every last drop of life had drained out of him. He looked down, to the wound in his gut. His shirt was covered in blood, but the flow had reduced to a trickle. Fallaize had given him a tea towel. Balled it up, told him to hold it there. Michael wasn't sure if he'd been trying to help or to minimise the mess made in Tanya's living room. Either way, he had probably saved Michael's life. Not for long. Michael was sure now that this was how it ended. Old and weak, trussed and gagged on a prison-cell floor. Not how he'd imagined it.

But then, nothing in his life had been quite how he'd imagined. There'd been a time when he'd had it all. A beautiful wife and daughter.

Seemed so long ago now. Sheila, at least, was happy. She deserved to be. He'd done a good thing, letting her go. Moving on. He groaned. Pathetic, lying to himself, even now, pretending he'd ever moved on. The closest he'd come to feelings for another person was Margaret Dorey, and even then he'd held himself back, because she wasn't Sheila. Jenny wasn't Ellen.

Footsteps. Outside. Michael moaned. The gag cut into the corners of his mouth, but he ignored the pain, tried to open wider, to moan louder.

The door rattled. The padlock being unlocked.

'Shut up!' It was a panicked hiss. 'I'll help you if you shut the fuck up!'

Michael struggled to focus. The light flooded in from the narrow corridor outside the cell. It was Martin Langlais.

Michael moaned again, quieter this time, shook his head from side to side. *Undo the gag.*

'No,' Langlais whispered. 'It stays on.' He looked behind his shoulder. 'We've got ten minutes, fifteen at most. I'm supposed to be checking on you. Waiting for the other two.'

Michael narrowed his eyes, questioning without words. This didn't make sense. If Langlais wanted out, he could have just run.

'I'm not a part of this. I knew about the drugs, same as most people. She paid me not to say anything. That's it. The rest is madness. I'll take you as far as the doctor. Then you're on your own.'

He helped Michael to his feet. Michael groaned, long and low as the full extent of the pain wracking his body made itself known.

'It's late. There's nobody about. But if you try to get anyone's attention, I'm dragging you straight back here, you hear me?'

Michael nodded.

'I could have just left. You know that? You'll tell them? That I helped you?'

That was it. Langlais wanted brownie points. Something he could use to mitigate his involvement in this. Michael swayed. Tried to express just a tiny amount of the contempt he felt for Langlais through the weight of his stare. Nodded.

'Let's go. Keep your head down.'

Michael felt the sting of sand and dust on his face as soon as he stepped outside. The streets were pitch-black and deserted. They passed houses, the odd one with the cold glow of a television screen escaping from between closed curtains. The further they went, the fewer houses they saw. Langlais used his phone as a torch, but only long enough to illuminate the way for a second or two each time before switching it off.

It started to rain, just a few drops at first, but soon his face was wet and it was even harder to see where he was going. Michael felt like he was walking through treacle, Langlais's tall, lean frame struggling to take the burden of his weight. They moved slowly, covering only a few feet a minute. Michael, with his hands bound behind his back, unable to reach out, to feel his way through the night, stumbled and swayed. He tried to remember where the doctor had said his house was. Up by La Moinerie. Far. They had been walking for twenty minutes or so when Michael finally stopped.

He was never going to make it.

'Fuck are you doing?' Langlais shone the phone on him.

Michael stayed still. Groaned through the gag. *Untie me.*

'Keep moving!' Langlais had to raise his voice to be heard over the wind.

He shook his head. *No.*

'What the fuck? I'll fucking leave you here.'

Michael moaned again. *Go ahead.*

'Shit. Shit.' Deep breath. 'They'll know by now. That I let you go. There's no time to fuck around.'

Michael shrugged.

'You make one sound and I swear you'll die here.'

Hands on Michael's face as Langlais fumbled to untie the gag.

'Fuck.' It came out as a hoarse whisper. The movement pulled at the corners of his lips, which were bloody and sore. He opened and closed his mouth, caught some rainwater, swallowed, tried to work it into his dry throat. 'It's too far.'

'It's less than a mile away.'

'Too far for me. Take me to the nearest house. We'll call the doctor from there.'

There was a long pause.

'What is it?' Michael coughed. Felt like he was being stabbed all over again. 'You've helped me, but you'll not get much credit for it if I'm too dead to tell anyone. Just dump me at a house and then run. Or stick around. It will look better for you in the long run.'

'I don't know who I can trust.'

'What do you mean?'

'The doctor. He's only been here a few months. He won't be on the payroll. Not yet. The rest of them . . . Anyone could be working for her. She has people. Watching. Listening. Everywhere. We turn up at the wrong house, she'll get a call.'

Michael couldn't believe it. 'You're paranoid, man!'

'He's not.'

They had failed to hear his footsteps above the storm. Fallaize's hand was wrapped in bloody bandages, and in it he no longer held a shard of glass but a knife, the wide blade glinting in the trembling light from Langlais's phone.

34

Jenny

She struck solid rock again. This time, she grabbed at it wildly, managed to get a hold. Pulled herself close to it. She was numb to the pain but knew that her body was covered in scrapes and bruises. It was only luck that she hadn't been dashed to pieces—luck and the fact that the water was calmer here, in the relatively sheltered channel between the two islands. The wind had dropped too. Not much, but enough that the waves were now only smashing into her face, not totally immersing her as they had when she'd first jumped in.

The jetty on Brecqhou was tantalisingly close. Two security lamps stood like sentries at the end, beacons in the darkness, throwing an eerie, silver glow on the surrounding water. In daylight, she might have had half a chance of reaching it overland—scrambling over the rocks, clinging to the coast or clambering up onto the headland—but under the cloak of night, it would be impossible. She had no way of knowing how high the cliffs were here, for a start. If she fell, she might break her neck, tumble into the sea, sink into the depths, fragments of her bones washed up with the sand in centuries to come.

She tightened her grip on the rock, not wanting to let go, instinctively feeling that the water was far more dangerous than the land but knowing that she had to get back in. No one was coming to rescue her. The only person who knew she was in trouble was Luke. And she was pretty sure he wasn't going to send out a search party. If he even could. She strained to see behind her, back out towards the open water, looking for any sign of his boat. She'd listened to his shouts, heard the engine splutter, but the sounds had soon been drowned out by her gasps, her ragged breathing, her pounding heart.

Her fingers ached with cold. Maybe if she screamed, they'd hear her at the Mansion. Maybe. But what if Luke was floating out there, lights off, engine cut, just waiting for her to do exactly that? The more she strained her ears, the more she became convinced that she could hear the creaking of wood, the slapping of the waves against a hull, the faint, rhythmical clinking of cleats and carabiners. As she stared out into the blackness, she thought that yes, she could see him—there was movement out there, coming towards her, closer, closer now, a rush of warm air, the lightest touch, an unearthly, strangled cry—and then she did scream, a pathetic, rasping scream, her throat burned by seawater, and it was far fainter than that of the gull that brushed her as it flew by and, no doubt terrified, broke into hysterical screeching and chattering.

She shook herself. So long as she kept up momentum, she could make it. With as much force as she could muster, she threw herself away from the rock, back into the channel.

The water aided her now. She felt it pulling her through the passage between the two islands. She just had to get herself out of it before it swept her back out to open sea. She started towards the jetty, but the current was too strong; it carried her, rushed her into the pool of light and through to the other side. If she didn't get out soon, she was done for. Already her strokes were weak and ineffective, barely keeping her head above water. She should have stayed on the rock, or better still, she should have stayed on Sark until morning. She should have left the pub without drinking too much, without leaving garbled messages on Michael's phone, without agreeing to a boat ride with a virtual stranger. And as she weakened further, she made a silent plea, sent it out into the night, that if she got through this, she would do something with her life, something good.

She slipped under. Held her breath. Water in her nose, pooling at the top of her throat. Chest aching. Pressure building.

Drowning was supposed to peaceful—that's what they said—but this was chaos and panic and pain. She thrashed and gagged, surfaced, just for a second, just enough for a gasp, half air, half water, then under again, deeper, darker, and it was like her soul was fighting to break out of her body, pushing from the inside out, and every part of her burned and ached until she had no choice but to open her mouth, to set it free.

35

Michael

'**W**alk.'

There was no way they could take him on: Michael was too weak, his hands still tied behind his back, and Langlais was too much of a chicken shit. They'd both end up dead.

'What are you doing, Fallaize?' Michael rasped. 'You must know your only hope now is to turn yourself in. Failing that, just run, man. Go on, just leave us. Let Martin get me to the doctor. We won't raise the alarm, will we, Martin?'

Langlais shook his head.

'Where's Tanya, eh? What has she told you? That you're all going to play happy families? She's going to try to pin all this on you—you know she is.'

'She won't need to. There'll be nothing to pin on anyone. Not once you and Langlais are gone.'

'You think the police force are going to stop a murder investigation just because I disappear? You know better than that Fallaize. They'll get to the bottom of what happened to Reg, with or without me.'

'I had nothing to do with that. Neither did Tanya.'

'Like hell she didn't.'

'I've no reason to lie to you. Tanya went to Reg's house that morning. Presume that's how the kid ended up there. He's always following

243

her around. Reg did a lot of work for the business, going years back. He was losing his marbles, she was worried he would talk. But he was dead when she got there.'

Michael shook his head. 'She's got you right where she wants you, doesn't she? How do you know she was telling you the truth? And what do you mean Reg worked for her going back years? She been running this since she was a kid, has she?'

'It's a family business.'

Michael tried to process what that could mean. 'Family? Like who?'

Langlais whimpered. 'Please, stop. Let me go, Richard. I won't say anything, I swear. You can trust me. Years I've kept quiet about all this—'

Fallaize's fist came out of nowhere. Langlais cried out, fell to the ground, dropped his phone, clutched his nose.

A whisper. 'That's how much I trust you, Langlais. Now get the fuck up and walk.' He stamped on the phone, crushing it under his foot, then took a flashlight out of his pocket and shone it on the road ahead.

Langlais went first, cradling his face in his hands. Michael followed, dragging his feet, slower and slower until he felt the prick of sharp steel in his back.

'Hurry up.'

'I'm going as fast I can.' He coughed, struggled to catch his breath. 'I was done in already by the time you got here.' It was true. It took all the energy he could muster to stay upright, never mind move, but Fallaize dug the knife a little deeper into the small of Michael's back, and from somewhere, he gathered the strength to put one foot in front of the other.

He tried to get a proper measure of where they were. Fallaize kept the light close to the ground. A rough pathway. It was flat and straight. He saw glimpses of grass on their right and felt, instinctively, that the land there was open. A field. Damn cloud cover. On a clear night, the light from the stars, a crescent moon would be enough to see by.

'What's that?' Langlais sounded congested. Michael suspected a broken nose. Or perhaps he'd been crying.

244

'What's what?'

'I heard something up ahead.'

They stopped. Fallaize lifted the torch. Shone it left and right. There were trees. Woodland. Michael knew where they were. The path to Port du Moulin. The Window in the Rock.

'Nobody there. Keep moving.' Fallaize moved on.

Langlais stayed still. Michael slumped forward, onto his knees.

'There's nobody there, I said—come on!'

'I can't.' Michael's shoulders ached with the strain of being twisted behind him. The rope round his wrists burned. The wound in his side still bled. And his head. The throbbing in his head, like the waves pounding the shore, relentless, all-encompassing. He closed his eyes. Drifted.

Pulling. Dragging. Langlais had one of his arms, Fallaize the other. They manhandled him into the woods, where the trees closed in around them so the path became more uneven, gnarled and knotted with roots, dislodged slate and granite shifting underfoot. Was it really so quiet, Michael wondered, or could he no longer hear? It was so peaceful. Or it would be, if not for the pain. It filled the silence. Each stab of it like the cracking of a twig inside his head. One, then another and another, until it was all around him, a cacophony of cracking twigs, and he wanted to put his hands to his ears, but he couldn't, so he closed his eyes, gave in to the darkness.

36

Jenny

Charlie didn't feel like swimming today. He hadn't felt like going to the beach, complained of too many grockles and too much sand, said he spent all week on the water, had had enough of it by the weekend. But Jenny had nagged him, and Margaret had said she wouldn't mind a couple of hours to get the house sorted, so he'd sighed, tried to persuade Jenny a walk at the reservoir would be more fun. She'd begged and pleaded for the beach and sensed his resolve weakening, so she'd run and put her bathers on before he could change his mind.

Now he was standing ankle-deep, newspaper tucked under one arm, the other hand shading his eyes, watching her, calling her back whenever he thought she was going too far out, which was often, even though she was a good swimmer, the best in her class, better even than the best boy. Not faster—he could beat her in a race—but she could go further. Ten lengths of the pool without stopping. She was the only one who could do that. And now she wanted to try to swim the length of Pembroke. It was much too far, she knew that, but if she was going to do it before she was ten, she needed to start training. But Charlie wouldn't let her go deep enough.

She stood and looked longingly out at the grown-ups, bobbing about way out to sea, where their feet definitely couldn't touch the bottom, which was much better, Jenny thought, because you never knew what you were standing on out here, and one of her friends had got spiked by a weever fish last week and said it hurt more than when she went to the doctor for her jabs, so Jenny definitely did not want to do that.

She waved to Charlie. Perhaps he would come in after all and play sharks and minnows with her. But there was someone with him now. One of the friends he played cards with. They were talking. They weren't watching her. She looked back out to sea. It would only take her a few seconds, thirty maybe, to get out to the proper swimmers. One lady, wearing a bright yellow swimming cap, was cutting through the water like scissors, arms like blades, up and down, head twisting shoreward every other stroke, so that Jenny saw a quick flash of her face, eyes covered in goggles, nose clipped. Jenny could follow her. Copy her movements. See if she could keep up. Just for a minute or two. Just while Charlie was talking.

She lifted her feet. She was standing in a warm patch, but her body had dried in the sun and the water was icy against her chest and shoulders. Cold on top, warm on the bottom. It felt funny. She went under to get her face and hair wet so she would be more streamlined. She opened her eyes. The water here was supposed to be very clean, but it looked murky, a soupy green with little bits of seaweed and sand whirling around in it. She peered at the seabed. She wished she had goggles so she could see properly. No sign of weever fish. She wasn't sure what they looked like, in actual fact, but imagined they must have sharp fins, like tiny sharks, which they stuck out of the sand waiting for a poor child's foot to spike.

The water stung her eyes, so she surfaced. Checked Charlie was still distracted (he was) and then looked for the professional swimming lady. (Jenny had decided she must be at least a Guernsey Swimming Club champion, if not a Channel Island one, with all that kit and such a confident technique.) She found her. She'd already swum quite far in the few moments that Jenny had been underwater, so Jenny wasted no time trying to catch up. She put her head down and did front crawl, but found it was quite difficult to keep in a straight line, much more difficult than in the pool. It was because of the currents, which Jenny knew all about: Charlie was always going on about them and how if you knew where they were, it helped you to find the fish. They could be dangerous too. People got swept away in them. She felt a tingle then, in her tummy. A little wriggle of nerves. She twisted in the water. She was further away from the shore than she'd ever been. Further, even, than the lady in the yellow swimming cap, who seemed to be heading back to the beach now. Charlie still hadn't spotted her, thank goodness. She would swim as fast as she could and get dried, and they would get an ice cream, and she would do some more training in the pool before she tried anything like this again.

She pushed forwards, arms nice and streamlined like her teacher had shown her. Head down. Straight to shore. Five strokes. Ten. Twenty. She didn't seem to be any closer to shore. In fact, if anything, she thought she might be a little further away. She put her head down again. Thirty strokes. Forty. Tired. She stopped again. And now Charlie had seen her. He was waving. But not in a friendly way. In a frantic way. She was too far away to make out his face, but she could tell he was cross. He wanted her to come back in. Charlie was pointing towards the tower on the headland. He was shouting, but she couldn't hear what he was saying, and now there were more people with him, and Jenny's cheeks burned and her eyes watered because everyone could see she'd messed up and that her dad was angry with her, and she hated making mistakes. She would act like everything was fine when she got back to the beach. She would keep swimming now until she got there.

Head down. Arms aching. Water tickling her nose. She needed a clip, like the lady. And goggles and a swimming cap. Then she would be fine, she was sure of it. She started to cry with the frustration. That was when she gulped down her first mouthful of seawater, and that was when she really panicked, started thrashing and yelling, until, out of nowhere, she felt a weight against her, like some great sea monster had attacked her, only instead of eating her, or dragging her down to its watery lair, it threw an arm round her neck and pulled her, sideways, parallel to the beach, towards the loophole tower, and suddenly they were floating. The water had lost its power over her.

Charlie let her go. They bobbed about for a few seconds. He looked furious, she thought. And terrified.

'Can you make it back?'

'I think so.' Her throat was thick with mucus and salt.

'Follow me.'

He swam in front of her, slowly, deliberately, turning his head to check on her every few feet. It was only when he got out that she realised he was fully clothed. Someone wrapped a towel round her; it was thin and scratchy and smelled of other people's washing powder. Someone got them both a cup of tea, the first one she'd ever had, milky and sweet. It made her feel sick, but she didn't say anything, because she'd caused enough trouble already.

That evening, Charlie explained what a rip current was. Told her that even the strongest swimmer would struggle against one. That the first thing you should do if you found yourself trapped was yell for help. If nobody came, you had to swim out of it, one side or the other. Never try swimming against it. You couldn't win and the tiredness, that's what would kill you. If it was really strong, he said, if you couldn't escape it, you had to let it carry you. It might be fifty feet long; it might be a thousand, but eventually, it would come to an end. You'd feel it lose its grip on you. Then you could find another path back to the shore.

He bent over her. 'Not a word to your mother,' he whispered.

She nodded. They both knew that Margaret would probably stop Jenny swimming for good if she found out about this, never mind the fact that Charlie would have hell to pay for taking his eye off her.

'And you'll remember what to do if it ever happens again?'

She nodded. 'I'll remember.'

He brushed her nose with his knuckle. Kissed her on the cheek.

'I'll have a few more grey hairs tomorrow because of you, Jenny Wren.'

The grip loosened. She felt the pull subside, the movement slow, the din quiet.

Underwater.

Seconds. Minutes.

Calm. No fight left. This must be the peace they talked about. There was nothing left to fear. The worst had already happened.

Pictures. Bright colours. A flood of images, of memories. Walking in the woods. A Sunday roast. A bedtime story. Leaving for university. Mum crying. Wet streets. An abandoned car. A bunker.

Black. Black. *Black*. But no panic. Just acceptance.

And then a light in the darkness. A speck at first. She thought of the anglerfish with its lure. But this was bigger. Brighter. Coming towards her. An angel, come to save her. She told her legs to move. To kick. They responded, half-heartedly. She drifted towards it.

Not an angel.

A ghost.

She reached out to touch him. To stroke his cheek. Cold fingers on cold flesh. He smiled. She closed her eyes.

And suddenly they were standing at the water's edge on a warm summer's day, breathing the sweet, fresh air. She saw a bright yellow swimming cap. Felt a rough towel. Swallowed a mouthful of sweet, milky tea.

You'll remember what to do?

She nodded. I'll remember.

She opened her eyes. He still smiled, but as she stared at him, his face seemed to bloat, his skin to loosen, and she pulled her hand away, and with it, a chunk of his flesh, exposing pale bone beneath, and his eyes were empty sockets, gaping black holes, and she could see inside his skull and it was filled with tiny, wriggling fish, which burst out in a stream of silver, darting around her, working their way under clothes and through her hair, and she screamed, soundlessly, endlessly, kicked and thrashed until she felt a weight against her, an arm round her neck, and it dragged her, still screaming, up, up into the sweet, fresh air.

*

Corey Monroe looked different. Less threatening. Perhaps it was the fact he was wearing checked pyjama bottoms and a loose-fitting T-shirt, his hair ruffled as if he'd been sleeping. Perhaps it was because he'd picked her up off the jetty, shouting a string of confused expletives, and carried her into the house, setting her down on a sofa, wrapping her in a thick white towel.

She shook. Struggled to hold steady the cup of steaming liquid he had given her. She put it down, fearful of making more mess. She'd vomited what appeared to be gallons of seawater over the carpet as soon as she'd sat up, and she presumed that the blood was hers too. She had yet to feel the sting of the deep cuts on her arms and legs. The soles of her feet were ripped to shreds, but the skin was still swollen, loose and bloodless. She shuddered at the thought of what she'd seen down there. What she'd dreamed, she corrected herself. Or hallucinated. Because none of it had been real.

'What the hell happened to you?'

'Fell off a boat.' It was little more than a whisper and was followed with another bout of coughing. She hunched over, spat up yet more water. 'Sorry.'

'Wouldn't worry. He can afford a new carpet.' Jenny started at the familiar voice. Turned to see Tuesday Jones, barefoot and wearing a dressing gown, come into the room. Margot, Monroe's assistant, followed.

'I'm having Ms Jones's clothes dried. Can I get anyone anything else?' Her tone was just-another-day-at-the-office bright and breezy. Jenny thought about the rumours the waitress in Sark had mentioned. She wondered what other weird and unexpected situations Margot had had to deal with.

'You wouldn't have some cigarettes, would you, love? Mine got a bit damp.'

'I'll be right back.' She smiled.

'Very kind.' Tuesday sat opposite Jenny, put her feet up on the sofa. 'Lush here, isn't it?

'What are you doing here?' Jenny croaked.

251

'She pulled you out of the water. Dragged you halfway to the house. At which point, I heard her screaming and ran out to see what the fuck was going on. I carried you the rest of the way.'

Jenny pulled the towel tightly around herself. 'How did you know where I was? What were you doing out there?'

'I was out on the RIB, planning a new route for a tour. It was getting rough. I was about to turn round when I saw a boat. We all know there's no right of way past Mr Monroe's house. Thought I'd better check things out. I was just being a good neighbour.' Corey threw a look in her direction.

Margot returned with a packet of cigarettes and a lighter. Tuesday lit up. Monroe took one. Tucked it behind his ear.

'As I was saying, I turned into the passage. Lost sight of the boat. I was just about to go back when I saw you. You're a bloody strong swimmer. Practically launched yourself at the RIB. I hauled you out. Brought you here. Now, I think the question that needs to be answered is, what were *you* doing out there?'

Jenny had no way of knowing if she could trust Tuesday Jones. And she suspected she could definitely not trust Corey Monroe. But she was out of options. She told them what had happened. When she finished talking, nobody spoke.

'Well?' Jenny asked.

Tuesday shook her head. 'I don't know anything about Luke Carré, not really. Seen him around over the years, every now and then. Know the story, his mum disappearing and that. Maybe he killed his dad. Not who I would have put my money on, though.'

'Who *would* you have put your money on?'

'Tanya Le Page.'

'Why would Tanya Le Page kill Reg Carré?'

'Because he was becoming a liability. She was worried he was going to talk.'

'About what?' Jenny felt like the water had swollen her brain too, making it slow and heavy.

'Drug running.'

'But that's ridiculous.' The thought of Tanya Le Page, frail and worried, running drugs, let alone killing anyone was preposterous. Except . . . hadn't Jenny detected an edge, a steeliness beneath the surface? And the fact that Tanya did not want Arthur to talk to the police, to describe the killer. Jenny had assumed it was a mother's protective instinct, but what if she was only trying to protect herself?

'How does this work? Who else knows about it?'

'She has a fair amount of Sarkees on her payroll for sure. I reckon the drugs come in from France, are dropped off in Sark and then from there taken to Guernsey, Jersey, the mainland. I'm betting it was one of her guys found those bones. They use the caves to hide the gear.'

'How do you know all this?' Jenny asked.

Tuesday shrugged. 'I don't, not for sure. But I'm out on the water all the time. I see things—boats that look a bit out of place. Saw a couple of guys on the rocks at Derrible a couple of months ago. It was the crack of dawn. They didn't look like they were over on a daytrip.'

'Why has nobody said anything? Why haven't you?'

'People who work for her are scared or in her pocket or both. The rest of us don't have any proof.'

'I knew something was going on.' Corey added. The pushback to bringing in reforms, to my investment in the island, people trying to keep me out of local affairs. At first, I thought it was just a small-town mentality, but the force of the resistance against me . . . I'd started to do some digging. I often do background research on people. I like to know who I'm dealing with. I have contacts, people who can find things out for me.' He threw a glance in Jenny's direction. He'd had someone look into her background, she thought. That was how he knew about the assault in London.

'What sort of contacts?'

'The sort of contacts a lot of money can buy.'

'Police?'

'Some. Some from the other side of the tracks.'

He paused. 'They haven't had much luck with this. Turns out the Sarkees are very good at keeping secrets.'

'We need to call Michael.' Jenny's voice broke above a rasp for the first time.

They both looked at her blankly.

'DCI Gilbert. We need to call him now.' She looked around for a clock. Not yet eleven. It felt like days had passed since she'd left the pub on Sark.

'He was going to talk to Tanya. He needs to know what's going on.'

'You trust him?' Tuesday asked.

Jenny nodded. 'With my life.'

Tuesday and Corey were silent, and for a moment, Jenny thought they'd tricked her after all. They were working together, and now that she'd told them everything she knew, they were going to throw her back off the jetty.

Finally, Corey spoke. 'I'll call him. Where's he staying?' His hands, Jenny noticed, were trembling.

'I don't know. Somewhere in the village. A B&B. Try the incident room at the church first. Or Tanya Le Page's house.'

He nodded and strode out of the room.

Jenny and Tuesday sat side by side in silence.

'That dressing gown fits you well. Looks exactly your size.'

'That's because it's mine.' She looked at Jenny. 'We got friendly. While he was trying to buy me out.'

'Do you trust him?' Jenny whispered.

Tuesday smiled grimly.

'I don't trust anyone, Jenny. And neither should you.'

'Police said the officers on Sark are out looking for him. There's nothing else they can do until morning.' Monroe had tried the incident room and Michael's B&B. No one had seen him since earlier that evening. At Tanya's house, the phone had rung off. Finally, Jenny had persuaded him to call Guernsey Police and report Michael missing.

Jenny shook her head. 'Something's wrong. He was going to Tanya's. He's in trouble.'

'We've done everything we can. The police know what's going on—let them do their jobs now,' Tuesday said. 'Can we get her some dry clothes? She's going to catch pneumonia.'

'We have to look for him,' Jenny insisted.

'You want to search the whole island in the dark? He could be anywhere. And it's pitch-black. We wouldn't have a chance in hell.'

'We could take the chopper.' Monroe said it like he was suggesting an evening stroll.

'Funny.' Tuesday didn't sound amused.

'I'm not joking.'

'You can't just fly over Sark whenever you feel like it. Can you?' Jenny asked.

'It's an emergency, isn't it? I'm sure I'll be able to clear up the formalities later. We can do a quick sweep with the searchlight, then land at one of the fields near Tanya's place, check it out. If he's missing, sounds like she has something to do with it. We'll be in the air twenty minutes, if that.' He looked eager at the prospect. Excited even.

'This is crazy.' Tuesday shook her head. 'I'm not getting in that thing.'

'It's me and you, then.' He looked at Jenny, eyebrows raised.

'Can you fly in this weather?'

'It'll be bumpy. But yes, I can fly in this weather.'

She stood. 'OK. Dry clothes, then let's go.'

37

Michael

When Michael finally opened his eyes, the trees had thickened and the din inside his head had quieted. The path narrowed and evidently it was a struggle to walk three abreast as Langlais stumbled over the raised edge of the pathway. He stopped.

'What's the matter?'

'I need to catch my breath.' Langlais's voice was thick. He had definitely been crying. 'I don't feel well. Pain in my arm.' His breathing was shallow.

'Jesus Christ.'

They let Michael fall forwards. The earth was cool. He could sleep now. They could leave him here, he wanted to tell them. He would be no trouble to them if they just left him here to rest. It came out as a murmur. He tried again.

'Shut up!' Langlais, sharp, urgent. 'Listen.' Michael heard him swivel. 'It's behind us now. Don't you hear it?'

Silence.

'Don't you hear it?' Langlais pleaded.

Fallaize was going to hit him again, Michael was sure of it, and he waited to hear the crack, but Fallaize stood still. He must have heard something too. Perhaps by some miracle, someone was searching for him. Suddenly Fallaize pivoted. Michael followed the light with his eyes.

The path behind them was alive with swaying shadows—it was quite possible to believe that there was someone—or something—hidden among them.

'Shit!' Langlais, scared. More so than before.

Michael strained to see.

There was something out there, on the very edge of the torchlight. The darkness seemed concentrated somehow. Denser, blacker than the rest. Fallaize lifted the torch slowly, and to Michael's exhausted eyes, to his oxygen-starved brain, the shadows seemed to merge, as though drawn to each other by magnetic force, layering one on top of the other, shifting, building but never fully taking shape.

'It's a bloody great dog,' Langlais whispered.

Michael shook his head. Tried his hardest to focus. But he couldn't see it. He heard it, though. It growled, long and low, and the sound filled him with dread.

'It's going to attack.'

'It's not going to take us all on,' Fallaize snapped, but his voice wavered. 'Just turn away slowly.'

They did. Michael braced himself, half expecting to feel the animal tearing into his back. He had come across a few dangerous dogs in his time, and numbers did little to discourage them—once their hackles were raised, you were best to get out of there sharpish. Or aim a well-placed kick. Neither of which Michael could manage right now. Instead, he was lifted roughly to his feet. Fallaize set the pace, marching down the shallow steps, each one sending a jolt of pain through Michael's side. Langlais struggled to keep up, stumbling, tripping, looking behind him, until they emerged onto soft, springy grass. The sound of waves crashing below. A glint of light over on Brecqhou. The Mansion. So close. But a channel of rough water stood between here and there, and even if he could get into it without dashing his brains out on the rocks, he could never swim it, not even on a good day, never mind in the dark with his hands bound behind his back.

They dragged him over the grass, quicker now they were no longer avoiding the trees. A flash of grey as the light bounced off granite. They stopped. Fallaize placed the torch on the ground, aimed it at the spot where Michael stood. He moved behind Michael, fumbled at his wrists until Michael's arms were free. He struggled to bring them forwards, his shoulders stiff, the movement in his hands slow. He flexed them, trying to encourage the blood flow.

'Now what?' he croaked.

'Now you go.' Fallaize picked up the light. Shone it in front of them, towards the cliff edge. 'That way.'

'You going to say I jumped? That we were taking a friendly walk and I decided I'd had enough?'

'I'm going to say you ran. Couldn't face the shame of what you'd done to Tanya. Plus lying to Dorey. Covering up her dad's death. Then there was the death of your daughter, your wife leaving you. Christ, why wouldn't you kill yourself?'

Michael laughed, a rough, hacking laugh. 'When you put it like that, maybe you have got half a chance of convincing people. But what about the stab wound? You know I'll wash up eventually. How are you going to explain that?'

'I'll fix it.'

Michael shook his head. 'You won't have a hope in hell.'

'That's not something you need to worry about, is it?'

He was stalling, Michael thought. He should be dead by now. If Fallaize really thought he could manipulate the evidence, falsify an autopsy, he would have killed him already. Throwing him off the cliffs dead would be a damn sight easier than throwing him off alive.

'You don't want to do this.'

'You know nothing about what I do and don't want.'

'You're not a killer. Charlie Dorey's death was an accident—I know that. I'm betting when you joined the police—when was it? Fifteen years ago? You were only a lad, straight out of school, I remember. You wanted to be one of the good guys, didn't you? And then Roger Wilson took you under his wing. Showed you how you could make a bit of extra money. Is that how you met Tanya? Is that how you got involved? He groomed you, mate. That's what he did—'

'Fuck off.'

'Can't. Even if I wanted to. You want me off that cliff, you're going to have to pick me up and throw me over.'

'Richard.' Michael had almost forgotten Langlais was here. 'Richard, it followed us.'

Langlais was standing very still, his attention fully focused behind them. Fallaize followed his gaze.

Michael grabbed the opportunity. He stumbled out of the torchlight. There was no way he could outrun them, not in this state. But he could hide. Fallaize yelled, but Michael kept moving, feeling the way with his hands. Grass—good; earth—good; avoid the rocks—they would be a sign that he'd gone the wrong way, that another step in that direction might be a step into nothingness, a two-hundred-foot drop to his death.

There was movement behind him, a scuffling, a strangled cry. Fallaize was going to grab him any second, or the dog was going to leap at him, rip him limb from limb with its teeth and claws. He knew he didn't really have a chance, but he wasn't going to give up without a fight.

But nothing followed him. Nobody grabbed him. He figured he'd gone a hundred feet, hoped that he was circling back towards the woods. He stopped. Tried to catch his breath. He did everything he could to swallow down the cough that threatened to give away his position, managed to stifle it with his hand.

He looked over his shoulder. Saw Fallaize, where he'd left him, standing in a pool of yellow torchlight. He was crouched, knife held out towards something in the darkness beyond. Michael saw it all as if it were playing in slow motion—Fallaize swiping, feinting, moving back, slowly, slowly. Then he stopped. Frozen. Dropped the knife. Turned. Ran. Straight through the Window in the Rock. Vanished into the black.

*

He was weak. Dying. How long had he been hiding, too scared to cry for help in case Fallaize was still out there, or worse, whatever the fuck it was that had chased him halfway off the cliff? He could make out shapes—twisting branches, shifting shadows. Noises. So many strange sounds. The creaking of the trees and pounding of the water, the fluttering of wings, an owl, maybe, or a pigeon. Insects, burrowing in the earth. And something else. Michael pressed himself against a tree. Tried to make himself invisible. Tried not even to breathe.

Beneath the night music, there was something that did not belong.

He closed his eyes.

Christ be with me, Christ within me . . .

It was getting closer. He smelled its rancid breath. He wrapped his arms around his head.

Christ behind me, Christ before me . . .

It brushed past him, ice-cold.

Christ beside me, Christ to win me . . .

He didn't believe in evil. He'd seen it at work, in deeds and actions, but it was abstract, not concrete. It didn't *exist*, not like this.

Christ to comfort and restore me.

He forced his eyes open.

Nothing there.

Of course there was nothing there.

He was losing his fucking mind.

He was going to die here, slumped against a tree, lost in the smallest wood in the British Isles, praying to be delivered from his own hallucinations.

He'd lost all sense of direction. Needed to move away from the sea. From the water. He listened for the sound of the waves. Heard the wind. Blustering. Rhythmical. Slow. Sweeping. Faster. Louder.

Light. There was light.

He staggered to his feet.

The pain was almost overwhelming, setting his ears to ringing, his vision clouding, head spinning. He lurched towards the light, crying out as the movement tugged on the wound in his side. He crashed through the trees, falling, crawling, dragging himself out of the woods and back onto the headland.

Brecqhou.

It was all lit up, the tiny island centre stage, and then the Channel and the cliffs and then the land around him, all became clear as day and he was a ghost, pale and ragged. He raised his hand, skin torn and filthy, and he knew that his rescuers were flesh and bone, just like him, but he had, for a brief moment, the most exquisite feeling that the heavens had opened, that his salvation had come straight from God.

He slipped in and out of the strangest dream. It was loud. So loud. And Ellen was there and she was worried, he could tell. She cradled his head and she was talking to him, but he couldn't make out the words and they were moving, through the air, and he felt sick with the motion and the pain, and she was crying and he wanted her to stop because he'd never been able to stand it when Ellen cried. He reached up. Patted her cheek.

''S'all right, love.'

She said something. It echoed around the roar of the engine, the chug of the propeller blades. A helicopter. He was in a helicopter.

'Will you tell her something for me, love?'

Ellen looked confused, like when he told her a joke she didn't get, and he realised she didn't know who he was talking about, because she'd never met Jenny. He felt sure they would be great friends, Jenny and Ellen. Ellen and Jenny.

'Will you tell her I'm sorry?'

She was shushing him now and he tried to sit up, to show her he was OK, but he couldn't lift his head.

'Tell her he's gone. He paid for it, in the end.'

'What are you talking about, Michael?' Her voice cut through the noise and it wasn't Ellen's.

Of course it wasn't.

'Fallaize. He paid for what he did to your dad.' The lights were bright now and the swaying settled and the roaring faded, but the sound of a siren filled the space and people were shouting and he couldn't bear it anymore.

He closed his eyes.

He could still hear Ellen crying.

Guernsey News Friday 15th July

DARK CRIME ISLAND

Sark reeling in wake of recent revelations and arrests

Mystery still surrounds murder of Reginald Carré

Twenty-nine-year-old woman in custody on unrelated drug charges

Sark constable suspected of involvement in
criminal activity found dead in woods

Guernsey detective implicated in crimes, missing, presumed dead

Police: 'Many' more arrests likely in coming days

Jennifer Dorey

Sark is reeling this week following the arrests of Luke Carré, 36, and Tanya Le Page, 29. Mr Carré, of Maple Wood, Icart Road, St Martin's, Guernsey, is suspected of brutally murdering his father, Reginald Carré, on the morning of Monday, 11th July. In a separate and apparently unrelated incident, Ms Le Page, of Beau Séjour Guesthouse, Rue de la Seigneurie, Sark, was arrested while trying to flee Sark for her role in a drug-smuggling operation organised and operated from the island. Neither suspect was granted bail, and both are being held at HMP Les Nicolles pending charges.

Police are still looking for Detective Constable Richard Fallaize. He was last seen at Port du Moulin, Sark, on the night of

Wednesday, 13th July. Police consider him dangerous and warn the public not to approach him under any circumstances.

On the same evening, Sark constable Martin Langlais, was discovered dead in the vicinity of La Moinerie, Sark. His death is not considered suspicious, although sources have confirmed that Mr Langlais was suspected of involvement in the drug smuggling ring headed by Ms Le Page.

Detective Chief Inspector Michael Gilbert, the officer in charge of the investigation, was airlifted from the scene and is recovering from a wound to the abdomen.

Anyone with information about the above incidents is urged to call Guernsey Police on 728024 or Crimestoppers on 0800 555 111.

38

Michael

Marquis brought flowers. A huge bouquet. Michael tried not to laugh, but the lad noticed the expression on his face and went beet-red.

'My mum said to bring them,' he muttered. 'I should have brought chocolate. Sorry.' He placed them on the floor, and put a manila folder, which had been tucked under his arm, on the bedside table.

'They're very nice, Stephen. Thank you. I'll get a vase in a minute.' Michael put down his book.

'How long do you have to stay home?'

'Few more days, they say. It's all a bit of a fuss over nothing. The stab wound looked worse than it was. Apparently a layer of subcutaneous fat prevented the glass from entering my abdominal cavity. Which is to say it's lucky I like the odd bag of chips. It's the concussion the doctors are worried about. They say I need to rest. I'm not going to argue. Anyway, enough about me. What's the latest?'

'Well, I know you hate anonymous tips, but seems they might be the key to putting Tanya Le Page away for a long time. It's like the flood-gates have opened. The Crimestoppers line is ringing off the hook. Nobody wants to give a name, but they've all got plenty to say. Looks like her dad started the operation. When he retired, she took over.'

'So Fallaize was right about that much, eh? A family affair. We got the father in custody?'

Marquis shook his head. 'Him and the wife took off. House looked like it had been ransacked—drawers open, clothes all over the place. They took their boat—it's one of those bloody great yachts.'

'What sort of a bloke leaves his daughter to take the rap like that, eh?'

'Sort that lets her take over his international drug-smuggling business, I suppose. We'll find him. We've requested all of his financial information, frozen his accounts—he can't run for ever.'

'What about Luke Carré?'

'The lads from search and rescue said he was just sitting there when they found him, waiting for the boat to sink. They never recovered the diving gear. Presume he chucked it overboard.'

'How did we miss the fact that he had a boat, eh? Assumed he didn't have enough time to get to Sark on the ferry, but on his own boat, he could have done it.'

'I did check actually—same time as I confirmed his alibi.'

'Well, why didn't you say anything?'

'Because he doesn't have a boat.'

'It wasn't his?'

'It belongs to a woman called Helen Groves. Luke boarded with her when he came over to Guernsey for sixth form. He says she let him use it sometimes. We've been trying to get in touch with her, but we've not had any joy. She's not reported it stolen. We'll have to charge Luke with something by the end of tomorrow or he's free to go. He's obviously lying, but with nobody placing him at the scene, no forensic evidence, we've got nothing on him.'

'You've explained it will help his case? If he talks to us now rather than waiting for us to figure out what the hell is going on? What does his advocate say?'

'The States have appointed him one, but he refuses to speak to her. This might help, though. It just came back from the lab. Confirms our suspicions as to why we've not been able to trace the mysterious Rachel Carré.' He handed Michael the folder. 'The results from the DNA testing on the bones. Familial match to Luke Carré.'

'It's her?'

Marquis nodded.

'What nightmares do we unleash on our children, eh? We've got Tanya Le Page groomed to take over a drug-running business by her father, and Luke Carré . . .' He shook his head. 'I don't even want to think about what that child might have seen. What that must do to a person.'

'You think he saw Reg kill his mother? The discovery of the bones triggered him into action all these years later?'

'Let's see if we can find out. Give us a hand, will you—bring me my shoes?' Michael shifted his legs over the side of his bed.

'What are you doing?'

'I'm coming with you.'

'You're on sick leave—are you allowed?'

Michael gave him a look.

Marquis went to fetch his shoes.

Les Nicolles Prison was in a pocket of green in an otherwise industrial area of the parish of St Sampson's, halfway between town and the bridge. The building was painted the same shade of buttermilk as the States' houses on the island, and was similar in design to a housing estate, except for the six-foot wall topped with six further feet of barbed wire that surrounded the complex.

Michael was doing his best to ignore his aching head and the bone-numbing tiredness that had settled on him five minutes after getting into Marquis's car. He was shaking, too, just a little, feeling cold despite the fact that the interview room they now sat in was obviously stiflingly hot. Marquis had little beads of sweat on his top lip.

'You all right, sir?' Marquis handed him a steaming-hot cup of tea and Michael took a grateful sip. It was thick as tar and scummy on top, but it still hit the spot.

'Fine, Marquis. Fine,' he lied. Resting at home, the wound in his side had barely bothered him. Sitting here, it felt sore and he wondered if he was pulling on the stitches. He repositioned himself, trying and failing to get comfortable in the hard plastic chair.

Marquis sat next to him. Put his own tea on the table.

'It's rough in here, isn't it? Smells like boiled eggs. And I always wonder what those splatters on the walls are.' He pointed to a dark brown patch in the corner.

Michael grimaced. 'Best not to think about it. It's supposed to make the suspect uncomfortable, not throw us off our game.'

'You think it's been done on purpose?'

'I think someone probably shat up the wall, Marquis. But it's not been repainted for a reason.'

The door behind them opened and Luke Carré was led into the room by a young female prison warden. He looked terrible. He'd had his hair cut, short and choppy. It didn't suit him. Made him look severe. Like a criminal. He wore the prison-issue outfit—shapeless trousers and a wide-fitting short-sleeved T-shirt, both in the same shade of royal blue.

'I'll be outside.' The warden smiled at them before she left. She was very pretty, Michael thought. Marquis had obviously noticed. He looked like he was about to burst into flames.

Luke sat, heavily, in the chair opposite Michael and Marquis. Eyes down. Shoulders slumped. Michael motioned to Marquis to start the tape.

'Mr Carré, before we start, I just want to remind you that you've been given the opportunity to seek legal advice from an advocate. Could you please confirm for the tape that you do not wish for an advocate to be present during this interview?'

'I don't want one.'

'Thank you. Now, if at any point you do want an advocate present or wish to speak to one, we'll stop the interview. Do you understand, Mr Carré?'

'Yes.'

Michael slid the file across the table. 'Mr Carré, I'm very sorry to inform you that the bones found on Derrible Bay are those of your mother.

Luke looked up. 'No.'

'I'm sorry, son.'

Luke picked up the file. Flicked through it. 'There must be some sort of mistake.' He turned the pages back and forth.

'The sample taken from the bones and the one we took from inside your cheek show the probability of maternity is over ninety-nine per cent.'

He shook his head. 'My mother left.'

'Did you ever see her leave the house, Mr Carré?'

He shook his head. 'No. I . . . She left when I was at school. But I remember her packing a bag the night before. She was crying. I knew that she was going to leave. She put the bag under the bed. Told me not to say anything, that everything would be all right, but I knew it wouldn't.' His voice cracked.

'But you never saw her walk out of the house? You said goodbye to her that morning, and when you got back from school, she'd gone? You don't know what happened in between. Do you, Mr Carré?'

He shook his head.

'There's been no sign of your mother since she left Sark, Luke, not that we can find. No trace of a Rachel Carré. That's probably not even her name, as it happens. We can't find any record of your parents' marriage, not at the Greffe, and your father had no paperwork in his house, no photographs.' He pointed to the file. 'Sadly, this here is the only proof she ever existed. Besides you, that is. I am sorry, son.'

Nothing.

'Did you ever look for her, Luke?'

'No.'

'Why not? Surely as you got older, you must have had some questions, must have thought about tracking her down.'

Luke did not respond.

'Unless maybe, deep down, you knew there was no point. The mind can do amazing things to protect us, Luke. It can block out traumatic memories and fill in the gaps with a version of events that are easier to process. I think you suspected all along that she was dead, didn't you? And then, when her bones were discovered, your fears were confirmed. You went to confront your dad. Things got out of hand. Perhaps you didn't mean to kill him, eh? You confess, get yourself a good advocate—maybe you'd be looking at manslaughter. Whole different ballgame.'

Luke looked at him. 'I don't have any false memories, Chief Inspector. My mother packed a bag. She left.'

Michael made it as far as the corridor outside the interview room before he had to stop. He sat where he was, on the floor, back against the wall.

'Sir, are you OK? What is it? Shall I call a doctor?'

Michael shook his head. 'I'm old and broken, Marquis. Nothing a doctor can do about that.' He patted the floor next to him.

'He seemed genuinely shocked, didn't he, that they were his mother's remains.'

'He did,' Marquis agreed, sitting next to him. 'Is it true what you said, about blocking things out? You think he might have seen his mum murdered and forgotten?'

Michael shook his head. 'I really don't know. I've read about it happening.'

'Luke was there in Sark that morning. The kid saw him.'

'Kid saw someone in diving gear that Jenny Dorey says she saw on his boat but was never recovered. That's not going to stand up in court.' Michael paused. 'But say he was there and he killed his dad. Why?'

'Either he's lying about his mum and he did it for revenge or, I don't know, money maybe? Reg had plenty and left no will—it was all going to Luke.'

'He doesn't strike me as the type. Reg was already sending him a good amount every month—if he needed more, why wouldn't Luke just ask him? And Reg was getting old; he was ill—why risk a life in prison for an inheritance that would be coming your way in the not-too-distant future?'

'Maybe he didn't do it.'

'Then why isn't he talking to an advocate, preparing a defence?'

'Could be protecting someone else.'

'Have to be someone he cared about a great deal.'

'The wife?'

'She's left him. He's got no kids. His mum's dead.'

The prison warden approached them.

'Good timing, love. Can you check something for me?'

'You all right? You can sit in one of the interview rooms if you want. Or the foyer at the front desk.'

'I just need a minute right here; then I'll be out of your hair. Can you just check if Mr Carré has had any visitors?'

She shook her head. 'He hasn't. No one apart from the advocate the court appointed and she didn't stay long. It's a bit sad.'

'What about phone calls?'

'I'll have to check on that. Give me a min.' She flashed Marquis another smile and he flushed crimson again.

'You know her?' Michael asked.

'Went to school with her, sir. Name's Kayleigh.'

'Seems nice.'

Marquis cleared his throat. 'She is, yeah. I see her at the pub sometimes. Same social group, like.'

Kayleigh returned. 'He's made three calls, all to the same number.'

'You got it there?'

'Yep. House in St Peter's. Belongs to a Helen Groves.'

39

Rachel

Three days he'd been in there. Three days and they hadn't come for her, not yet. She'd heard the voicemails, the police, asking her about the boat and would she please get in touch, but they hadn't worked it out. They can't have done or else they'd be here, battering the door down, dragging her out of the house. She'd heard Luke too, his voice wavering. 'Helen. Are you there? Can you pick up the phone, Helen?' He would understand, she thought. He must. The calls from the prison were recorded. There was nothing she could say to make him feel better. Not yet.

Now there was someone else, knocking on the door, calling through the letterbox.

'Ms Groves? Ms Groves? I'm from the *Guernsey News*. I wondered if you had a minute to talk?'

She stood behind the door, small and still, waited until the woman had gone.

What did the *News* know? she wondered. What did they want to ask her? It was only a matter of time. She felt the panic well up inside her. She balled her hands into fists, forced them into her eyes. She had to go back. Find the letters, the photographs. He wouldn't have destroyed them. He'd have hidden them. Ready to produce if she ever broke her promise. If she ever came back for Luke.

271

Poor Luke. He would be scared, but he would be strong. He'd always been so strong. Cried so much as a baby but hardly at all as a child. As soon as he could walk, he'd been happy. Grazed knees, broken toys, lost pocket money—he'd always kept his cool. Except that one time. The last time.

The silence, that was what she remembered most about that day. The silence ringing in her ears; after the screaming and the screaming and the screaming, it was all so quiet. And then the sound of his little footsteps on the lino—God, how she'd hated that lino; the pattern still haunted her dreams—and he'd heard her crying. It had frightened him. He'd tried to run away from her, from his own mother. And when she'd caught him, the look on his little face. He had burst into tears. It was the last time she'd held him properly, mother to child. Because the next time she'd seen him, he'd been a man. An almost-man. Taller than her. There was something obscene about it, she had thought, that he could have grown inside her belly and sixteen years later tower over her.

She had to go now. She'd waited long enough. Luke would keep his cool—he always did. She would find everything and destroy it, and tomorrow they would have to let Luke go and this whole, decades-long nightmare would be over. It would be just the two of them. The way it always should have been.

40

Jenny

Helen Groves left the house and got into her car. Jenny followed, at a distance. She had only wanted to talk to someone who knew Luke well, to ask what sort of person he was. She would say it was for an article, a quote about the man suspected of killing his father, but really Jenny wanted to know how she'd got it so wrong. How she'd willingly got into a boat with a killer.

It turned out nobody really knew Luke, at least nobody who would talk about it. His wife had slammed down the phone. No doubt Jenny had been one of many journalists who had tried to speak to her. His friends were vague—he was quiet; he kept himself to himself—the sort of thing everyone said about murderers after their crimes had been discovered. But then one of them had mentioned a woman Luke had boarded with as a kid. How they kept in touch. It hadn't taken much to track down Helen Groves. She would know him, Jenny thought. She would tell Jenny what a lovely man he was, how she never would have thought him capable of such things, how he was sweet and kind, and Jenny would feel better. Less duped. Less stupid.

But Helen Groves had not answered the phone. She had not answered the door. She had hidden in the front room. Jenny had seen her rush behind the door. She wanted to know what she was hiding from.

She followed her through the winding lanes of rural St Pierre du Bois and St Saviour's and into St Andrew's, where the roads widened and the traffic increased as they joined the steady flow of cars into town. At the roundabout, Helen Groves took the exit to North Beach, parking her car in a ten-hour zone. Jenny came to a stop a few spaces away. Reached for her phone.

'Jenny?' Michael sounded out of breath.

'Are you OK? Are you out?'

'Marquis took me for a drive. What's up?' He was still unsure of himself with her, despite the fact that she'd told him over and over again that she'd forgiven him, that there was nothing, really, to forgive.

'I'm fine. Maybe nothing but I went to see someone, to talk to them about Luke—'

'For God's sake, Jenny. I've told you—you made a mistake. Everyone makes mistakes.'

'Michael, I know. But she wouldn't talk to me anyway—didn't answer the door. I waited, watched the house, just felt like something was off. When she came out, I followed her to North Beach. And now she's buying a ticket to Sark.' She waited for Michael to berate her for harassing members of the public, but he was quiet. She could hear his laboured breathing. 'Michael?'

'Who is it?'

'A woman Luke boarded with when he was at school here. Name's Helen Groves.'

'Shit!' She held the phone away from her ear at Michael's exclamation. 'When does the ferry leave?'

She checked her watch. 'Half an hour.'

'Keep an eye on her. Text me when she's on the boat. I'm on my way.'

'Here?'

'To Sark.'

'Michael, you're supposed to be in bed—'

The line was already dead.

41

Michael

They heard the hammering before they reached Reg's cottage. Michael, stooped forward—the only way he could get any relief from the pain in his side—stopped at the end of the path to the common.

'How did you know she'd be here?' Marquis asked.

'Just a hunch.'

'You go round the back.' He directed the two officers who had accompanied him and Marquis on the police RIB from Guernsey. 'Keep your heads down—don't want to spook her—but be ready in case she runs when we confront her.'

They nodded, jogged ahead.

'Sir, no offence, but you don't look like you're in a fit state to confront anyone.' Marquis had been fussing since they left Guernsey. 'I can handle this.'

'I'm sure you can. But I need to be here. I can't explain why.' He didn't want to think about the reasons for this recklessness. His need to control the outcome of this investigation, to make sure nothing slipped by him. To see his final case through to its conclusion. He forced himself to stand up straight.

'Come on.'

They walked to the front door. Knocked. The hammering inside continued.

'What do you think is going on in there?' Marquis looked nervous. Michael knocked again. Pushed open the door.

The linoleum on the kitchen floor had been rolled up, exposing bare wooden floorboards, many of which had been smashed to pieces, leaving jagged-edged holes dotted all over the room, splinters of wood littering the remaining floor. Helen Groves was not there. The hammering was coming from the back of the house. One of the bedrooms.

Marquis went first; Michael followed, peering into the holes as he stepped towards the door that led to the back corridor. If she was looking for something, she obviously hadn't found it yet.

They followed the noise, past the main bedroom, where he could see through the open door that the floor here had had the same treatment as the living room. He stopped in the doorway of the spare room. The bed had been pushed to one side and a woman, presumably Helen Groves, was crouched down, back to them, attacking the floor with a particularly vicious-looking claw hammer.

'Ms Groves?'

She stopped. Didn't turn round.

'Ms Groves, I'm DCI Gilbert. This is DC Marquis. Can you put the hammer down, Ms Groves?'

She stood. Turned to them, hammer by her side. Her knuckles were white she gripped it so tightly. She looked at Michael, who was panting, sweat on his brow, bent over, hand pressed protectively over his side. Then to Marquis, who was young and fit, and who, Michael knew, was a hell of a lot braver than he looked, but perhaps, with the freckles, the mop of bright red hair, was not the most intimidating of adversaries.

'The cottage is surrounded, Ms Groves. We've two officers at the back. I've more only a phone call away. If you could just put down the hammer, tell us what you're doing here, maybe all this is unnecessary, eh? Did Luke ask you to come here, to find something for him?'

She dropped the hammer. Sank to the bed. Put her head in her hands. No tears, though. No wailing.

'What are you looking for, Ms Groves?' Michael stepped over the broken floorboards and picked up the hammer.

She took her hands away from her face. Splinters of wood clung to her hair, and her skin was grey, and her eyes—her eyes were dark and terrified. This, Michael thought, was what broken looked like. Not an ageing cop with a few stiches and a sore head but this woman. Whatever she had seen, whatever she had done, it had destroyed her.

Michael sat in the back garden surveying the house. Marquis emerged from the back door, dust in his hair, something black and greasy on his hands.

'There's no space in the roof—it's completely flat. She'd already torn up the floorboards in every room. I just had a feel around the back of the boiler, the pipes in the bathroom. It's a tiny place—we went through it with a fine-tooth comb the first time. Whatever she was looking for isn't in there.' He walked over to the guinea-pig hutch. 'Who's been feeding them?'

'One of the neighbours.'

'Shouldn't we take them to the animal shelter or something? They smell pretty bad.'

Michael joined him at the chicken wire. 'Mangy little things. Never liked them myself. Luke said they used to be his dad's pride and joy.' He stopped. 'Don't suppose anyone thought to search in here, did they?'

Marquis shook his head. 'Don't think so, boss.'

Michael opened the latch on the door to the enclosure, poked his head into the animal's sleeping quarters. The bedding of shredded newspaper was wet through and covered in droppings. Michael rapped on the wooden base, setting the guinea pigs out in the run to squealing. Definitely hollow.

'Where's that hammer?' His voice echoed in the small space, and the urine-soaked air caught in his throat. He pulled his head out and took a couple of breaths, waited for Marquis to return.

'Here.'

Michael took a few more deep breaths before sticking his head back inside the hutch. He prised one of the wooden slats with the hammer's claw. It was damp and pliable. Came up easily. He pulled up another. And another. Handed them back to Marquis. Reached into the space below. Felt earth. Gravel. Plastic. It took a bit of an effort for him to pull up the package. It was wrapped in old, thick bin liners and brown packing tape. He dropped it onto the grass at Marquis's feet.

Marquis pulled at the tape, tore at the plastic. 'Photos, boss. And looks like letters. What is all this?'

Michael walked over to the wrought-iron chair and sat, a little heavily, wincing, yet again, as the stitches in his side pulled.

'I'm hoping, Marquis, that it's all the bloody answers.'

42

Michael

'Can you confirm that you are Helen Rachel Groves of Westwood, Rue des Vinaires, St Peter's?'

Michael and Marquis sat across from Helen Groves and her advocate, Jim Bradford, an earnest and capable man in his late thirties, in the stuffy, windowless interview room at Guernsey Police Station. Advocate Bradford had loosened his tie, and both Marquis and Michael had their shirtsleeves rolled up, but Helen Groves sat stiff and straight, hands clasped together on the desk.

'Yes.'

'And can you also confirm that between the years of 1979 and 1989, you went by the name of Rachel Carré and lived at the Cottage, Rue du Fort, Sark?'

'It was never my name.' She spoke quietly.

'Can you explain?'

'I was always Helen Groves. Reg and I never married. People just assumed we had.'

'And Rachel?'

She shrugged. 'My middle name. I always preferred it. Used it for the first time when I visited Sark as a kid.' She paused. 'Not a kid. I was eighteen. It was when I met Reg.'

'What were you looking for at the cottage this morning, Ms Groves?'

'Letters. Photographs.'

Michael placed an evidence bag in front of Helen, containing a yellowed piece of paper, the writing on it faded, barely legible in places.

'Were you looking for this?'

She nodded.

'Can you tell me what it is, Ms Groves?'

'It's a letter.'

'From whom?'

'From a woman called Catherine.'

'And why did this woman called Catherine write to you, Ms Groves?'

'She wanted money.'

'What for?'

A deep breath.

'What for, Ms Groves?'

'She gave him to me.' Her voice was strong and clear now.

Michael held the letter at arm's length, squinted at the words. '"You took him from me. You need to pay."' He looked at Helen.

'I didn't take him. It wasn't like that.'

'Why don't you tell us what it was like?'

She looked at her advocate. He nodded.

'I wasn't myself. I was depressed. I'd had a miscarriage a few months previously. I was only with Reg because I was pregnant—we both knew that. After I lost the baby . . . he wanted me to stay. I did for a few months. But there was nothing for me there. There's nothing for anyone there. I left in the summer. Went back to my father's house.'

'He was a vicar.' Michael scanned his notes.

'He was. But sadly lacking in the values he preached. He didn't believe that I'd lost the baby, and even if he had . . . The church ran a charity—the Christian Pregnancy Advice Centre. He thought I did everything to spite him.'

'And this advice centre was where you met Catherine, Luke's mother?'

'She gave him to me. I'm his mother.'

'She just handed him over?' Marquis looked incredulous.

Helen's stare was cold and hard. 'She was going to have him adopted. She didn't want him. I did.'

Marquis shifted in his seat. Michael's throat was dry. He needed to lie down. He took a sip of water. Pointed at the letter. 'But then this arrived.'

'Yes. Five years later. You only read the beginning. She wanted money. She asked for three thousand pounds.'

'And you paid her?'

Helen nodded.

'How did you go about finding that sort of money?'

'I asked Reg.'

'He knew that Luke wasn't yours?'

'Not at first. Not until this letter came.'

'And how did he react when you told him what you'd done?'

'He was . . . very upset. Devastated. But I knew Reg loved Luke. I knew he'd do anything to protect him. And he did. He got the money.'

'How?'

'I don't know.'

'Anything to do with what we've recently discovered about the Le Page family business?'

She shrugged. 'He told me he'd won it playing cards. I knew he was lying.'

'This wasn't the end of it, was it, Ms Groves? There were more letters asking for money.' He placed two more evidence bags on the desk. 'And then this.' He placed the last of the four letters they'd found in front of her.

Michael summarised the contents. 'Catherine said she was coming to Sark. Said she wanted to see Luke. That she regretted giving him up.'

'You see,' Helen said, an edge to her voice now. 'She admitted it herself—she gave him up.'

'But you never made any of this legal, Ms Groves! You must have known that you couldn't just take someone else's baby and be done with it. There's a process. You say you were depressed when all this happened, but what about this young woman, eh? What state was she in? Alone, confused, just had a baby. She needed proper help, proper counselling, not to hand him over to a stranger!'

'It wasn't like that! She was only interested in money. When she came—' She stopped abruptly.

'What happened when she came? What happened when Luke's mother came to Sark?'

Helen rubbed her eyes. 'She was very thin. I hardly recognised her. And she was dirty. I remember looking at her filthy fingernails and her hair—it can't have been washed for weeks. The thought of her touching Luke . . .' She swallowed. 'She'd been in and out of temporary housing, she said. Homeless for a while. Blamed it all on giving up Luke. Said she wanted to see him. I explained he was at school. She said she would wait until he came home, that he deserved to know who his real mother was. She was disappointed, I could see, that our house was so small. She was looking around, sizing the place up, trying to figure out how much more she could ask us for.'

'She asked you for more money?'

Helen nodded. 'Said she'd go quietly if we let her see Luke and gave her ten thousand pounds.'

Marquis let out a low whistle.

'She wouldn't have. She would never have stopped, you understand?'

'What happened, Ms Groves?'

'It was Reg. He lost it. He used to get so angry. He'd been drinking—it was only ever when he'd been drinking. Ever since I showed him that first letter, ever since he found out that Luke . . . Luke wasn't his . . . he was different. He came at her. She fought back. He fell, and she . . . she was vicious. I thought . . . I really thought she was going to kill him. I'd been ironing. It was the first thing I picked up. I hit her. I had no idea it would kill her. I was just trying to make her stop.'

Advocate Bradford ran his hand through his hair, undid another shirt button. 'I'm going to suggest, at this point, that my client be allowed a break and a chance to confer with counsel.'

Michael thought perhaps it was Advocate Bradford who needed the break. He was doing an excellent job of acting like this wasn't already the biggest case of his career, but the slight shaking of his pen as he lay it on the yellow legal pad said otherwise.

'You want to stop, Ms Groves?' Marquis asked.

'No. It's been twenty-seven years. I just want to get it over with.'

'So what happened after you realised you'd killed Catherine? Why didn't you go to the police? You had a good case for self-defence.'

'And have you take Luke away from me? It was Reg that sorted everything. I don't really remember much of what happened after . . . after . . . There was so much blood. And Luke.'

'I thought you said he was at school?'

'He came home. Not long after it happened. Reg had gone out the back. I don't know what he was doing. Panicking. Looking for something to start . . . cleaning up. I was behind the counter. Numb. Couldn't move. Then I heard him. His little footsteps. He was terrified. We told him she was a bad lady. That he must never say a word to anyone. I don't think he ever did.'

'So you killed her and Reg hid her body in a cave. She was no longer a threat to you or your family. Why did you leave?'

'He made me.'

'Who did?'

'Reg. Said I was a danger to Luke, to myself. Said I had to go, for everyone's sake, and that if I didn't, he'd go to the police, tell them everything. It was his way of punishing me for what I'd done,' she said bitterly.

'You don't think he was genuinely worried, Ms Groves?'

'About what?' The thought did not seem to have occurred to her.

'That you might be a danger to Luke.'

'I'd never have harmed him. Reg knew that.'

'You stayed in touch with Luke—did Reg know that he came to live with you?'

She nodded. 'When he moved to Guernsey for school, he asked if he could. Reg said no. They had a terrible fight. Eventually Reg realised he couldn't stop Luke from being with me.' She looked a little triumphant at that.

'The bones being discovered in the cave. Must have had you worried.'

She looked down. Twisted her hands.

'As I'm sure you're aware, Ms Groves, the prime suspect in Reg Carré's murder is your . . . is Luke. We've only got circumstantial evidence so far, but—'

'Luke had nothing to do with it.'

Advocate Bradford had aged five years in five minutes. 'Ms Groves, I have to advise—'

She held up her hand to stop him. 'The night that Catherine's remains were found, that constable had been in the pub, telling everyone about it. There were always rumours about my disappearance. I suppose people presumed it was me in that cave. One of Luke's friends phoned him to break the news. Luke called me. I took the boat over at first light.'

'You went to see Reg?'

She nodded.

'Why?'

'His mind had been wandering, I wanted to make sure he knew to keep quiet, that as long as no one said anything, it would all be fine. When I saw him, he was very distressed. He was insisting that we told Luke everything. Said Luke had a right to know. I went to the bathroom, to think. Luke's diving gear was hanging over the shower rail. He'd been over a couple of days earlier—he often left his stuff at Reg's. His bag was there too. His fishing knife inside it. I just . . . It was my only option, don't you see? I put on the wet suit, the mask, to protect my clothes, my hair and . . . afterwards, I changed, went back to the boat, but it wouldn't start. I had to take the ferry back. I called Luke that evening, asked him if he could go over and fetch the boat for me.'

'He knew that you killed the man he believed to be his father?'

She shook her head. 'No. Luke has done nothing wrong—you have to believe me. He must have suspected, when he saw his things on the boat, but he didn't know for sure.'

'And what about Reg? What did he do wrong, eh?'

'He was going to tell Luke that I wasn't his mother. Reg took my son away from me once. I wasn't going to let him do it again.'

43

Jenny

She joined him on the bench looking out over Bordeaux Bay, the ruins of Vale Castle behind them. It was the same spot where she'd first met him, what felt like a lifetime ago. It was strange even to think of a time before she'd known Michael.

Fishing boats dotted the horseshoe-shaped harbour, their hulls splashes of bright blue and red against a pale sea. A haze hovered over Herm and Sark in the distance; seagulls rose high over pockets of warm air looking for the first of the day's catch to arrive.

'It's ice-cream weather.' Michael stretched his legs in front of him. He'd already rolled up his shirtsleeves, and his jacket lay across the wooden tabletop.

'I'll get them.'

She ordered two cones from the kiosk. Guernsey ice cream was like the butter, dense, dark yellow, the rich cream providing most of the flavour, just a hint of vanilla. She carried them carefully back to the picnic bench.

'You're just about wrapped up, then?'

Michael nodded. 'Suppose you want an exclusive?'

'I'm a bit tired of them, to be honest. Everyone hates me at work. No one else has had a look-in at front page for days.'

'No one else was running around Sark like a lunatic getting the stories.'

'There is that. Did you confirm the identity of the woman? Luke's mother?'

He shook his head. 'We've only got a first name and Helen's description of her, which was vague to say the least. We're going through missing person reports. Although, Helen seemed to think this woman had been in and out of foster care, had spent some time homeless. There might not even be a report.' Michael looked troubled at the thought. 'Doesn't bear thinking about, does it? Walking this earth for how many years and leaving no trace, no one to miss you.'

'Plenty of people would miss you, Michael.'

'I wasn't talking about me.'

'Weren't you?'

He gave her one of his looks.

'What about Fallaize and Langlais? Anyone going to miss them?'

'Hm. Sure Langlais's wife will miss him. No kids thank God. As for Fallaize.' Michael sighed. 'Always had him down as a bit of a wally, but I actually thought he had the makings of a good copper. Beneath all the bragging and bravado. Never for a minute thought him capable of—what happened with your dad. And then the lies. So many lies.' He shook his head. 'I'm sorry, love.'

She and Michael had not talked about Charlie since she'd sat with him in the hospital and he'd told her what Tanya had said, what he'd seen, out on the cliffs.

'You think he's dead.'

'I do.'

'Something must be looking out for you Michael.'

'How so?'

'Three men went into those woods. Two of them likely wanted you dead. And yet you were the only one who made it out. Maybe all that praying really works.'

'Don't joke about things like that Jenny.' He looked rattled.

'I'm not joking.' She said, gently. 'How's your recovery going? The recovery after the recovery you messed up, that is.'

'Didn't mess it up. Not unusual to have a wound like that re-stitched. Even the nurse said.'

'Passing out cold after an interview usual as well, is it?'

'That was the concussion. The trip to Sark was potentially a little too much movement for my already-jarred brain. All fine now, though. I'm officially allowed to be out of the house for an ice cream.'

'How is Luke doing?'

'As well as can be expected having basically lost three parents in as many weeks. He's gone to Shropshire to try and sort things out with his wife. He's been carrying around too many secrets, Jenny. Could never tell his wife about Helen, or about what happened all those years ago. You can't build a marriage on that. Now everything's out in the open, maybe they can start again. He's only young.'

'He's older than me.'

'You're still a baby.'

They finished their ice creams in silence, the sounds of the water rippling on the shoreline tempered by the hum of traffic on the road behind them. The sharp, tangy scent of seaweed drying in the late-morning sun carried on the breeze.

'I'm moving out of Mum's.'

'About time.'

'Hey!'

'I'm only joking, love. But your mum needs to start managing by herself. You know that.'

'Hm. I'm pretty sure Mum can manage fine. She's been different, since she found out what happened to Dad.'

'Different how?' Michael sounded worried.

'Not in a bad way. Just, more settled. I think she needed to know, just as much as I did. It's not in her nature though, to ask questions, to challenge authority.'

'Lucky she's got you then isn't it? You moving in with Elliot, are you?'

She sighed. 'We're having a break. I think it might be permanent.'

'Told him that, have you?'

'It was sort of his decision. I need my own space anyway. At least for a while.'

'Well. Good for you.' He gave her one of his reassuring pats on the shoulder. Cleared his throat self-consciously. 'I'm taking your mum out this weekend.'

'I know.' She smiled.

'Thought we might go to that new Italian place at the top of Mill Street. Think she'd like that?'

She laughed. 'No way. Absolutely not. I am not giving you tips on dating my mother. You're on your own there.'

'Well, don't be asking me any more favours! Bloody ungrateful you are.'

'Pretty sure we're even on the favours front, DCI Gilbert. Seem to remember you being pretty grateful for your airlift to hospital earlier this month.'

'Fair point. Suppose we're even. And you can drop the "DCI".'

'Since when?'

'Since I finally decided it's time to retire.'

'Is this official?'

'Will be in an hour or so. I'm heading to the station after this.'

'Oh.'

'You sound disappointed. Prefer I work myself to death, is it?'

'No! But I'll miss this. And where will I get all of my exclusives? I have a reputation to uphold now.'

'You might want to start being nicer to that cousin of yours. I've a feeling a promotion might be in the works for him.'

'The dog shit!'

'That's no way to talk about DC Marquis.'

'You know what I mean! I can't believe I nearly forgot about it. Was it that guy who worked for the seigneur? And why was he doing it?'

'You'll love this. Turns out Len Mauger, Reg Carré and Sir William had a long-standing card game. Sir William had been on a losing streak, ended up heavily in debt. Accused the other two of cheating. Apparently decided the best way to retaliate was to throw dog crap all over the place. There was a lot of it on the path outside Reg's house—Luke even mentioned it when I first spoke to him. I should have connected the dots.'

'What a horrible man.'

'He's not admitted it. He's blaming his private secretary. But I wouldn't be surprised if Sir William was responsible for the spate of vandalism on Sark. I think losing his role on the island unhinged him. Too much time on his hands. He decided to settle old scores.'

'There's a story there.'

'I'm sure there is, Jenny. Right. I've got an appointment with my pension. See you later, love.' He walked, slowly, back to his car.

Jenny looked out at the bay.

Just knowing what had happened to Charlie had quieted the hum in her brain. She was still angry, that he was gone, that he had been taken from them. Angrier still that his killer would never stand before a judge. But Michael was right. Fallaize was dead. He had to be. Maybe his body would wash up somewhere along the French coast. Maybe he was lost, for ever, to the sea. Either way, she had to accept that not all justice was handed out in a courtroom.

She went back to her car, opened the window, let the warm air in. She followed the coast road towards town. The sea shone. The traffic slowed behind a group of cyclists, bikes laden with buckets and spades. A cruise ship was moored in the harbour. Tonight the bars and restaurants would be full, people would spill out onto the streets, drinking chilled wine, eating freshly caught seafood, and for the first time in so long, Jenny felt like joining them. Guernsey in the height of summer. There was no better place to be.

Author's Note

I spent three weeks every Summer on Sark when I was a child. It is a truly magical place with its dramatic coastline, secluded beaches, hidden caves and dark, star-lit skies. I have been lucky enough to travel widely since I left the Channel Islands nearly twenty years ago but Sark remains my favourite place in the world. I have made use of its stunning scenery and unique history as a back-drop for Dark Sky Island but of course, the events and the people depicted in this book are entirely fictional.

Glossary

Advocate—An officer of the Royal Court in Guernsey who performs the role of both solicitor and barrister. An advocate must be qualified in English law, obtain the Certificat d'Etudes Juridiques Francaises et Normandes in France and pass the Guernsey bar exam.

Chief Pleas—Sark's parliament, originally comprised of the seigneur and forty tenement landowners. Since 2008 has been made up of twenty-eight democratically elected members, known as Conseillers.

La Coupée—a natural causeway which joins big and little Sark.

Euchre—A trick-taking card game, originating in Cornwall. Popular in Guernsey where it is played competitively in leagues.

Grockles—Tourists

Loophole tower—Towers built by the British in the late eighteenth century to defend Guernsey from French invasion.

Quarantaine—The original forty parcels of land leased to tenants by Helier De Carteret in the sixteenth century. Leaseholders were given a seat at the Chief Pleas.

RIB—Rigid-inflatable boat.

Seigneur—Head of the feudal government of Sark.

Le Seigneurie—Ancestral home of the seigneur.

The States of Deliberation (commonly referred to as "The States")—Guernsey's government, made up of Deputies from each of the island's ten parishes.

States' house—Council house

Tchico—A large black dog with fiery eyes. Said to be a sign of death. Also known as La Bête.

Toast-rack—name given to the open sided carts which carry visitors to the top of Harbour Hill in Sark.

Acknowledgements

Dark Sky Island is the product not just of my overactive imagination, but of the love and support I find myself surrounded with on a daily basis. A non-exhaustive thank you list as follows:

To the inimitable Sam Eades, who as well as being (probably) the most approachable and enthusiastic editor in the world, over the last year has gone above and beyond the call of duty, accompanying me on not one but two trips to Guernsey and at this rate is in with a very real chance of being given 'local' status. A big thank you too to Lauren Woosey, Mireille Harper, Katie Brown, Laura Collins, Debbie Holmes and all of the Trapeze team who work tirelessly to turn sprawling Word documents into beautiful books.

Sophie Lambert at C+W has, once again, been a rock, guiding me through the terror that is 'difficult second novel syndrome' (turns out it's no easier than writing the first) with grace, patience and good humour. Thank you also to Emma Finn and the rest of the team at C+W, and to Luke Speed at Curtis Brown who navigated the very exciting but equally complicated world of film and television rights on my behalf.

I am grateful to so many people in Guernsey—Mike Watson for answering my questions about Guernsey policing, Tim Bamford for the legal advice, Susan Ilie for championing The Devil's Claw, Catriona Stares and all at the Guernsey Literary Festival, the Guernsey Geekon podcast and especially to the Guille-Alles Library, which is everything a library should be (i.e. full of books and people who love them). It is really something to have so much support from the very place I first dreamt of being a writer. Special thanks to Adam Bayfield—librarian, event organiser and interviewer extraordinaire.

Thank you to mum and dad for the summers in Sark. I remember the incredulous looks people would give us when we told them we were, once again, spending three weeks on Guernsey's neighbouring island, but I have the best memories of endless sunny days spent bike riding, rock climbing, fishing, rescuing frogs from the swimming pool at Stocks Hotel and my first taste of Orangina (which I still think of as an exotic beverage). Magical.

Across the Atlantic, thank you to Anderson's Books, the Larchmont Public Library and to Francine Ludicon at The Voracious Reader, whose love of books is infectious, and to Rhiannon Navin and Eloise Parker, who have helped to make writing a slightly less lonely pursuit.

I have lived an itinerant sort of life since I left Guernsey nearly twenty years ago. I find myself now far away from 'home' but home nonetheless, in Larchmont, New York. Thank you to the wonderful, strong, supportive women I have met here—I am so fortunate to call you my friends—you know who you are.

And finally, as always, thank you to Andrew, Lily, Charlie and Lena. How lucky we are to have each other. I love you all so much.